Rage Against The Game

Matthew Brookes

ISBN: 1983801569
ISBN-13: 978-1983801563

This book is a work of fiction. Names, characters,
businesses, organisations, places, events and incidents either
are the product of the author's imagination or are used
fictitiously. Any resemblance to actual persons, living or dead
or events is entirely coincidental.

for Fate

It is important that my family know how grateful I feel, for all the support throughout the process of writing *RAGE AGAINST THE GAME*. They have never stopped encouraging me to chase my dreams, even when money comes into it. So, for understanding that this means a lot to me, I thank you. One day I do intend to somehow pay my family back because I believe you should always get what you give, and they have given so much, without receiving anything in return.

Towards the end, when I was close to completing this story, I turned to the angels, seeking them out via a pack of oracle cards. I did this because I began to doubt myself, wondering if it had all been a waste of time. I mean, being rejected by countless literary agents certainly did have a negative effect upon me, in my times of need and when I felt weak, I would do what's called a 'reading', hoping to receive divine guidance from the angels. Suffice to say, the angels made sure I knew, without doubt, that in writing this novel, I have been on the path of light.

I thank the angels just as much as my family, for being there, when I needed them most.

PRELUDE: THE DEATH OF A DREAM

What of future endeavour bring to light?
When the light itself shines against not for
Truth, that which was the way of life
From whence Christ came to become more
Than man knew was possible but man knows
Only too well without a warm heart or an open
Mind and so see not the light within which will
Be blinded by the brain made of darkness

Soul-black like the colour a great white's eyes
Stare at all and yet nothing but its sea of prey
Where remains to be seen, indeed does it exist?
This place is not for the ones nice in nature
We are last and least. First and foremost man
Of money known as God to he who worship
Such a thing, then so be he a slave to it at once
Lost

As for yours truly, lusting after a better world
One of out and out truth, if only, only human
After all else slips away with every breath
That is such a whimper the prevailing loss
So these sweet nothings, this dim me, I am

MATTHEW BROOKES

Not what I want to be but the blackest shadow
Was I once somebody bright and beautiful?
Of course it's in the windows which will behold
Whose words are alive, mine unto you

Day by nightfall faster than the last
Time my bane until the bitter end delighted
Itself of a win over mortal life from fallen
To finite, autumnal nightmare may you yield
Your horror over my dead inside fibre of being
But breathe this fresh air for the love of it, I do
So hopefully feeling spirited away by my mindful
Fantasies sure enough from whence such an atmosphere
Full of itself; share your evergreen goodness now and
Always

Dream might I try and do so lucidly yet to no avail
Vain! In light of futile desire for what want is
So self-indulgent, it must matter therefore where I am
And thus far here I am, naming it simply a place,
Opposed to paradise dwell with the deepest despair
Prevails such sadness as I gasp for the good life
Like an ungrateful fool see not what is so, only feast
My hungry eyes over the rainbow, but to be beyond
Worldly need seek out that which is within instead of
Holding onto the heartfelt false hope, oh hooray for
All things physical!

There is no escaping this system of things
So obliged and disgusted at it, I must endure
Every rage gesticulating in spite of my morbid
Bones existing to humour my hateful body

And so of woe is me it will not do! To be
Blackened down descending deathlessly
Lake-like fires so lonesome from one lost soul

2

Lest to the next, not at all aware, we as each
They are alone under endless influence of a
Forever vexed disposition and thus far
Torments them this sick consuming inglorious
Sorrow rages against nothing but itself!

For everything else is non-existent to us
Such sufferance comes as if by quite the
Conundrum doesn't cease! Still feelings
Loss of bodily function continues its state
To have pain not felt but be in and of fear
Remains one's own unrelenting limbo born
Now as now knows no other, other than now!

Whereby I am an infinite nightmare made from
Nothingness manifest eternal loss as a monstrous
Sight to none but becomes me, real albeit between
What is rock-like and the hard place so-called and
Quite torn only by my make-believe last gasp grasp
At reaching for more or other than this sordid darkness
Known not yet well; hell will never end and the everlasting
Agony grow within, then out of all that remains as just enough
Fibre forever reborn of formless horror reverberating in a
Space saved for the fallen

Great beauty to me feels like the closing in of winter
Tremendous ice cold and the look of frozen faces
Suffering instead of basking in its sweet, sweet freeze
Hear, hear to the festive cheer! From the bottom of my
Heart I have and hold December dear, Merry Christmas
Amongst a market that is buzzing, as I sip a cup of mulled
Wine I can hear the choir singing. Indeed these days as they
WAY TO GO by beautifully fallen unto starry ravishing night
Light of my face smiley-eyed and warmth this inside of mine

3

MATTHEW BROOKES

Shines out to you all

All the lights so many nights spent planning now we feel
The fireworks, count down from 10 to 1 where strangers
Verge on newfound friends sing singalongs . . . Still to come!
Somewhere the one with her broken smile will drink until
She's gone, gone from here to there without a care, tomorrow
Never comes as it were - Happy New Year'

Summer rain feels good against the hurting pain I know
Will never cease so many a day by the wayside doing this
Still waiting for the one to take me away from my oh my
Becoming undone and the rest is just so I can stay young
A sweet dream made up of wishful thinking makes no
difference
Instead I did some more drinking, at night the darkness
consumes
Misguided desire, I might as well sell my soul lest set it on fire

If love is all we need do nothing more or else just so you know
When I feel I feel from deep inside and what will be will be
my own
Don't get me wrong I won't let it lie I sing a song on the
seasons
Change of heart and mind, no time like mine, being here right
now
With your soul light the way, my way out

It is within then, that I am much more than the rage against
Such a silly little game made up of us all playing our part
Let me be one long song of selfless celebration unto life, death
Thereafter but before of what I like, and not of rigid word
Born more for the bittersweet feeling seducing my senses
So often than not to be but thus far remain on behalf of the
hate
That I have and hold and yet for what?

What will I have of love if only by hate, rage makes me feel alive!
Of course I can contradict myself without even knowing it, to be
Is as good as being not what one was - lost at once – so seize the day
I did! And yet yesterday has since slipped away, wherefore art thou
'Now' of newfound glory reborn by every breath then not to end
But be eternally lost to the life force coursing through these veins

Yes, oh no shalt not gently leave the night to its silence so I rage on
For all against me is me, my own worst enemy may still serve to trouble
But of course thoughts as do feelings pass, by what will I stand at a place
Set in stone? When words are profound for the few who wander dangerously
Close to the truth, that of this, as I am in love with the darkness' caress

Something incarnate taken from nothing-infinite of a pure form therefore
Formless in the first place, so to be, is innocence swallowed whole - lost
At once shape of self suffocates space peacefully free being no other than
None and no one but oneness thus as a thing brings us into out of space
Black of white, white of black, colour the colourless light to the darkest
Night

*Oh, what night does, as of now I feel found, down upon me
such stars shine!
I need not know how or why any more than they are there for
what is itself life
Of course as if by magic it is in my mind where wander
daydreams sweetly
Leaving everything and more, with regard to being, behind
hence desire cease
Exist outside my means, see because nothing then enters
somewhere within me
May I somehow have the view from up above, escape self,
find out of body is,
Is simply the place we are all looking for – paradise –
destination unknown and so
Go beyond my make-believe, overshadow weak needs such a
thing as this isn't it just
To be*

*Feeling a feeling of everlasting lightness shine senselessly yet
still somehow aware
Without this shell feel pure around soulful all and for once
within an atmosphere free
Dreaming in lucidity take shape of perfection from me as a
lasting moment made by
Timeless lovers singing the song only angels dance to – true
love reverberates as essence
Is its spirited away wanderlust la-de-da dream of a dream of
a dream come true*

*Tomorrow won't take me away from my ceaseless suffering,
bid it not farewell with a smile
Hello horrid despair please don't go . . . only imagine can I
fathom that which is so very void
At least to feel, albeit sick of self so should I loathe with all my
limbs still fully functioning . . .*

*Fuck the obligation and no I won't be grateful, for why was
such a thing as me even born?*
*Ever so sexual! Lusting after great beauty but of course
settling for much less; needs must!*
*This is as a man, one knowing his strongest urge just so
happens to turn and thus something*
*Else entirely becomes me . . . we resist it – the surging subtle
twang when a woman knows*
*Too well what to do – good God down with what has since
sprung some game we play like*
*Intellectually-inclined idiots disguising disgustingly lush lust
lest, then, I for one will not do*
*To deny my animalistic nature – never forget girls secretly
love it – but, yes, alas as long as*
*Society fronts twisted worldviews with shimmering smugness
stem they have from media's*
*Downright wrongdoing amongst other wrongs wrapped up in
silly little rules blah blah blah*
*There can be no inglorious uprising without that which is
action instead of brave vain none-the-wiser words . . .*

Such was this sure-fire fucked up epic poem
spoken in its own newfound rhythm that the jazz
band came to a spontaneous stop. Not a minute
into the man's exquisitely real recital, all around
him was golden and thus silence lent itself fully
for all the time it took to stun his astounded
audience of stuck up couples, until then,
delighting at the subtle stench such kept company
creates each to one's own unique flavour of foul-
mouth mimicry. For now nothing but an
awakened state of freedom came over those who
heard him and so off with the shackles keeping
couples 'coupled'.

   This jazz room is pitch black but lightness
shone out from one and all's so very eager eyes

feasting on a natural high he created at the pen's peril albeit mightier – proven in his performance – than the sword of old. A new feeling lingered around the room. The man responsible stood still while a sax started to play. People got up. They all did. And went on their merry way they were strangely loose as if by magic like monkeys swaying from tree to tree. Straight to the dancefloor, for a different reason than that which would have been obvious, had it not been for one man's mysterious talent to seduce the senses into animalistic action.

What transpired proves the power of poetry that is simply pure. Thus touching the hearts here, forcing souls to find a home from whence something spiritual took control. All the people let sparks fly – they made love with each other. This was an orgy born of beauty. The man with the golden tongue watches on. The band's jazz gets louder and all the more daring when the collective voice of ecstasy too went up in volume.

Moan upon moan. Sound upon sound of sax to the sex on fire right now *'Now we are free'* he thought, before exiting the stage to 'get involved'. The man undresses entranced by a beautiful woman of middle-age and an olive skin complexion as she lies naked on her front with her arse as if inviting him to join her. Her derriere remains stuck up in the air above all else's sexy 'goings on'. He gets to his knees, pulls her cheeks so far apart that she makes a sound somewhere in-between pain and pleasure. Suddenly he spits at her anus, simultaneously letting go of her lovely little arse.

And to his bliss, his erection is bigger than ever before! Raunchily she turns her head to admire the man's sizable behemoth of a cock. Her dirty face says it all, and then in no uncertain terms she ecstatically pulls her arse apart to await his imminent entry.

18th of October 2008

Maximus Lucifer Phoenix suddenly and in a fit of sweat wakes with the jump happening when one least expects it, to come alive via an unconscious state that has been under wraps since such a thing as sleep put him out of touch with where reality is right now and almost always concerned. The first feeling coming back to his senses is discomfort, for now he has a numb bum from being sat on hard ground. Secondly, he feels sheer panic consume him, compelling his now worried disposition up.

Rushing over to the nearest screen where departures are listed, it is soon upon him in a sinking feeling. He's missed the last train home. Then, in a flash of subconscious stuff surfacing, something along the lines of his sick and twisted dream comes back to make Max remember *'There can be no inglorious uprising without that which is action instead of brave vain none-the-wiser words . . . '*. Which in turn led him to the most part of what followed on from such a statement, but instead of basking in its explicit content, the present moment must be dealt with.

Kings Cross London and it's now 1am. Max has a night to kill, well, that was his initial reaction to this situation anyway. He twists his rucksack around and undoes the zip to remove a movie script, 'The Rise and Fall of Folklore' 'written by Maximus Lucifer Phoenix'. With regret, he flicks to his favourite bit to feast his eyes for one last time.

                    PRIEST
        Jim, things don't just happen
        for no apparent reason. Destiny
        doesn't dance all over the place
        like a godforsaken drunk, does it?

                    JIM
        What do you mean?

                    PRIEST
        I mean we are already predetermined
        bodies of flesh and bone born in order
        to do well for ourselves, so why not go
        one step further? Here we are, struggling
        until it gets better or stays the same.
        I'm talking about the one thing that we
        need for our future to even exist . . .
        with 'hope' there is vision and we breed
        dreams from it. But without hope all hell
        would break loose, so what's the use of
        life from having hope, if for fear we
        choose only to acknowledge the idea of
        a future, therefore never really achieve
        the true reality of it! That will require
        our wholehearted hopefulness, so much so
        that that hope you or me felt hellbent to
        have evolved and became something else
        entirely. . . eternity, to the extent of
        exceeding even our own wildest dreams.
        I'm talking about transcendence,
        'somewhere over the rainbow',
        beyond body, mind and above all else -
        soul
                    JIM
        Well, when I lost Wendy, I lost
        Heart. Hell, I lost it all

                    PRIEST
        It's better to have loved and
        lost than not to have loved
        at all

Jim lifts his eyebrows as he lets out a forced
laugh of nothing but bitterness.

                    PRIEST CONT'D
     It's built into us — somehow we
     are hardwired survivalists!
     Man's most basic instinct is
     an animal's whole life! We share
     our woe, which is this struggle
     for survival; with love as an
     answer to the one and only question
     in the world worth knowing —
     WHY — ARE — WE - HERE?

                         FRANK
     Because of Eve

The priest bursts into laughter from across
the table, banging his hands on the table
because of his fit of kneejerk ecstasy.

                         PRIEST
     Oh despair for a woman and
     her wrongdoing

                          JIM
     We can't live with them and
     we can't live without them

                         PRIEST
     But it begs such a question
     then, why did she do it?

                         FRANK
     The serpent played a devilish
     trick on poor old Eve

                         PRIEST
     'Poor old Eve' gave the serpent
     her every fibre of being
     because she got bored of Adam

                         FRANK
     Maybe Adam didn't have a very big
     thingumajig!

Max smiles to himself before throwing the script in the bin. Then he removes from his bag a box of business cards. He takes one out to look at, and turns such a thing over revealing the back of it *'TRUST IMAGINATION'*. Putting it carefully back in the box of many more where that came from, Max drops the box in the bin, thinking back to the time when he was so sure of himself as a writer that had what it took. Back then, having just written a scene from his script, taking a break outside for a cigarette, letting his thoughts settle. Suddenly he starts to cry.

ACT 3: NEW BEGINNINGS

SCENE 13: FATE MAKES FOR A CHANGE OF HEART

EXT. LOCH NESS LAKE, DAY

Mary-Jane and Jim have taken time out from being at the psychiatric hospital. They walk along the loch; the day is not at all beautiful, it's bleak.

MARY-JANE

I know the priest means well, yet I can't help but feel like he's hiding something

JIM

Mary-Jane, just remember being a priest must take its toll from time to time; I don't doubt the dedication in doing not just any old job, but a duty. Because I was just the same, except I wasn't at loggerheads with God day in, day out

MARY-JANE

And how are things - on the farm I mean?

JIM

Funny you should ask — actually,
it's not at all a laughing matter,
the less said about it the better.
But what is it they say about death?

                    MARY-JANE
They say many things about death.
Though when the end is near for
them, those so content to make
quips up about how we can but let
it be. . . Believe me, I was a nurse
once upon a time and from what
I remember of witnessing the sick
take a truly long-lasting turn for
the worse, well, not one went 'gentle
into that good night,' no. They
'raged and they raged against the
dying of the light!'

                    JIM
That was it; 'After your death,
you will be what you were before
your birth'

                    MARY-JANE
What does that even mean?

                    JIM
I don't know

                    MARY-JANE
Sounds profound

                    JIM
I think it came from a fortune
cookie

Mary-Jane laughs as a somewhat comfortable
silence continues to bring them closer
together.

                    MARY-JANE
Jessie is sorry for the way
he, well. . .

                    JIM

13

Really you don't have to say
anything on his behalf. If it
was me, and at that age. . . he
was young but still, old
enough. Now he has you and
a baby on the way

                    MARY-JANE
When I first met him, huh,
getting to know your son
was a struggle. Right from
the beginning I sensed something
was missing in his life. I mean,
then as things got more serious,
cos I kept asking the same questions
and soon enough he told me
everything. Then we talked about
Texas. It's just I guess some
things are easier said than done

                    JIM
Wendy was his rock, mine too, but
I spent most of my time on the farm
and so Jessie became more a mummy's
boy. I don't blame him for trying
to find his own way in life. . . after
all, he found you

                    MARY-JANE
Jim, I'm not being facetious,
I just want to understand. Because
all of this feels beyond me —
our suffering brings us closer
together. But why? I wanna know why!
Has it always been this way? Pain,
I mean, instead of something else
something within us. There must be
more to life than a futile feeling
of love for fuck's sake!

Mary-Jane sounds so very emotional now.

                    JIM
'I hurt myself today,
To see if I still feel,
I focus on the pain. . .

Jim sings some of a song made famous by Johnny
Cash, 'Hurt', to answer her question and in
doing so chokes up before being able to finish
the first verse.

                    MARY-JANE
    'The only thing that's real'

Mary-Jane finishes it off for him. She
suddenly stops, holding her pregnant stomach,
writhing in pain.

                    JIM
    What's wrong?

                    MARY-JANE
    I think my waters just broke

It was as if this was Max saying a long goodbye.
But not just to his story, a story that stayed with
him for many months of false hope. He shakes his
head, holding back the tears. Max shifts his
recollections forward in time, to today. Today he
pitched his project – *The Rise and Fall of Folklore* – to
producers. This was at The London Screenwriters
Festival, albeit to no avail.

"Sounds like *Free Willy.*" Were the words of one
big name Max sat opposite, listening to him make
fun of his story. After five fast minutes pitching,
picking his best bits, this was what he came here
for, only to be belittled on behalf of something
that Max spent months making-believe. £300 on a
weekend of bitter disappointment, but life of
course goes on, and yet at twenty nine, no sense of
direction can overturn now what has since become
– Max is still lost.

His rucksack feels weightless. What with a
washbag and a notepad, and not what a dream was
made of, page upon page of soulful deliverance

from the time misspent in a sleepy little village. Max exits the train station. It's cold outside. He feels it take him away from his thoughts, least of all for a few seconds somewhat delighting in the bitter chill.

Smoking a cigarette attracts the attention of a homeless person as such a thing thinks it can come up to Max and beg for money. He blows smoke into the face of desperation. The skinny man in black rags and bare feet starts to cough. Max walks away. Suddenly he feels a shove from behind. He turns around.

"Who do you think you are?" The homeless shadow of a man can barely raise his voice.

"What do you want from me?" Max asks angrily.

"An apology, some money and a cigarette, since you're asking the question," he says shamelessly.

Max drops his hand into his pocket, gripping a fistful of change before letting it all go onto the floor. The man is reduced to his knees as he picks it up. Max watches on not knowing what to do next so he does nothing.

"Give me a cigarette," he says displaying a toothless smile.

Max hands over the whole pack and then turns to walk away.

"Wait." The homeless person hasn't finished.

"What?" Max asks complete with a distinct lack of patience to his southern tone of voice.

"Say sorry," he says seriously.

Max takes a prolonged drag of his cigarette, tilting his head up before blowing out the smoke, throws it to the ground and then stamps it out. In a flash of having enough, and not just taking a breath before all the hate and heartache fade,

Maximus lets fly from his purest place possible, a place where rage reigns supreme. He punches the homeless person, knocking him down to the ground.

"Sorry," Max says spitefully. Suddenly a police officer restrains him from further wrongdoing.

Email Message Sent: 03:35am, 18th of October 2008

Belle,
It is important that you read the attachment. My writings will give you an insight as to why I must leave the country. Seeing the world for the life of me I hope changes my current state of mind. As you will find out upon reading page upon page of my rage against . . . to tell you the truth I have lost sight of whom or what I was fighting for. Understand that I left the country first and foremost, not you, you will always be with me in my heart. There is nothing more for me to say, so I bid you farewell.
With love,
Max

Belle meant more to Max than she'll ever know. However, there is something independently imperative to him, something indeed meaning much more than anything else, even more than his love of Isabella Antoinette, and that's meaning itself. His 'writings' suggest bitter discontent at that which was his job, but much more than that, there is a seeking in his brash, hell-bent vent taking shape page upon page of ferocious rage against the game, the game we call life. This seeking smacks of a perspective otherwise sheltered and thus so very far from having personal experience inform him. Maximus must dig deep into his heart for the way he feels calling him . . . indeed it is the path that arrives at a righteous place.

Max is spending the night behind bars for lashing out at a homeless person. Upon one click of a button comes the end of his relationship with Isabella. There was no goodbye and no face-to-face explanation, just a moment of madness now the predominant time of his unfulfilled life.

He has the urge for going. In truth he's been punishing himself for too long now, working a horrible job at a posh hotel as a night porter. Not even needing the minimum wage it pays; since his adoptive parents passed away, he was on the receiving end of enough money not to worry about being in work. But working somehow gave him the fire to write, and write he did. Max used to live with Gwen and George at their B&B in Newquay, Cornwall, working for them when it suited him. For he was loved by them both, but not necessarily needed where work was concerned. As for what it means to go home from here, he doesn't see fit to live on the grounds of a stuck up place like Belton bloody Woods is anymore. Max will leave his worthless possessions, and his even more worthless work colleagues, as well as his sweet little girlfriend behind.

The sound for Belle's incoming email messages goes off on her smartphone and yet she is fast asleep. Tomorrow, Max will be long gone and as for Isabella, well, only time will tell. Love hurts. She will read his message (subsequently take no notice of the attachment) and in a fit of shock, scream her heart out with hurt, having every fibre of her being consumed by that strange, sick sinking feeling.

Message Deleted.

Attachment
I don't despair anymore, for time has healed me and my incensed sadness: now I am merely feeling numb . . . numb of fixated ambition and devoid of farfetched dreams. Such redundant remains makes me breathe a bittersweet sigh of relief – from the useless pressure a self-imposed pressing issue I sought to see before me as something that could quite easily be realized. 'Success', fancy that! That, which I would wonder and worry about becoming 'somebody' because status, society says, is everything.
And what is society but a bemused, dismal, make-believe effect from the cause caressed by our ever-present trappings, self-satisfied fear, surface fears prevailing against that thing called love. I've learnt to look 'out there' from whence such a sense was born unto itself, within. And I have felt the vast space of infinite untouched nothingness as it simply becomes me. Above and beyond my silly little thoughts stemming from my needy mind of want, for the gratification taking shape upon shape but made of the same 'missing feeling' like a lack

of getting 'it'. It is sex yet diluted down into other satisfactory 'requirements' 'seeking to be seen' and so noticed as an attractive functioning member of this shambolic la-de-da destitute society.

I 'look out' not in need but repulsed by my dwindling disposition; indeed I do feel like an animal misled and made to believe I have evolved from something inferior. However there is something else entirely lurking inside,   a sinking feeling reveals itself; fallen and now not at all aware of where or when one was once whole.

(The way it is)

'No one's perfect.' But if everyone's idea of perfection differs, and it does, this statement fails to make much sense at all. Except such a thing indeed does make some sense after all . . . no one's perfect quite frankly because 'perfect' itself ceases to exist. This expression fools us into a false sense of what it is or means to be 'perfect'. The idea is, I want to be this way when I am in fact that, but of course I can be the way I want to be if perfection is a becoming process. So we arrive at being perfect from whence we see ourselves as imperfect. But what about beauty being in the eye of the beholder, and if so, we shall not see what we actually are to others? Is beauty perfection? Or is perfection simply peace of mind?

I want to be a better me. 'Better' to me will differ from what's better to you. For arguments sake, let's say I reach my idea of being perfect. To at least someone else my idea of perfection fails therefore reducing me to a self-proclaimed place of perfection, not perfect itself.

We all know how and why we use such an expression, in order to excuse ourselves from things like sin, temptation and making mistakes. The fact of the matter is this, if we can safely say Jesus was perfect for instance, then no one will achieve being perfect. To state the obvious, only Jesus was

Jesus. So, if we live in the lifelike light of Christ, does this make us perfect? Imitation is the sincerest form of flattery; it is not a path to perfection. I am imperfect but I strive to become closest to my kind of perfect. And my kind of perfect effectively begins with us as a whole people, living in a righteous future.

Enter RAGE. It will not do to use such an expression as 'don't believe everything you read' in the truthful future. There will be no more lies. Why, oh why, have we as a society settled down at a place of comfort where newspapers are concerned? Regardless of how we read the news nowadays, I dare stress such a downright wrongdoing it is to sensationalise stories otherwise masquerading as true. Print, the ink of the inglorious, basking in its own wayward world made from filth that has been dressed up as sometimes respectable but is always wrongful. The truth, that which will fuck falsehood up its soiled derriere, raping it of wrongdoing until it is righteous. Yes, your mouths may open wide with shock, horror . . . hear hear to your kneejerk reactions and please do disgust at my wordy way!

I have only just begun to craft rage into a beautiful monster of out and out truth. This is not knowledge. This is certainly not a song and dance. This life of mine won't just sit pretty at the peril of all else as they make excuses to themselves as well as to others, about being in the fake cold light of day doing whatever it takes to come across as a beautiful soul. Yes, your money buys you cosmetic surgery so to enhance such a physical position of false agelessness, and fake confidence of course. True spirit, that which is within in order to obtain a better frame of mind, doesn't come from pumping up your lips with the similar sort of jelly they put in pork pies! Disgusting pigs sniffing out the next best fix to calm an agitated mind, blinded by a self-obsessed outlook on life.

The way it is, is what exactly? We wander around aimlessly, all the time manifesting make-believe truths to ourselves, because of course the actual truth will hurt your ego, won't it? That dress does make your bum look big, but stare into the mirror long enough and you'll soon somehow hypnotise yourself for the sake of retail therapy and believe this dress is just right after all. Why do we do it? Oh how weak can a mind become when we feed on the scraps rammed down our throat thanks to the goddamn media. If in doubt – blame the media? When in doubt – blame human nature for always choosing the path of least resistance. And that path has been carefully constructed for you to go down, done so, to deceive even the most perceptive of us from feeling the need to at least be curious towards what we are witnessing on television, let's say.

Everyone is looking for something or someone in life. We spend it searching. This is curiosity but it is also desire and a lack of fulfilment. To strip us all down to what happens in any busy city – it is experience experiencing experiences experiencing experiences experiencing experiences etc. One and many, simultaneously, we are experiential individuals all at once experiencing the same manifest but in a unique kind of way. We call it the rat race. Because we live in a system of things inherent to what is survival of the fittest. That has been the way since cavemen needed meat to thrive. And of course a cave to survive, therefore cavemen played survival of the fittest with animals and sometimes other cavemen depending upon what was up for grabs at that time.

Surely we have moved on from once upon a time when man was more like a monkey than anything else. Surely we have, haven't we? It is dog eat dog out there, for what? Well, 'better' or 'more' mostly - more money, more stuff, better opportunities etc. It's a fight not only for survival, but for status as well. Why? Why is it so important to appear 'better than' someone else? Because quite frankly from an early age, we are born into this system of encouraging competition - think schools for instance. Thus doesn't such a thing as being competitive bring out the best in you? Believe in me, I will bring to life a better world. One where we can be the best, without bringing it out to play a fool's game. Money need not have the power to enslave us anymore. I am in my heart of hearts sure there is a path that we are at once and for all, but have forsaken.

We lie. We cheat. We steal. We are very much gutter-ridden individuals albeit staring up at the stars for a moment's respite, apart from ourselves so we seek peace of mind. Yes, we live on to fight yet another mundane day in and around a mad world of money-hungry go-getters. Dressed as if appearance is everything, hence so very hard they try to look the part. It's a shit for brains race of the rats out there, wherever you may be, especially London.

I've been from job to job, being an average Joe for the system long enough. Now is the time to rage against this sorry excuse for a way of life from a western perspective. I've had enough of all the soul-destroying times misspent at this perilous system making me into a tool for the tedious industry, whatever it may be. Because it's all the same; I have seen death in the face of others as they plod along being killed from the inside out. That's the way it is.

CHAPTER 1: HER BRAVE ENDEAVOUR

18ᵗʰ of December 2018: 10 years later

This was supposed to be an epic cause for celebration, not one of shock, horror or concern. And in such a striking, quite beautiful place as Prague, as dark and gothic at night, as it is a subtle but brilliant beam of light by day. Isabella Antoinette stood with her back to an astonished audience as she mesmerised and moved them almost to tears of a spontaneous stream born of beauty; it was music to their ears. She feels this music from her heart of fire – therein is such sheer effortless ease as she scans and sways yet without doubt does what she does best to within an impending second of perfection. Plucking it would seem strange but beautiful fragments of what is in the air, an atmosphere phased only by its own manifest of magic.

Her orchestra are totally tuned in to her hypnotic stance and exact as she is, so very precise with her moves of fierce strength that match the soft touch she feels from her right hand holding her black baton like a diehard wizard. Dance as to do so, indeed it is such a thing, since the term orchestra derives from the Greek word "orcheisthai" and everything that they make happen upon sounds for the superior ear is a dream come true. Municipal House holds inside it The Smetana Hall, surrounded by beauty all around. Art Nouveau decorations paint a picture of motifs Slavic in nature. The stained glass ceiling is such a haunt at night when one will look up at its magnitude and become drunk with wonder and awe.

But now the time came for Belle to turn around and face the music of another form, one of adulation from her audience as rapturous applause so nearly consumed her senses that she almost felt compelled to cry with relief. She is still in the zone from whence music came to life, therefore her ear for everything and more was very much alive. Looking out at the collective of a crowd now they were, brought to their feet, it was a moment to remember for Belle. She turned again in order to acknowledge her hardworking orchestra and then once more for the audience she encapsulated. But something was wrong. In the midst of all that jazz such an excited audience exerts, was a noticeable breakaway. A frantic separation in turn met with gasps and panic.

The applause was short-lived. For now the air turns into a heavy heady setting, distraught and chaotic. Belle drops her baton and heads for where the audience have broken away.

"Father . . . FATHER!" Her cries consume the confused audience as she brushes past them all and gathers speed amid a deafening silence.

She remains somewhat out of control, reaching the space made for a fallen man. Her father lay on the floor face down. With him is a younger woman, now bent over, try as she might desperate at his motionless state, shaking him with frantic fright.

"Joseph, Joseph, for the love of God get up!" Belle pulls the young woman off her father. A security guard arrives at the scene.

"Get help!" Belle says, as her voice breaks into terror. The security guard gets his walkie talkie out and calls for help.

"What the hell happened?" She then vents towards the young woman whilst audience members disperse.

"We got up to applaud you and he just fell down." She is stunning to look at but her voice sounds troubled and her hair has fallen out of place.

A man from the audience turns Joseph over.

"What are you doing?" Belle says shockingly.

The man, who appears dressed down on this occasion, ignores her. She is filled with the utter chaos surfacing as of an emotional rollercoaster and therefore tries to pull the man off of her father. Then in doing so, she recognises his scent straight away, which for a brief feeling takes her back in time to the adventurous days they spent together protecting foxes from the deathly clench of hound dogs. This man is Maximus Lucifer Phoenix; he was Isabella's first love and her former leader of the 'Hunt-Trap Rat-Pack', the Cornish foxhunt saboteur society.

"Hello, Belle." Max, with some trepidation, dignifies his old flame amongst such an unbecoming chaos. Isabella is quite frankly taken aback but gathers her thoughts for her father's sake. The young woman begins to walk away.

26

"Where are you going?" Belle wonders, as a stream of sweat trickles down the side of her vexed disposition.

"I can't take this. I'm going outside for a cigarette." The lady in red, with the same shade of lipstick to match her flawless looks, takes her bag from the seat and leaves the scene.

Belle looks like a lost soul; she went from being in her element to this travesty. Two paramedics arrive and take over from Max. They strap Joseph onto a stretcher and carry him out the exit, followed closely by Belle.

30 years ago

Joseph Symonds stands tall at the Kingdom Building delivering one of his sermons.

"'Have you believed because you have seen me? Blessed are those who have not seen and yet believed.' I am one of those blessed few who have not seen and therefore felt not the spiritual awakening; I can only imagine it is something supernatural. But what I can see I will feel and what I therefore feel comes from my heart. I have and hold onto life from whence such beauty, such a miracle came into being - born of a gift from God."

Jehovah's Witnesses as these modest few fill the room with hopeful love. Among them sits Joseph's fiancé, Wendy Danielle Antoinette. A rise of spontaneous praise escapes some of the townspeople, followed by a cry of sharp pain from Wendy at the front of the room. Joseph watches on in disbelief as she falls forward off her chair. Those sat beside her try to help her up but she cries out in pain.

"JOSEPH!" Wendy's waters break.

Joseph stops his sermon and all of a sudden comes to his fiancé's aid. Everyone else watches on as he helps her out the door and into his car. The drive felt long for Joseph but like an eternity to the expectant one of Wendy; breathing heavily she huffs and puffs from the backseat. At the hospital Joseph hands his fiancé over to whom it may concern – nice nurses are at hand to help deliver her baby. He is squeamish. So when asked if he would like to be in the delivery room, Joseph shakes his head. He walks into the waiting room, sits down and begins gathering his thoughts.

It's an empty waiting room today, Sunday, day of rest as if it were such a thing on this occasion! His mouth feels dry while his mind races nonstop. Joseph gets up unnervingly, and goes over to the water dispenser. There is no water left. He sits back down and starts to rub his knees displaying all the obvious signs of nervous excitement. This room is small and bleak. There is next to no light but for the merest ray of sunshine creeping in through an unkempt blind, and then even that soon enough just disappears as if a foreboding gloom looms.

Such a wait! Waiting rooms feel like a limbo for the living. Outside life goes on, but in here there exists only your thoughts to keep you company, and of course outdated magazines showing you what your better life looks like, if money was no object that is. Suffice to say worry reigns supreme. He doesn't know what to do with himself. Without his trusty Bible, Joseph feels all the more unsure of what the near future will bring. Fiddling with his engagement ring, he purposefully loses himself with deep thoughts of meaningful scripture to ease his bittersweet suffering. But nothing springs to his otherwise worried mind. Only worry.

For a peculiar reason unbeknownst to him, Joseph suddenly receives a flashback. It was one of his secondary school biology lessons structured around the reproductive system – making babies. But it wasn't so much the content of such a lesson, than that which he remembers most about it. In the afternoon of a hot summer's day, one fan from the corner of the room did little to cool anyone down. But it did do just enough to make the students abundantly clear that their biology teacher, Mr Prendergast, wears a wig.

And so, while the teacher quickly lost his temper at the sound of smirks coupled with jubilant fidgeting, his wig inched all the more out of place. Mr Prendergast pretended that his pupils were laughing at the subject matter, to spare his own blushes as he repositioned his silly little wig. Joseph always enjoyed the sciences, aside from the sometimes comical moments made possible by teachers such as Mr Prendergast. It is in science Joseph found joy. The joy of discovery and the joy of discovering this universe is seemingly limitless; his awe was always with the brain. When it came to making a decision regarding university and course selection, neuroscience was at the heart of his spirited pursuit. The fascination came from his innocence as a bright but quiet child. Curiosity at a natural high, he would be the one to ask a question that his teacher could not answer with a definitive explanation. Indeed the other pupils always delighted at Joseph's uncanny ability to ask such stumping questions, but to Joseph this was not a victory over his teacher, more so a defeat in

MATTHEW BROOKES

the eyes of a bright child looking for answers at a very early age.

His questioning nature carried on through his university years, yet here he was ready to be redirected and very much encouraged to keep being inquisitive. To the extent that at the end of his studies, his lecturers recommended he take up an evening class in psychology. I guess you could quite easily say Joseph sucked the life out of science – so much so that soon enough, he took his sense of emphatic enthusiasm elsewhere. And when the questions keep on coming, sooner or later there will be the time to branch out, or explore other pathways. Pathways which, different though they seem, all lead to the same outcome in the end, obtaining enlightenment (truth, finding God).

But his becoming a Jehovah's Witness was impassioned by a beautiful woman and not the religion itself. Suffice to say, she is the same woman as the one giving birth in the delivery room right now. And to gain her hand in marriage, he did so after making an agreement with Wendy's cautious parents. Such an agreement is the reason as to why Joseph stands before other Jehovah's Witnesses and says the word of God on every Sunday, except for this one of course. Because of course, Joseph remains pacing up and down the waiting room, along with a hundred and one things racing through his throbbing brain-dead head. And then, the waiting room door slowly opens - enter the doctor to reveal all.

Joseph shoots up from the seat, standing in wait to the doctor's undivided attention. It reads 'Dr.H.McCarthy' on his identity tag attached to his white coat. He is mid-forties, respectable-looking, full head of silver hair, healthy tanned skin and friendly green eyes. His hands are in his pockets. His eyes turn from friendly to a deadly serious stare. Joseph reaches around to the back of his neck with agonising uncertainty taking over his average Joe frame. He shrinks in light of the doctor's stature. Dr. McCarthy takes one hand out of his pocket to stroke his Adam's apple adorned with silver stubble.

"It's not good news, Joseph." The doctor keeps eye-contact with him and after a dramatic, quite uncalled for pause, he continues.

"How can I put this, with respect to your religion . . . um . . . ?" Dr. McCarthy looks ill-at-ease.

"Just spit it out, Doctor – regardless of my religious beliefs this is a personal and private matter." Joseph finds it within himself to assume a false sense of calmness.

"Your baby needs a blood transfusion," the doctor replies, with absolute certainty taking over his softly spoken manner as Joseph's face drops into one of a long look coming from fear and disbelief. His sunken dark brown eyes fall from the doctor's graceless stare. He feels like crying yet keeps it together. Then something comes to him in a flash before his eyes, as such a thing hit his thoughts straight to a stop. He heard the words 'Love conquers all' rattle his cage and shake him to the core.

"Do it." Joseph, without a moment to lose, speaks straight from his deepest place possible.

"You're sure?" Dr. McCarthy makes sure before proceeding with the treatment.

"Do the damn transfusion!" Joseph finally snaps out of frustration.

"By the way that wasn't the bad news, Mr Symonds." The doctor takes his hands out of his pockets, putting one on Joseph's underarm for comforts sake.

"Wendy didn't quite have the strength to pull through. After giving birth, she passed away." The doctor squeezes Joseph's arm and strokes it with his thumb. But Joseph shrugs him off aggressively, like a startled animal in the wild, feeling threatened and violated. He is stunned into a silence soul destroying him from the inside out.

"I'm sorry. For what it's worth; Wendy gave birth to a beautiful baby girl." The doctor tries as he might to soften the blow but the damage has been done. Joseph feels like the life force has been beaten out of him. He goes over to the water dispenser and lashes out at it in desperation. The big empty water bottle falls to the floor and rolls across the room. Dr. McCarthy walks away with a look of concern on his self-satisfied face. Does the Bible command us to abstain from the ingestion of blood? And by avoiding blood do we respect God as the giver of life? Questions such as these should perhaps have entered the mind of Joseph before feeling the need to answer the doctor's prognosis. Or perhaps his mind had already served its purpose upon bringing to light the scripture from Corinthians. Yes. It's true. Love does conquer all.

19th of December 2018

"Miss Antoinette, the doctor will see you now," the receptionist informs Belle regarding her father's condition.

"Shall I come with you?" Max asks.

"Yes, please do," she says.

They enter the doctor's office somewhat separate from the hospital itself.

"Have a seat." The doctor is tall, slim and Indian.

"I am Dr. Chopra. Are you the son and daughter of Joseph?" His voice is surprisingly high for a big man.

"I am, Max is my friend." Belle appears nervous so Max puts his hand on hers.

"Isabella, your father has an inoperable brain tumour, terminal in other words, do you know what this means?" Dr. Chopra removes his glasses so as to maintain a serious edge. Her first love, Max, has her hand held tight. She rubs her forehead with her other hand, distressed.

"Does Dad know about this?" Her whimper of a question nearly fell silent with the sadness she feels.

"Joseph knows what he has, as we informed him when we knew for sure that that's what it was causing him to collapse," Dr. Chopra responds sharpish, fiddling with a pen in one hand, like a craving mad smoker can't go without doing something with his or her hands.

So delicate a dream is, Isabella's sweet dream became victim to the cruel world we live in. It did come true for all of an evening's splendor, shattered after fate took a twisted turn for the worse. She can choose to have her father cared for by 'professionals' somewhere which will accommodate the dying in a big disenchanted facility, but Belle will not neglect Joseph even if all else fails. So she has not got a choice but to take her father home and watch him die a debilitating death. The music in her heart has been broken until all that remains is silence of the suffocating kind.

(Attachment continued)

'You are born and the game begins. You grow up playing along. And then one day you find yourself feeling lost. Your mind wanders, as it does, but then it begins to question the game. 'Am I lost?' 'What does this feeling really mean?' Then you realise something that turns your stomach, making you stop doing whatever it was which just so happened to bring you to this place of inquiry. It's dark. For the first time in your life, you become made fully aware of the darkness surrounding you. You are not afraid of the dark because the darkness has always been here. Then you try to think back, but its useless consolation against the ever-present blackening. Instead of searching in the past for a false glimmer of hope, you accept the reality of your situation and start to move on. Now the universe knows you know how you got here – reckless disregard. And so, you see the error in your ways as clear as day. Suddenly, something else happens, this self-perpetuating nightmare, your waking life, for as long as you can remember being in control of your own destiny, and then it hits you. You have heard words such as 'destiny' and 'fate' thrown around in an abundant attempt to answer for everyone else's existence except for your own. Why? When all else has failed to move you forwards, you're hereby begging the question. Somewhere along the scribbly little line of your life, you not only lost control, but you forgot how to get it back. That blackening, blinding, mad, mad world of your own manifestation, in other words – this ignorance suddenly ceases to exist. It has been taken over by your wonder alone, and in doing so, you are filled from within, without doubt but a feeling like never before overcomes any sense of uncertainty. You hear yourself say 'Anything is possible' but it is so spontaneous, as if by your very own newfound, cleansed stream of consciousness, was such a thing singing a praise for *finally feeling free? You're free from the trappings of 'playing along' and now your nature tells you to rage against it. To keep questioning this so-called life from an open place – yours truly, you have the heart but do you have the time? The presence of mind? And as you ask an honest question, when in truth the answer is already yours for the taking, this sincere sense of inquest is exactly that! The quest inwards will continue to prove wise, while the universe plays out your future for you.'*

I am a philosophical questioner, whatever that means. Amongst other things, this self-proclamation comes of course as no surprise; I can call myself a fucking cunt for all anyone else cares! Quite frankly, if and when one can and will at once as if by magic think me 'this' or 'that' then this or that I AM albeit in the moment within which I was such a thing. And so, you too will think highly, lowly, maybe even heaven forbid godly of yourselves! Simply put, it will not do, to be but a thought that can catch fire from whence one's self found, felt, then adored and thus far forever grooms such an ego. Oh God, help us. This is not right. To parade around in circles as a self-perpetuating peacock! Or wrongly lull yourself into a false sense of certainty until believing in no uncertain terms this life has assurances above and beyond death, that you then know better than anyone else, is self-deception. Indeed do you even know yourself, first and foremost? As for me, I know not what it means to be at one with the truth. The truth is I had a beer for breakfast, just so you know . . . oh despair for woe is me! I really am an out and out contradictive vex self-destructing in the wake of making sense. Where's the sense in killing brain cells while writing about . . . wait, what am I writing about?

It means nothing now. It was just an impossible dream. It is what it is, and it is forever futile. To know now why we as a whole will not try and live a life of truth . . . this destroys my righteous soul. All else fails me albeit in vain the game goes on   and we play, maybe not consciously lying yet to deceive even ourselves sure enough of what will be, will be because needs must. And need becomes us all. Indeed dare I need not to write would I write at all? But I don't need to hate, hate mutates out of an absence, something that lacks its capacity to be a dance dancing in and of itself, if not for or from love then only hate with regret reign raging against this system. A system of things misshapen hence westernized and aesthetically pleasing, so to compensate for its soullessness existing within, that which is instead filled with the pure evil void, deathless limbo forever reborn an unending disease. These people all around are playing along but I look deep within and thus far before my ever so sunken until colourless eyes finally see the light to be at once brightest because of what I seek - meaning, not money, reality, not a game made of fools moonlighting as professionals and of professionals spirited away by their own sense of bias self-importance. Most of all, let truth turn our future righteous so we can bask in being living proof of the greater good   and delight at the paradise we made possible here on planet Earth.'

CHAPTER 2: ENDING ON A LOW NOTE

20th of December 2018

Festive cheer falls on her heartbreak, like an acapella plays without the sound of music; it longs for the heavenly voice of the voiceless, such as music is. She wheels her father home, knowing not what to do next, but quiet as a mouse she grieves underneath her heavy breath.

You really didn't have to help me here . . . after all, now I feel guilty taking you away from your travels." Isabella and Max make their way into Joseph's detached and quite quaint Cornish cottage. It's cold but frosty, yet the light looks special since the sun is in and so something else glistens, as if in the air remains the most wonderful time of the year, regardless of such suffering. And yet still her pain brings out the beauty of being an imperfect part of the perfect full circle – life is beautiful forever and always.

"Nonsense, Isabella, you're my friend and friends stick together this time of year, or are you not my friend?" he jokes softly, leaning into her side and gives just a nudge of his elbow while letting out a twinkle of youthful innocence as his hazel eyes widen at her soft face.

"So while I'm dying, you two can converse sweetly, like nothing has happened. Don't mind me! I'll just sit here and have my brain rot from your mindlessly lethargic conversation. Continue to act like everything is ok, play at being the 'happy couple' you once were before he had to fuck off and 'find himself'. If there's one thing that I have learnt from my time on this somewhat warped planet, it's in everybody's best interest to be real . . . speak your mind! Don't waste time trying to 'keep the peace' because it's a futile lie. And because 'nice and normal' small talk makes my skin crawl." Joseph is sat positioned at the foot of the kitchen table, while Max watches on from the head of it not knowing where to look, listening to Joseph find words for his frustration at the cruel consequence of being born. Belle leans down, bent over the kitchen worktop, putting the kettle on and closing her eyes for a moment's respite from the harsh reality that is crushing her. She weeps for one second of weakness consuming her fragility. But then, upon gathering herself, she approaches Max.

"Can I have a cigarette please?" she asks, sweeping her tears away with both her backhands.

"But you don't smoke," he says, surprised by her question.

"Just give me a goddamn fag or you can get the hell out of this house!" Belle loses it. Max gets out a cigarette. She takes it from him, along with his peace symbol lighter and then walks outside through the front door for a smoke. She slams the front door with feeling, lights the cigarette, then breathes out, desperately losing the will to accept such a sick twist of fate.

Her phone rings; it's her agent.

"Hello, Lucy. Yes, yes I'm fine, don't worry about me. No, really, Lucy, please, there's no need to act like this is the end of the world. Ok . . . thank you. I had the time of my life. If my father's health improves I'll be sure to carry on in the same vein. I mean," she composes herself as she stares lifelessly at a naked tree brought to warmth from whence such a striking beam of sunlight hit it in the heart. "I mean . . . I can't come back. I can't carry on with the rest of the tour . . . yes of course this is not what I want but no one can account for where or when one of your loved ones just falls down and almost dies, damn it! This is my father. This is my family. That which I did was just a dream come true. This is something else entirely. Lucy, listen to me, I'm ok. Put the champagne on ice as it were . . . I wish you a merry Christmas as well, Lucy. Give my love to all the orchestra for me please . . . yes, you take care too . . . goodbye . . . bye." She cancels the call, inhales her cigarette with disgust at life, looks up at the shining sun and shouts, "FUCK YOU!" Max and Joseph hear her cry for help from indoors.

"Shouldn't you go see if she's ok?" Joseph says coldly. Max snaps out of his strained disposition and joins Isabella outside.

"Is everything ok?" he asks hesitantly.

"What kind of a question is that?" she answers back, blowing smoke in his face.

"Well, I was just wondering . . . " Try as he might to make sense of such a question, Belle feels compelled to butt in and interrupt.

"It's been ten years and you 'was just

wondering' . . . well, how about that! Your sincere concern means so much to me! For your information, Max, everything is not ok." She throws him back his peace symbol lighter.

"Is there anything I can do?" Max sounds sheepish.

Belle laughs as she stamps out her cigarette and then goes back inside, leaving him on the receiving end of her whirlwind attitude. He has a cigarette to settle his thoughts.

Max always saw himself as something of a game changer where the world was concerned. Indeed it was his discontent at the westernized zeitgeist that played a pivotal part in making him a man of the world and not merely a slave to the ways of western society. He was born an orphan but grew up being loved and adored by his adoptive parents. Whom managed a successful business on the seafront, host and hostess to their charming B&B.

He is on the wrong end of thirty these days, lest he forgets, but of course try as he might he can't do so. No escaping time. No escaping one's own sense of success and failure measured up against friends, enemies, peers, people the media bombard us with – the fame game from whence one average Joe general public cunt can somehow break away and become a famous fucking cunt instead. There is no doubting this once upon a time trailblazer lives and breathes for the greater good. But Max, having travelled far and wide, has since misplaced his sense of belonging. In other words, this man is lost.

Max therefore feels filled with a sudden sense of being intrusive with Isabella and her life in mind. His cigarette long since burnt out, but unwittingly the butt is still between his freezing fingers as he speaks on the phone. Joseph and Isabella are re-joined by this man a shadow of his former self, certainly not in the mood to drink tea and talk about the weather.

"Who were you on the phone to, if you don't mind me asking?" Isabella's curiosity is still alive even if everything within her has a distinct and deadbeat feel of being broken, unto what exists at the moment as nothing more than her flightless soul.

"It doesn't matter." Max lets out a whimper for feeling the way he does, down and out. Belle raises her eyebrows, surprised by his unwillingness. Max continues to stand amid a dying old man and a broken woman, sat down on the receiving end of eventual death and the surrender of a childhood dream. There are no words, but a piercing silence instills deep thought for all three.

Knock, knock, knock at the door makes Isabella jump and wakes Joseph up from being half-asleep. She answers the door to a taxi driver. Max readies himself for a short goodbye.

"Sorry for everything, Isabella. Bye." He makes the merest of eye contact with her, upon passing through the front door towards the taxi. She has frozen, not knowing what to say or do. He gets in the taxi.

"You should stop him before it's too late." Joseph says sincerely.

Isabella runs out of the house as the taxi begins to move. She catches up to it just in time, banging on the back window with his name on her lips.

"MAX, WAIT!" she shouts violently.

He winds down the window.

"I lost you once, I'm not losing you again," she admits desperately.

"It was more than just a coincidence . . . destiny brought us back together for a reason, Isabella," Max says, sure of himself.

"What's going on back there?" the taxi driver asks, staring into his rear-view mirror.

"You're staying with us this Christmas, Max," she says, as it starts to snow.

"Ok." He gets out of the taxi.

'Stay not the same; change one's ways. May my eventual death give a whole new meaning to the way in which was, and always will be, but to know not now anymore might I bask then at an all-encompassing place surrounded by beauty beyond what this life had and held dear, dreams . . . do I ask of you, universe, so much so there will only be deep profound feelings misspent at my peril longing for your warm embrace, as if I were to once and forever realise I was just a question away from the answer I was seeking, in spite of not at all looking within, without doubt, to be freer than these sweet nothings and transform from my masquerading disposition into timeless essence itself such an equivalent of love but much richer than that of earthly love.

Fuck it. The truth is . . . I don't know what the truth is. What's within me I know not but for my imagination and its fashion inform me by many more ways than one? Was I an outsider? Did I care not for the way it is? And the way is what exactly? 'The way, the truth and the life' if only I knew how to be. . . real always. What do I want? I want truth. I want not to be a hypocrite. Happiness, sex, a great big cock, a smaller nose, nicer skin, and the rest! What was I thinking? I was thinking I could change the world and make it into a truthful future just by writing what I thought was righteous.

To think, it is bittersweet when one will realise his thoughts simply promote what one knows now was small-minded and ignorant. I can only think for myself! That's not true. I can think for others as well. But because of being a selfish fuck I commit to being 'me, me, me' in all my godawful glory. And in all my godawful glory here I am making sense of me. I smoke, ok. I smoke socially, I smoke so to help gather certain thoughts, I smoke as a 'fuck you' to a few things. Basically I smoke because I cannot see the harm in me, but only feel a superficial sense of satisfaction from it. I drink, I drink, I smoke some more, while I think, and I think until taking great heart from the thoughts that give me feelings of profound truth. And yet, I think enough to know not therefore I am! And that which was thought wasn't so set in stone, only by my way of wanting; wanting until feeling the need to know what is real. And what is real is right, therefore falseness is wrong. But of course can I really be saying that all things make-believe, every profound feeling from fiction alone and no matter just how much such a thing, a film for instance – such a thing! It will move you to tears, tears of being moved. Moved from making you believe in the unbelievable because quite frankly anything IS possible. And if anything is possible, but by if I mean when and by when I mean when anything is physically proven possible, then in no uncertain terms - 'simply put' - what is real is also wrong and what is false is also true, right?

No one wants to live a lie but no one wants to live the truth either. Therefore, from mind and thus thoughts that are reinforced as time marches on, one will lull oneself for feeling the need to exist at an agreeable place of peace, as in simply being rest assured where one's reasoning is concerned. Would you open your mind enough if it meant to consciously clear the way for what could quite easily be an experience of feeling vulnerable by a rude awakening? Instead, let what will be but a coping mechanism in force not for your better judgement; to 'see the light' out of a blinded mind is impossible! Becoming closed-minded and all that which is as opposed to jazz's spontaneous stream of playful fucking around, requires killing off the firing neurons not in use, so those 'things' that are there for your growth have been neglected until all that remains stays the same. Why would you not want to free your mind? I have a feeling it is simply fear from what we believe to be our own ego, grasping at your every fibre of being, gripping an innermost 'me', making senses seem more or less separate motions of what on the naked eye you cannot possibly see as all-encompassing experience personified by energy.

By 'living a lie' I mean when a way of life finds solace as an acceptable substitute for feeling the feared repercussions stemming from what one knows is just so, or 'righteous' as it were; where the truth will hurt there won't be a soul in sight! Why am I doing this? Simply because as of when one writes a book, any book, along comes the flood of better women wanting to have sex with the writer. By better, that is exactly all I mean, maybe not in every way but on the surface, perhaps better by the way they make themselves seen as striking, and then in the way of being well-spoken. So all in all, better is a severe reference of the physical.

What am I doing? I am attempting to articulate rage. Therefore 'rage', not as in 'violent uncontrollable anger', or else this is a betrayal because by trying to articulate it, I am of course somewhat at least in control of it. But this is the rage of being a 'vehement desire or passion' and that vehement desire or passion comes alive via the hate that I have for the way of the western world. It is also a rage against one's own human condition.

My indulgency here leaves everything else as simply being everything else separate from me. Be it at night then when I think to myself 'Have I got you horribly wrong world?' 'Do you, "universe" whisper your precious sweet nothings so as only by my spirit to pick up the pieces of your universal truth?' If it is written in the stars as manifest finite to that which oneness looks like, coming from an all-encompassing essence, such was and always will be; by your highest place cast but one lonesome star down upon your ravishing, shining night;   take great pleasure showing me the only way of life *worth dying for - where righteousness reigns supreme.*

They go back inside. The December day quickly becomes a cold night. Isabella helps her father as best she can into bed but he has a lot of forsaken acceptance still lurking on the outskirts of his troublesome mind. Max and Isabella are relaxing in the living room. A fire burns in its rightful place, as well as perhaps somewhere more vulnerable, but the night is still young. The news is on:

"Rio de Janeiro has been hit with a severe earthquake. Measuring in at 10 on the Richter scale, all that remains is Christ the Redeemer amid a city reduced to ruin. But survivors are proclaiming this natural disaster to be an act of the divine kind, and as a spontaneous celebration breaks out amid devastation there is something in the air here, not a carnival atmosphere however, more like a crazy party at that which awaits its life and soul, from what these people of Brazil believe is a sign. . . a sign indeed of the second coming of Christ."

"Oh my God," gasps Isabella.

"God's got nothing to do with it," Max says swiftly, sipping on his glass of mulled wine.

"How can a statue withstand such force?" she asks, gazing into the television screen. He gets up from the armchair and turns off the TV. He then bends down and pokes at the fire's embers before returning to his seat.

"I've seen the face of the future, torn to shreds thanks to us so-called 'civilised citizens' cos on that day, the day of your performance, I was waiting to board a plane from Prague airport to Rio de Janeiro. But before Prague, I made a visit to Madrid and feasted my eyes over a vision of our ill-fated future. Have you seen 'The Garden of

Earthly Delights'?" Max's eyes glow in the dim room losing its light from the dying fire.

"Only in print but what has such a thing got to do with this atrocity anyway?" Belle sounds offended by the way he has assumed such confidence in his stance that otherwise opposes her 'more normal' mind-set.

"I was sat there thinking about it on the whole . . . have we any idea what the hell we are doing with freewill as our weapon of what is in no uncertain terms mass destruction? Human beings losing sight of self-respect; it is a dying breed to be at one with the truth. These days, and maybe even long before my time, we are a people living in spite of everyone else's mistakes as opposed to taking responsibility for our own actions. As for our dwindling identity, we've lost the will to be anything but men and women of business, industry; it's a digital age jollying in online lunacy - such is limbo born from the womb of a man-made machine - an imitation will always fail the real thing. I'm talking about the beauty of Mother Nature here being in great danger, for I am not a tree-hugger more so a struggling trailblazer. Business is at once and for all about business itself, obviously. Suits dressed to redefine life from a blind mind and a black heart set on money and more of the same. Man has the means to make-believe, if it fits with his agenda, his game plan I mean . . . " Max seems to be declining towards the edge of his scatterbrain but Isabella adores his passion and humours him.

"You mean what exactly?" she asks, sat on the sofa as she sips her hot chocolate.

"I wouldn't be at all surprised by our scandalous ways, as a government but also as a people we reduce ourselves to living on the prayer of false hope . . . " He thinks he has time to build up his point of view but Belle is getting tired.

"Spit it out, Max, you're losing me to my sleepy head, have you got a point to prove here or am I only on the receiving end of your rant for no apparent reason?" She finishes her hot chocolate and places it on the coaster positioned near the centre of the table.

"Different forces are at work here. The one which kept me in Prague, ultimately leading me to you and the one which has caused destruction in Rio. It is possible the beginning of a shift in power will soon happen and yet emerge as something else entirely. Because we live in a mad world posing as 'nice and normal', no one bothers with what has slowly but surely become an art form unto itself and that's questioning the television's version of events. Suffice to say, the media are all puppets . . . who's pulling the strings? I don't know, not yet anyway. All I do know is this; that that earthquake cannot possibly be natural." His eyes scan side to side rapidly looking within himself for an answer.

"What if it's supernatural?" Belle's eyes light up, prevailing against her tiredness.

"What if it's artificial? What if it's a set-up?" Max wants the facts of the matter at hand and not some kind of throwaway miracle dealt out to the desperate public by the powerful few.

"By whom?" Belle wonders.

"The powers that be . . . the ones who will come to Rio's rescue," he says openly.

Belle leans over and grabs the remote control from on the armchair. She turns the news back on, obviously keen to know more about the meat of the matter.

"President of the United States of America Ronald Flump has issued an offer of great help to Rio. And by that I mean this man, a man of funny money by the way who before rising to the heights of presidency, was once a billionaire businessman, now will pay out of his own pocket to help rebuild Rio around its miraculous Christ the Redeemer. Here's what he had to say from The White House . . . 'We are all on the same team, divided only by country, we will stand side by side in the face of adversity . . . together . . . together we will make Rio great again . . . any questions?' 'Bruce Jennings NBC: is this a sign of the second coming?' 'I'm a president not a prophet, next question . . . ' 'Natasha Henderson FOX News: is this an act of God?' 'Are all you guys gonna ask me the same question in a slightly different way? What can I say? God did not come to me in a dream. God has not found his way into the White House. How do I know what this was exactly? All I can do is act fast; for the sake of Rio de Janeiro but also as a fellow human being this feels like the right thing to do. Thank you.'"

"He knows something. Did you see how defensive he was? And why waste his own fortune on a country that has been of no significance to him in his whole life? This makes no sense, unless of course there's an agenda here. " Max is on the edge of his seat, startled and fascinated, disturbed but inspired by his own conclusions.

"Listen, now it's the Prime Minister," Belle politely tells Max to shut up as the news continues:

"I'm sure I speak for all of Great Britain when I express such sadness and disbelief with regard to Rio right now. We must come together and unite as one strong unit of support. Take a leaf if you will out of President Ronald Flump's book - give everything you can. This is a desperate time for Rio so please let us unite in the name of human kind ."

Belle turns the TV off, kisses Max on the cheek and goes upstairs to bed.

"It's late, get some sleep. Goodnight," she whispers from halfway up the stairs as she advances to her room. Max soon falls asleep on the armchair.

21st of December 2018

Belle wakes to the feeling of being shaken. She opens her eyes as Max turns on the bedside table light. It's still the middle of the night.

"Can I talk to you?" he asks, disregarding the inconvenience of it all.

"Is it important?" Isabella asks, as she yawns and rubs one eye.

"Very," he says, sat on the side of her bed.

"Let me put something on and I'll see you downstairs." Belle can hardly believe this, but there was always, and still is, such an innocence to dear sweet Max. He gets lost with what goes on in his head and how hard it must be for him to comprehend the world from a sane place; he comes across as a compelling and endearing madman at times.

They sit back down in the darkness of the living room. This time he sits next to her on the sofa. She turns on the sidelight.

"Your pupils are dilated - how much sleep have you had?" Belle looks concerned.

"I fell asleep for a bit but my dream woke me up." Max is wide-eyed as he wriggles restlessly.

"What's so important that it can't wait until tomorrow?" Of course, it's already 'tomorrow' but Belle is too tired for anal accuracies.

"Noah . . . Moses . . . and now me . . . you know too well what a dream is made of . . . your dream was achieved and I saw how much it meant to you up on that stage . . . everything must have made sense in that moment when you made it happen . . . when you made it come true." Max's scatterbrain is back and firing on all cylinders. Isabella still feels ill at ease speaking of such a bittersweet recent past event but can see how much he is dialled into something going on in his head.

"Yes, Max, my dream became my destiny and now life goes on." Belle looks taken aback by her own words as she still has not come to terms with it, that which is a shattered dream.

"Yes! Destiny in a dream!" He leans into her with open arms and holds her for what a one-sided kind of embrace is worth.

"Max! What's going on with you?" Belle smiles surprised and yet senses something is up.

"Remember when I left the country for pastures new?" he asks, so very rhetorically, all the while with shimmering intensity, yet without doubt. Therein is such subtlety to his passion, an understated edge.

"How can I forget? I fell in love but you just had to fuck off for 'pastures new.'" Belle looks sad as she recollects such a time gone by.

"Did you read my writings?" Max asks excitedly, devoid of time and place.

"What writings?" Isabella looks confused.

He raises his eyebrows but continues to pursue his innermost thoughts that are surfacing as he speaks.

"I dreamt then like my dream came over me last night, both have the same strong quality. That winter I went chasing such a dream and so such a dream brings me back to you but last night . . . a new dream . . . same feeling . . . this is something undeniably real, Belle, believe me please because I can't do it alone." He has past the point of intensity; indeed he now looks to have captured the essence of passion in his hazel eyes.

"Can't do what alone? You're yet to make sense!" Belle is losing her patience.

"HELP ME! BELLE!" Joseph screams from upstairs. She runs up to the bedroom.

"I can't feel my fucking legs!" Joseph says desperately, pulling the covers from underneath him. He stinks of piss and there remains a wet patch between his legs.

"MAX, CALL AN AMBULANCE!" Isabella at the top of her voice screams downstairs as Max jumps up from the sofa and phones for an ambulance.

"Dad, try to remain calm . . . an ambulance is on its way, ok?" Belle comforts her frightened father.

"Get him up here, there's something that will set Max free from his wayward world of fucked up unrest . . . get him up here right now!" Joseph has such a look of desperation on his pale face; Isabella has not seen him in this light ever before but does as he says straight away.

Max enters the piss-smelling room. Belle puts the bedcover back over her father to hide his penis from sight.

"Belle, wait downstairs for the ambulance," Joseph says clearly.

"But Dad . . . " Belle doesn't want to leave his side.

"Go! Now!" Joseph raises his voice straight at his daughter, who concedes as she makes her way downstairs.

"Max, Max, Max . . . first and foremost, I forgive you for breaking my daughter's heart. Water under the bridge but now is not the time to nit-pick. I think the time has come for you to find your way home - wherever your soul feels most at peace, that is. So without further ado, open up my Bible . . . it's over there." Joseph points towards where his bible is as Max goes and gets it.

"Turn the light on and have a look inside," Joseph says, scanning Max's movements as he turns the main light on and sits back down on the side of the bed. Then suddenly, Belle comes back with two paramedics.

Max gets up, clutching the Bible. Joseph is startled but the paramedics are professionals and make sure he feels somewhat at ease. Isabella signals at Max to leave the room with her. They go downstairs into the kitchen. One of the paramedics soon joins them in the kitchen.

"We have no choice but to take Joseph with us, just so you know what's going on." The paramedic is tall, well-built but not fat and speaks making eye contact with Isabella.

Max is sat at the kitchen table looking mesmerised as he stares down at the Bible.

"Can I come with you?" Belle asks the paramedic.

"Yes, of course. Excuse me while I help tend to your father." The paramedic goes back upstairs right away.

"What's that doing down here?" She asks him why he has her father's Bible.

"Joseph gave it to me, he says something is inside and I should take a look," Max answers honestly, for there is no reason to deceive her.

"Now's not the time for fucking scripture! You're unbelievable! Bloody hell, how did I ever fall for such a . . . such a blissfully foolish little lamb like you . . . all lost and forever vexed by life . . . you're a hopeless case, Max. Jesus Christ." Belle lets off some steam as she paces up and down the kitchen. The same paramedic comes into the kitchen.

"We're ready when you are," the paramedic addresses Isabella.

"Look after the house please, Max . . . can you do that?" Belle belittles him in front of the paramedic.

"Yes, of course I can. You go, I'll be fine." He is still entranced by what could be in the contents of Joseph's Bible. Belle follows the paramedic out the front door and into the ambulance.

'The game is a grey area reinforced from numbers breeding an endless strength that will work together therefore prevailing against the greater good and thus disregarding the definitive truth. The black or white matter of fact that our moral compass least of all senses, so it still exists, if only by a bittersweet whisper of feeling it in the first place. Lest we forget to feel from our heart, at that which is indeed heavier than it should be, because I can determine many things, as if by a tragic truth of the truth, then land like I am a fish out of water upon one certainty – apart from the obvious one which will always take us in the end – death. The other certainty that has been many times soul-destroyed and then even effortlessly rebuilt by the mechanics of cunning common sense, yet still blinded are the minds made dark, coldblooded are the ones whose windows open only to the fellow wrongdoers, so don't get me wrong when I mean greedy, deceptive versions of a network corrupting itself for the purpose of power that will always reduce truth to a desperate plea being answered with

the same old empty promise personified by liars. Players like to play God for more control over our better judgement.

Thank God for Sunday, day of rest from the game and its sickening grip over greater good. Yet to what end when that hopeful future never even happens? So we could quite easily self-destruct but not for today, today the world slows down. When our heads hurt for the false feelings from which we were under the influence of liquid courage just hours before the cold light of today came. Came it did to bring us back at least until the next time comes around and then again, consumed by booze, as an enabler, loss of our whimpering former selves sober no more to the bore reality at least is for those of us suffering with a blinded mind.

Not all see Saturday night through the wandering eyes of a wasted predator, or from a throbbing boner behind trendy trousers remains nothing but a tipsy sex pest. There are the braindead telly addicts delighting in a shallow wayward world of famous fucking cunts and self-satisfied damsels dancing to a tune worn out but still skipping, parading about town, no, not a town, indeed it is my capital city, these thespians and those serious about business – still all are very much monkeys of money. Monkeys masquerading in spite of our want, to be seen and heard as that which we are not! But it is within thinking, it is as we envision such a thing to be real or right; therefore from whence Descartes took care realising this mistake: 'I think therefore I am!'
And add alcohol into the mix of your make-believe mouthpiece, is simply saying yes for your conscious stream, may it take on an animalistic mindset, speak not sober but more from your heart's desire. So to sum up Saturday night it is, or over time manifests as, a means of wilfully killing brain cells/losing sense, instead find yourself feeling the bittersweet falsehood of freedom from being victim in the working week. Because systematically speaking, we are all trapped. To live for the weekend and yet you will only ever exist as a self-perpetuating team of individual players, playing your part in

the system kept together through fewer than those sat at a secret meeting, making your life a living hell albeit to further fund an all-encompassing businessman and his much loved playboy lifestyle.

The privileged and proud, despicably well-off and by classy shamelessness surround themselves within an intricate, intimate, select circle of celebrity puppets, but still puppets that know not their place. As if by black magic making themselves believe because of course that's what they do best, isn't it? Actors act therefore players play, playing the game at its own game. 'Playing the game at its own game', imagine then that art not only acts as an imitation of life, but it becomes exceedingly life-like, creating yet more of a falsified form than the illusion being believed real when we 'wake up' in the morning. If in life we are encouraged to 'play the game' because that's its nature, therefore actors are playing the game from a nuanced disposition. Indeed actors are, from imagination, imagining and at the same time becoming someone else entirely. Why? Why not! It pays to play the game at its own game, simply because 'imitation is the sincerest form of flattery'. Actors are, in essence, flattering the game of life itself, celebrating it, but we mere mortals welcome with open arms this special deception, hoping to obtain greater understanding towards what one and all exist as by being human.

Life made art as an effect from being caused or created and life therefore became made aware of what art was – simply light within which there dwells darkness. Darkness does not know itself; if darkness 'saw the light' it would at once cease to exist as darkness. Is light related to dark? Did dark come first before light? Life, from being born of sin, knows itself already and thus far not for a name to say "you are 'this'", or "you are 'that'" at birth, but your life before your identity manifested itself from experience was simply your pure experience experiencing experience itself after having inherited the unseen intelligence; essence seemingly solidified by and contained inside such a thing as your body. Your body is being personified by the human condition. An actor, or my personal preference is as a 'player' does nothing but play, playing a part that asks you to make-believe in it. 'It', as each and every character created inside a story of its own doing. This is all a player does; she or he befits such a story that will always aim to move you in some way shape or form. For a story to work and thus far for players to play as per usual, there requires a certain something in simple terms, such is this so-called 'game'. And a game more often than not needs rules. As for its definition, a game means 'a form of competitive activity."

CHAPTER 3: BREAKING BAD FOR THE GREATER GOOD

Max opens up the Bible. Not to scripture, but cut out to hold inside it certain documents instead. He unfolds the documents to discover such things have been rendered classified by the US Government. The contents of which include drawings; diagrams containing notes and calculations deciphering an equation - an equation for free energy. He flicks through the documents discovering that the last page is a letter addressed to Max. The letter reads as follows:

Max,
By receiving this, I should already be dead, either that or knocking on Heaven's door. Documents such as these must be taken care of, for they are precious. As a scientist I was spirited away by my own wonder and awe at what on Earth this world is, or more importantly, what this world could be. Belle tells me about you and your vast appetite to see the world around you for what it is, as opposed to what the western world will have you believe it is – a consumer driven dreamscape, make-believe bullshit basically. Let me be real right now. I went from a wonderful life of science, straight into the world and word of God, not with love but through

fear reigning over me.

A week before my graduation, it was my birthday, and being the way I was, one lecturer whose name I may not state took a shine to me. These classified documents were a gift from him. He thought he was giving me a head start after graduating but on the day of my graduation news broke out of his death, which was without doubt a contrived suicide by the powers that be . . . I soon went on to receive a death threat, and a word of advice: destroy the documents if you value your life.

If you are afraid and fear for your life, Max, destroy the documents, maybe even marry my daughter, to live out a life of happiness instead. Or are you willing to do whatever it takes to make the world a better place? 'Push the envelope' go 'beyond the pale' . . . 'OVER THE RAINBOW!' What you are reading, indeed feasting your eyes over, is the vision of a righteous future. The documents concern Nikola Tesla's pursuit of free energy. Please, Max, act NOW and illuminate the world with the colour of truth. You know what to do. You're the son I never had. And look out for Isabella's best interests at heart; she cares deeply about you, Max . . . she always has . . . she always will.

With love,
Joseph

Attached to the letter looks like a poem. Max recognises its handwriting to be Belle's. He reads on:

This is the life we feel from our heart's discontent
Out in the wild, we watch on, to see country folk and their time misspent
Playing a game of cat and mouse, much worse than that which is, as if by a tragic Tradition continues . . . it's foxhunting to the rich, it's sick and twisted to us

High horsemen and women in much the same vein
Train dogs up to betray true nature; the chase is on . . . run
away!
Run away my dear sweet fox, it's not your fault or the dogs
It's us . . . just blame man and his misguided desire for
bloodlust

But here I stand with our great leader . . . Maximus Lucifer
Phoenix of out and out righteousness
It's in him we trust
So to you my enemy, these people of fucking cruel heartless
shit for brains
They may have a status to uphold but only amongst their own
kind
Kings of self-proclaimed kings, queens of self-proclaimed
queens . . .
Be gone once and for all

Isabella leaves the hospital alone. The sun is up. The sky is blue. But all is not bright to Belle. All has been nearly lost this Christmas. She buys a pack of cigarettes from the nearest newsagents and then takes a sombre stroll into a park. Belle sits down on a bench and opens up the pack of cigarettes, but to her heightened annoyance has forgotten to buy a lighter. Frustrated and upset, she throws the pack of fags away and remains seated.

In the distance she can see an altercation between what looks like a homeless person and two police officers. The scruffy-looking man is middle-aged, black and big in stature. He looks to have been stopped for feeding a kit of pigeons lashings of birdseed. She watches on as the black man is bundled down to the ground by both officers. Isabella jumps up. Her instincts kick in and she paces towards them. The pigeons are startled by the black man's hefty fall and fly away.

"Hey! HEY! Who do you think you are? He's done nothing wrong! Leave him the hell alone!" Belle wholeheartedly lets her feelings be known. The officers stare at her. The big black man remains embarrassingly left for a fool on the floor.

"We are police officers or are you blind as well as bat-shit crazy, lady?" One of the officers speaks out at her with his horrid rotten tongue in full swing. The other one watches on as the black man stumbles back up to his feet, but before he can do so, the officer kicks him back down to the ground right before Belle's eyes.

"Hey! You corrupt fucking pig! That's assault!" Isabella, astounded at the officer's sheer audacity, tries to shield the man from further trouble.

"This is police business so if you don't mind walking away now we'd appreciate it." It's like both officers speak in exactly the same way – stuck up that is – using an appearance to put forth their futile illusion of power.

"Oh, is it? Alright then, I'll walk on by like nothing happened here . . . perhaps I should stop by the station on my way home . . . maybe your superiors should know what sort of officers you two really are . . . or am I blind as well as bat-shit crazy? Cos quite frankly you guys are one witness statement away from being unemployed pigs – as opposed to just pigs . . . so is this still police business or have you two got better things to do than degrade your power for the purpose of sick and twisted tomfoolery?" Isabella has just put a smile on the black man's face as she humiliates both police officers for what was unjust, but her words are raw and her beautiful face is of thunder today.

The police officers are silenced and shamed. They walk away. Belle offers her hand to the man and he accepts. She helps him up to his feet.

"May I?" Isabella gesticulates at the birdfeed hanging out of the man's coat pocket. He gives her a handful along with his great big smile. She scatters the feed all around her and soon after there are pigeons galore loving every bit of it.

The black man's appearance is in accordance with the way she feels, a million miles away from his predicament. But that being said, she doesn't shy away from attempting to make a connection with him, if only out of being polite.

"So what's your name, if you don't mind me asking?" she asks with a certain degree of caution - he is a homeless stranger after all.

"Francis Smith." The man holds out his big black hand and she shakes it without a moment's hesitation.

"Isabella Antoinette," she says somewhat worryingly, wondering what at all possessed her to get involved with a homeless person in the first place.

"It's ok, you can leave me be, I am at peace so long as these pigeons are here." Francis carries on feeding them from his hands as he crouches down to make contact with the pigeons.

"But Francis, it's almost Christmas . . . where will you go?" Belle asks, as if to worry herself with his troubles so for respite from her own.

"I will be here . . . where else is there for a guy like me to go?" he says, staring at the pigeons surrounding him.

"You cannot spend Christmas without the company of others . . . that will not do and I won't allow it." She feels determined to do a good deed. Belle puts her hands back in her pockets after feeding the pigeons. It's a bitter winter's morning in a picturesque park located on the outskirts of Plymouth. Joseph is being kept at Freedom Fields Hospital until further notice – more tests must be done in order to establish a certain timeframe for how long he has left.

"Look, lady, I am thankful for your intervention and yet you have a life above and beyond me and my sorry state of affairs as it were." Francis seems content to continue feeding the pigeons instead of imposing himself on her.

"Nonsense, Francis, the less you know about my broken world the better. After all, appearances deceive even the most perceptive of us sometimes. So I ask you, for my sake more than yours, spend this Christmas with me and my friend . . . we'd appreciate the company you keep. Please say yes." Isabella looks Francis in his big brown eyes, asking him to stay over for Christmas.

"But I have no money. I have nothing that would suffice as a gift for your good nature." Francis is surprisingly well-spoken for a homeless person and this in itself interests Isabella.

"Francis, just come with me and I will make sure your Christmas is full of festive cheer," Belle pleads with him. Christmas spirit has certainly touched her tainted heart.

Francis nods his head, scatters the rest of his birdfeed away and then walks alongside Isabella whose mood has taken a turn for the much better. They take a walk through the park on the way back to her car.

'Ring, ring, ring, ring' Belle's phone rings. Its Max. She cancels the call and then puts her phone back in her black bag. Francis notices this but makes nothing of it.

Max turns on the TV. He sits down in the armchair. Breaking news has since interrupted the otherwise soul-destroying *Doctors*, despite such an episode being a 'Christmas Special', all that jazz aside, and so for once the news comes as quite the relief, of course. He lets the news unfold before his eager eyes, sighing with sheer feeling, the brief but satisfying kind of feeling, making you appreciate fate when it works out in your favour. Therefore, it is safe to say, he dislikes *Doctors* and so he should!

"This just in: One of the Queen's current butlers has released a statement to provide the general public with the reason as to why there has yet to be a law passed at Parliament to make foxhunting legal again. Butler Charles Swinton addressed journalists this morning from outside his home and here is the video link with footage of just what he had to say . . . "

"There was a near-death incident at Buckingham Palace concerning the Queen and one of her great-grandchildren. Indeed I did witness such a close escape as it happened, at a charity event on the outer grounds, surrounded by family members and special guests. The great-grandchild, who I will not name, had in hand a tennis ball, about to throw it for the dog in question. Said dog ran at the Queen's great-grandchild suddenly and in no uncertain terms pounced upon the great-grandchild goring him down to the ground. Gasps of horror reverberated around the green and just as the worst was on its way the dog got distracted by a fox in the distance so instead chased after it. This twist of fate forced the Queen from her otherwise occupied position, as she came to her great-grandchild's safety, taking him away from the scene immediately. Needless to surmise, I strongly suggest since such a thing has happened, the Queen herself is having a crisis of

conscience, knowing too well it was the appearance of a fox in the distance that saved her great grandchild's life."

Max feels compelled to call Isabella again and does so from the discomfort of an armchair he is now fidgeting on.

'*Ring, ring, ring, ring*' Isabella and Francis are approaching the hospital carpark. He notices she is ignoring the sound going off in her handbag.

"It might be an emergency, Isabella," Francis speaks out from under his homelessly smelly breath. She humours him and answers her phone.

"What is it, Max? That's nice of you to ask but he's not ok no, he must stay at the hospital until further notice . . . tests etc. I should think. Oh . . . ok . . . yes, we are on our way home now Well, let's just say I have invited a special guest to stay with us over Christmas . . . you will soon find out . . . its cold and so I will have to cut this short for now. Yes, I'm fine, don't you worry about me, we'll be back soon . . . goodbye." Belle terminates the call, drops her phone into her handbag and approaches her car. Francis hesitates slightly, yet gets into the passenger side and she makes a move.

The drive is silent at that which from Francis' perspective feels somewhat way out of his comfort zone. Belle silently reassures herself of what this is - a nice and normal Christmas gesture of goodwill. The homeless man finds in him some courage, just so he can break the ice.

"Is someone in your family unwell?" he asks quietly.

"Yes, Francis, it's my father," she answers, with her eyes firmly fixed on the road ahead.

"What's wrong with him?" Francis asks, looking over at her, but she doesn't meet his glance.

"He's dying," Belle whimpers, before fiddling

with the radio player.

"Aren't we all?" he says definitely. She gives up on the radio and turns it off.

"Well, Joseph seems to have very nearly reached the end of his life if you must know. Now how much clearer can I be?" Her stare remains on the road. Francis shuffles in his seat.

"I know not what it means when we die, I only know what it is to be alive," he says indefinitely.

"Feeding pigeons makes you feel alive?" Belle surmises sarcastically.

"Feeding pigeons makes me feel peace of mind," Francis says seriously.

"I know what you mean . . . I mean, I knew what it once meant to have peace of mind – doing something that you love." She briefly loses herself with thoughts of the recent past, as a magnificent conductor controlling her orchestra at every movement she made. Francis notices she is drifting back in time to something in particular, but doesn't humour her on this occasion, as she must concentrate on the road ahead.

It's not a long drive, for her father's Cornish cottage is situated in the sweet little town of Tavistock. They soon arrive. The traffic from Plymouth to Tavistock was not bad at all, considering it's a Friday. Isabella gets out of the car first, followed by Francis as he follows her into the house.

Max excitedly stands in wait, welcoming them on the other side of the door. He has in his hands a tray of freshly made mince pies, he has on his head a pair of antlers and he has on his nose a red bobble resembling Rudolf of course.

Belle lets go of her worries for just one second and relinquishes such a warm smile. She takes a mince pie and passes through into the kitchen. Francis can't help but physically loom large over Max, as he too takes a mince pie and then follows Isabella.

She puts the kettle on.

"Not for me." Max says sharply.

"What about you, Francis?" Belle looks over at him; he is standing at the door of the kitchen and appears to be feeling out of place.

"Have you got any mulled wine?" Francis must be feeling braver than his appearance suggests. Belle smiles for the second time in quick succession as she pours Francis a mug of mulled wine. He takes a seat next to Max.

"Max, mulled wine?" she asks, all jovial and cheery for once.

"Yes please, Isabella." He has the Bible next to him but it is closed.

"Are you a holy man?" Francis asks scratching his stubbly chin.

"No I'm just Max, nice to meet you." Max offers his hand across the table for Francis.

"Francis." Francis accepts and they shake hands.

"But the man who gave me this book . . . he was holy . . . and I hold him in high regard . . . God bless his soul," Max says, as Isabella passes him his mulled wine, smiling with her eyes this time, at the kind words on behalf of her dying father. She gives Francis his mulled wine and then sits at the head of the table.

"I'll get a call first thing in the morning and then we'll know what we're dealing with. Meanwhile, let us hear from you, Max . . . I can see something burning in your eyes." Belle doesn't want to talk in ifs and buts about her father, so she shifts the conversation.

This is his moment to put across all the wild ideas he's been having of late. There's his dream, the documents inside the Bible, the breaking news and now he does not know where to begin. It's in his eyes; such a bombastic kind of self-perpetuating dizziness sprung from feeling the weight that has come about because he cannot contain the sense of self-importance consuming him.

"Max?" Isabella echoes his name, in the wake of knowing something is not quite right. Francis is opposite him, he can see him staring at and yet all the way through his every fibre of being. Such intensity leaves Francis raising his eyebrows as Max's instincts take over and he downs his glass of mulled wine in one. Then he closes his eyes as if in an attempt to gather his thoughts.

"Sorry, you know when you have everything and more on your mind but the words just won't come out . . . it's like there was some kind of traffic jam happening in my head! Anyway where was I?" Max sounds and appears every bit as lost as the way he has made both Belle and Francis feel – stupefied. And the resulting silence says it all!

"I have something in my possession, something that will ruffle the powerful few of their precious feathers, something that will rattle all the egomaniacal cages as they dance and parade around themselves, safe in their carefully constructed and thus so self-satisfied a social circle can be . . . but beware of the darkness as it is darkest just before the dawn, indeed the dawn of a new day. Today, in the wake of what will be, will be a near future for the greater good and in that cold light of a brand new day, dare I may by saying so myself, seek as I see fit, to therefore find us basking in the glory of truth . . . the truth to set us free from the unrighteous." He is impassioned in speech, clutching the Bible with both his hands; he has certainly got the undivided attention of Francis and Isabella.

"Suffice to say, I have an ace up my sleeve. All will be revealed. But for now, I wonder where the will within me exists so to thereby find a way I can know for sure whether the powers that be – 'this not so Great British establishment' that is – practice exactly what they preach. Or whether they are, as I fear them to be, corrupt to the core." Francis and Belle both watch on as Max grows high and mighty at his seat – not fit for the mere dreamer he is!

"There was an incident at Buckingham Palace concerning one of the Queen's great-grandchildren and since then such a thing has put on hold Prime Minister Pricilla Fay's most dastardly plan to make foxhunting legal again. Now we all know what happens on Boxing Day, but will the privileged elite take matters into their own filthy hands and break the rules themselves? Only time will tell. What I strongly suggest is a way we can catch them red-handed and thus, cometh this Boxing Day, cometh the truth of the few who have the power to do as they please." He takes a breath. Belle gets up. Francis smiles knowingly. She tops up both men with more mulled wine and then sits back down at the head of the kitchen table.

"I'm from a small town in South Africa called Alldays. It's in the northern province of Limpopo. An indigenous community nearby, they laid claim to some land and then rented it out to certain 'individuals' whom were hosting hunts as a way of earning income. These indigenous 'people' built platforms that line the bush for the hunters to stand on, and have employed locals to walk in a straight line while beating metal drums, as a consequence chasing the animals into the slaughter strip. The hunters take pot shots at the animals. The animals are put in a hopeless position and cannot possibly survive such an onslaught. As for me I was just a boy at the time, but old enough to know the difference between right and wrong, not letting any amount of money cloud my better judgement. But that being said, I did let what I witnessed fill me with the utmost hate I had, and have, for all the people involved with the killing of animals."

Belle has since been engrossed by Max and now with her heart open can learn more about Francis, his voice so very deep but upon pronouncing certain words one can detect his place of birth.

"What did you do?" Max asks coldly.

"Do? I don't understand?" Francis insists that he should elaborate for the purpose of making sense.

"With your pure hatred . . . what did you do with it?" he asks again.

"I put it to good use . . . at least that's what I thought about it back then . . . but now, I'm not sure whether revenge is enough, not without justice." Francis sips slowly on his mulled wine, letting its steam warm his face.

"Francis, did you murder the hunters for their crimes against nature?" Belle tries to put it in a way which is siding with him ever so slightly.

"I did not. What I did was supernatural 'black magic'. I, I knew an elderly man in my hometown of Alldays and I quickly learnt a certain kind of 'karma' for we merely let the power of spirit take shape and so in an 'undead animal form' these creatures great and small, slaughtered just for the hell of it, they came back to life for one purpose . . . this is an act of righteousness, Isabella, and I don't expect you to understand, but as I said . . . I was young . . .I was angry at the world around me for being so, so . . . " Francis fails to find the right word, one to describe the world in which he was a part of for so long.

"So sick." Max finishes Francis' sentence. Francis concurs, closing his eyes slowly, while nodding in the same vein.

"So how old were you when you got involved with this, this . . . 'black magic' business?" Belle shudders to think but this man is in her father's house so she demands to know what Francis was like and if he still harbours any misplaced sense of hatred at life.

"Between the ages of twelve and fifteen, he taught me things - he showed me ways of fighting these 'crimes against nature' from the comfort of a raging fire. We were two shadows with one and the same spirit." Francis is being looked at with the deepest intensity by both Belle and Max; hanging on every word they are expecting him to continue the conversation.

"There is a way you can know whether the powers that be are behaving themselves as it were, or whether they are rotten to the core." Francis finishes his mulled wine. Belle looks at Max and he senses her concern from across the kitchen table.

Her phone rings. Such a thing gave her a fright. It's the hospital. Belle gets up and goes outside. Max pours Francis some more mulled wine and then tops his mug up, finishing the last of it off.

"Your past troubles Isabella," Max says frankly.

"It would appear she has her fair share of troubles already," Francis answers back.

"Appearances are not always what they seem sometimes." He doesn't feel comfortable discussing Isabella's private life with a newfound friend.

"She told me about her father . . . that being said, I don't intend to intrude," Francis says honestly.

"Then what are your intentions, Francis?" he asks, taking a sip from his mug of mulled wine. Francis watches on, above and behind Max Isabella can be seen from out of the kitchen window; with feeling, he sees her crouch down and then curl quite hysterically all the way up into a ball of woe. His instincts force Francis into action and he leaves the kitchen in order to go outside.

Max turns around in his seat. He sees Isabella all curled up and at once knows what has happened but doesn't get up from his seat. He turns back around and takes a slow sip of his mulled wine while deep in thought.

Francis stands next to her, staring down at what she has been reduced to . . . tatters.

He holds his hand out for her to take. Belle looks up at him with the eyes of a frightened child and yet takes his hand. Francis pulls her up and then into his embrace.

She holds him tight, crying on his shoulder and he holds her back, caressing Isabella albeit with a colder kind of failing warmth that has since succumbed to this bitter December.

They think there are no strings attached to the good life. They are hero-worshipped for the wrong reasons. So what if William Shakespeare proclaimed life to be but a stage! Rage against this sorry dream devoid of depth, enough not for a nightmare to manifest itself – forget about a pure paradise! As of when money buys such a thing it is at once 'owned' and attached to the needy little thought patterns polluting one's mind until the bitter end.

So, can the question 'to be or not to be' remain relevant today or 'contemporary' by asking us all to choose, as it is not an open question at all. William Shakespeare simply poses such a question as an important ultimatum coming to terms with that of his time. To be or not to be, but now, with the systematically corrupt picture of moving images, 'these people' prevailing in an unjust fashion and as an ugly glitch in the system of a game called life.

I think the question now which begs to be made quite clear for there will only follow one true answer or else face a life locked inside the prison of your own perchance manifest, swallowed up by your own shallow trappings persisting to further shut down an already closed mind . . . live in and of the truth, to die righteously . . . either that or live with the fear of dying unto nothing but dust.

I am aware of politicians as much as they are all aware of the public eye being on them. That being said, depending on what party you support, and the big issues such a party try to tackle, there are certain expectations upheld by the common man on certain representatives of that particular party. The fact that it has now become common knowledge, 'lingo', regarding any politician and his or her 'nuanced' if not phoney way in which one answers a question is so far over the edge of reason I'm not going to dignify a fraudulent defence mechanism with an example. Can I call it a 'calculated type of lying'? I think I just did. Do politicians practise the art of answering a question indirectly while trying to please us with what will be yet another broken promise? Yes, they do.

I feel challenged and I know why. My mind is being occupied by a belief, if I can accurately say, taking into consideration certain factors that are promoting what I consider 'pressing'. Pressing buttons inside my brain and causing me to see the world in a way which gives birth to the inconvenient truth of our times. Things, this 'system of things', is so very beyond the pale. 2 Corinthians 4:4 'among whom the God of this system of things has blinded the minds of the unbelievers.' This is the beginning of a betrayal against the justifiable brightness as in spirit expressing itself from the purest place possible.

It is easy for me to have hate on the one hand and yet it will be much more meaningful for me to hold dear in the other every wavering voice of a forgotten time, every dream from your heart's desire, every feeling you've ever felt the full force of on behalf of the inexcusable broken promise society tries as it might to cover up – pussyfooting around one's own words is what politicians excel at. Therefore forgive them, because, simply put, they have lost sight of what it means to be men and women of their true word. Indeed, being a person of one's word will assume a certain trait at that which is an idealist thought pattern. To be an idealist, it is in accordance with the very definition I find from Google, telling me who an idealist is: 'A person who is guided more by ideals than by practical considerations'. Fancy that! When was it even considered, and in doing so decided upon by I don't know who, but chances are the people behind this certain definition are old or privileged and therefore prone to perchance complacency. So by being, I imagine, 'complacent' at best, it is for everyone else seeking meaning, going onto Google (note: meaning in general! Believe me, 'Google' is not a big enough 'thing' in itself for where we are headed) and then getting an idea agreed upon from men and maybe even women as well, who have one thing in common: they all think the same. So when I for one, 'found out' that an idealist is supposedly 'guided' by ideals as opposed to practical consideration, isn't it in other words saying you are far too busy dreaming of a 'perfect world' to be in the 'real' one which exists before us all? Well, what I deduce is this, that without one idea alone, there cannot be reason in order for reasoning. In fact, quite rightly, we will lose such a great big system of things itself! If an idea to create this system of things ceased only to exist as a passing thought at that and that alone, then society might never have found its feet in the first place! 'Practical consideration' once upon a time came from the very same place as an idea did; the only difference is with the nature of having a 'good idea' and by the way of our own imperfect nature there are also bad ideas as well.

What grabs you? Your undivided attention I mean, and that itself is a simple indication of what matters most to you upon being caught up in the crossfire or created moment that comes from any media source. Your senses are being fed, whether it's sport or celebrity news, 'world affairs' or a terrorist attack. But, of course, spending time in solitary confinement literally makes one's mind wander outside of one's head! Let's say you committed a crime which warrants prison punishment but then in absent minded disdain and as you shout at the top of your voice 'FUCK THE SYSTEM,' you act like an ape and trash the place!

So you're thrown into solitary confinement for a whole month, that's blackness personified by the way. You have nothing but scraps as food and hardly any water to drink; there will be no contact with cellmates since you are forbidden from leaving your little hole of blackness. Soon enough, when your mind wanders around every last bit of your brain's capacity to think things inside yourself, essentially and sensually starved of your real world, what happens defies 'nice and normal' minds because your mind quite literally paints its own picture against the darkness destroying your soul from the inside out.

Can you really keep playing along and not know, deep down, when all is said and done and as your days draw closer *to the end, and as the time comes for your meeting with your maker, your final glimpse upon your deathbed brings you to a bittersweet realisation, an awakening one moment too late, but of course, since you resist going gentle into that good night, it's with rage, and yet more rage against the dying of the light, to no avail all endeavour victoriously swallowed whole – life for death; the dream, the system, the family, the friends . . . disappear from your sight, at the peril of all things finite.*

Why does the universe listen to me? Because I've found my one true love – voice of reason. . .

CHAPTER 4: DECISIONS, DECISIONS AND DEATH

22nd of December, 2018

The recently deceased Joseph never married, after coming closest to tying the knot with Wendy, yet at her premature end, death had the final say and so he went through life from one lover to the next. Isabella feels very much at that age now where she should be able to cope with the ups and downs of life. Her twenties were spent perfecting her craft as a conductor, dating 'this and that' within the field of her choosing; classical music. But Maximus Lucifer Phoenix never left from the forefront of her heartfelt thoughts. She grew up appreciating the transition her father made from science to religion, based on the knowledge of how Wendy made him feel. She knew Joseph wasn't a man who would happily make a sing and dance about the greatness of God. But she also knew how passionate a man he was and as for matters of his heart, he always followed the way of it without much thought to what would be 'better in the long run'. A realist Joseph was not, but a lifelong dreamer and avid lover of life.

Today is Saturday. Isabella has slept late, not that she shouldn't but it's understandable, besides she hasn't got anywhere else to be at this present time. Francis was up first followed closely by Max. Both have decided to skip breakfast for a cigarette outside, overlooking the view of this picturesque Cornish countryside. Afar are fields of farmyard animals while a river runs down in the distance where there is a bridge leading into the town of Tavistock.

"You said you have something in your possession, something that will, well, 'fuck shit up' for want of a better way to say such a thing." Francis makes conversation standing next to Max as they admire the snowy white fields in the distance.

"And you said you have a way of finding out what the establishment get up to in their spare time." He glances over at Francis, who in turn acknowledges him with a straightforward nod.

"Are you sure you're ready to experience something that goes against the grain of 'nice and normal' daily life? Black magic is not for everyone." Francis issues a fair warning, while Max just shrugs it off and exhales smoke at the same time.

"Francis, this is me at a time in my life where I am wondering what the hell to do with it and at thirty nine to have a thought like that . . . let's just say it troubles me, ok," he says openly, while still looking into the distance.

"I am forty nine and homeless, so I still think about that . . . that's just the way it is," Francis responds, as in doing so he gives further insight to what might be ahead of Max.

"Suffice to say my newfound friend, I am ready

to receive such a thing as black magic. If it informs me of the Prime Minister's whereabouts this Boxing Day then bring it on." Max says excitedly. Francis puts out his cigarette.

"On the night of Christmas Day, we will make a fire here, somewhere out in the open, and then, with a few necessary 'ingredients' - so to fuel the flames as it were – we can make the magic come alive," Francis says as a matter of fact, to what will be if fate takes course this way. Max glances at him with great expectations, as he then stamps out his cigarette. They go back inside.

Isabella is sat at the kitchen table. She appears ready to go out.

"I was waiting for my breakfast in bed but it never came." Belle makes a joke as both of them return from being outside.

"Going somewhere?" Max notices she looks to be on the edge of her seat somewhat.

"We all are," she answers forcing a faint but beautiful smile.

"What, right now?" Max says, surprised by her sense of urgency.

"Yes! There's the Christmas market today in town . . . now come along boys, it's time we experienced the most wonderful time of the year!" She seems to be forcing the issue but her urgency doesn't go unnoticed as both Max and Francis ready themselves.

It's a short walk into town. The sky is white, with every intention of snow to come falling down at any moment. Max and Isabella are wrapped up warm while Francis is wearing the same rags as always albeit with fingerless gloves.

"Francis, consider me your personal shopper for today," Belle says, as a false sense of enthusiasm comes out to play.

"Whatever you say, for I am just pleased to be here, therefore your good nature need not spoil me, but that being said, I could do with some new clothes . . . so thank you, Belle," Francis responds jubilantly.

The busy streets are filled with families and friends shopping like their lives depended on it. The high street road has been closed off for the market stalls to do business on either side. It's awash with this sea of cheer-ridden individuals swept up in nothing but such a consumerist shit-storm; there is no time for calm amongst these people. Treading footsteps upon and over the merest-set snow, walking in the wake of overzealous thoughts misspent, a townspeople like every other; brainwashed and hungover.

Fathers that are young and fathers that are old but both comfortable behind an unnaturally well-groomed beard and tightfitting puffer jacket, these media-driven men of modern times moonlighting as silly little trendsetters. To who but their own flesh and blood and yet further still, life the stage, they are men ready for one another's senseless style. All in the name of having a very subtle but evermore present is this sick and twisted need for the competitive edge over your fellow man.

Mothers that are yummy and mothers that have given up on coming across as sexy, yet mothers they are all the same, masquerading against each other's misguided idea of perfection, putting on their Oscar-winning smiles falsified by a subtle bitterness at life. Why so spiteful from on the inside and yet deceptively 'la de da' to the naked eye? Guys and girls of this day and age are driven round the bend by TV telling them things that are on a need to know basis, showing them how to live in a manufactured wonderland.

Kids distancing themselves from their redundant parents as they venture out into the open playground of a seemingly beautiful life for the young, but also all who have an ignorant outlook. Creatures so innocent yet still fall victim to being misled by media-mad men and in the same vein venomously self-driven women wilfully fooling the untrained eye, youngsters deceived. Very braindead children getting spirited away by app-tastic creations stillborn from nothingness – this is the life of a modern day land drunk on its own westernized whimsy.

Francis walks around now with a newfound social status; he's been bought for free by Belle but just for Christmas of course. Max has not yet mastered his own torn sense of feeling cynical where Christmas is concerned and so allows himself such a guilty pleasure as being sucked into this plastic take on what once was a celebration in light of our newborn king. Isabella lets her long dark hair down and allows anything that is festive take over her suffering disposition. People here dress fancily especially as its party season and all. Belle looks quite to die for, for she is used to being in the company of pretentiousness personified. Of course that's not to say everyone in the classical field adores their own tone of voice, it's just the vast majority that do.

"Ooh, this is a very gentlemanly place! Let's go in here, Francis, it's time to work a Christmas miracle!" Belle grabs Francis and pulls him into a posh shop, one which has a slight sale on certain items of clothing.

"I'll be sat on a bench then, drinking mulled

wine like a homeless person would." Max says such a thing in jest, but truly feels left out of Belle's visions and is drawn to the refreshments stall on the street corner.

He must first withdraw some money and checks on his balance. It's not the healthy chunk of what George and Gwen left him when they died. That amount has been on a steady decline for about ten years now. But it is still enough not to be worried and he decides to take out £100.

People really are all over the place this afternoon and it's getting under his skin. Hence the reason as to why he buys a large plastic cup of mulled wine. In the distance, amongst the drum of mass-chatter at the same time, Max can hear a choir ringing out; it almost makes him smile upon paying for his drink.

It seems like a lifetime ago now when Max saw Isabella for the first time. He was in his mid to late twenties still living with his adoptive parents at their B&B in Newquay. Yet Gwen and George, although able to carry on doing what they love, were slowing down somewhat. As for Max, he was busy riding the wave of a fashionable phase . . . surfing. After helping Gwen and George throughout the day, by before sunset there would be a beautiful light to bask in and he just loved to surf when the sun was so big with its glorious shade of red.

Isabella was not yet twenty but upon finishing her final exams before graduation from a prestigious classical college of fancy music (it's in Exeter but goes by a different name), she and her friends were celebrating on the beach. They had made a fire for marshmallows, while guzzling on a cheap brand of fake champagne between them four excitable young women drinking bubbly from straight out of the bottle – classy as hell. Her three friends were very impressed by the surfers catching waves, as opposed to Max and his onslaught of epic fails. But Belle felt sorry for such a trier and after finally calling it a day, Max was invited to join her as he walked back up the beach.

Such fond memories he has but of course, squandered by his misplaced sense of adventure, that which cost him and Belle a future together. Here he is sitting on a bench while Belle leads a dance as she prances Francis from one shop to the next. Yes, Isabella is making much more of an effort to feel the festive cheer but is she simply deflecting the fact that her father has passed away, with an immediate distraction in the shape and form of Francis Smith?

It's meant to be the most wonderful time of the year for a reason. And we all know why we gather together for a jolly good time . . . to remember the birth of the one and only Jesus Christ. Father Christmas is a necessary nicety . . . no . . . he's the stable substitute to Christ almighty but why? Why do parents prefer their kids to hero worship a big fat man instead of the one who died for our sins?

Max is people watching. It amuses him how we all latch onto the commercial shallowness that Christmas is for the common masses. Men wearing ridiculous Christmas jumpers pass by, as they carry all the bags of overpriced presents for the brainwashed women in their boring little lives. Brainwashed by shops basically, but not without the deceptive appearance of being in control. In control of all the credit cards aside, such women Max can see strut ahead of their tender, distressed hubbies being hounded by their children.

He catches his own sense of cynicism make him feel dead inside and so shudders as a way to snap out of it at once. With one more sip of mulled wine, he winces, surprised by its stone-coldness. This causes him to make a stand and in doing so, throw his drink away.

Max, this is my special gentleman friend, Francis Smith." Belle presents the new and improved Francis, as if she is showing him off. Yes, he looks better for it in his fancy new clothes, opposed to old rags, and yet he appears severely unable by these so-called brand names alone to transform from homeless loser into something else entirely.

"Ah Francis, dashing springs to mind." Max plays along for Belle's sake. Francis smiles while he looks at her for approval.

"Let's go for coffee shall we?" She sounds so false it's untrue, but at least she is giving good spirit everything she has got. Max nods at her; he knows it's just a matter of time before her front collapses.

Isabella, Max and Francis enter into Costa, a coffee franchise speaking for itself if ever your heart desires such a thing as cheapskate coffee. Francis sits on the comfy side of a small table. But Max doesn't submit to sitting opposite on a mediocre chair and instead budges Francis up with his backside. Belle joins them both, but doesn't hesitate to sit straight down on the mediocre chair.

"Francis, such swanky apparel really becomes you, but I must endeavour where your bright future is concerned." Isabella suggests she is to have a say in his way of life from now on.

"'My bright future'," he humours her, after taking his sweet time with what was a pronounced and yet cautious sip on his coffee.

"After Christmas let's create you a CV. Have you worked at all in your earlier years Francis?" Belle's eyes are wild with big ideas for Francis; somewhat at his innocent enough peril Belle can on this occasion be forgiven if she is accidentally treating him like an adored dog.

"This and that but nothing notable enough for me to make a sing and dance about, Belle." Francis answers swiftly yet with a worrying hint of flippancy attached to his quick fire throwaway statement, shedding little light on what sort of working life he has had before becoming a homeless person.

"Well, I'll help you create your own, when the mood takes us past the festive cheer, but a bit before the storm of New Year's celebrations, because let us not get carried away with all this spare time . . . we must make sure we're productive even if the most wonderful time of the year allows us some complacency." Belle will always speak like she knows best but don't get her wrong, for this is not at all arrogance creeping into her nature, her heart remains in the right place.

"Meanwhile, what about your dead dad?! Pardon me for being frank but all of this smacks of a fearful diversion from facing the truth." Max has had enough of her dwindling lie, try as she might to come across all cheery . . . he wants the real Belle and not a brave face.

"I'll have you know, Joseph's death certificate is in my bag, thank you very much, Max." Belle looks less than best pleased as Max is put back in his place. She feels compelled to continue.

"Speaking of a 'fearful diversion from facing the truth', then let us consider your life choices shall we, oh high and mighty Max, the moonlighting traveller but for how long? Look at you, your way was well and truly lost the moment you gave up on the Hunt Trap Rat Pack and in doing so, you gave up on us as well." Belle folds her arms so to demonstrate discontent at Max. All the while Francis sips on his coffee keeping quiet.

"We won, goddamn it. We were a pivotal part of what became the bigger picture; the ban on fox hunting had a whole lot to do with our pursuit of saving lives I still feel the same way . . . nothing much has changed." He seems to be defending himself, sat opposite the upright stance of a woman catching fire.

"You've changed. And that in itself is more than enough for me to realise just how foolish I was when . . . well . . . I won't go there. It's ancient history." Isabella unfolds her arms and takes a sip of her coffee.

"Please, Isabella, enlighten me, these severely lost 'life choices' you seem to know so much about . . . and what about your own? Don't you have a tour to get on with? Your father would want you to carry on chasing your dream." He snaps at her, clearly keen to stand his ground and not back down.

"You know next to nothing about what my father thought of me. You were far too busy 'seeing the world'." Belle flicks her hair back behind her. Francis feels caught up in the crossfire.

"My mother was a whore for whatever she could get her poor hands on. And as for my father, after losing his job, he became one of the men involved with the killing of animals. I still remember when I saw him out there for the first time, beating the metal drum like a madman who was possessed by the power of filthy money. At sixteen, it was to be my last encounter with the elderly black magic man and of course we had grown close so he knew enough about me . . . 'You will see a different light to your parents as of when you enter the afterlife, for now, you must leave here and I will make sure of it.' That's what he said. And then he gave me a sum of money, enough for a ticket out of town, out of my country." Francis opens up in an attempt to cool both hotheads. Isabella and Max stop at once.

"Why here?" Max asks.

"I was a tall lanky kid back then. Tommy Cooper was my hero. There was one pub in my local town and the owner would let me in to watch his show on the TV every Friday night. I wanted to be just like him, making people laugh for being myself. I saw you didn't have to know jokes but it was about timing and tomfoolery. I left home with him in my heart. But a dream remains such a thing, it was childish of me." Francis' eyes turn teary; he wipes tears away and excuses himself from the table.

"I'm just going to the toilet," he says sheepishly.

"You're coming back, aren't you?" Belle asks as a kneejerk reaction to what she feels inside - something of a soft spot for Francis.

"Yes, Isabella," Francis says as he walks towards the toilets.

"I'm sorry, Belle. For everything," Max says desperately.

Belle says nothing in return.

"It's Christmas, my life, lack thereof, oh woe is me! I have nothing to show for my middle age of being a drifter." He descends using her silence as a means of feeling sorry for himself.

"Did you not hear a word from Francis just then? Are you so self-centred that it is impossible for you to let anyone else in? I can't believe you can sit there and worry yourself over, you've seen the world and yet you still feel . . . well . . . I would ask but I'm not here to be on the receiving end of your useless brooding." Isabella crosses her legs aggressively while she drinks her coffee.

You should call your agent. I don't know what this thing is with you and Francis, but it's getting in the way of your life," Max says finally. Belle gets up, brushes herself down and then responds.

"Life is what happens when we are all busying ourselves with silly little plans Max, this is life! I'm hungry, do you want anything?" she asks, her attention elsewhere, waiting for Francis.

"No, thanks," Max says sharply.

Francis comes back.

"Ok, can I trust you two boys to be about town on your own while I tend to an arrangement?" Belle asks, resting her right boot (Ugg) on the chair while she flicks a feather from it.

"An arrangement?" Max echoes curiously.

"And so your curiosity continues to be as it always was, on fire. For if you must know, I have a hot date with the one and only Johnny Depp . . . " Francis smiles as Max tilts his head and raises his dark brown eyebrows – such things stand out in an alluring manner, strikingly weird and yet fitting against his messy blond hair.

"Fear not, Max. He's one of the last things on my mind. I've arranged to meet two old friends from my time spent at Exeter Classical School of Music," she says swiftly, passing Francis a £10 note like she had done such a thing nearly all her life.

"What's this for?" Francis asks.

"If you get hungry on your way home," Isabella answers, as she gives Max her house keys. Francis picks the small white feather up from the floor before offering it back to Belle.

"What's this for?" Belle looks puzzled.

"Guidance, Isabella . . . you're being watched over from above," he says sweetly.

"I'll see you both back at home . . . won't be long." Belle places the feather in her bag. She kisses them both on the cheek and then leaves Costa in a flash.

"This coffee fucking sucks," Max says distastefully.

"Mines fine," Francis responds, putting the money in the inside pocket of his new tweed jacket.

"I hate it in here." He goes further with what is now a growing discontent.

"Why?" He humours him.

Bleak décor for one and the coldest of lifeless breezes becomes me every time I try to sit back and relax. I catch bits and pieces of people's lives left, right and centre . . . blah blah blah about this, that and the other . . . it's all the same monotone type of 'nicety talk' . . . quiet not to know any details but always loud enough that these people speak making a song and dance about boring little plans . . . like . . . like . . . " Max is losing his train of thought to his fistful of hate.

"Like the unhappy couple sat to your far right. See how he's doing all the talking to his nodding dog of a wife while she couldn't care less. Look how he has her hand from across the table . . . he's holding onto her for dear life, huh? Her hand is loose as she holds onto nothing but the false hope of her desperate daydreams; she wants out and yet he is blinded by his own sense of mistaken contentedness stemming from mediocre coffee and comfortable living." Francis is ice-cool, looking straight forward while he questions a couple's happiness just for the hell of it.

"You should be a security guard or something along those lines, I'm impressed Francis!" Max's eyes light up in the wake of what Francis just said.

"I've lived long enough not to let lazy ignorance destroy my world view," Francis says softly.

"Well . . . let us leave here before I feel the last of my life force spirited away by so-called Costa and its bewildering disenchantment," Max says so gracefully, like he is giving a line on stage somewhere far from here.

'Only us humans as we get together for the collective creation of 'your privileged position' amongst friends and/or professionals, forming your carefully constructed schools of thought that are arising and sadly stinking of smugness, nevertheless this separation not only keeps stupid people at bay, but what begins to happen and it can be conscious or subconscious, is an intellectually inclined ignorance forms or mutates out of an 'agreeable feeling' growing in strength, then becoming a false sense of certainty that otherwise blinds the third eye of all members making up your very special social circle. Simply put, you, as an individual, will either have to stop yourself from feeling the need to be or appear better than everyone else outside your circle, or make your real feelings known inside your circle, consciously creating a bridge of brilliant truth that you will offer your friends as a lifeline, before your friends force you gently down the stream of self-satisfied fantasy. As of when the moment presents itself, refer to one of your friends/professionals as a 'highness' instead and

then study his or her reaction. Because by bringing into your circle real feelings instead of false senses, this will challenge each and every personal reality that is present; to be real or not . . . what will it be?

'All truth passes through three stages before it is recognised as a matter of fact. First it is ridiculed. Second, it is opposed and then third it is accepted as being self-evident.' Arthur Schopenhauer went on to write 'To truth only a brief celebration of victory is allowed between the two long periods during which it is condemned as paradoxical, or disparaged as trivial.' Before we can create a collective, truthful future, that clarity comes from our own will to want what is right and therefore never wrong. We need to know what we have done in order for us to truly know what we are doing and only then can we make a great big difference.'

(At one with all)

'If feathers that are forever ruffled look like Lucifer's suffering disposition, then imagine just what it is to be eternally fallen; not born of sin and cast down from whence sin was but still the prevailing inbred condition. Don't get me wrong, we are for being itself so to soon enough feel free, realise such a reachable light that at once manifests as Christ-consciousness. Should it be we are worn down by scientific cantankerous reasoning? Rise not against, but above and beyond your material lack thereof what is supernatural. Let us go so far as rejoice such supernatural, albeit subtle lightness shone of our inner divinity.

Fear not but breakout of habit bringing you back to your cold, destitute reality. Yet you're reading this thing in what way? Any nuance is not welcome when one's words are rejected or more agreeably brushed aside by lazy eyes skimming over perhaps such an inconvenient truth as that which will be brought to light at my demand for a real life and righteous existence in one.

I'm inclined, compelled and moved to be exactly as a beautiful feeling suggests, so far from my life of surface flippancy is this irrepressible belief, for there are forces at work making me see the light. Not a fascination. Not a falsehood. How could I quite easily leave feelings passing away only to return with interest? To act out of feeling it in the first place is simply you and your heart having a fantastic conversation. Connecting within oneself for the greater good of doing feelings justice is as it should be, because disregarding a bodily reaction in my eyes seems so very wrong.

What led me to believe I was Lucifer? A personified fallen angel gradually realises such a thing, and then what? Well, let me at least start from an earlier reluctance to accept the true reality of myself. For my style of writing indicates somewhat without doubt thus bask as I do in a romantic relationship between me and the written word. From feeling not a need and so it is a soulful firmament instead; inside, I am an old soul. Reluctant might I add to accept this as a teen, even then though, oh how I felt it in me . . . an undercurrent hinting at depth that I knew not all are aware of having.

Love everyone unconditionally. Why not? True love after all and therein lies why we will give of ourselves over only to the one we really, really love! Believing this selective love is special, since one will feel it to be between only lovers. Lovers have already made it to each their own underlying love, like a pact preventing tenderness except for your 'significant other' that rattles those bones of yours yet just as an image fades fast, so do bones slow but sure enough fail you, yes, every fibre by bone alone laid down and degraded. Before mortal truth hurts your every all, feel, as you do desperate in your need deep down and manifesting these three sweet words/nothings . . . 'I love you.' I love you. The Holy Grail grasped. The ego groomed. From the flight of three words resplendent together, then destined to do wonders for your heart; at least short-lived if not even sincere . . . ever since we have very much mastered the artless craft of conniving and *corruptly lying in all our swagger-gross-out unto blue in the face. As coldness comes home from home – hell on earth thereafter your wrongdoing, indeed the devil is in the detailed deceit of fallible braindead and absolutely lifeless lies.*

Lucifer! For art thou thy one and only by way of wane, bane not God but the heartless essence still lingering inside, desperate to do what will be redeemed divine? No. Never ever elevate to thy highest place such suffering rage just so seething in silence misconstrued; does gold delight in its own wonderful golden disposition? And does Lucifer feel all the more or less of a fallen fool albeit not so sublime a mindset to mutate terror inwards as if fearing his own numbness first? Even heavier a burden in no uncertainty, timeless limbo but much, much worse is where one so-called Lucifer fell at a fall from God's great big will all-encompassing. Strike! Stricken; quite frankly left to one's own unclean and devilish devices as damnedest descent unto take shape of formless sickening thing. So homeward bound now and a newfound down in one foul swoop! With this simply lost least bit of fabric bringing its blackness, not at all alight. Angelic lack thereof frowned upon pure reminiscence as rendezvous venomous self-perpetuating inglorious ooze is in revengeful foul mouth that thanks itself ex-elixir-Lucifer: from now on what will be will be everlasting stings, squalor lurid and disgustingly real beyond ought not to be but for a rotten nobody. Jeers as a horrid hooray for all fallen unto hate itself swallowed up but spit out to complete the repeat process circle of horror reverberating in and around an eternal evil, ill-fated darkness thus far forever forsaken. One alone cannot conquer everyone else's sickly fears, sweet dreams, merciful forever afters, but before your fall from once again grace, rage against greater good and thus destined to fail only by divine right quite apart from God; dying of degradation inside out at eternal lust after your nightmare masquerading itself as an impossible dream. May you suffer well, Lucifer!

Hell really IS other persons as opposed to one existent

point of view; whereby 'I' am 'me' and all else simply appears around about 'being itself' from not what will live, if I'm my only way of having an experience so how can I possibly prove without doubt that at another perspective within which there remains something similar? Therefore, 'essence', 'soul' like mine may well embody but come from a human condition different thus far physically. Yet still all else exists as an image made to feel real albeit at my senses sending and receiving information unseen in nature or by brain then entertains such superb brilliance accepted except open no less for further reasoning. Reduced downwards, as in descending; not a freefalling living breathing body, your soul - let us use the imagination now. What will fall from the ground down unto a depth of fathomable but bodiless despair, where one's senses cease as by being free from embodiment itself? If, in the air or as an essence experiencing such a twist of fate, to be somehow heinously least bit at your perilous last life-affirming moment literally feeling itself fall from here therefore whereabouts is this 'self'? Further still let us surmise one's soul left for death thereafter certain end, destroyed by a beautified form of suffering. Indeed, it won't be long before feeling itself is forever rendered back to the beginning and thus nothingness not at all aware will simply be.'

CHAPTER 5: HOME IS WHERE THE HEART IS

23rd of December, 2018

It's Sunday, day of rest to some, but Belle is up bright and early, clearing away the contents of what was consumed the night before. Francis, Max and the beautiful Belle spent last night talking, drinking and laughing for the most part. There was no TV, no movies, only sweet music in the background of a talkative trio brought together this Christmas. Last night the outside world didn't exist, at least not to two of them. Max is inclined to let his feelings be known on the subject of worldly affairs, especially while under the influence of red wine.

Francis sits opposite Isabella at the kitchen table.

"I am attending church this morning. Will you join me?" Belle asks.

"I have nothing better to do but of course, regardless, yes, Isabella . . . are you a believer?" Francis asks with interest.

"My father was," she deflects softly.

"What about you?" Francis asks again.

"Sensitive subject, but to this day I do believe in something that is in control of our . . . struggle, shall we say," Belle says honestly, as her eyes drift off into the distance.

"I came from a godless place where people put all their energy into the pursuit of financial gain – not so much on a spiritual path to being free from their own undoing in the end," he says, as both his palms rest flat on the kitchen table, relaxed and yet present to the moment.

"Such a place sounds so very familiar . . . are you sure you're not from around here after all?" She is, of course, suggesting that her country of origin, England, can come across as godless. Max enters the kitchen. He gets a glass from the cupboard and fills it to the brim with water from the tap.

"Morning, Max," Isabella says with a smile on her face. He does not answer back but gulps down the water in one.

"I take it you're up for the same purpose as me and Francis this morning?" she says suggestively.

"Is it safe for you to elaborate, or are you about to crush my spirit with something along the lines of, oh I don't know, church?" Max has such a smart mouth; he at least likes to think so.

"See, Francis, this is exactly the reaction us English have become infamous for . . . but to bask as we do in our own inglorious sense of humour, my goodness, doesn't it just get under your skin?" Belle's smart mouth makes Max's seem simple; she is awesome as of when the mood takes her – more often than not to going in the one direction that affords feeling best pleased, and that's when she pisses all over his sense of humour.

"So you are going to church. Forgive me, I

decline not because I don't care but because as George Harrison once sung 'You don't need no church house and you don't need no temple, you don't need no rosary beads or them books to read, to see that you have fallen.'" He ascends as if by magic breaking into song, but it still doesn't redeem him from his unbecoming sense of humour.

"And as John Lydon once sung. . . 'I am an Antichrist' but what has that got to do with whether you, Maximus Lucifer Phoenix, will attend church today or not?" Belle looms close to catching on fire from whence such words are playing with the mood of Max.

"Little Miss Smarty Pants wins again. But you can't force me to clap my hands and jump for the joy of Jesus Christ, ok." He will go with them simply because his time spent with Isabella is always worthwhile.

"Max, we are going there more for the awkward business of letting the people at Kingdom Building know that Joseph has passed away, and not the pleasure of receiving the word of God, but of course can you be at all selfless just this once?" She knows she has him against the ropes as it were and so he cannot possibly say anything but yes to the church, otherwise he's just a selfish little moron.

Kingdom Building hadn't changed over the years. Yes the faces have aged, but the way in which Jehovah's Witnesses go about their business is still the same. Families gather, the small talk of daily life reverberates around this modest space. Isabella approaches a middle-aged man near the front, just down from the stage. He is dressed immaculately, slicked back black hair, grey sideburns, clean shaven and with big bulging green eyes.

"Yes, Isabella, I learnt a lot from your father . . . a very interesting individual indeed. He always had something to say about the brain and that in itself fascinated me. You could quite easily feel yourself get carried away by his spark of enthusiasm; his eyes were always wide and alive with every intention to learn from his experiences. So how is Joseph?" The man appears pleased to be speaking of Joseph, but little does he know what Belle is about to reveal.

"Joseph passed away very recently. Its why I am here really . . . you good people deserve to know so if you don't mind, I'd like to address everyone on the whole." Belle looks to be keeping it together, but that being said there are racing thoughts taking place behind her bright bluey-green eyes.

He nods his head and opens his arm directing her to the stage. She smiles at him and then gets up to the pulpit, tapping her hand against the microphone in a sheepish manner.

"Good morning everyone and season's greetings to you all. I am Isabella Antoinette, daughter of Joseph Symonds. Some of you, well, all of you I hope, know who he is . . . who he was." Belle wipes a tear away as she gathers herself.

"Joseph Symonds is dead. His last act as a then healthy, elderly man was the applause he gave me seeing his daughter realise her dream. I don't want to dwell where my dad and my dream is concerned; here he would speak highly, mightily of what will become in good time. He believed and yet he did not see. Not from the place of a spiritually inclined believer but from his heart he always was for the greater good, regardless of having seen the light or not. Being in his precious presence as I'm sure you'll all know too well . . . Joseph spoke straight from his sheer inner light. I loved my dad and still do and I hope he will live on in your hearts and minds, as well as in mine. Thank you for listening." Belle steps down from the pulpit to an uncomfortable silence, soon pierced by everyone's shuffling with shock and discomfort. Max goes to her, puts his arm around her shoulder and leads her out of the building.

"Francis, you are my designated 'tree hugger' for today. I've already ordered a sizeable one, we are going to get it right now," Belle says, as the three of them walk back towards town. It is snowing softly. People are out and about again. Sunday day of rest – not for the wicked.

"Are you OK, Belle?" Max asks somewhat worryingly.

"Yes, Max, thanks so much for your ever so sincere concern but can I have a cigarette?" she says dramatically, displaying a certain degree of being a bit not so ok, but still alive and breathing in the cold frosty atmosphere. He passes her a cigarette with his peace symbol lighter.

"That was a brave thing, Isabella, whether you're in the mood to appreciate it as such a thing or not. You've had to handle a lot of late . . . take it easy today." Francis speaks up in light of what he saw her do at Kingdom Building, but Belle remains silent while they walk to where the Christmas trees are.

Another market, another reason to be cheerful, and another day closer to Christmas day. Everyone appears alive with feeling something in the air, especially since it's been snowing; such people here are in jolly good form, dressed in their best, and speaking with a spring in their step personifying an all-encompassing sense of joyfulness as families, friends, and strangers alike smile at each other for 'tis the season to be jolly!'

Francis carries Isabella's tree home for her. She seems preoccupied by the flippant and yet prevailing goings on on her smartphone, while Max soaks up the atmosphere, pondering upon what Belle will do next – amongst other things.

This day came and went with a whimpering misery, since Isabella barely said a word after her performance at the Kingdom Building. Indeed she decorated the tree within the limited disenchantment made from her false smile, while Max and Francis just let the Christmas mix CD do its thing on repeat. She did not join them both for dinner, instead retiring to her room. Life for both boys feels lacking a spark; she has lost the will to be cheerful for one, but it is much more than that.

Knock, knock, knock at Belle's door.

But Max doesn't even wait for her approval, opening the door to her room. Isabella lies face down on her bed, sobbing into her pillow.

"Belle . . . " He sits at the side of her and shakes her shoulder softly. She turns over from her front to face the wall, with her back to him.

"You've hardly said a word since Kingdom Building this morning . . . is something on your mind? If there's anything that I can do to help, Belle, please say so, ok, cos I hate to see you like this . . . " Max chooses his words quite carefully considering Isabella's present instability.

"Like what? The weak hypocrite that I am? Well, Max, this is me, deep down I'm just as lost, just as lonely and just as selfish." Belle opens up facing the wall, with tears streaming down her face

– she feels very vulnerable.

"Where's this coming from? Maybe you need a drink of water . . . are you hungry?" His concern is born of fear for he has never seen or heard her like this before Belle looks and sounds defeated.

"Ha-ha-ha-ha-ha Max! So clueless it's almost touching . . . indeed, what would I do without you?" Isabella breaks into a fit of hysterics as she turns over and faces him sat beside her. He looks confused from her reaction to his sincere concern and remains silent albeit with the appearance of a discombobulated dog on his tilted-sideways face, as she continues to talk.

"Why should we feel guilty any more than we have to? You were right to take off on your travels, it's your journey, not mine. There were hard feelings, yes of course there were . . . yet not now . . . now I've come to my senses. See, I chose to chase my dream all the way down that rabbit hole of who but only the brave become made aware – realising such a thing if and when one digs the deepest. Oh sure, I worked hard at it but back then I wasn't to know what a sacrifice I was making, in light of my childhood dream. Because quite frankly you can't have your cake and eat it after all." Belle gets up, enters her en suite bathroom for some tissues, blows her nose, wipes her face and then stands over Max, still sat on the bed.

"What do you mean?" he asks, looking up at her foreboding body of hurt and pain.

"I mean, given the choice between being with you and making my dream come true . . . Max, I was born to be a conductor . . . destiny did indeed bring us back together here and now, but not for long, not forever, I've been on the phone to Lucy my agent. After the funeral I will go back on tour where I belong." Upon revealing just what she has in mind, Belle leaves her room and heads downstairs where Francis remains sat at the peril of yet another Christmassy costume drama from none other than the BBC. Max is left to digest Isabella's plan of action and in doing so, gives thought to his own future, or lack thereof if he's honest with himself. Such serious consideration compels his body to shut down and so Max soon falls asleep albeit on Belle's bed.

Belle enters the living room with a mug of mulled wine for Francis. She switches the TV off before taking a seat next to him.

"Thanks for that, being homeless has its perks after all because the more I see of what's on TV these days the less attached to such surface flippancy I feel. Television is like an old friend that has changed and yet not for the better. I fear for the mass mess of us as brainwashed media-addicts, these people of nothing but popular opinion; do they not even know how hollow a world driven by money and status is? It's exactly like what Oscar Wilde once said, 'Most people are other people. Their thoughts are someone else's opinions, their lives a mimicry, their passions a quotation.'" Francis rests his head back against one of the sofa's exquisitely coloured cushions, as Belle leans forward appearing to be deep in thought.

"Excuse me and my stupidity but what does mimicry mean?" Belle looks embarrassed asking a homeless person to be on simpler terms for the purpose of making sense. She should not let her ego go so far as colour her feelings in, when this moment's place of purity remains at stake.

"To live, is to discover your own way of life and

yet many make a bad habit of losing themselves so far gone that they desperately feel the need to come across as something that they are not, and what better way to hide your decreasing sense of persona than imitate someone else's strengths, such as a charisma most to die for. Are you following this or should I just shut up?" Francis is on fire right now, but being modest means his concern is more so on how Belle hears him, and not on how he hears himself because of course, as stuck-up people know too well, oh how easy it is to fall in love with one's own tone of voice, so much so that these people of a practised demeanour don't care for what they say, so long as it sounds convincing.

"So, Oscar Wilde was passing comment at the time on just how easy it is instead to get swept up and then taken aback by being made victim of what others say. 'Brainwashed' with the same old drone drowning out in numbers the few from their own potential 'light', the light to shine on and against all those surrounded but also seduced by the black chaos of darkness as it misguides us from . . . from . . . " Belle almost made complete sense of Francis' spirited quotation and yet towards the end of her sentence she falters somewhat.

"The truth." Francis finishes Isabella's inspired point of view for her.

"You're a very smart man, Francis, isn't it time to make use of what you have, this gift that you've been given, in a way with words so potent? Don't waste your life feeding pigeons. Please, let me help you?" Belle looks Francis in his deep, dark brown eyes for a glimmer of hope.

"It is time . . . I've agreed to assist Max in his search for a better world," he says, staring right back at her.

"What does that even mean?" Belle looks confused.

"It means he's helping me get to the bottom of what goes on when the cameras are off and indeed beyond the media leading me astray; it's time I knew the truth." Max talks the talk walking downstairs with an air of fleeting tenacity to his strong words, as he has in his hand the Bible given to him by Belle's late father, Joseph.

"What truth do you speak of if I may reduce such a thing into terms most simple? Please enlighten me, Max?" She watches him sit on his favourite armchair, accompanied by an ever so subtle smirk making him look like the cat that got the cream from somewhere only he knows.

"I want to light the way for a righteous future where we are free from greed-breeding, corrupt-polluting individuals doing a disservice to us all." He speaks from way down deep, while his eyes gain animation unto his heart's desire for a world without wrongdoing.

"And how will you achieve this 'righteous future' or is your head well and truly sky bound beyond comprehension?" Belle knows how to get the most out of Max; she is stirring him up.

"Your father gave me this, so I can and will make a great big difference in my lifetime," he says, holding up the Bible.

"And yet you were forced into attending church just this morning so what's changed?" Belle looks bamboozled by what she has deemed a major contradiction on behalf of her old flame Max. He opens up the Bible and gets out the documents inside.

"What's that you got there?" Isabella asks

curiously.

"See for yourself. " Max passes her all of the documents. She feasts her eyes over the notes relating to Tesla's cause for free energy. And then at both the letter addressed to Max from her father, followed by the familiar handwritings of her former self – such is a certain poem. He watches for a reaction from her but she appears pretty much unimpressed by it all.

"What do you think?" he asks seriously.

"What am I meant to think? I think . . . if you think classified documents such as these feel like the right answer you've been looking for then who am I to say anything else other than good luck to you my friend." Belle passes all of the documents to Francis, including the letter written to Max by her father and her own poem from back in the day.

"But surely you can fathom the magnitude, and grasp at quite the compelling implications these, these . . . " He is losing himself for the sake of creating a hype he feels is necessary now.

"Pieces of paper... pieces of paper, Max, that's all it is . . . " Isabella belittles such things because she has not got the heart to care for matters that are simply beyond her world of classical music.

"How can you say that? This is history in the making!" he bites back, pushing himself forward onto the edge of his seat, clearly feeling impassioned.

"Francis, what do you make of Max's fantasy?" Belle really likes rubbing him up the wrong way and is an expert at it.

"Max, I ask you, just like it is in the letter from her father, are you willing to do whatever it takes?" Francis asks seriously, sat beside a troubled

Belle.

"Yes, of course," he says, so sure of himself.

"Tell Belle what we're doing in two nights time." Francis is ordering him to tell her the truth.

"Is there something I should know?" Belle asks as her attention shifts from Francis onto Max.

"Yes, you should know what we will do in two nights time because quite frankly I have nothing to hide. Do you, Francis?" Max goes from being on the edge of his seat to standing up intently.

"Certainly not . . . continue," Francis says straightforwardly.

"On the night of Christmas Day a vengeful fire will rage against the powers that be; we, me and Francis, are to act as shadows dancing in the light of flaming karma." Max sacrifices sense for the more cryptic, attractive tone of poetry in motion, from whence his piece of mind is since awash with big ideas masquerading as some kind of self-indulgent monologue-like take on what is to happen soon enough, if black magic makes an appearance.

"Francis, from what I make of Max with his crazy eyes right now, your talk of black magic is a bad influence so please refrain from dwelling in a dark place. Shadows don't dance in the light of 'flaming karma', at least not around here, therefore any attempt to summon such stuff will force me into taking legal action against either one of you responsible for your wrongdoing." Belle addresses Francis as both remain seated on the sofa. Max is still standing and yet shrinks with disappointment at being told what he can and can't do by a bossy Isabella.

"Francis, say something." He sounds desperate.

"It's not my place to say anything," Francis answers back coldly.

"Max, why fight fire with fire? You're better than that . . . or after all these years have I got you horribly wrong? Here I am, forever thinking highly of your righteous stance in the face of injustice but now what I see before me looks like a lost shadow of your former self." Belle looks disappointed at Max; her words hit him hard and he remains silent, sitting back down in the armchair.

"Belle, we both know he has his heart in the right place. Perhaps I should keep parts of the past to myself from now on." Francis is shouldering the blame because he feels responsible for Max's misguided ideas.

"Francis, it's my fault. Yet still the error in my ways is at once redeemed by my intentions; not exactly honourable, but for the greater good I'd do anything," Max says, staring into Belle's bright eyes as he looks at her for a change of heart and mind.

"Francis, if you don't mind going outside for a cigarette right now I would like a word with Max in private please." Isabella appears, exactly as she sounds, deadly serious. Francis nods once and then takes himself outside. Max is still, silent and sat back in the armchair awaiting her every word to follow from Francis' exit.

"You were once the love of my life, therefore feelings like the ones within me do not just simply pass . . . yes, I still think you're the same man I fell for but it's me who has changed. Jesus, Max, I'm worried about you, you're nearly forty now and . . . " Belle tries as she might to get through to him, but hits a raw nerve, forcing him to retaliate.

"Hey, you're the one who invited a homeless stranger here for Christmas, Isabella! And we both know why . . . you busy yourself with anything that can be but a necessary distraction and thus far away are the very real goings on – neglected out of the fear you feel from facing your father's death, let alone going back to being a conductor. Sure you may have made plans, albeit in the company of Francis. I feel sorry for him, and I feel surprised by your thoughtless actions as well." Max stays seated but makes his feelings fly across the room. Belle watches on in the wake of receiving his strong words. She does not move a muscle, for far from feeling a sense of sheer paralysis instead she is simply thinking about how to respond.

Belle walks away, out of his sight, to go outside for fresh air and a breather; her pulse was racing since he can clearly give as good as he gets from her where an earful is concerned.

"That's right, walk away . . . you're good at that these days," Max says spitefully, still sat in the armchair while holding his head in his hands.

Isabella went to join Francis outside, but to her surprise he has gone. She looks down the night-fallen lane and yet to no avail. Belle is left feeling lost at what to do. But the last thing on her mind is Max and so she heads toward town in search of Francis.

I fear gory details will get lost on those fortunate not to feel the exasperatingly lonesome clench of mental illness. So let me skip to two instances, most frightful, forever etched and always a wonder for my mind. On the brink of a breakdown, indeed I was not to know what has hit until the blow flashes before your being and desperately leaves you feeling an emotional vulnerability beyond comprehension. Yes, you don't know what's coming until it's just so happened and all that remains is in one long moment of madness, as such a state exists seemingly like quite to die for the ferocious ghost getting under your skin.

It is so very raw. But it is also a challenge in terms of constructing what will come together as sense being made from madness – this vexes my mind and ability to comprehend. Therefore, writing about being in a delicate state of despair as opposed to writing while in a delicate state of despair proves testing at least for me. Because I cannot put down on paper the true extent to that which I was well and truly rattled by my fear of being alive.

Forgive me, I feel like I've failed you already, dear reader. Do you know what I know? I know only my own mind and even then that in itself fills me with worrying unease. Utter courage just does not feature hereafter that which I will gather for the greater good of self-discovery. Sorry for not finding the strength within, when I was at my worst, to make more than a mental note of my mad mind and my hungry heart. Starving void dead and never of fullness, not at all willing to write down what was such a scare for me. Even now, I write without the foresight to know what will make more sense. So, is this simply my conscious stream masquerading itself as something else entirely?

Why, oh why, would you need to know how I felt when I went out of my mind anyway? Well, we are all for digging deep; put yourself in the soul of a soulless vessel . . . now how do you feel? I was without hope. Hell all around. There have been bedazzling feelings stemming from my horribly wrong thought patterns turning inside out with a pure form of fear personified by itself as opposed to the 'real me'. The only way I can capture your heart to resonate with my extreme experiences is probably by prose and prose alone. Although prose is the poor man's experience simply because, let's say for argument's sake, such a life as mine never ceases to sweat with my richness experiencing everything around me –

bleeding brilliance or crying a compelling charm from which I will feel free therefore fly high.

How are you to be me? I ask openly, my perplexity taking precedence as if from not knowing one's self is experienced as a tragic conundrum. I'm me. You are you. But I want you to get me by my bones and know what it is these sweet nothings say from the bottom of my heart.

In my early twenties, twice I went through horror for want of a better word. Once, when I ran out of the house half-naked clutching hold of a compass in one hand and a Bible in the other, thinking I was 'a newfound disciple of Jesus Christ'. I was running away from my eventless little life, having very really created a reality unto itself, distorted and yet sensitive. After being caught by my guardians, I was taken to a mental hospital and that was where what I went onto experience simply failed me of my right mind. Now again I must go back to how this extreme manifest of an experience is wasted on my words. But watch the Devil's Advocate (Al Pacino and Keanu Reeves) and feast your eyes on the horror of evil; only then will you get a glimpse of what I got in 'real life'. Faces distorting into the expression of longing, of suffering, and of ghostly evil; this is what I saw before my eyes and believe me, because who was at work to deceive the world around, turning it inside out? Satan? Indeed the devil? I don't know.

The other experience was when I studied Creative Writing in London and after a few months of inner turmoil, mixed with distancing myself from friends, I wasn't fit to continue the course. Most potent about that time; I'm crying on my bed and praying for the truth . . . everything else was non-existent to me.

Bipolar Disorder: a mental condition marked by alternating periods of elation and depression. In my troubled past, there were moments of pure mania, where for no apparent reason I would break into hilarity. And fond memories such as those are riddled with the long suffering depression in between. We all have our highs and lows, don't we just! But for the bipolar sufferer such things simply feel much more extreme and are a frequent trait tainting ones personality, or colouring it, that all depends on one's certain outlook of life.

Schizoaffective Disorder: a condition in which a person experiences a combination of schizophrenia symptoms such as hallucinations and delusions, and mood disorder symptoms such as mania or depression. This disorder is not as well understood or well defined as other mental health conditions. It's interesting to think like I do at a time like this as I try dissecting a certain part of my personality, that which sprung to mind was just an expression 'If you haven't got anything nice to say then don't say anything at all.' If the same thing is said of a writer's writings then perhaps I should stop now!

CHAPTER 6: CHRISTMAS SPIRIT

Belle realises something that at once stops her from walking on in the dark wake of Francis' disappearance. She realises such are her feelings forcing her into action – now what a stinging sense of futility to that which she moves so fast at her own undone body being broken down and a mind misguided by nothing but taking this sweet time, in vain, not from her heart hence headstrong circumstance presents itself for all she endeavours here is simply redundant.

Still, she feels repelled to rejoin the juxtaposed prat Max, such a man as he remains wavering on the outskirts of her consciousness now she feels Francis has gone back to where he belongs. And this makes her all the more aware of where she should be – on tour with her orchestra. It is early evening now, not that Belle knows the time, since she never wears a watch. But her body clock can do wonders for knowing what the time is close to being, because nonetheless she feels free of a time frame right now. For here there remains nowhere to be but of course killing Christmas time.

Isabella brings herself feelings footloose and fancy free as she enters The Great Goat Inn on her own. And so, such a familiar aroma makes her smile, albeit inside, as she enjoys this sense of some things staying the same. Belle goes straight to the bar. For party season, she is surprised such a place as this pub be anything but busy. Sure, The Great Goat Inn is cosy and traditional, with a beaming reputation of being the best around for ale. And then it hit her; ale, at least these days, has not got the gift of being a trendy drink, until the time arrives at a crafty advertising campaign in order to change everything you think you know about ale.

Everything therefore remains as it should be here; there are no young couples showing off a fake kind of posturing romance and no group of middle-aged 'friends' from work (colleagues) together drowning their sorrows. 'Nice and normal' are the hypothetical collective troubles born of a suppressed disgust at one's time misspent perilously, seriously losing the will to live via a very meaningless, least of all soul-destroying, not to mention mundane beyond boring, average Joe job. Not even a pool table, just the worn unto old dartboard positioned in the corner which remains unused.

"What will it be?" The obese bartender robotically retorts, talking in 'working tongue' mode and thus far from what is on the ear clear as can be but an unbecoming croaky kind of tone to fit his distinctly lifeless voice. Isabella looks around her. There is an elderly couple sat opposite each other while they enjoy the cosiness sprung from the fireplace, as well as their alcoholic beverages of course. So her attention turns to the bar area, but then Belle notices that a plain man has been sat on the furthest stool from where she stands. She immediately returns her attention to the fat and balding bartender, but out of her peripherals she can see that the plain man is staring at her.

"Sorry, what did you just say?" Belle sounds distracted.

"Are you here for the ambience alone? Or are you going to buy a drink with that?" Out of the blue, the bartender sounds sarcastic in his way with words. She turns to her left, looks straight at the plain man and he gives her the grossest smile, showing his severely yellow teeth. Belle leaves the pub with immediate effect.

Ten minutes pass since Isabella left Max to his own devices. Such a man gets up from the armchair and goes outside. Dark is this night, yet a gorgeous shade of red adorns the sky, making it brighter tonight. To his surprise, Isabella and Francis are nowhere to be seen. He meanders down the front garden and leans on the fence whereby beyond it is an empty field. Suddenly appears before him something that is up above and big together as one, but only illusory resplendence exists in the eye of the beholder therefore this false wholeness has stemmed from his limited outlook. Beautiful fierce spectacle taking shape made of starling . . . it's a stunning murmuration. Max is spellbound enough not to take away any of his undivided attention and thus doesn't smoke a cigarette. He watches on, as the black wave-like dance gathers speed of movement to shift from one weird and wonderful form to another . . . the starlings simply create quite a curious, aesthetically pleasing sight at Max's amazement.

It indeed feeds his imagination and yet utilizes his memories as he is taken back in time. To when the red sky complimented a darkening Newquay sea and Max was sat on his surfboard waiting for the next big wave. He reminisces, focusing on the special silence now and then, this essence as an ingredient to what was made up of a golden paradise devoid of time. The murmuration reminds him to appreciate the little things in life; of how one whole will always come from many a force somewhat working together.

"What are you doing down there?" Belle raises her voice as she stands at the beginning of the garden, near the front door to the house.

"Look up at the sky and see for yourself, " he says, still full of emotion from how the spectacular murmuration makes him feel.

Belle looks up at the reddish sky taken over by the beautiful arrangement of starlings. She smiles straight away, effortlessly leaving behind her now redundant troubles. Max makes his way back up the garden and stands next to her. He lights a cigarette, before offering one to Belle but she declines, keeping her attention firmly fixed skyward at the gorgeous goings on up above her.

"So when is Joseph's funeral?" he asks her, after breathing out a mouthful of smoke.

"The 27th. He is to be buried beside Wendy. And then, when all has been said and done, on the day after that I go back on tour – for what it's worth." She breaks off from being in the sky's company and appears to be feeling cold back on the ground. Max notices Isabella looks cold and offers his arm around her shoulder, but she shrugs it off before going indoors. Rejected, not to mention downbeat, he stays standing, smoking and thinking of what to do next with his headless chicken-like life.

Belle readies herself for bed, with every intention of getting an early night. Max eventually feels the cold and comes inside. He is sat in the familiar confines and comfort of his favourite armchair. He is not watching television, instead dwelling over the documents that his mind continues to wonder 'what if' about. But soon enough his sense of adventure is replaced by a brush with reality. Slowly yet surely, he folds the documents, so to put them back inside the Bible, because now all he can think about is his life of fluctuation, frustration and foolishness.

An estranged father from birth who abandoned his responsibility, and a self-destructive mother who lost her life to an overdose soon after Max was born. But of course, George and Gwen made sure he had a good life for the most part. After their death he cashed in on the B&B business as well as everything that they gave him in the will. All of which would fund him on his travels Max is not a man about business, neither has he the normal mind-set necessary for starting a family. Because as he sees such things, that's the systematic trap pinpointing the beginning of the end of freedom.

Max spent ten years seeing the world from a point of view well and truly lost at what to do. At the expense of financial loss, hence is an oh so long holiday away from England and its self-deprecating parts of our country here nevertheless softened/made bearable by comedic charm from our 'national treasures' to say the least. Yet still the collective heart of us English has been hardened numb until the tragedy of it all feels lost on our practised suffering. Something that Max has not at all missed is this way of life from a western disposition now westernising itself further still so other countries can copy because us English (and Americans!) have a very meaningful worldview . . . *wink.*

Prime Minister Pricilla Fay came to power on 13th of July 2016. To pass a law legalising foxhunting would mean to attain the Queen's signature (her approval). No one but the Queen knows how the Queen feels about a blood-sport such as foxhunting. But after what happened at Buckingham Palace recently she, sorry, 'The Queen' could well be experiencing a change of heart, that or her mind has been made up on the matter. After all, you don't just watch a fox save your great-grandchild's life and then make foxhunting legal like nothing happened. And so, there exists a clash which has the makings of a crisis. The Prime Minister is yet to get the Queen's signature, therefore foxhunting has not been legalised. Charles Swinton felt compelled to reveal the very real Royal ordeal and risk his job being a butler. But now in the public knowledge, such a thing will divide us as a country, for better or worse.

Speculation surrounds our dear sweet Queen and her Majesty's Christmas speech. Will she address the public concerning the rift with the Prime Minister? Perhaps not, but stranger things have happened . . . President Ronald Flump and Brexit spring to mind. Thursday 23rd of June 2016 to be exact, was the date that the UK voted leave (52%) as opposed to remaining in the EU (48%). The EU itself is an economic and political partnership involving twenty eight European countries. It began after World War 2 to nurture economic co-operation and help prevent another war from breaking out on the basis that by trading together, each and every country part of the 'EU' could build up a potential relationship born in order to thrive of trust.

Since our sour departure, Pricilla assured us it was for the best and that Great Britain would definitely benefit from parting ways with the EU. But of course she did this in the same strained way many, if not all, politicians are forced to act when under such scrutiny and pressure to perform for all else as we watch on in the wake of public affairs showcased daily/nightly/always. She has a stern verging on stubborn manner, matching her appearance so very grey and aged.

Christmas Eve, 2018

Max wakes up in the armchair again. Getting to his feet he heads for the kitchen in search of Isabella but she is not there. It's just gone 10am and she is not in her room either. He goes back downstairs to the kitchen and has cereal for breakfast. Sitting down at the table he notices a note . . . *Gone Christmas Shopping xx*

Belle is back at the hospital to confirm a certain date and time for her father's transfer from Freedom Fields hospital to the same cemetery as where Wendy remains. It's all been sorted but the issue of Francis is still lurking somewhere within Belle's brain. Indeed she wonders whether it is wise to go back to the park where Francis and her first met. But before she can find good reason in order to betray her better judgement, Belle approaches the park on foot, having left her white Audi TT at the hospital carpark.

Francis stands at the exact same place as where their first encounter took place. He's too busy feeding his pigeons to notice Isabella lurking in the distance. She takes a deep breath before walking towards him amid the merest of snowfall. Belle is in all black and wears her hood up for some warmth otherwise she'd freeze – it's such a bitter chill out there. She walks in the path of the pigeons on purpose; as they fly away Francis gives her his undivided attention.

"Hello, Francis" she says, subsequently revealing herself after removing her hood.

"We meet again." Francis says such a thing with his face straight, but underneath the fancy clothes she bought him, he opens his heart to her.

"Here is where your heart feels whole . . . home. I know not to meddle like I have been but you're more than welcome back for Christmas, Francis, please . . . me and Max miss the company you keep," Belle pleads with him hopefully. Her eyes like a child's, she appears sincere.

"What do you want from me?" he asks, as if it is a simple question to answer. Isabella looks somewhat taken aback but doesn't flinch in her response.

"I want a silver lining." Belle opens up.

"You want what you can't have . . . everything is as it should be, but you're forcing the issue with me as your way of feeling better. A kneejerk reaction to the death of your father, that's all I am in your eyes." Francis in the same vein opens up.

"Sorry, Francis, this was a mistake coming back here . . . Merry Christmas." Isabella turns around and walks away.

"Isabella," Francis calls out to her. She turns around.

"Give Max a chance . . . listen to him . . . he wants what's best for the future . . . our wayward world needs people like him in it." He proceeds to feed his pigeons again.

"Your pigeons don't need you like you need them . . . come back with me . . . please." She sounds desperate.

"I'm homeless, Isabella, and you're a highflyer . . . why would you want anything to do with a guy like me?" Francis asks, perhaps fishing for a compliment.

"'Do we not even know how hollow a world driven by money and status is', Francis." Isabella remembers his words and uses them to her advantage. Francis smiles, albeit with his eyes, as he spreads the last bit of birdseed around him, before joining her. He is greeted with a warm embrace by Belle and then she leads the way back to her car.

A taxi pulls up outside Joseph's cottage. Max leaves a note next to the one Belle left. His bag is packed and his mind made up, but he feels sad all the same. He holds the Bible tight in his hand and gets inside the taxi.

"Where to?" It's a middle-aged lady with short black hair, husky voice and the lingering smell of smoke for her scent is strong but underwhelming.

"The train station." He whimpers putting on his seatbelt.

And off he goes. Unbeknownst to Belle, for she is Christmas shopping with Francis, as Max stays silent throughout the short journey. The taxi driver glances down at his hand clutching the bible, before turning her attention back onto the road ahead. She says nothing but the cost of the journey upon arriving at the train station.

It's busy; people here resemble headless chickens as they race past each other from one platform to the next. Max gets a miniature bottle of red wine from the coffee shop and drinks it as it is – in one foul gulp. He goes straight to the ticket office and waits his turn. The man in front of him smells of booze and BO; while shapely, he too appears Christmassy, as Max stares depressively verging on indifferent at this stranger for all he's worth. Thus far where the better man is concerned and, of course, it's his egocentric mistake to make judgements based on a bad mood, but alas shows no sign of an outer-reaction, when under his skin remains much ado about a bludgeoning intensity soaked in an altogether horrid downfall flooding his feelings with nothing but bitter revulsion upon one long look of fierce displeasure affords, from whence such a newfound fandangle gathers a gross stench testing his patience. Soon enough, the stinky stranger goes away and it's his turn to buy a ticket.

"A one way ticket to London Kings Cross, please," he says seriously. The ticket person does her thing and then prints him his ticket.

"What platform?" Max asks.

"Platform 3 . . . the 12:27 train to London Kings Cross." She says it with the straightforward sound of the system ringing in his ears, appearing all the more like an impeccably programmed robot.

"Thanks." Max looks at the time on his mobile phone and then heads straight to platform 3.

Belle brings Francis back to the cottage with her. She places her shopping on the kitchen table, only to discover a note next to the one she had left for Max.

'*Destiny in a dream . . . a dream away from being the*

real thing. This is for your father. I have gone to do good and right. With love, Max xx'

Belle doesn't want to lift her head and face Francis. A tear escapes her, dripping onto the note. Francis watches on, not knowing what has happened.

Meanwhile, the world doesn't know how to react to the bittersweet natural disaster taking away everything in Rio - all but Christ the Redeemer which remains standing tall. Many an expert within the field of science seem to be receiving the vast amount of media exposure, proposing certain explanations as scientists are quite capable of but still failing us in simple terms of providing a basic answer for how this 'accident' happened. And why the statue of Christ the Redeemer survived such severe devastation.

It would appear the media doesn't want a balanced thesis with regard to revealing all the possible likelihoods. There has been no coverage of Christian reasoning, only the cantankerous gibberish being force-fed from all walks of science. This, however, far from means people are anything but the small-minded majority jollying in a collective ignorance enough not to use their own imagination. And thus they do wonder, for the media prefer the ever so subtle but constant technique taking shape as sheer propaganda via a manipulative mouthpiece masquerading itself as popular opinion. Indeed people all around world are very much aware of what Christ the Redeemer means for many believers. Even if for they themselves as atheists or agnostics, at the end of the day nobody but God knows how and why this seemingly natural disaster did not destroy a significant statue.

Max is on the train taking him to London. He's sitting in a seat that is positioned opposite two seats with a table between them, but the other passengers are of no importance to him when reading a newspaper. Well, 'appearing' to read a newspaper, because inside it he has put the documents concerning Tesla's pursuit of free energy. For obvious reasons Max feels a precious sense of possessing such things inconspicuously.

"If you're not reading that newspaper, please let me have a look at it," says the voice of a woman sat next to Max, snapping him out of his fixated state of mind. She is dressed smart, but not overly, clearly stylish yet subtle with it. Her glasses have a thick black circular frame complimenting her heavy use of mascara, whereas her eyes are dark green and yet bright blue also – strange but beautiful.

"Of course, sorry, I was just . . . " He has gone blank at what to say, so instead carefully fiddles with his documents before giving her the newspaper. She refrains from making a thing of it, takes the newspaper and smiles knowingly at his sheepish wince. Max closes the Bible and puts it in his bag before feeling the need to stare vacantly out of the window. Out of his peripherals he can see she has yet to take a look at the newspaper, but then quickly convinces himself so to think nothing of it.

"It's Max, isn't it?" The woman checks her smartphone and then puts it in her silver designer handbag. Max turns facing her with his undivided attention, and in doing so does his best not to look down her inviting cleavage.

"And you are?" he says, as if feeling unsure of

her intentions.

"You don't recognise me?" Her voice gets higher while she removes her glasses and puts them on the table. He takes a moment to picture her in his memory, but appears perplexed.

"No, sorry, should I know who you are?" Max asks directly.

"Perhaps not, but I remember you from uni. Oh my God, what a coincidence this is! We were in the same Journalism lectures, although that being said, we never sat together . . . the name's Macey Cena. Nice seeing you again after all this time, what's it been since back then? Like, fifteen years?" Macey smiles, showing off her immaculate white teeth that are set against such a sexy shade of deep red lipstick.

He squints into her, hoping for a recollection, and in doing so surrenders such bewilderment because he has become quite transfixed by her impeccable beauty.

"Yes Macey, such is life for what happens when time passes us by. I don't mean to be rude but I really can't picture you . . . did we ever have a conversation in the past?" His eyes start to wander down her body; she is dressed as a serious businesswoman would, but allows enough leeway for the ever so subtle element of hotter than hell allure being given off from knowing what she can and will do using such powerful features she has been blessed with.

"For a time I worked in the student bar and there you were very much under the influence asking me what time I got off. Flattered, that which I was, I was also seeing someone else." Macey says, smiling at Max, who now looks like he's cringing inside.

"Silly me." He cannot recall this, though that being said, such a thing is best supressed so he can't really deny it not to have happened and instead endures his embarrassment.

"No, not at all, you were very sweet . . . it made my night," Macey says suggestively.

He does not know where to take the conversation next. It is far from encouraged by society to make connections away from the designated confines of a bar for instance, and yet Max is feeling lonely this Christmas.

"So what brings you to London on Christmas Eve?" He sits back, comfortably lulled into the ease at which she makes him feel.

"I've been assigned to cover the goings on in and around Rio following what has happened," Macey says seriously.

"And what happened, in your humble opinion?" Max asks, assuming an unbiased stance at least until after her say has sunk into his curious state of mind.

"Well, Max, it's all over the news . . . a severe earthquake caused devastation and yet left Christ the Redeemer miraculously untouched." She sounds just like a reporter reading information off of a screen.

"But do you have an opinion on what caused such a thing in the first place?" he asks again.

"As far as I am aware a natural disaster just so happens to happen spontaneously." She seems stupefied by his irregularity.

"I see, so you don't think it was something along the lines of an artificial earthquake caused by the New World Order . . . or an act of God?" Max wants to know what she really thinks about it, but tries hiding his intense interest.

"Of course we can wonder, and yet, yes, such a fitting time to come back, but that in itself answers for all the hysterical chaos. As for the former, there will always be reason to think quite wrongly along the laughable little lines of conspiracy theory; we people have always been incomprehensible!" Macey seems fully engaged within his thinking and gives as good as she gets.

"Ah, but did you know that the 25th of December became the date for Christmas not because Christ was supposedly born on that day, but because it was already popular in pagan religious celebrations as the birthday of the sun?" Max sounds pleased to be showcasing such knowledge.

"I did know that, but if God is all seeing and all knowing, then it would make sense to set a date for Christ's birth, whether accurate or not, otherwise when would the believers have a special occasion just to make a spirited song and dance in light of such a self-fulfilling prophecy?" Macey is in a manner most arrogant, taking great pleasure from cleaning her glasses as she shoots down the likes of Christ and God.

Max suddenly feels an urge embody every last bit of his weariness now replaced by a child-like excitement. To the extent that he reaches inside his bag and gets out the bible. But Macey fears the worst as she raises her eyebrows with a preconceived notion of the kneejerk kind and wonders what's to come from him next. He opens it up, passing her the precious documents with a glint in his hazel eyes.

She spends a good ten minutes silently looking through them, while he watches her face for any expression in order to indicate what she feels about that which she feasts her wondrous eyes on.

"In your own time I strongly suggest listening to the late journalist John Smith's interview with Nikola Tesla from the year 1899. Just type in 'Everything is the light' via YouTube, but this is interesting in itself. Classified documents I see . . . so what are you to do with this information now? And can you comprehend his use of formula and scientifically inclined language?" Macey's eyes light up as an effect of being intrigued beyond what her usual looks suggest.

"Um, well, all I can gather from it right now has already made me realise there's something going on behind closed doors, perhaps inside Area 51." He reduces his voice all the way down to a precious whisper, which she finds endearingly sweet, smiling at his spirited reaction.

"Nikola Tesla the enigma, Max . . . there's a Chinese proverb about how seriousness reduces life. It's like even now, in this day and age, we have yet to let go of our trivial feelings, so much so we are imprisoned by them and this is a perpetual trait . . . thoughts born of fear; we contract to our own inner version of who we think we are, from having the same experiences painting the same picture over and over again instead of expanding our awareness of everything in and out of our control Tesla said he simply 'played' and enjoyed doing it. This is a man who could quite easily solve problems by dreaming up the solutions in his sleep. He was a self-proclaimed failure but a driven genius, driven by the power of love, of visualisation. In all honesty, I don't think you know what you're getting yourself into . . . do you believe fate brought your enquiry here, or is this just a mere coincidence?" Macey has certainly made an impression on him as he now allows a moment to consider her vast point of view.

"We will soon be arriving at our next stop: London Kings Cross, which is where this train terminates. Please make sure your belongings are with you upon departing the train. Thank you." The train driver makes an announcement, letting all passengers know that they have very nearly reached their destination. Macey readies herself for leaving the train and this snaps Max out of his head immediately.

"Wait. I mean . . . when is your flight to Rio?" he asks almost desperately.

"There are no more flights to Rio so I fly to Sao Paulo. My flight is tomorrow afternoon." She can sense his interest but doesn't shy away from it.

"Oh right. What hotel are you staying at?" He has lost all inhibition now.

"I will tell you, depending upon what this is in your eyes . . . a chance encounter or something more?" Macey must be into playing games, the games us adults indulge in for the purpose of fun and fancy.

"I think this is something more than I can comprehend," Max says honestly, albeit displaying an obvious sign of desire via his starry-eyed wonderment. The train grinds to a halt. The doors open and everyone is up on their feet approaching each exit.

"Let's get checked into a hotel and then talk more over a drink or two . . . do you like cocktails?" Macey looks to have a mischievous side and Max is loving it. He smiles at her warmly before readying himself.

"To tell you the truth, tequila always comes first but that's just stating the obvious." he says, as they exit the train together.

"My sentiments exactly," she answers back, with the look of fire in her eyes, as both become immersed by everyone else's goings on around them. They have arrived in London and the quest for a righteous future has begun.

'Waking up is a so very vague phrase for 'seeing the light' of truth take shape and take control over your conditioned mind. I know why we as a society try to domesticate the chaos within, with nothing but braindead telly! (And outdated worldviews as well.) If for instance, everyone were to 'wake up' but only by going through the emotional distress I was a victim of, it would not be a bright future that I foresee. So why is an extreme experience 'bad'? Because the lucid and mundane mind of the mass collective is exactly that! Your lucid mind feels free of the nuances stemming from the brain's unlimited potential to manifest absolutely anything. And yet your mind is being brainwashed by the mundane media mouth-piece police, letting you know in all of its arrogance masquerading as certainty that you should be thinking like 'this' so you are able to do 'that'.

'The fool has said in his or her heart, "there is no God."' To act unwisely as a jester or a clown and deceive, even play a trick on someone; dupe . . . definition of fool flash before your eyes! You can quite easily live your life of comfort from a fictitious, twisted and sanitary way whereby lies pass as second nature, not knowing what nature itself flourishes simply because such a thing is without the want we have of money and the need we feel for pleasure. As a matter of fact Mother Nature deserves so much more nurture not from us, but from animals. Is it ignorance really stopping your right mind from knowing without doubt that animals feel the same way we do? To have a heart must mean something other than a means of satisfying an unquenchable blood-lust after meat. Make no mistake about what I put to you; you've been an animal all your life!

If, of course, this is disagreeable because your brain busies itself subconsciously building up an ideal identity based upon one conceptual construct that exists as if by ego alone, then when will you take a quiet moment to consider Descartes resounding notion of 'I think therefore I am' ? And in doing so, suffice to say inside yourself first and foremost, make clear something along the lines of, 'If I think, this thought that sprang to mind, my mind had been but still without what was seen to be by me and only me.' 'Before feeling the need and by fibre of being become my thought; what was I when there exist not a thought to think?' Thinking is a way of processing something; something simply became created out of nothing, therefore everything that has since spent its time, and your energy on embodying an idea upon personifying your existence as real reflects not reality, yet your personal reality; this isn't true to all things, just you.

I take great heart from the story of Moses setting his people free from slavery. If Moses, as a baby, be he not sent down the river, there was no other escaping from death by order of King Herod. And so Moses was rescued and cared for from the safe hands of Egypt's elite; he grew up to fight battles but in the end exiled as of when the true reality of his situation came to light. He became made aware of what it meant to fight for a power which was unjust, took it upon himself forever after that, with the help of divine intervention and so saved very many people from a long life of slavery. Therefore the truth will always set free from being victimized as less than that which is still the same when all has been said and done.

Indeed I too was adopted as a baby, but the parallel will not stop at that. There remains slavery, yet not of the body but mostly of the mind. And do we really believe because such a thing as an ability to perceive everything else, its mechanics are as unseen as 'sleep sees dreams' . . . mind may well be out of our sight but a mind out of its mind will always cause concern, not to mention an out and out chaos. So how will *we heal and grow? Within this system that at any given moment might see itself financially viable, better off from managing your money, your mind and then end up in no uncertain terms soul-destroying your hope of having a dream realised. So I ask you now, what has the system done in order to deserve the vast majority of your waking life? We know not a waking one anymore, but at our peril it is a working one instead.*

Winter, not a wonderland but a town of no importance to me. Here I have died inside so many a time I can't quite believe there is still the will within what consists of a comfortably numb body made from mundane pain and lifeless suffering.

I write this misery from the comfort of a cheap and cheerful Wetherspoons, sat next to a display of empty beer bottles, once shelved with books but now a soulless shadow of its former self. In the month of November but the Christmas decorations do not adorn here therefore more so a sentiment out of place. I love this time of year. In truth, if I found myself somewhere else entirely like London, then I'd be happy to see such a spirited indication of what festive cheer looms just around the corner, premature though it is in November after all.

And so, from one soulless place to the next now with the help of red wine, I find myself sat in 'Eden Wine Bar', but Eden indeed it is not at all that! Dead, definitely lacking anything and everything whatsoever where paradise is concerned. This place masquerades as swanky yet it is shit manifest from whence shit came, out of nothing but a bad idea. There is no sign of any interesting individuals . . . does this mean to say I consider myself such a thing?

There is also nothing much for me to rage against in the flesh, like a carefully constructed circle of friends, fuckwits with every intention to come across as superior via an intellectual la de dah dancing over the graves of those they speak highly of. If only they knew not to be basking just above a cesspool for the stupid. Don't make me rethink that which I write! I write to be beautiful from the inside out! Today (Thursday) I went to the local doctor's surgery so I could order my repeat prescription of antidepressants, antipsychotics and Viagra! Get me wrong why don't you! But I won't waste my time trying to excuse myself from further embarrassment, it is what it is and it is certainly not what you think! There was an old man in the way of the order forms as he slowly but surely filled one out. I waited patiently by his side and after a while he noticed I was stood in wait. What then went through his elderly little head and failing brain came to mind and thus far brought that which he did into being a breath of feeling the need to excuse himself from the time it took to fill out a form. 'Whatever you do, don't get old' were the words spoken in jovial vexed surrendering to an unbecoming shame. I said nothing worthy of a mention and then watched him walk away.

'Gather all your pain and suffering, turn them into strength and weaponry to overcome the enemy that's in you. Come face to face with the war that rages in you.' Jessie Leach (Killswitch Engage)

The rage which I will use so to shit on what is such a waste of space comes from many things going on in and around me. I have to admit to being bitter, jealous, weak and the rest, lest I know not what it is . . . whence such rage came to be.

I 'suffer' from bipolar disorder. I say such a thing simply because it's true, but also today I had a fling with that fantastic thing called an awakening. An awakening of what was sure enough already somewhere within. Nevertheless an awakening it was. I know not what it was in words whence such a thing, an awakening is, simply, magically and quite beautifully opened my eyes to the endless possibility that can manifest for and from me, if and when I continue to <u>keep questioning things.</u> This is, if you like, my magic potion and so the more I question, then the more I rage at the western *and westernized world around me.*

I bring bipolar into being, specifically via my innocent ignorance of sorts, so you see because of 'suffering from' bipolar disorder, perhaps I experience such an awakening in a much more vibrant manner than your average Joe. I am not an average Joe so I do not know how to feel from an average Joe point of view.

In keeping with the questioning nature, that which brings me out to play in the light of truth, this from my former self of a falsehood headless chicken confused and so hopelessly lost in the shadows stemming from a forced, self-indulgent rage, here I am in not all but much of my true glory . . . being real. And being real feels good. I don't want to write that which I feel feels 'better than' that which I haven't felt, but write still in a way which would have you – the reader – believe I have felt things even if in truth I have not. That would be a lie but furthermore a betrayal. I choose to be real rather than not, not out of pride, indeed I don't feel proud of myself for being a man of my word. Why should I? I simply feel alive via my heart's surefire rage; such a thing is as of when I write from my purest place possible.

CHAPTER 7: SPECIAL DECEPTION

Max and Macey check themselves into a hotel at Waterloo, soon after he made recommendations concerning certain night life around that area of London. To his surprise she took the liberty of checking them both into one room, and a nice surprise it was. Exiting the hotel, both have decided to skip dinner and head straight for the cocktail bar Cubana.

It's a short walk from the hotel but because the hustle and bustle is constant, they take their time. After all, London on Christmas Eve was always going to be busier than its usual state of systematic chaos. Max notices Macey struts with the air of self-importance fit for a misplaced princess, and she can certainly turn heads especially upon adorning an oh-so-skimpy pale yellow dress.

He steps aside at the entrance and allows her to enter first. It's jam packed. But her beauty forges a path that otherwise wouldn't exist, leading them straight to the bar without any effort at all.

Max watches on with simmering jealousy as the tall, dark bartender grins her way.

"A Cosmopolitan and . . . " Macey says excitedly.

"A tequila and a Mojito," Max says forcefully, while feeling the contact that comes from being in a busy place like this. There are partygoers everywhere here.

"And another tequila." Macey feels compelled to keep up with the man in Max, as the handsome bartender gets to work.

"Shall we sit down?" Max asks hesitantly; he wants to get away from the friendly furore wreaking havoc on his sober senses.

"No, silly, let's dance!" She beams from being beheld beautiful; it's all in the eyes of others after all and Macey seems to feed off the attention her gorgeous self is getting. They down the tequilas and then she takes his hand, leading the way to the dancefloor. Of course, this being a Cuban cocktail bar, there is an exotic mix of men and women in perfect timing with the rhythm. Max's movements are uneasy on the eye; he can't dance to save his life. Soon enough the inevitable happens and just as Max at least lulled himself into thinking that he was doing ok on the dancefloor, another man makes himself fully felt.

Macey smiles seductively, shaking her hips like there will be no tomorrow, and in doing so she makes contact with the other man's moves. Max surrenders. He takes his drink from the side and goes out for a cigarette.

Christmas time, mistletoe and crime, consumer-driven dreams such a disease self-destructing in the wake of being itself shattered here, there and everywhere. The most wonderful time of the year yearns for more than this system-manufactured trap preventing us from reaching a higher place of consciousness and understanding.

Of course there are mere moments that come to clarify

your struggle for survival as just, but it's nothing more than a coping mechanism lest you forget to look on the bright side. What bright side? Death? 'Til death do you work for a fucking pig of a boss sucking out your life force from whence she or he has a superior position undermining your every fibre, belittling your every move. Rise above but rage against at the same time my friends . . . these days are dawning into the nightfall from grace, especially after the long grind but before your storm of a face like thunder reigns supreme.

Rather that which I will be more inclined by my prince of darkness-esq quality, than a king of self-proclaimed kings in days to come undone. We exist in wait for what exactly? An honest politician can and will rise up through the ranks of wrongful 'la-de-da' deception and all things such as that which is so very corrupt. Russell Brand can talk the talk of a sophisticated yet excitable troublesome chimpanzee, he feasts on your feelings entranced and thus far fooled by your very eyes, simply betrayed unbeknownst to you upon pretty little sweet nothings falling out of his misguided gob.

I must stop, not my rage against the game, but to rethink that which is my goal. Will my rage make a difference? Scrap such a stupid question. The question is, is a truthful future worth fighting for? I fight myself for the answer first. Then, depending upon the answer, I either rage forth with every fibre of my being or cease from feeling the need to put down an out and out assault towards what I consider wrongful.

Certainty remains in the absence of doubt. Death, that is certain. Truth, that is not. Want. Where in the world does want come from? Can we do without it? Want is what drives us to get. But when we get what we want, we will soon enough feel the need to have something else. So want is somewhere within us, perhaps existing inside the ego, and so long as we want, we carry on wanting until we get.

I want truth to overshadow shitty little lies. I want people to realise lies of every level are wrong. Why do I want a truthful future? What is a truthful future? No, no, no! I know exactly what I am doing with these kinds of questions. Because of self-doubt, uncertainty or whatever you want to call it, I am making an uncalled for effort to justify my rage before I carry on in the same vein.

I don't have a vision of the future. I have fucking shit to rage against, at my peril of lost time. Why should I impose upon you a predetermined picture of what I would like the future to look like? I don't know what a world without lies feels like, I can only imagine it as something better than one which is riddled with them. Maybe I should learn to accept things just as the way they are – people lie, people cheat, people steal because they can and will, in order to get what they want. And not everyone wants what I want.

Another awakening and this time such a thing did not make me feel all warm and fuzzy at the festive cheer. It's December, but I adore the cold. What came over me has now sunk in and I am ready to articulate it. This is the way it was, from a believer's perspective. My dwindling belief of being created in the image of God and yet what if? What if indeed! To rage against the game I must first and foremost make my rage break through from being in the wake of the game's players . . . you guys.

Me too, for the times I am reduced to humouring this sick joke of a game, playing along while I bite my tongue at its ridiculous, serious, self-centred disposition. Bring it on. For I have no such pride to swallow when I question my faith. That is the power of truth taking over every fibre of my being by the way. What if my ancestors ate each other for the hell of it, what if once upon a time we came from some kind of cannibalistic cave dwelling people?

Hah, how do I even view myself? For what is this rage made of? Yes, righteousness is the only way yet what will the path to righteousness look like? The pen may well be a bit mightier than the sword but the sword itself represents such a thing as our bloodlust. The lust for blood to be shed and sometimes swallowed but why? I am answering a call of the wild from my heart of fire. Therefore the question again goes back to the battle between creation and evolution. And who am I to ask that of myself for the answer? How many books will it take before I find my way to the truth? God made me a slow reader for a reason! Such a wicked sense of humour, right?

Religion: the belief in and worship of a superhuman controlling power, especially a personal God or gods. This can be characterised as a particular system of faith and worship, or an interest but more so the pursuit to that which is soon enough followed with great devotion – an end then answered for by your one and all-encompassing God.

Revolution: a forcible overthrow of a government or social order, in favour of a new system. Must it be but much a choice? Surefire I find not of one, when the other therefore follows on from my willpower, which chance has it at times speculative even naïve a flame came to be burning bright by beautiful, illusory story . . . we end up at the beginning again and yet take great heart are we reborn sinless vessels sought after a soul? Oh, how weird and wonderful life of finite; trappings prevail over your long lost spirit perhaps? Cannot then henceforth think highly you despair! First it is with hellbent beauty towards such a righteous stance; tall from being real, taller still for fear not of falling victim to sorry pride and tallest therefore true to oneself! Foremost to say so I should and shall have victory yield. And dare I dream it to be of glory realised. And so far as if by magic, make-believe revolutionise my life, feels for forever everyone else's sweet, sweet truthful future revelling in itself a perfect world! Once and for all we are but one, with each beating heart to the same rhythm, from my soul somehow written in the stars is such sacred dreams. May us at once wilfully find a way we can catch quite betwixt this exasperated desire by blood, sweat, tears, feelings, its instinctive if not the moral rare breed dying inside I have of every fibre being, wishing I were free!! Free from mental slavery, these people. My people will not be brainwashed with a wicked and fishy shit sight for falsified eyes since shat on from high above, but below lays Lucifer, forever the dark side of the light. It is in unknown nothingness nestled and how one naughty feeling grew Lucifer's fearsome montage of monstrous manifest.

Superhuman means someone whom has such a supreme manifesting thing, inside, supernatural, albeit outing into an extraordinary super-power, whereupon no uncertain terms most miraculous is this gift to quite frankly 'break through the fabric'. Reality exists as per usual limit, except for the one who will reach beyond dispositional limitless grasp and do wonders; thus far the resulting inconceivable becomes so very true to life after that.

Therefore, religion need be born out of an imagined deity greater than our own kind known as simply being the mere mortals that we are, a human in form and dually anything in fantasy. As for revolution and why I have found footing to stand such a thing in the same sentence let alone next to what religion means, 'Superhuman' might I add was a pleasure reiterating yet necessary here-now with interest but also inspired by beautiful fire from my lion-like roar, heart of gold honest innocence spirited away where essence knows not but just itself forever perfect! Back to what it may well all importantly mean when one considers, or goes ahead with, the unveil lest then venerating towards, whereby bringing this so-called brand new religion into being, simply because as we use words so we can find a way beyond words, so we will worship such a newfound thing in order to move up one more from our worship hopefully leaving behind science-based reason and arriving at the purest destination manifested for our journey's end.

Once we overthrow this system of things, such a thing will be wiped clean in favour of a new and improved, if not perfected, system manifesting itself as my truthful future for all. Realistically, leaving living in the wake of woeful lies behind us so to arrive at truth – this is possible but unlikely.

Faith: the complete and utter trust, or strong belief in something or someone. We 'believers' are for the divine in every way, without or regardless of proof physical to Mother Nature presenting itself as a material world. I will exercise my faith in one day doing everything and more for there to be a way of life from what is righteous. Truthful future reveals itself from men and women wanting above all else peace, prosperity, true love of real life. Let us too open possible doors swinging in the favour of a fairer currency than one which gives birth to putrid greed. Sweet nothings lost on modern dwellers desperate lust, to be forever young and yet with or without a heart matters not for our generation since it is fixated on what we are as skin deep people of our own inclination. And what is skin deep but only an appearance. And it is such an appearance presenting itself as the human condition deceives us all into taking life so seriously!

A lie is like a cigarette. It feels nice and normal, looks ok, tastes safe enough, but by being seduced as we suck in its stuff of abject juiceless sort, to blow smoke at each other's self-perpetuating tricks used as we do deceive even ourselves, so what possible beauty fronts the face of such a smoker?

There are times manifesting into moments past that will come over us so we see the light acting as our guide and yet not all look for it. What some see will blind them of others resplendence, darkness as a way of life looking with the light off. Within which is simply left to itself, for want of vices such as sex and drugs.

Truthful future, you're a futile fantasy. Why haunt my right mind and make me see the light that is at once lost on all else? These people of money know not the price of freedom, for freedom must have been long since sold to the devil. The value of life itself far from forgotten but truly lost to your weak whims, well, fancy that! And if only your willpower would just lose heart on menial lusting, let us just stop being so shallow, won't you just grasp at all else as everything in essence is – eternal.

Do you know what your real problem is? I'm not on about any personal problem being none of my business, but the big problem man has and faces is in fact a testament to time, I'm talking about the desire for control. Time, man-made, gives us all an illusion of order and so far as it gave birth to the belief of there being a real-life future whereby we have hope for a better one than that which is at this present moment. Nothing is wrong with make-believe, if you are more than able to take it with a pinch of salt. Perception itself is both outward and inward. Deep down, modern man must know what he is made of – it's chaos personified. And somehow, by divine right to be or a miracle of Mother Nature, everything comes together, working towards what we say and do. And what we say may persuade us to do as our heart desires, so long as we desire 'control', well, that in itself is a rage against nature! But here is where 'who we are' comes into play. Please see past the surface living condition now, we are all physically 'special' yet still the same mechanics inside us all apply when we strip apart the ever-fading dispositional nature of being a human body (and a cosmetically modified body for that matter!). And so, if we feel the need to disregard our guilty pleasure for sex, silencing it in the cold light of day only for it to break free between the sheets at night . . . let us consider sex as evidence stating the obvious: we are ANIMALS.

Smoking his cigarette, he let his eyes wander around London. Naturally, a mass swarm of people are the predominant feature here, all going places. But it was the pace in which these people kept up, brushing past each other's self-driven dispositions, spirited away by what? What were these city tempestuous people thinking? Indeed, did it at all matter what goes on inside the mind of a stranger?

There was now a queue to get inside the bar. All the seats outside are taken. Couples loved up;

oblivious of all else except for themselves, they talk and laugh and talk and laugh like people possessed by a superficial feeling moonlighting as love but unmistakably fake. Then there are the groups of friends scattered around; loud and proud and yet pretentious in the way they behave here.

Max thinks back to dancing with Macey. He looks down at the ground grossed out by his whimpering embarrassment. He drops his cigarette, stamps it out, downs his Mojito and then turns to go back inside.

"There you are! I was looking for you." Macey steps out of the bar, towards Max. She gives him a Mojito, toasting his glass.

"To chance encounters!" Her eyes pierce his. She downs her drink in one while Max watches on.

"Let's go," she says excitedly.

"Where?" Max asks, keeping his cool.

"Back to the hotel . . . hint hint," Macey smiles suggestively.

Max wastes no time and downs his drink.

A latino-looking man taps Macey on the shoulder. She turns to face him.

"Un último baile, " he says softly, offering her his hand. She gives her bag to Max and then lets him lead the way back inside.

Max sighs, finds a seat outside and waits patiently. He feels his frustration take over from the tipsiness seducing his senses. Suddenly a sound from inside her bag goes off. Max looks inside her bag and finds a phone . . . *1 new message: from unknown . . .* and the message reads as follows '*Do you have the documents yet?*' His heart beats fast as he looks up from the phone in fear of being seen by Macey.

The frustration and the tipsy feeling have taken a turn for the worse. Max feels dizzy. He puts the phone back in her bag and finds her purse. He takes out her driver's license only to discover her name is not Macey Cena, it's Oksana Kuznetsov. Not wanting to get caught red-handed he puts her purse back and closes her bag.

She comes out of the club, brimming with energy accentuated by her effortlessly lush looks. Max stands to his feet, putting on a forced smile. He hands her bag over.

"Ready?" she asks frantically.

"Yep." he answers pensively.

"Sorry about that," she says softly.

"What?" Max doesn't know what she means, since his mind has just been blown to smithereens.

"Dancing with that man when I should have been with you." 'Macey' caresses his arm and then takes his hand as they make their way back to the hotel hand in hand.

The short walk back to the hotel was dominated by Macey. Max has been silenced by her deception and does not know what to do about it. They enter the bedroom. She strips naked. He falls back against the wall, struggling to stay on his feet.

"You're drunk!" she says smiling.

"Come lay down." Macey gets into bed.

"Who are you?" Max slurs his words.

"I'm your wildest dream come true." She lifts the covers, inviting him in.

Max goes to the bedside table and takes the Bible but try as he might to walk away, he falls face down onto the bed. Macey opens up the Bible and takes the documents from inside.

CHAPTER 8: GAME-CHANGER

What's wrong with the game? Games are fun! But not this one, this one sucks out the very essence of who and what you are, all for a fucking payslip! Money, money, money and the alternative is . . . being fair? Being equal? Killing greed? Killing corruption? Something in us wants more of the same, money that is, because there exists a competitive trait that we learn from a young age. But before that, and that which makes me wonder, your birth came to be, from whence sperm competed against each other for the obvious reason of being born.

It annoys me when I watched a certain comedian descend into comedy because his intelligence just can't cope with such subject matter that Mr Gervais was tackling, religion and being an atheist. What annoyed me most was his certainty, stemming from an arrogance existing in the wake of making a name for himself. So is this what happens to any and many a man when fame comes calling? Will my ego grow so big that I think my voice of reason is above and beyond anyone else's? Stop. This is what happens when I watch a 'recommendation' from on YouTube. What annoys me more is this; that I only know what is essentially a 'talking camera' and it is the irrelevance of therefore each and every man or woman in front of the camera more often than not, playing up to it for a reaction. And I reacted, like an angry gorilla.

I cannot continue to rage against all but a media device showing me bits and pieces, because this is not a good read. Write what I know? I know from experience this life is shit to you if you're not up for it. This feels the most futile it has ever felt, but why? My heart wants to hate what is wrong with the world whether it be a person or the system, so why does this feel really wrong right now?

Every rage comes from the same place, somewhere without love? There is no woman in my life right now. But there are things that I love, such things I must have, for they keep me feeling like I can make a difference somehow. When Mary runs to her son Jesus, as he drops down to the ground and is thus crushed by the cross he carries, she sees him as she saw him once before but as a child who one day fell over, out of her control. Her memory recollects his innocence then, as she was once again witness to his innocence upon that fateful day of death and yet resurrection. Passion of the Christ compels to move you, as it did me.

I cried uncontrollably while surrounded by my friends on a beach; the sun in the sky looked picture perfect setting amongst such delicate clouds and I remember the colour red present at the time. I had just overcome a breakdown. I went to my friend's wedding and quickly became overwhelmed by the power of love. But to recollect beauty that you cannot possibly imagine unless you were there, or as me feeling it, what will words bring but a betrayal along the lines of this present moment.

To be real right now, well, friends set me free from my suffering, for that I thank Kam, Diana, Alex, Nick, Nikki, Nat and Marian. As for all of my old friends from back in the day, you know who you are, and I'm not sorry for neglecting the likes of Facebook but I have better things to do with what is limited time on Earth than spend it on social media. I endeavour with all of my heart to live the truth, the whole truth and nothing but the truth. What is living in the wake of the truth? I have given my life to Christ at a Christian festival called SoulSurvivor but even so, I didn't feel the love overcome my sense of feeling lost.

Jesus existed but the only proof of his life lives on in my heart and/or soul. I believe because such a story takes my breath away and affects me like no other story has. I have been through things that make me safely say I was touched by a force, or forces were at work on me unseen in nature therefore supernatural. Still and I imagine in a long time to come, I will wonder what happened upon being broken by life itself. For God's sake, when I saw a face change from normal into something else entirely, and then another stranger's face do the same, what was happening in that moment of horror?

Most of us must at least lull ourselves into a false sense of escaping this dire reality. It is as such a system takes control that we feel ill at ease, desperate to break free from what becomes mundane and truly tedious. Today I went back to work in a warehouse, surrounded by bloody good people I'll have you know, but as for the job I do, don't get me started! I could quite easily describe being stripped of my soul all over again, every time I step foot into oh what a wicked warehouse! While I wheel a trolley round in a circle all day, doing orders for the business I just don't give a damn about, listening against my will, albeit to Heat radio. Born of Heat magazine, DJs sounding so self-satisfied by the fluff from which they report to us, such trivial goings on in the warped world of fame. It makes me sick. But I stomach it, as do my work colleagues bless them, circling sewing products left, right and centre, taking away our right mind in order to make a living, dying from the inside-out.

What am I to do? I know there is no escaping this present reality trapping me, ok yes writing feels good and right but I want to explore reality, not escape it. I cannot take anything that is of worth from my time misspent at the warehouse. I spend nine hours of the day being numbed from head to toe. This is not what I would call 'living' in any way, shape or form. I am instead 'existing' in the wake of a worn and haggard game made from nothing but money.

I suffer from being delusional albeit spirited away by my wild ideas of making a change for all. Truth is, I don't care enough about you to try and convince you otherwise. This is not offensive; it's a matter of fact. I care more for myself than I do you. And anyway, why should I try to convince you that I know best? I only know what I've been through and where it has got me – ergo nowhere. Reading this won't make you a better person. I wrestle with things flashing before my eyes as I see fit to articulate these thoughts so you can see where I am coming from.

Working in a warehouse gives me more than enough rage to take home with me. The rising hatred turns over and over again within, then on occasion outs itself from my mouth, that or here where I write the way I experience such a dull reality by day. Yet out of the blue it occurred to me; I need work for the raw reaction and the rest, as if by tragic circumstance, so I vent at my lovely little colleagues gross-out insight. Like why has Justin Timberlake received an Oscar nomination? When the song in question comes across as ever so stupid at least to me "Got this feeling in my body" . . . ok great, but of course your feeling is in your body! Feelings exist inside the body, by singing "Got this feeling" alone is itself enough for me to know where that feeling came from. But by going on to sing "in my body" you, Justin, just sound silly.

An average Joe job forces me to foolishly wish the day away. Because quite frankly if it weren't for falling victim to this sorry system, I would quit work first thing in the morning. It troubles me, being in a godawful workplace for nine hours of feeling dead inside. Time is of the essence after all and at twenty nine I'm in my precious prime. I don't want to merely live for the fucking weekend! And thus far the false feeling of freedom looms large for two whole days . . . that's just not good enough.

I am guilty of avoiding media sources such as television and newspapers, for obvious reasons. When at work however, my better judgement is at once bombarded by daytime radio and its excruciating array of toxic-ridden adverts. Short storylines are attached to whoever the hell kind of company buys its airtime in an attempt to manipulate but also deceive. I am not and never will be, moved to act according to that which is so false it's untrue; therefore every single advert in the world can go fuck itself for all I care.

Hate doesn't work. I spend my day being rubbed up the wrong way by a monotonous task as I listen to the unbearably pleased sound of self-satisfaction coming from the radio. Oh sure, there and then, I am my own worst enemy, feeling compelled to take spoken action against such surface-driven drone ringing in my ears. I want beauty to consume me. I wilfully welcome anything that will fill me with love. Frankly, I feel sick and tired of my self-perpetuating hatefulness. I listen to some of the Gladiator soundtrack and it changes my mind. I appreciate and adore the life-affirming music from one of my favourite movies.

I look at the time with fear of what tomorrow will bring because I know what to expect, pretty much more of the same mundane doings in a dreamless warehouse. I hate my life. I am about to write a novel, with every intention of changing my life for the better. Beauty happens as of when I write from my imagination.

Today is Tuesday. And goodness gracious me, I got the shit kicked out of my mind by this sick system. From 8am until 5pm I'm nothing but numb. Being made to feel like a zombie because of fucking business, ridiculous sewing equipment picked and packed many times over oh my God, give me strength! Heat Radio, oh woe and despair, prevailing against at least me to be but one of a few who have the tremendous displeasure listening to sex-mad music and gossip-driven DJs making mountains out of famous fucking cunts. When will this scary rundown nonsense cease to exist?

I must endure the heartache and channel the brain pain in order to make use of what this average Joe job does inside myself. I suck on a vape device every break because it's my kind of dummy, making me feel better about being in this sorry situation. Sure there are work colleagues I can have very meaningless small talk with, wow, what a treat to take me away from my task as a 'warehouse assistant'. I won't write a bad word about any of them, this is not at all personal, no, my venom must at once sink into the system; murderous, sanitized and devoid of any meaning whatsoever.

I feel myself succumbing in spite of what is such a shallow, lifeless system. Trapped, prevailing against the effort I give of me in my entirety, exists this systematic attempt to destroy creative endeavour. The working week makes me out to be but a zombie, either that or a broken robot. By the weekend, needs must be met, at my peril killing brain cells, losing inhibition, on the edge of becoming simply a foul-mouthed drunken wreck. I will not at all 'live for the weekend', good God, what a depressing piece of shit sentence stemming from my hungover head. How has it come to this? This is an outrage right here, right now.

I see people all around me. I hear people speak, putting forth their whimpering patterns of ever so small la-de-da discourse for fellow friends and family only to nod in lazy agreeance. And so I feel the severe insignificance of it all leave me gasping for a breath born unto something, anything, that is at once worthwhile. I mean meaningful life-affirming moments magically manifesting from fierce hearts righteous, strong, good and beautiful. But of course, as is instead it's not that at all. Only the dull colourless conversations arising and yet at the same time dying of nothing but a bore from within these people being 'nice, normal', mundane daydreamers fantasizing about going on holidays spent sloth-like; living it up somewhere far away, abandoning a daily life of utter futility for an exotic getaway which will encourage even more of the same meaningless lounging about albeit in the sun. Thinking that a change of scenery may make a said daydreamer 'happy' and so distancing oneself from a horrible job, boring friends, a disenchanted town, when in the end discovering it is these people, each and every one, which are suffering a foolish little life of no life, existing until all has been said and done.

I often find myself considering Dylan's lyric 'The answer is blowing in the wind' and it doesn't take long for me to know what he was on about. Basically he is singing in praise of life itself. If Shakespeare proclaimed us but 'to be' I wonder whether then Dylan sang in light of feeling free, or simply 'going with the flow'. For what has rage given only by my misplaced passion and tremendous persistence to be but mistaken when others are more or less like me regardless of this passing surface charade. . . do I care enough about being in a truthful future? Or am I writing with an agenda hidden between the blurred lines of a manipulated place basking in being clever, dare I say it, to deceive every reader from my true intentions? This I put to you, always within the knowledge of a heartfelt plea, please be real.

The system in simple terms equates to what cost is living, as we are, altogether a part of it. If that makes sense, so does it? I did not ask to be born but because I am, I have to inherit what went on in the past. I have to play along with what it is to live in a dog eat dog game. I have to compete if I am to get ahead. Well ha fucking ha in the face of this westernized deathtrap. Because make no mistake about it, 'system', I'm referring to you as a whole while I imagine just what kind of cretins in individual terms make up your organised crimes against the greater good.

Friends soften the blow I feel when I'm all alone in my bed, wondering why the world is so fucking cold. Tossing and turning and thinking that what I need in order to forget about this sickness is a sexy squeeze of flying sparks, coming from the caress of her breast, at the same time taking my erection and shoving it straight up her lovely little ass. A kiss in itself has the power to take me away from my mad world of fucking hatred. And gone now is my people pleasing fear of feeling the need to come across as 'just right' (politically correct). If you can't even sense where these words are born from then don't bother reading on. Go buy a children's book by David Walliams instead.

Laugh at me for wearing Pokemon pyjamas. Laugh at me for listening to KoRn at an unholy hour for the pumping up of my outdated teen angst masquerading itself as surefire rage. Laugh at life first, for failing me. I have hit rock bottom a number of times now. I've seen evil perform its scary play all over my then frozen point of view. I've felt literally like I was the walking dead in a rotting limbo of frightful numbness. The times I was so low were the most extreme and alive of my life. Of course I wouldn't wish these times on anybody, except for Richard Hammond maybe, oh, and Piers Morgan.

Monday to Friday you should go to work. Wait. We live in a box. We make babies. We create for ourselves certain responsibilities. Bills to pay and a job to grind, one wife to fuck while your mistress is waiting in the wings . . . this cynical bullshit tastes disgusting but that's life! Listen to the television drain any unique take on the world way out of your morbid body. Watch the worst excuse for killing time on the planet, that is, the One Show and let it ease you into an evening of comfortable living. Go be with your special friends, hence experience such fun and laughter; at least for a few moments forget about all the mistakes you've made.

Feel the relief of Friday take you out that night, cheat on your overweight wife for the hell of it! Drink beer, cheer for your team, drink more beer, neglect your kids, insult your wife, slam the door on your way out, meet your mates at the pub, drink more beer, flirt with whoever the hell takes your fucking fancy! Truthful future . . . what truthful future? Where are you? You're a million miles away from manifestation. Bring me Claudia Winkleman instead, let me disregard her happy family life, her lovely little circle of quirky friends, just give me her for as long as I like. I will make her ruin her life (by cutting her fringe off of course) just for me and then leave her.

I am made of many things, as I'm quite sure you're the same . . . daydreamers, wasters, professionals, musicians, artists, office monkeys, etc etc. This is a sick and twisted world of contradiction, deception, sex, drugs, daytime TV, suffering, loneliness, togetherness, sexual frustration, fear, failure, disappointment, Viagra, blah blah blah. Let me open up like a can of worms . . . I wear make-up sometimes to conceal certain imperfections, I don't watch porn, I do imagine and I do masturbate over famous fucking cunts such as . . . use your imagination! In thinking about what happens next with this thing, my mind goes gaga blank.

I walk down the street but need to cross, so I wait with the other strangers at the designated stop. Someone has long since pressed the button and we all wait to cross the road but there are no cars coming in either direction. I cross because I trust my eyesight over a beep, beep, beep piece of systematic shit. I leave them to wait for it. Have they been brainwashed? What's going on in their nice and normal minds, I wonder. And then I forget about these people, especially when I see a beautiful woman walking towards me. Where am I going? I'm going to Wetherspoons for food and an energy drink. It doesn't matter what the time is because I have nowhere to be.

There is no hope for me here. I drink Red Bull because I wilfully buy into the claim that its contents give me more energy. Yeah right. I walk around town in the cold light of day, gaining no inspiration from what I feast my eyes on, nothing but many the morose face I see before me, holding themselves together for the false hope of having it all, all that a weak heart desires is an escape plan in the name of imaginary money. Because surely there exists not one soul that wants to stay put in such a shitty little town, but for what it's worth, I have learnt to bask like a sicko, oh yes, as a sicko I actually like being here from time to time. I can but love the suffering faces as each and every body of woe wishes life was not what it is.

Today is Thursday, not that it matters but still, hooray for Thursday! Today I look forward to yet another appointment at the job centre but at least the mix of heavy metal, red bull and my unending distaste makes me feel the need to continue where my rage left off. I've lost touch with most of my friends from way back in the day, when life was so much more bearable. But of course, it's my fucking fault! I should have loved this social media age of everything and everyone at our fingertips to connect with. Instead I chose to detest such a thing.

I roll my eyes at Facebook, Twitter, Instagram and the list goes on. What is it that we need to display exactly? Oh la-de-da my dear fake friend of no importance to me, won't you click on my profile to look at just how fucking fantastic my shitty little life is? Facebook quite encourages us to compartmentalise life; like ludicrous organisers try as we might to make our life look fucking amazing, it is in fact not that at all. But because we all play along, and by that what I really mean is we are at once sucked into this twisted outlet of self-satisfied fantasy-turn-make-believe-life-affirming-insipid-people-pleasing-shit-for-brains-nonsense.

And as for Twitter, well, what a fucking think tank that attracts the attention and then opinions of oh-so-stupid people. Stupid indeed, because quite frankly these users of such a website must not be able to speak their mind in real life, for fear of upsetting an ambience I imagine. I mean, come on! What is it with you guys? Yes, life feels better when we all agree with each other, but being in agreeance is not the be all end all! Why, oh why, we must wait until we are in the safety of our own smartphone in order to truly say what goes on when we're not telling it like it is face to face? Surprise surprise people, let me tell you what you already know: your precious conversations spent talking in confidence to your friends . . . these sweet nothings simply pass the time, and have a lack of feeling attached to your throwaway words safe from causing disagreeable bullshit albeit that which is least of all real; conflict.

It must make me laugh, for if I were to let life move me to tears of hopeless disarray, well, where's the fun in that? This is not worthy of any award at all. I write what I feel like because this is fun for me. People these days are so fucking insecure, regardless of whether they admit to it or not. Why else feel the need to update one's status so often? Facebook, Twitter, whatever . . . I for one couldn't care less whether you're my friend or not, but please, PLEASE refrain from telling your virtual world of followers what's going on when you're not online trying to tell everyone what's going on! NEWS FLASH: No one cares.

If life is a stage, sadly we are ALL LIARS. This truth reveals itself as the reason behind my rage. And my rage just so happens to be but the ugliest of monsters, existing inside my unbecoming body of confused distress. This sad fact that is as make-believe as it is sick and twisted – what a world we live in! I wish I was an actor to be honest. Always have, and yet there is an uphill battle to fight before I can channel my 'feelings' as it were. I want to be alive and living in the true essence of what existence is. It will not do to poke my rage against that which I wish I was, unless strictly necessary.

There remains so much stuff of me yet to see the cold light of day, and such stuff for sure exists somewhere within, awaiting its time. I'm not content to put down men and women of fame based solely on my envy. If a dream remains inside, such a thing will not come alive via my incessant discontent at life for the famous. I must rise above but first follow my rage down the rabbit hole of hate, to see what will become me when all is said and done.

Why am I obsessed by my idea of an absolute truth? What sort of heart wants a world without its stage? We played as children and thus playing is a part of us as adults as well. This rebellious streak smacks of Lucifer, fallen from grace. So to stare up at the sky and know never there be me, I cry for what will become my undone destiny, destitute until ill-fated downcast only ever further from now, where I remain an unholy lost soul sinking in a black abyss of self-inflicted torment. Oh, despair for being the woe which is me. Where am I to take my uncalled for feelings? Against what more is there for rage, taken in a body of my misjudged being, back I cannot conceive of going when upon past the point of no return . . . then the rage must go on.

Be 'somebody'. Do 'something'. Whether from peer pressure or from society playing itself from a media source, there is a struggle to establish ourselves as a 'respectable' people. Because struggling with the craft of self-respect takes us to settle for the next best thing, that is, respect from others. To be taken seriously, why? Well, deep down, many know how we could quite easily, all of us, rest on the sheer ridiculousness this so-called life feels 'nice and normal,' all of a sudden 'weird and wonderful', from one moment to the next, 'things change'.

The mood of a room, good vibes and the bad, between us, we decide deep down whether we are aware of our power or not. To diffuse a situation from erupting into violence, firstly creating an atmosphere before all hell breaks loose. Celebrities are accepted and then welcomed by the bias, blinded and heavily mediated/mindlessly self-absorbed public eye. They are a commodity fitting into the system of things as an attraction and escapism from the more mundane elements making up our waking life.

Of course, as we are, hero-worship is necessary for obvious reasons. What's lost in translation seems each and every journey from being an average Joe to the best thing since sliced bread. The media and society together create a divide, by separating the mere mortals from the 'untouchable brilliance' of the famous few; we become as blacked-out as an audience at the theatre or cinema. Admiring them from afar, our only connection to these superior creatures is through TV, magazines, newspapers or the internet.

It is sources such as those that we know and buy into,

telling us just how great fame is. And the agenda always with money in mind; make mental note now: this is not rocket science so don't think I'm just stating the obvious because I have nothing better to write about. I want to know why our dreams are being shaped up for churning out more of the same: movie stars, singers, rappers (yes, there is a difference between rapping words and singing them). Not to mention professional footballers, boy oh boy!

Being a celebrity, not that I know, but believe me I can imagine! Being a celebrity takes you into a whole new world of worship, private parties, self-satisfied feelings, paparazzi ridiculousness and so on. What does this say about our nature to reality? We create nuances, distorting but worse still, this instigated diversion, away from a more meaningful focus (like finding out what we are really made of) prevents spiritual growth with one foul swoop of the celeb-obsessed, stupid mindset of a mass affair revelling in its own manifest. For so long as the media aim to distract the many by ramming more of the same make-believe-mouth-piece propaganda down our throats, this is an overdose of a surface-fixated time misspent pampering aging skin; indeed either that or pumping iron and for what? To keep up an appearance!

An appearance slowly but surely failing you day in, day out and one day you will look in the mirror fearing your own reflection, since your futile strive for feeling 'physically complete.' 'lol,' how can one possibly be a physically complete specimen when all the time your human body is basically laughing (if it could) at your misled mind, and so with every single unrealistic thought that creates each fleeting feeling of positive vibes coursing through your veins, just remember where you are or more to the meat of the matter what you've been doing with your time . . . a treadmill maybe? Brilliant! I believe David Icke once passed comment when he drove past a gym full of fit treadmill men and women running nowhere fast. His words were somewhere along the lines of

'Fancy that! There they are, running nowhere fast, and it's all thanks to society taking them for a ride, a ride which I will state yet again goes nowhere fast!'

Men 'hero-worship' a woman's 'assets' such as her arse and tits as well as her 'ever-present' pussy, because a man's mind is his best friend, and yet at times his worst enemy. Women 'hero-worship' a man's penis in its erectile glory because obviously as a 'boner' grows, such a thing shows his excitement towards a woman and her womanly way. They also admire our body for being defined and thus showing what a 'real man' 'should' look like. After all, modern man has his roots as a hunter-gatherer, whereby back then he needed to be physically capable of fending for his own and for good reason (survival).

Both men and women depend on a selective viewpoint to choose wisely, we want what we want and everything else is disregarded, rejected, ignored or resented as an insignificant existent, getting in the way of our struggle to obtain what we think feels desirable. But, so long as we embark lacking intelligence, excelling instead from a physical place of fancy, yes, this is our nature for the most part, yet if we openly ignore other areas existing inside us, 'subtle beauty', we will miss out on the many more fruits to who we really are, regardless of physical looks.

Media, or in other words devil's advocate, a kind of cupid coming from our relationship with all things physical, can and will try to tell you in no uncertain terms just what you want out of life. For single men and women wondering why they haven't found 'the one', there appears countless solutions and 'attractive avenues' to venture down. eHarmony, Elite Singles, Match.com and so on offer you a chance at finally finding that special someone. Divide and then conquer your quest for true love! Of course, this comes at a price obviously. We are aware and indeed I am, that it is a tremendous task and then some, when we seek such a figment of our perfectly crafted 'dreamboat' becoming from one's wild and vivid *imagination. Narrowing down, weeding out, getting to the meat of the matter - there are websites especially accommodating to your personal needs.*

So why is it that the pure universe is being ignored instead for a virtual reality? We would much rather have our love life existing at our fingertips as opposed to letting fate decide where and when your superman or wonder woman comes from. And so, once again, another form of control parading itself as just another power play altogether; that is, courtship for the desperate. The famous have the fellow famous, whereas the mere mortals get fed an impure propaganda and out of a jealous spite we are reduced to eating it up as our only hope, the supplement that will leave us feeling an odd sense of satisfaction for how long?

Science as a means of making us see the world for what it is, this isn't such a bad worldview. What does strike me as 'bad' has next to nothing in the name of science itself so far 'wrong' with a quite cold-hearted nature taking course; results and findings are figures or facts. It's when many people of differing beliefs feel the right to convince us, as in everyone else that science is the only way of figuring out truth from falsehood. Advocates saying science is simply neutral will also advise us to be of a balanced mind and have feelings based only on an equilibrium experienced by all who are 'normal enough' not to believe there exists such a thing as 'God'. Being 'normal enough' refers of course to what acceptance means as members of a general public concerned and consumed by material matters (or the complete and utter rejection of all things supernatural).

Let us just make quite clear before I continue to change minds as well as reinforce others that it is unacceptable blowing oneself up in the name of 'God' and all that jazz. As I can gather, there are very many mistaken kinds of person in the world. Whether a religious person puts countless lives of innocent bystanders at risk with certain death, if only for a warped and wayward worldview to persist until literally self-destructing, it's either that quite drastic inconvenience manifests so much until enough is enough or on the other hand have ourselves a so very well-informed 'master of science' suggesting in no uncertain terms 'from animals, may we one day yet evolve into out and out robots.' Basically, because of media doing its thing, this leaves me cold in the knowledge and broken is my heart having witnessed what television programmes promote. The same old debate rages on and on and on and to what end? A fight to the death of one over the other, resulting in a totalitarian regime mindful of religion and so mindless of science, or vice versa. Is that what it will come to? Low-blows based on an unbridled belief of being right to whomever else believes otherwise are at once wrong.

One will soon enough, (if, of course, feasting on nonbelievers versus believers is not entertaining anymore) make a conscious effort to question then why does the media not move on from encouraging this discourse? Is it but only the conspiracy theorist thinking something else entirely may well be spoken in whispers put between the powers that are prevailing like ninjas of the night? Why would you not want to know what goes on when the cameras are turned off? If anything then the media desensitizes us from feeling compelled by crimes against a greater good. Indeed we are force fed and yet starved of the true reality that is simply kept a secret.

Outrage just the one reaction necessary for there to be but a beginning of an uprising. Against what exactly may we rage? Well, how about a rage against not wanting to be made the victim of a crime you didn't even know about, let alone commit! This so-called crime became you the day your willpower was lost on what material pleasures are thrown our way to distract us from more important issues as opposed to the basic satisfaction of a short term primal urge. For what is right, it must come from my heart; to me I see but one standalone need and that's simply being of the truth. How will I achieve living the truth if I am surrounded by liars?

Jesus said it himself; if he is still 'the way, the truth and the life' what comes between one man or woman and his or her freeing insight of Christ? Vitally, yes, this must stand up profound and alone unto itself: if this certain something within us is simply the same manifest so as to not stop a believer from believing, as the nonbeliever from disbelieving, then that which has been manifest first and foremost must before your eyes see a similar light to one another's darkness. So to know without doubt what will be, will be of light; therein lies darkness. Now can you say safely: 'Jesus is just the made-up superman of a forgotten time.' I think that you cannot safely say such a thing.

People like Francesca Stavrakopoulou, apart from not being able to take great pleasure greeting them in full, for the obvious reason - anyway what path am I on? In no uncertain terms Francesca quite rightly laps up her professor status, teaming up with the unlikely lot, atheists so as to prove religion is wrong and we are here for the hell of it. Did you know how she describes herself? From Wikipedia, and so don't take my word for it but apparently she has 'huge respect for religion;' indeed she then goes on to determine men and women of olden times simply knew not the difference between fact and fiction.

When I went onto her Twitter account and scrolled down out of interest if nothing else, I was surprised by what I saw. She had retweeted an image of Jesus Christ, tied to the cross just so we know not to take crucifixion in any way whatsoever other than deadly serious ('I'll never know how much it cost to see my sin upon that cross.') This image I'm bringing to light not only looked light-hearted but it was also a social commentary regarding modern times' self-obsessed disposition. Upon this cross was Christ, at least as a caricature, taking a selfie of himself 'suffering' for our sins. Is Francesca therefore respectful of religion? And does she even have the heart to be but a woman of her word?

Why have the media fed me a wholeheartedly lost monster? Francesca, a confused and geeky Greek, regurgitating misspent time, try as she might to make sense of the Bible but from an emotionless place. This is basically like having the key to unlock your door from one side, while on the other remains the same kind of key (a spare one if you will) left in the lock itself. I've come to find Francesca quite easy on the eye. Yet still she prevails persisting with her interesting mix, this impressive veneer refined by an academic kiss and tell. Letting her hair down and thus escaping is her power play albeit sprinkled in an ever so subtle lexicon, not of fancy words just pretentious posturing. Until this descent takes shape upon personal preferences she has as an atheist, with a righteous sense of self Francesca cannot at all help her human condition. And from coming a cropper or revealing in its least bit to me I see her contradictory truisms: 'Show us atheists as we lack an imagination between us, so if you believers should be so kind as to provide evidence suggesting it true, we will follow your God and therefore our God from hereafter that!' Bad vibes surely become my feelings sick and tired of Francesca, making her mouth open only for spirited drone! So she disbelieves in the existence of God . . . and don't get me wrong when I strongly suggest what she says is simply lost on my mind made up of 'fantasy!' She may well be seeking her journey's destination now, which I would like to think is a sense of an out and out truth. The truth however of her airtime comes down to looks and looks alone I'm afraid. Frankly, anyone can come across as having a viewpoint that is at once controversial, just for the sake of feeling the falsified need to be your own worst enemy masquerading in desperate places as a professional provocateur. But of course, blessed by beauty, she has been many times made media's Miss Not So Sat On The Fence, swung one way inclined by her nonbeliever rendition. In truth, the party parading downright atheism is not fit for our purpose as Shining Ones; we will leave the nonbelievers dancing in the dark.

To eat, drink and be merry, seize the day, and gather rosebuds while ye may. Must it be because pleasure reigns simply beyond any need we feel? Is the reason being in spite of why we witness still the same old debate between science and religion down to a pure pleasure principle? Do we delight then in one downfall from the other? Risen such strength then in numbers believing 'this' way over 'that', therefore are we willing to kill all things religious just so we can have ourselves rejoicing science? So as a doctrine instead of an investigative form from which we are always curiously lusting after the facts as opposed to truth that is sacred and kept within.

Christ: I am the way and the truth and the life, no one comes to the Father except through me.

Atheist: Why must I go your way? Why are you the truth? What makes your life a life to be beyond everyone else's existence?

Christ: When you question me, are you already ready to receive me, only yet to your means as an answer for your end of further inquiry? You want to know without doubt that I am as I attest to be, but still you listen and not even hear me out of the truth that outs itself. If you hear your thoughts first, forget about all things as an experience of wonder or profound feeling. Listen not to your heart? Then let your head be full of lifeless knowledge and instead dream as you do, of never ever waking up.

Atheist: I don't know what you mean. Does your 'Father' have a 'funny tongue' like you do?

Christ: Let there be light to your darkness. Taste sweet, but still, bitter is your poison. When you love over fear, reason speaks for itself – from your mouth there be no more resistance.

Atheist: But aren't we all fighting for the truth?

Christ: To fight, what for? You will not win the heart of truth through great debate, but for an ego boost to simply reinforce falsity. It is in not material, albeit at arm's length, therefore reaching your own, and only your own, sense of being true to what God do you grasp?

Atheist: I grasp at all the clear, real things. Since such things simply appear before my eyes, I need not take a great leap of faith for what is already real and apparent to me.

Christ: To you, your life. . . what is it?

Atheist: It is what it is . . . an existence towards what will be evolutionary in nature.

Christ: And as for the world?

Atheist: I don't know what will happen when I'm gone.

Christ: And yet you seem so sure of yourself, speaking about a supernatural, all-encompassing force such as my Father.

Atheist: 'I think therefore I am', and by my freewill, whether or not it is a gift from 'God'. 'God' does nothing but stand back like a coward watching his big mistake cause chaos.

Christ: Listen, and this time may you hear me from your heart . . . 'I am the way and the truth and the life, no one comes to the Father except through me.'

Athiest: Ok so how can I find you?

Christ: Easy. Seek me out not with your eyes, as appearances deceive. If your vision fails you, how will you see me?

Athiest: If I go blind, then what do you feel like?

Christ: How far are you willing to reach out? Out of the ordinary and into the extraordinary maybe? Fear not the unknown, only love is the light.

Atheist: I don't feel like I am in the dark.

Christ: Then why ask what the light looks like?

Athiest: I am but one and yet your God is all.

Christ: All is one and one is all.

An atheist wants material truth. The out and out atheist is not yet ready to receive something that cannot be but a watered down manifest of the unmanisfested. What form must truth take to be real? Jesus was, still is, and always will be. 'How' and 'why' are the weaker questions stemming from fear or worse, ignorance. Experience is in the experiencing. Thus truth is in the truth of truth, therefore the truth of truth is so very pure. Your idea of it is an idea of it indeed and that can quite easily become manifest as a personal reality. Yet you cannot comprehend, let alone know what the truth is, if the truth to you has been reduced as an appearance of what once was. Because quite apart from being in the wake of the truth, the truth that came to be Jesus is simply here to stay. You either free yourself of surface shackles or you simply remain enslaved by a beautiful illusion and so the seducer of your senses is still in and of itself seduced.

I am 'for Christ' to show me the way. She or he who

opposes such a choice, so to choose the lightless passage of confusion and confidence based solely on one's self-perpetuating ego . . . not only are these people fools as a collective, but as individuals against God or to reject Jesus. I safely say of someone set in the brittle stone of our material world 'Go! Be gone, end up down and out as an Antichrist.'

Nothing comes close to the conscious stream revealing itself, before being rewritten in all of its self-foreboding rage. One will get no glory realising his surrounds are as twisted and ill-fated as these sweet nothings, descending down a current created by all around, inside a sanitized toilet almost overflowing with wrongdoing stinking of smug-grotesque excrement exiting the foulmouthed mother of all accidents, as if by being given the gift of life for free; treat it to a price you put on your own head and thus destroy any sentimental value you have of yourself, sell your soul! All for a petty media done and driven dream come true. Who am I to rage against your kneejerk reaction of a self-fulfilled and realised dream, while I worship my own! What will it take to live a life of out and out truth? This shit life of lies, lost love, of players prancing around and dillydallying in new dreams more so self-indulgent than ever before. Or does death hold the ultimate twist of fate to come not undone but finally free?

I read books too you know, not that I can class myself well-read yet, but at least now I know what I'm up against . . . all the more reason in order for my rage to gain momentum. Methods of madness masquerading inside strained one way written attempts to answer for human kinds questions such as 'does God exist?' 'Is there life after death?' There will not be a book to end all books based on not one but always a few select points of view. Any view within which the writer of said book – hypothetical – compels said writer – hypothetical, to only include a handful of heads (whether they are already dead and buried heads doesn't matter); what matters is sense being made in the wake of what one or more 'enlightened individuals' sought to contemplate, ponder and then produce as manifest thought patterns (paragraphs of philosophy for instance).

Yes, this means, as I add a pinch of ignorance not against my will, albeit to save my average reader from becoming confused, so help me God! Do you know how to use such a thing as parallel reasoning? It is, if not a complex method of identifying in no uncertain terms exactly how to ask the 'correct question' in order to obtain a distinct answer also 'correct.' So much so not to debate what was written down as being 'right' therefore irrefutable, bloody brilliant truth! Then it is somewhat the way of having the devil in the detailed downright result to that which was ascertained and argued around an intellectual narrative – truth, having been intellectually elevated at once will only reduce the amount of men and women from 'getting it' or 'getting to it'.

Now one might like to make clear, are we really ready for what would be extremely painful if you're full of pride? I'm making clear here the sacrifice necessary, especially we as artists, almost expected to be bonkers, come across as almost always unreasonable by guilty pleasure therefore frowned upon from more a mundane kind of man and a plain woman only here for one reason amongst nothing much more than that which is to make up the numbers, breeding greater numbers of offspring. This sacrifice I strongly suggest possible, but must you fight it with your ego, don't come anywhere near me! Because quite frankly long gone and so ever since such a thing did indeed definitely fail me as a man of my word and my word is truth, then an ego can get the hell out of here for all I care.

Are you searching for the truth? If so, is it an ultimate truth? Whether the truth is little or large, the truth is still the truth. The sacrifice is a sacrifice because as of when one and all will look not down on each other, but at one another as equals, casting out the ego from whence it came, then your conditioned mind can breathe thoughts that are pure. Reason now will wake up to profound unfathomable beauty of being, existence, and God (or the universe as it is). Do not get me wrong, ego can but come from us at an early age, and yet it is in our power to be everything and more; where did 'all' arise out of? Nothing. Therefore for everything that you will come to know now and later forget, or feel, see and experience as you are, all there is, you must first accept the true reality of life; nothingness as a worldview will set you free because it's the truth – that out of nothing everything is as manifest.

In terms of ego, but first as a baby, we are 'pure being' experiencing the experience of experience itself, for no other reason than the effect of birth. Therefore, since 'ego' is basically an accepted concept to answer for our collective, initial realisation, 'sense' of what we are personifying as an apparent separate state within which other separate states exist as well. When we are aware of what it means to be we feel, from being, a freedom mindful of self; 'freewill' playing with what it perceives as life. Of life, we learn from experience as an action and utilizing parts of the body because as nature requires us to be but a physical form in a material world.

How will we heal and grow within this system that at any given moment might see itself further more viable by emptying your pockets at the same time as brainwashing you away from your right mind; managing your money and more importantly your mind but ultimately destroying your soul. So I ask you now, what has the system done in order to deserve the vast majority of your waking life? We know not a waking one anymore, but a working one instead.

To be rejected at nothing but the ignorant intent of avoiding an unattractive feature; 'crazy eyes' and beer bellies beware! Beauty taken then, only by face value, albeit in the eye of he or she beholding his and her prerequisite. Time flies so rats race against it to obtain the one and only love worth dying for – true love. If we know what we want, what we want is first a fantasy before finding a way of realising such a thing. The perfect gentleman of your dreams exists as exactly that! A beautiful illusion, and yet you make it so over exaggerated that this 'Mr Right' turns into an impossible dream because deep down we lose sight of what we want when time marches on. Nightmares manifest as bad dates present to you the all-important but subtle enough factor that we either forget or cynically laugh at: fate.

True love exists, but on the one condition of actively engaging in a truthful future. Free from devilish lies, so surmounting today a day of yet more corrupt subtlety. You will live to love but love of course at your convenience. Create rules as a kneejerk reaction to past failings such as divorce or separation. When we know love conquers all, that includes your rules as convenient and quirky; they are a betrayal against the quest for true love. If you do not know now how to take a chance, chances are your conditioning is controlling your every move, even your heart's desire!

Fear of loneliness negates the need and the need becomes a must, but must you settle for second best? It is still a world in which we are born in order to work and work we do for our survival! Aside from this sad fact, let yourself feel free to experience the limitless possibility but also the eternal bliss love itself is.

I want to reference a film starring Mel Gibson but fear not – next to his greatest achievement in the movie industry, directing the quite epic and profound 'Passion of The Christ', 'Tim' is a lovely little film. Tim suffers from a learning disability yet can grasp the gift of love when he experiences such a thing towards a woman much older than him. It is a happy ending because quite simply they belonged together regardless of what our misguided ideas are about age gap relationships.

Sick and tired definitely feels like quite the understatement to me at least, let down gently because of a meaningless little number. Bloody hell, who has a right to betray true love? I've been rejected countless times just because of my age and yes its ageist but more importantly I worry about the outdated mindset some women in their forties and fifties have. Sad that they feel the need to limit their life experience simply because of becoming victim to one's past mistakes, two words: move on.

Ah, have an eye on society; together these people of some sense let themselves see one and all young men as simply the same thing – toyboys. Because being a cougar is sexy I suppose, certainly the word 'cougar' comes across as such. But so long as we live in a vapid world of shallow buzzwords and flippantly lazy thought patterns, times may not change just yet.

The definition of real, from Google again, goes like this: 1. actually existing as a thing or occurring in fact; not imagined or supposed. 2. (of a thing) not imitation or artificial; genuine. 'Not imagined' I'm sorry, but who wrote this? God knows how many of us use Google, bloody hell! How can 'a thing' bring itself into existence without being imagined as an idea beforehand?

CHAPTER 9: IT'LL BE LONELY THIS CHRISTMAS

Christmas Day, 2018

The Queen's Speech

"Life is full of uncertainty. But when we believe in better, whether that means to be a better person or to embark on making it a better world, we at once share each other's sense of togetherness. Indeed, we are brought together by our hopes and dreams because of course we all have them in some way, shape or form."

"Christmas is a time to celebrate, to be grateful, it's a time for giving and receiving; it is also a time to reflect upon this year, before we begin again next year. There has been much said and then speculated, with regard to my position on foxhunting. In no uncertain terms, I for one will not sign a new law to legalise such a thing. The statement made by my butler, for the most part, was true to a certain extent. But I wish not to dwell where my memories are concerned."

"Now, we must more so consider the sad state of affairs affecting the lives of those residing in and around Rio de Janeiro, a city destroyed by the most severe earthquake. Nothing can prepare us for the wrath of Mother Nature; let it be a reminder to you all. Although we are more than capable

of creating great things, lest we forget God giveth and God taketh away. Am I suggesting then, that this tragedy was God's doing? In my eyes, as of when I watched on and saw such a miraculous sight – Christ the Redeemer there, whereas everything else was gone – what logical explanation can one come up with, to answer for how on earth a statue withstands such sheer force? Suffice to say, for whatever reason unbeknownst to us all, God did this."

"As for Brexit, just trust in Prime Minister Pricilla Fay and have faith that our relationship with Europe prevails because of our decision to go our own way. May they – the rest of Europe – prosper without us in the European Union and with a mutual respect let us do business regardless."

"Merry Christmas"

Isabella and Francis sit in silence while watching the Queen's speech.

"I miss Max," Belle says, sipping on a glass of red wine, turning her attention outside to the beautiful falling snow. Francis acknowledges Isabella by letting out a long sigh, since he hasn't got anything to say about it.

"I can't believe he's gone again and now we have the Queen on our side! Max should be here for this, this was something that would have been better to experience as a, well, you know what I mean." She refrains from using the word 'couple' to stop her from dwelling in the past. That was the idea anyway, yet still Belle dwells with her ex in mind.

"No, I don't know what you mean, please explain," he humours her.

"Remember when I told you about being in the 'Hunt-Trap Rat-Pack' back in the day, fighting for the lives of foxes against the heartless elite etc," Belle says, with a distant look to her bright blue and glowing green eyes.

"Yes," Francis remembers, slowly bringing his mug of mulled wine up to his lips.

"Well then, there was the Queen in all her glory, denying the cruel elite from killing foxes for the hell of it. If Max was here he'd be jumping up and down now, I know he would." She pours herself some more red wine and then is so very reminiscent towards Maximus as the hero he was, once upon a time.

"Why don't you just give him a call?" Francis suggests.

"Well, why hasn't he been in touch with me? It's Christmas Day!" Belle says, as if it's some kind of game.

"Maybe he's in trouble, Belle, call him," he says seriously, before blowing on his mug of mulled wine. She downs her glass of wine and then gets out her phone, only to notice she has a missed call and a voicemail message from her agent Lucy.

Francis turns his attention away from the television and watches on as Isabella listens to Lucy's message. Belle slowly takes her phone away from her ear and places it on the table, before pouring more red wine into her glass, this time until the glass is overflowing with wine.

"Belle . . . Belle?" He gets up from the armchair and sits next to her. She stops pouring, puts the bottle down and then lets herself sink back against the sofa. Her phone begins to ring. She ignores it.

"What's wrong?" Francis asks, looking concerned.

Her phone rings again. Francis leans over to look at the screen.

"It's Max," he says, picking up the phone and

handing it to her. But Belle stays sat back, looking lifelessly at the TV. She leans forward, but not to answer her phone, instead downing the full glass of wine in one.

Francis calls Max back. Belle gets up. She leaves the house. He watches her get into her car from out of the window.

"Max," Francis says sharply.

"Where's Isabella?" Max sounds needy.

"She's in her car." His strange tone of voice says it all.

"What? Where are you?" He is confused.

"At home . . . at her home . . . at her father's err . . . her late father's . . . " Francis is watching the car from in the living room.

"So what's she doing in her car?" Max asks quickly.

"I don't know," he says sincerely.

"Have you upset her?" His voice takes a turn.

"No! I've done nothing." Francis is defensive.

"Ok, can you go get her for me," Max says straightforwardly.

Francis walks out the front door with her phone in hand. He goes around to the driver's side of the car and taps on the window but Belle ignores him.

"Um, she won't get out of the car." Francis is looking at her. She appears lifeless, albeit with her eyes fixed forward.

"Open the door and pass her the phone." Max can't quite believe this.

Francis tries to open the door but it's locked.

"I can't, it's locked," he says, with panic consuming him.

"What the fuck, Francis?" Max loses it.

"Sorry, I really don't know what's wrong with her." Francis feels helpless.

Suddenly she gets out of her car and snatches the phone from Francis . . .

"YOU KNOW NOTHING BUT THE BREATH YOU TAKE TO MAKE SURE YOU'RE STILL ALIVE! EVERYTHING ELSE HAS PASSED YOUR BRAIN BY BECAUSE QUITE FRANKLY YOU ARE DEAD INSIDE." Belle lets her feelings be known and then cancels the call. She goes back inside. Francis takes the keys out of the ignition and locks the car before following her.

Maximus is on the receiving end of her rage. But before he can answer her back, she's gone. He takes a look at the time from on his phone; it's just after 3pm. Max has just woken up and goes straight to reception so he can check out.

"That'll be £50, please," The pretty receptionist says with a smile.

"But the room has already been paid for," Max says, as a matter of fact.

"You were supposed to check out hours ago. Our policy is if you fail to do so within the time limit . . . " She starts to sound like a robot to his horror, interrupting her for the hell of it.

"Last night I was drugged, Goddamn it . . . this is not my fault," he says desperately.

"I'm sorry sir, there's nothing I can do about that, this is just me doing my job," she says, forcing an insincere wince of pity out to play. Max hands over the money in cash and then leaves the hotel.

It's snowing while the white sky darkens. Christmas lights shine brightly and all the people here walk with a spring in their step printed upon the ground softened by the snowfall. Lost, torn, alone and devoid of festive cheer, he meanders around Waterloo looking inward for direction.

Belle is sleeping on the sofa. Francis is listening to a Christmas mix CD sat in the armchair. Her phone remains on the table next to an empty bottle of wine. He picks up her phone, turns it on and listens to her voicemail message. His heart sinks. Francis turns her phone off and puts it back on the table, before getting a blanket and delicately placing it over her body. He sits at the fireplace, starting a fire with good intentions.

Max is in a pub garden, head in hands. There's no one else here. He downs his pint of beer before turning his attention to his phone for the obvious reason, Belle.

"*Belle here . . . leave a message after the beep . . .* "

"But you're not here are you," Max says, to himself, sunken and defeated. At the beep he begins to sing a song.

'*How many mistakes does it take to change a man?*
When good is all you got to lose there ain't nothing left to gain
Now I thought I knew who I wanted to be – but boy I'm still the same old kid
Can't catch a break like the luck I had was bad . . . and became me, my dear sweet bitter end'

'*Still I find myself forever where I wouldn't know*
Why all the hubbub being here I have a home!
There is a saying so I was saying they say the saying goes
No time like the present this moment right now with an open mind
can you see the world?'

'Old age shame, shame on me my dearest deadbeat by the wayside
    Cold dark night, nothing changes stay alive like a long goodbye
    All for one and one for. . . Oh so close, just too far apart
    To be my own worst enemy . . . mighty fine time in the end, did it even mean anything?'

'Believe it or not I don't mind my body dies dust to dust
    Death is just too much for some say they can't go on and that's fair enough
    Heaven and Hell la-la-la-la-la limbo before the chosen ones rise
    Silence kills us softly, let's speak of the afterlife tonight!'

'It doesn't matter so long as laughter breaks the ice
    If the cracks start to show where we came from don't get me wrong, I've seen the light!
    I'm sure there's still a choice, guess again and think twice twist of fate feels nice
    Science explains yes, no in-betweens, something strange, a funny feeling left behind'

'Old age shame, shame on me my dearest deadbeat by the wayside
    Cold dark night, nothing changes stay alive like a long goodbye
    All for one and one for... Oh so close, just too far apart
    To be my own worst enemy . . . mighty fine time in the end, did it even mean anything?'

Max hangs up, putting the phone in his pocket. It's still snowing so he tilts his head and pokes out his tongue to catch the flakes as they fall.
    'Clap, clap, clap, clap, clap, clap, clap'

He turns around.

It's Oksana Kuznetsov.

"It wasn't meant for you 'Oksana'. Where are my documents?" Max asks angrily.

"All in good time, Max. Merry Christmas! Can I buy you a drink?" Oksana asks almost sarcastically.

"So you can drug me again . . . hmm . . . how about no . . . now give me my documents back." His anger grows. She laughs at him.

"Have you been following me?" Max asks seriously.

"There's a tracking device in the heel of your right boot." Oksana answers sincerely. He sits down and rips the heel right off his boot to discover a tracking device . . .

"Destroy it," she says swiftly.

Max stamps on it.

"How long have you been . . . " he wonders, while still in shock.

"Long enough." Oksana hands him back the classified documents.

"Who is Macey Cena?" Max asks curiously.

"A journalist, like I said," Oksana answers straight away.

"But you said you were going to Sao Paulo today?" His memory serves him correctly, as he places the documents inside the Bible before putting the Bible back in his bag.

"Do you seriously believe Jesus Christ is coming back?" she says seriously, lighting up a cigarette, offering one to Max as well.

"Is it poisonous?" Max asks, with a fearful look to his hazel eyes. Oksana laughs.

"This cigarette or that certain belief system put in place for the purpose of control? 'Cos quite frankly if I wanted to kill you, you'd be dead already," she says softly. He takes the cigarette from her and then gets his peace symbol lighter out.

"Who do you work for?" Max asks, as he edges closer to her.

"Are you sure that's the question on your mind 'Maximus Lucifer Phoenix'? Now where the hell did you get a name like that from?! I'm jealous!" Oksana smiles menacingly.

"I changed my name," Max says, while trying his best to keep a straight face.

"You don't know what you're doing here, there or anywhere for that matter. Your heart is in the right place, yes, yet you are a headless little chicken when it comes to the truth and what to do with it." She drops her cigarette in the snow and then puts her black leather gloves back on.

"I don't claim to know all the answers, Oksana . . . I just want to do the right thing." Max says swiftly. He too drops his cigarette into the snow. She squints at him with interest.

"Then go back to the one you sung for." Oksana turns around and goes to leave.

"Wait! Where are you going?" Max asks, with a degree of need attached to his voice.

"Inside . . . I'm cold," she says softly.

"Oh . . . ok . . . can I join you?" He feels less lost with her around.

"Yes you can Max." They go inside the pub.

Belle wakes up to the warmth of a fire burning brightly. She smells something good coming from the kitchen. Francis is busy preparing their Christmas dinner.

"Merry Christmas, Isabella," he says softly.

She smiles.

"More mulled wine?" Belle lifts her spirit to feel the festive cheer.

"Why not?" Francis dishes up.

"So, what did you think of the Queen's speech?" Belle asks, sipping on her red wine.

"It was honest . . . nice and normal," Francis says, as he tucks into his Christmas dinner.

"Not sure we should 'trust' Pricilla Fay though," she says, staring at Francis so to await his reaction.

"Do you think she will still go foxhunting on Boxing Day?" Francis asks curiously.

"Of course – yes. Speaking of which, is there anything that you can do to intervene?" She speaks while looking down at her plate of food, almost ashamed of herself. Francis stops eating, puts his knife and fork down, has a sip of mulled wine and then waits for her to face him.

"Belle, look at me," he says seriously. She faces him ingloriously, resisting the urge to look away from his deep dark brown eyes.

"I know you're hurting, it's in your eyes. I'm sorry . . . I listened to your voicemail message. Forgive me, but I wanted to know if I could help you," Francis says sincerely. "You can help me," Belle says swigging aggressively on her red wine.

"It won't make you feel better," he says, shifting his stare from Belle back down onto his plate of food, before picking up his knife and fork.

"It's not to make me feel better, it's for the foxes. It's for those who haven't got a heart to finally feel something, something else entirely . . . like the wrath of their own wrongdoing." She feels on fire from her words. Isabella finishes her glass of wine and goes to pour another. Francis reaches

178

out to put his hand over her glass.

"If we're going to do this then I want you in your right mind," he says, staring at her. Belle gets up to tip the rest of the wine down the sink.

"No more mulled wine then," she says, stood over him. He gives her his mug and she gets rid of it.

"So what is it you do?" Oksana asks Max a simple question.

"I'm a writer. . . well . . . I was," he says defiantly, like fighting himself for the answer to her question.

"A writer of what exactly?" She notices his uncertainty.

"I once wrote a movie script, but it failed to make an impression," Max says, staring down his drink as he drowns his sorrows some more.

"What was it about?" Oksana asks, with interest.

"The Loch Ness Monster tied down at the bottom of the lake. It's about setting Nessie free but there's obviously a lot more to it than that," Max answers, as he signals to the bartender for the same again.

"And for you, Miss?" the bartender asks.

"Nothing, thanks," she says, still keeping eye contact with Max, sussing him out.

"Like Free Willy." Oksana, unbeknownst to her, has said the magic words!

"Exactly." He smiles knowingly, yet Max is crying inside.

"I can make a hypocrite out of you yet," she says menacingly.

"I don't know what you mean." He feels confused by her claim.

"'Players playing the game at its own game'" Oksana quotes his writing to him and it raises his eyebrows.

"Where did you read that?" Max asks soberly.

"I was with Isabella's dad the day he penned a letter to you; you know the one, 'act NOW and illuminate the world with the colour of truth,'" she says, laughing out loud after quoting Joseph's spirited words.

"When he told me what his intentions were regarding the documents, I took the liberty of tapping into your phone . . . hope you don't mind!" Oksana looks smug. Max is speechless.

"I was with Joseph when he collapsed. I was there watching your ex realise her dream. Do you have any idea how long we've been trying to obtain those documents?" she says seriously.

"Who's 'we'?" Max says, squinting at her.

"If I told you, I would have to kill you," Oksana says, sipping on her drink.

"What do you want from me?" he asks, nervously getting up from the stool.

"I want the documents back but I'm more than willing to do you a deal." She smiles at him. Max downs his drink.

"Humour me," he says spitefully.

"I can make your dream come true." Oksana humours him.

"Which one?" Max asks with interest.

"The one you deserve," She says sincerely.

"What about the one the world deserves?" he asks, looking down on her.

"Sit down." Oksana glances at the stool and then back to Max. He freezes.

"We recovered your script . . . it's a good read . . . and yet you gave up hope. Max, this world deserves to be on the receiving end of your writing." She reaches out to him.

"Don't you want the world to be a better place?" He stays standing.

"My life is on the line and so is yours." Oksana stands up.

"I don't have a life. I have nothing but this moment, to do what is righteous." Max turns to walk away.

"Do you love Belle?" she asks, stopping him in his tracks.

"It's none of your business," Max answers angrily.

"If you do then I strongly suggest you rethink your 'righteous stance', before it's too late," Oksana threatens Max.

"Why toy with me? What gives you the right to treat me like a game?" he speaks desperately.

"Give me the documents, Max and you can have your cake and eat it," she speaks devoid of feeling.

Max removes the documents from the Bible, walks against his will towards Oksana and attempts to hand them over. But before doing so, suddenly, he sees her face change. Just like he saw when he felt possessed by a Bible and a compass years ago, now such an extreme experience has come back to haunt him. Max flinches with the utmost terror, turning away from her in horror. He keeps hold of the documents, stumbling back and falling over a chair, dropping the documents onto the floor. Then he tries to retrieve them. When Oksana bends down and does the same, Max looks at her to see she has a face of ghostly evil, longing and lusting after the documents. Scared to death he has a panic attack. Oksana approaches him and puts her hand on his shoulder for comfort's sake. Max freaks out to the sound of his own scream coming from the most severe fear he has ever felt.

"What's wrong with him?" The concerned bartender watches on.

"He's passed out. I think he had a panic attack. Call an ambulance." Oksana answers the bartender before walking out the door.

Francis stands in the centre of the field down from the fence separating it from the back garden. It's stopped snowing and the sky has been brightened by the stars. His first attempt to call a fox is successful; Francis squeaks like a mouse for not more than a minute and one appears in the distance. He then continues to squeak, having crouched down now, awaiting it to approach him. And approach him it does. Francis feeds the fox from his hand before grappling it to the ground. Somehow he sends the fox to sleep with ease. Slitting the fox's throat, he gathers the surging stream of warm blood in a bottle.

Isabella prints a picture of Prime Minister Pricilla Fay from on the internet, taking it with her to where Francis has started a fire in the centre of the field.

"Pass me the picture please," he says seriously. She gives it to him. He pours the fox's blood all over it and then drops the smiling image of Pricilla Fay onto the fire. Francis speaks out in an inconceivable but nonetheless special language, lasting for a matter of minutes. Soon after that, he pours more of the fox's blood straight onto the fire. Belle watches on, taken in by the fire as its flames rise, suddenly and for a split second turning bright blue, to her entranced state of golden silence – she is amazed.

"What happens now?" Belle breaks such a silence and asks, buzzing with anticipation.

"Tomorrow will come, unbeknownst to those sick and twisted, and with a mistaken sense of elitist entitlement; delighting in the death of innocent creatures. These people, privileged and proud of it, they have hell on the way. We relight this fire when night falls same time tomorrow . . . that is when what will be breaks loose, as if by magic, black magic, but the kind coming from a karmic principle: You reap what you sow and so you shall suffer for your crimes against nature." Francis is spirited away with what he has just done and speaks passionately. All the while Belle listens in with her undivided attention.

Darkness this Christmas Day has in it a starry night fit for the greater good. Belle and Francis bask in the feeling knowing what's in store for the few who choose to break the law. That which is justice, true justice, not just an eye for an eye, but the powerful few will fall, all in the name of righteousness.

CHAPTER 10: FOXES OF FIRE

Boxing Day, 2018

Max wakes up in a hospital bed. A nurse pulls the curtains open. It's not snowing today. He gets out of bed and goes over to his bag.

"Take it easy," the nurse says softly.

"Where are my documents?" He raises his voice.

"What documents? Just calm down." She goes to touch him but he shakes her off aggressively. The nurse presses a button. In comes a doctor with backup. Max is restrained and forced back on the bed before being injected.

Belle listens to her voicemail message from Max singing his heart out. She gives him a call but there is no answer. Francis knocks on her bedroom door.

"How are you feeling?" he says softly, peeking through the crack.

"Fine, I'm fine. I can't get hold of him," she says, sat on the edge of her bed, drifting back in time to better days spent with him and the 'Hunt-Trap Rat-Pack.'

"Breakfast is on the table." Francis leaves her to it. She hears him go back downstairs and shouts, "Francis!" She gets up and goes to open her door. Francis turns around midway down the stairs.

"Yes, Belle," he answers her cry.

"Nothing," she says, standing at the doorway with her pink pyjamas on.

They take a walk into town. The rain is washing the snow away. It's a light drizzle, less pleasant than that of falling snow but much more bearable than heavy rain. Belle holds Francis' arm in vain, needing to feel the love she sees all around her. For there are happy families strolling in light of festive cheer here, whereas Isabella has been broken and needs fixing. Francis knows this as he feels her crushing instability take his breath away.

"Where are we going?" he asks as they walk along the riverside, approaching the bridge that will lead them into town.

"Nowhere . . . let us just pretend to blend in with the nice and normal . . . let us just bask like kids do, in this bittersweet freeze, as if it's the most wonderful time of the year after all," Belle says, staring at the riverbed, letting her wishful thoughts go gently down the stream.

Wakey, wakey . . . you have a visitor!" A nurse shakes Max out of his chemically-induced sleep. He glances at her groggily.

"Max, nice to meet you." He turns his head to see a smart man standing over him, smiling, showing shiny white teeth, holding a movie script against his chest.

Max lifts his arm and reaches out to the smart

man, who shakes his hand. Max doesn't want his hand and instead uses it for leverage as he tries to take the 'documents' from him.

"My documents," Max says desperately.

"Yes, you can call them that. Hey, go ahead, it's your story." The man, in an American tone of voice, lets Max take the documents from him. He feasts his eyes on the front page, but to his surprise, these are not the documents concerning Nikola Tesla's spirited pursuit of free energy.

'~~The Rise and Fall of Folklore~~ *NESSIE* written by ~~Maximus Lucifer Phoenix~~ *MAX MATHEWS*' Max flicks through his script, to notice such a thing has been, in parts at least, rewritten. It forces him to sit up and take note of the changes made, before feeling compelled to question the American man.

"Who the hell is 'Max Mathews'?" he asks angrily.

"You are. Let me introduce myself; Rick Nixon's the name, I'm an agent, I represent some of Hollywood's leading writers." Rick has slicked back black hair, dead grey eyes and an over-the-top pitch to his American twang.

"Is that so? Ok, 'Rick', who is responsible for the rewrite?" Max is not groggy anymore, for now he feels seriously violated and this has woken him up. Rick makes a face showing off his sickeningly glossy smile, like he's about to say something special.

"Michael Gay." His face lights up upon saying such a name.

Max laughs out loud, and then gathers himself all of a sudden.

"What's so funny?" Rick is confused by his reaction.

"Michael Gay aka 'crash bang wallop' and that's

a wrap! What's such an artless son of bitch got to do with my script?" Max sounds deadly serious as he voices his concern in an arrogant and offensive display of self-satisfied hatred.

"Michael's directing 'Nessie' as we speak." Rick quite frankly says such a thing in matter of fact terms most smug. Max's eyes widen and his eyebrows stick up like that of a frightened cat.

"You threw the script away. Technically, we don't have to include you in any of this but that's not my style. I believe you've got a lot to offer Hollywood which is why I'm here." He speaks slowly but surely, along with an air of self-importance. Max is still speechless.

"Michael's quite content to have his director credit stand alone, despite his written input . . . that means it's all yours – you're the writer after all. Shooting began in Scotland today. You are to oversee the movie being made and where necessary feel free to share your vision of the story. Sound good?" Rick explains the situation and Max sits with a blank look on his face.

"I guess this is a good thing, isn't it?" He feels bedazzled.

"Trust me, Max, this is just the beginning," Rick says swiftly.

Night has suddenly, finally fallen. Belle and Francis stand before the fire's ashes of last night. He puts sticks and screwed up paper on top of it, talking in a tongue unbeknownst to Belle. She stands back. Francis lights a match, crouches down and places it under the paper. Raging and rising high, the flames shoot up as Francis falls back. Bright blue, but so too a sound unlike anything they have heard escapes such fantastical flames.

A howling, loud and of ferocious rage breaks out. Together they are not many yet at one with this sheer reverberating noise so ghostly. All of a sudden, from the highest of bright blue flames flies out like a firework a dark red fox, its fur of furious flames, followed by another, and another, and another, and one more in the same vein breaking free from the bright blue flames. They are literally galloping in the air above. Below, Belle is spellbound and so is Francis for that matter. Moments later they are out of sight, gone. Now the flames fall, flickering from bright blue to dark red. The fire falls all the way down from whence it started and suddenly ceases to exist, burnt out, out of the blue now nothing but ashes and dust.

Darkness, no stars where once there was more than ever before brightly shining; now the night has turned into utter darkness as black as can be becomes such a sky. Belle bear-hugs Francis in fright of the night sky; she holds him tight. He holds her back, looking out into the blackness up above.

"What have we done?" Belle trembles; breathing fear into Francis' ear she keeps hold of him. He gulps as if for a moment lost at what to say.

"We have called upon spirit to catch fire for the greater good." Francis keeps his arm around Belle, before both begin walking gingerly back to the house.

In a manor house surrounded by well-kept countryside there is a party taking place. The Prime Minister and her rich associates are very merry drinking champagne, and wilfully succumb under the influence of festive cheer. Fireworks blast off outside as such superior partygoers watch on from the terrace. Talking in a way which is practised and pretentious to the sound of self-satisfied flailing laughter, letting the collective tipsiness sing its own song in the air here of humungous smug egomaniacal conversation.

"Look . . . a shooting star . . . everyone make a wish!" A well-dressed woman points up above the fireworks display.

"But it's red . . . maybe it's a meteor!" The man next to her appears somewhat taken aback by it.

The sound of an all-encompassing sure-fire reverence has since become more a wondrous wheeze, as the people here huff and puff panicky. From fun and fancy to fright and fear, the 'meteor' nears, now the sound of hound dogs in distress has drowned out all else as mass panic consumes these people privileged and since disturbed by the beckoning unknown. Everyone runs inside the manor house. The fireworks have finished. The party is not a party anymore. The Prime Minister stares out of the glass doors separating them from a now lifeless terrace, as foxes of fire are closing in for the kill.

Earlier on in the day, around the countryside of England a tradition took place. People watched on, altogether gathering in their families and amongst friends; as festive cheer reigned supreme, so did the anticipation, the excitement of seeing an upper-class display of foreboding murderous resplendence celebrated by bloodthirsty 'people'.

These people will watch with eager eyes as the wealthy wave while riding high and mighty to satisfy a desire so basic, backward and disgusting, it betrays the present day we live in. And yet, yes, this happened today! A day of horrific killing - killing in the name of nothing but to simply show off; fancy clothes, horses, hounds . . . it's all for the superior appearance of the powerful few who want to make sure everyone else knows this is what the 'good life' looks like: quite frankly a fucking hell on earth – that's what it looks like.

Crash landing on the lush green in the cold darkness, foxes of fire burn brightly a shining in single file, fast and furious rage against the wrongful few fearing for their over-the-top-posh-proper-pompous-shallow-little-lives. Such an unbecoming mutated sound of the spirited away along with the animalistic terror roaring in fear or horror, hound dogs going insane and foxes of fire raging against the 'great big killers,' since shrinking, quaking, crying out in vain. They are not on a high horse now. Now they tremble. Now they are afraid and so they should be! Oh how her face is a picture of pure fear, realising the end is near, the Prime Minister freezes because quite frankly she can now see what's to come. Others as well, silenced by this twist of fate, watch on, not knowing how to be themselves . . . they are paralysed.

Suddenly the fiery foxes take flight to reach the terrace, still full speed ahead, and then, nonstop, shatter the terrace doors, screams, barking, but the piercing sound of five foxes on fire reigns supreme. Wreaking havoc, hellacious chaos. First to feel the wrath of black magic is the Prime Minister, taken down and torn apart by all five foxes feasting on her fear. The screaming is severely loud, blood has been shed, dogs are barking constantly, here hell for the hunters exists this surreal albeit righteous nightmare manifesting in out and out outrage. Men and women guilty of their crimes against nature, for each and every savage act on an animal, killing in the name of nothing but bloodlust; these people are not even people, they are merely creatures crestfallen unto existence alas blackness.

They can run, and indeed they do, but it's futile. They scream not for help, but out of a fear never felt before. All dressed up in hunt attire, pride out of place, such savages, it's a masquerade! And yet it's a bit more than that right now, right now no more masquerading, dancing the last dance of life like headless little chickens, creatures such as these, screaming, bleeding, dying in the way of a well-deserved death. The manor house has gone up in flames from foxes of fire; here they came to give back a lasting taste of the huntsmen and huntswomen's own medicine. Unrighteous actions not always see the cold light of consequence, so it is with thanks to Belle and Francis for courageously leaping past the point of no return in order for true justice to be served.

Francis is sat in the armchair. Belle leans forward from being sat on the sofa, staring crazily at the television's black screen. She has in her hand the remote but is hesitating to face the music. Her phone rings, making Belle jump. She looks at the screen and then answers straight away.

"Max, where are you?" She stands up, pacing around the room while Francis watches on.

"I'm on my way to Scotland," he says excitedly.

"What? Scotland? Why?" Belle stops pacing.

"You know that script I took to the festival, well, it's finally being made into a movie!" Max sounds pleased.

"That's great, but what about the greater good and the classified documents from my father . . . " Belle refrains from congratulating him and instead wonders where his heart has gone.

"I . . . I lost the documents . . . well, not exactly lost them – they were taken from me," he says sheepishly. She sits back down on the sofa and turns the television on.

"Belle?" Max wonders why she is silent. It's the news. Isabella looks scared. Francis gets up and goes over to her, taking a seat on the sofa. She passes him the phone.

"Max, it's Francis, listen to me . . . the Prime Minister is dead . . . Belle misses you . . . can you come back?" Francis says staring into Belle's lost look of lifelessness.

"Dead? Did you . . .?" Max sounds astonished.

"Yes I did, with Belle's blessing . . . she's scared . . . can you come home to her or not?" he asks, as Belle breaks down into tears.

"Sorry, tell her I'm sorry but I have to do this, it's important," he says, swallowing in the wake of what Francis said.

"More important than her?" Francis asks, taken aback by his answer.

"I'm sorry, ok. Don't hold it against me. I feel for her, I really do," Max says desperately. Francis cancels the call and places the phone on the table. Belle continues to cry, her head down hunched over the arm of the sofa.

Max puts the phone down and stares out of the passenger's side window, while being driven to

Scotland by Rick Nixon.

"Everything OK?" Rick asks, keeping his eyes on the road.

"Yeah fine, I'm fine," Max answers, not letting his feelings show but still he faces away from Rick's outlook. In all honesty, he feels like he has let Belle's dead dad down. He realises just how weak he is and of what little importance are the words that have come from him in the past. He feels reduced to closing his eyes. Try as Max might to fall asleep he is not tired. But still, his eyes stay shut.

2005

"Hunt-Trap Rat-Pack, quite rightly I salute you for your unrelenting effort, but of course also the sacrifice each one of you made, as a member of my team, to fight for foxes' freedom. The ban on foxhunting is a direct result of our bravery; we prevailed against injustice, serving the greater good and so, no! We do not delight at dancing in the wake of what was wicked and wrong and worse still killed for nothing but bloodlust. This was never personal, nor was it a vendetta against the upper-classes, despite them being tremendously dislikeable and without any redeeming feature whatsoever; we fought not to satisfy a superficial feeling. . . we fought to do right by nature! And now, we can celebrate this victory together, but tomorrow go our separate ways taking with us, in all our walks of life from now on, not only a sense of fulfilment, but a belief born of the beauty to come from the few who had the heart to defeat evil! All of you, united by believing in a better future, a future where the unrighteous cease to exist! Raise your glasses, as we toast to living in the light of righteousness."

27ᵗʰ of December, 2018

No rain, no snow, just a bitter chill to contend with while the burial of Joseph Symonds takes place. Isabella looks down on the coffin, having been put in the grave, and then turns to face Francis as well as those closest to Joseph, for the most part consisting of Jehovah's Witnesses from Kingdom building.

"Who shall separate us from the love of Christ? Shall trouble or hardship or persecution or famine or nakedness or danger or sword? And so, as it is written: 'For your sake we face death all day long; we are considered as sheep to be slaughtered.' No, in all these things we are more than conquerors through him who loves us. For I am convinced that neither death nor life, neither angels nor demons, neither the present nor the future, nor any powers, not height, not depth, nor can anything else in all creation come between us and the love of God that is in Christ Jesus our Lord." The priest looks at Belle and nods, as now she will say a few words with regard to her late father.

"'The Lord is close to the broken-hearted and saves those who are crushed in spirit.' Must it be in death that we are saved from our suffering? I for one wish to be free from my pain, now more than ever before because it hurts inside. I suffer from having a soul, longing for more than this, . . . this . . . sorry; I can't do this. Speak like I can keep it together, for what? I don't know you people. I don't owe you my right mind. My dad not only did what he loved, but did what he didn't necessarily love, let alone understand and yet, for love, he delivered the word of God. And with love, studied the brain; indeed he delighted in its infinity but to die ironically from a brain tumour makes me sick." She folds a piece of paper being held down by her side and drops it into the grave. Belle falls to her hands and knees, clutching the cold damp soil with both hands. She cries uncontrollably before throwing handfuls of soil into the grave.

"YOU'VE LEFT ME! I HAVE NO ONE! WHAT'S WRONG WITH ME? OH GOD WHY! WHY?" She sinks back on her knees, letting her head fall back as she looks hopelessly up at the white sky. The priest stares down at the ground disapprovingly. Francis approaches Isabella and stands before her. Everyone else just watches on in silence, while Belle lets it all out. Francis puts his hand on her shoulder and bows his head. She continues to cry while releasing handfuls of soil down into the grave below. Beautiful suffering; for what we once held dear, there comes a time to let go. Belle has been on the receiving end of divine intricacy, as such a strange sacred secretive twist of fate takes her right by the heart to have feelings surface from way down deep.

18ᵗʰ of October, 2008

Joseph enters Isabella's bedroom to the sound of her crying.

"What's wrong?" he asks, sitting down by her side. She has the covers over her head and continues to cry. Joseph uncovers her crying, to which she turns over and faces the wall.

"It's Max . . . it's over," Belle says,

disheartened and distraught.

"Belle. . . " He wants his daughter to face him.

"Belle, look at me, please . . . " Joseph says softly. She eventually turns over and dignifies her father with her undivided attention.

"I know how you feel . . . he . . . well, Belle, being as Max is, this was bound to happen sooner or later . . . " His words are from the heart but Belle feels the need to interrupt.

"And Max is what exactly?" she snaps at him.

"He's a dreamer. And a dreamer like Max has reckless disregard for 'matters of the heart.' Don't get me wrong, we all have feelings regardless of who we are, but with Max in mind and with his history of mental illness, let's not forget, Belle, whereas music is in you and it gives you your love, your meaning in life, I think Max has been lost for a long time. I think he is looking for something . . . something other than the love you gave him."

"Like what?" she sniffles, sitting up to be on the same level as her father.

"I don't dream his dreams, Isabella, and nor do you . . . 'Do not love the world or the things in the world, for if you love the world and its things, then the love of God is not in you'." Joseph takes Isabella by her hand and kisses it.

27th of December, 2018

Max is in Scotland. And upon meeting Michael Gay, gets on well with him. It would seem such a producer specialising in mainstream movies has every intention to this time come from his heart.

"'The Rise and Fall of Folklore' felt to me too much. I mean, don't get me wrong it's a nice title, but with 'Nessie' we can not only appeal to a wider audience but we can pack a surprising punch in the way your story appears because 'Nessie' suggests 'nice and normal', not the weird and wonderful of what's to come." Michael is dressed down and wears a Nike cap. Max listens intently. They are on a boat, taking a trip around the Loch Ness.

"Yes, I see where you're coming from. I'm just happy to be here," Max says sincerely, looking around him, thinking it must be a dream. He is surrounded by beauty. The lake creates a calming influence, mysterious as it is; still a sense of peace has since instilled in Max this somewhat welcome comfort from the chaos his life was.

Belle leans against the fence separating her garden from the field she is absent-mindedly looking at. It's getting colder and there is little light left of today, a day despairingly lost on loneliness. Francis stands beside her. They lean on the fence for more support than it can give them; something inevitable becomes this bitter time misspent at the peril Belle feels.

"I take full responsibility for the foxes of fire I can't go on like this, Isabella. There are no regrets, just the consequence of my actions remains to be seen. And so, I have decided . . . " Francis is interrupted before he can finish his heartfelt sentence.

"Don't leave me. Please, Francis, I beg you not to go. . . " Belle drops down to her knees and clings onto Francis. He strokes her long brown hair, before feeling compelled to hold the back of her head against his side.

"You have your whole life left to do beautiful

things, Isabella . . . I gave up the ghost long ago. And now . . . now I must face the music." Francis pulls Belle up to her feet. He has a hold of her by both arms.

"What do you mean?" she asks sadly, looking into his eyes.

"I will tell the police what happened. I will leave you out of it." He lets go of her.

"They'll make you out to be a terrorist, Francis, is that what you want?" Belle says desperately.

"To live for the greater good, is to die righteously." Francis puts on a brave face for Belle, and then turns to walk back up the garden.

"Albeit behind bars, is that righteous? Francis, this is not the end. My dad didn't think I was cut out for fighting injustice hence Max has betrayed my dad's better judgement, and now, now you wanna go forth defeated into this good night. Well, I for one won't let you fade away without a fight! It's time, time to rage, rage against the dying of the light." Belle catches up to stand in front of Francis, speaking quite frankly from her heart.

"What about your musical career?" he asks, as it starts to snow.

"What musical career? According to my music teacher, a conductor's endeavour verges on obsolete! We are a 'dying breed' as he put it to me in no uncertain terms, despite my then teen angst and an utter reluctance to accept such a statement. But of course, as a victim of puberty not to mention passion, I persisted to argue my ambition and I remember it well . . . 'musicians play their instruments sir, so I shall play the orchestra – after all . . . you can't have sound without fury.' That's what I said and he merely laughed, scoffing at my childhood dream because quite frankly he was just a teacher and I was just a kid, " she answers scornfully. Francis raises his eyebrows, silenced.

"How old were you when you said that?" Francis wonders.

"I was twelve at the time." Belle says sharply.

"Remarkable," he says, spellbound by her magnificence.

"Yes, there are more important things in life. Why should I be but a conductor to the upper classes? Pleasing a certain type of people, people who only think of themselves. I was one of them, thinking it was good and right to be performing in front of such, such smug ignorance." Belle shakes her head and looks away from Francis so to solidify feelings discontented and disgusted at what once was something special.

"But, Belle, I imagine that what you were doing, it was making people happy, it was making you happy, so why stop?" he asks, rubbing his hands together from the cold.

"'Do not love the world or the things in the world, for if you love the world and its things, then the love of God is not in you'" Belle remembers word for word what her dad had to say when she was in her time of need and feels compelled to share such scripture as an answer. Francis puts his arm around her and they walk back to the house.

Max is in his hotel room. His phone rings. It's Isabella.

"Hello, Belle," he answers her call.

"Max, who took the documents?" she asks with intent to her wavering voice.

"Her real name is Oksana Kuznetsov but she

goes by the name of Macey Cena." Max sits up, with a look of concern on his face.

"Do you know where she is?" Belle is sat on the sofa facing Francis who's sitting on the armchair.

"She said something about going to Sao Paulo but she may have been lying to me." He gets up from the bed and walks over to the window, closing the curtains.

"Do you think that's where she is?" she asks, looking through Francis. Isabella appears deep in thought.

"I don't know. What's it to you? You're back on tour tomorrow." Max is confused.

"No, I'm not. I've been replaced. 'Destiny in a dream . . . a dream away from being the real thing . . . .' I should have known not to care where your words are concerned and yet you can come across as such a convincing seeker, 'cos quite frankly I felt compelled to believe in your quest for a better future, but of course this is Max! Suffice to say, you have chosen to do 'good and right', not for the many in need of it but for personal gain." Belle lets him have it.

"Macey Cena is a journalist. Oksana Kuznetsov is something else entirely. Be careful, Belle. Bye." Max cancels the call, falling back on his bed, downhearted and defeated.

"He hung up on me." Belle puts her phone on the table. She remains on the edge of the sofa, feeling lost at what to do. Francis senses her bewilderment from across the room.

"I don't doubt the importance of the classified documents but Belle, even if you do get them back, what then?" Francis poses his question from a position of discomfort, for he too feels somewhat lost.

She drops her head down into her hands as Francis continues his questioning.

"This is not your dream. And it's not your duty either. Your dad . . . " He hits a raw nerve, forcing her to interrupt.

"My dad is dead, damn it. The least I can do is . . . the least I can do to, to feel closure from this . . . this shitty sequence of events; actions speak louder than words ever will. All I knew was music, and now I know nothing but the burden of being broken by it." Belle's phone rings. It's Lucy, her agent.

"Hello?" she answers her call.

"Belle, good news . . . you're back on tour from tomorrow," Lucy says excitedly.

"What about my replacement?" Belle says cautiously.

"Your replacement committed suicide. I will text you all the flight details this instant." Lucy cancels the call.

"Lucy . . . Lucy?" Isabella looks surprised and somewhat taken aback.

"What's wrong?" Francis sees she appears to be beyond bewildered.

"Nothing . . . that was my agent . . . I'm back on tour from tomorrow." Belle keeps her phone in hand and awaits the text message.

"I think it's for the best, Belle, I really do," Francis says sincerely.

She receives a text message from Lucy.

"My orchestra are in Sao Paulo . . . the same place Max said 'Macey Cena' is . . . " Isabella can't believe her eyes as she reads the text message.

"Who is Macey Cena?" Francis is confused.

"Macey Cena is Oksana Kuznetsov . . . she stole

the documents from Max . . . there must be forces at work here." Belle sounds excited.

"When do you leave?" There is a sadness softening his strong tone of voice.

"First thing in the morning." There is also a sadness softening her words as well.

"I am happy for you . . . you deserve to spread your wings, Isabella . . . let us celebrate." Francis stands to his feet, as does Isabella. They go into the kitchen and Belle opens a bottle of wine.

"To you, for taking me in when no one else would dream of doing so. " Francis raises his glass.

"To you, for being my best friend and a truly beautiful soul." Belle toasts his glass.

28th of December, 2018

Belle drives Francis back to the park in Plymouth. She gives him some money and pleads with him not to go to the police. He gives her his word and then they part ways. She drives to Exeter airport, upset but determined, and avoids being on the receiving end of the radio by turning it off. Belle feels relieved to be leaving England, and with it the mess she has made in the wake of the Prime Minister's death.

The victims just so happened to be each and every person involved with the Boxing Day hunt. The survivors, consisting of friends and acquaintances to those closely associated with the Prime Minister, all claim the blaze was started by 'a pack of foxes on fire'. The media, however, have edited down the segments from survivor and in doing so suggest that the cause is 'undetermined' but for a full investigation to take place as soon as possible.

This significant death has since triggered 'protests' in and around London. For want not to call it chaos, supporters of both the Conservative and Labour party and also just the general public on the whole have taken to the streets.

Meanwhile, Max is in la-la land. Watching his film script come to life fills him with pride and joy. Just being in the presence of thespians, these people 'playing the game at its own game' makes Max rethink his writings. His rage came from an impure place of envy. Yes, the world is still in need of saving, but now he has a sense of belonging replace his outlandish delusions.

CHAPTER 11: PLAYING THE GAME AT ITS OWN GAME

ACT 1: BEAUTIFUL SUFFERING

SCENE 1: LOSS

EXT. FARMLAND, TEXAS, DAY

A farmer brings his cattle, totalling thirty cows in all, up the narrow lane and through the open gate to a field.

This morning is bleak at best. But the weather itself is a stark contrast to the sombre, broody mood of the morning. Indeed it does shine and yet the sun sheds light on Jim's sorrow.

Closing the gate, he makes sure his dog stays put on the other side.

                    JIM
    Home, boy

The dog tilts its head to one side and stays standing there.
                    JIM
    Go home

The dog sits, staring at him.

                    JIM
    Shep, I said home — go on!

The dog jumps up placing his paws onto the
gate with its tongue hanging out, tail
wagging.

The farmer yanks the gate, making the dog fly
back.

                    JIM
    HOME! NOW!

The dog runs down the lane (tail between its
legs) and into the distance as his owner turns
around.

The farmer takes just a glance at his cows,
before facing the lane again, turning away
from them.

He bows his heavy head, placing both hands
wrapped around the gate with outstretched arms
as he lifts his head and looks up at the sky,
taking a moment.

Slowly he turns around and faces his cows as a
big digger drives up to the middle of the
field.

A young man, not yet thirty, gets out of the
digger and casually limps up to where the cows
stand, stopping suddenly. He remains somewhat
at a distance so to give the farmer much
needed space.

The farmer herds his cows as he carefully
forces them into the cattle pen. All thirty
cows cram into the pen. The pen is attached to
a passage through which there is another pen.

Then, having contained the cows in the pen, he
turns around and walks towards the young man.
The farmer walks with his head down and,
gazing in absentminded disdain on the grassy
ground, senses the shadow of a man standing.

The shadow is seen to take a big gun from the bulge of his belt, held in one hand and now forcing the farmer's undivided attention at least for one long moment that lasts seconds.

And in those seconds from raising his head, he does not stop in his tracks as he looks straight through the young man's eyes.

The farmer sharply nods at the young man in giving him a signal.

And so the young man approaches the cattle pen.

Upon giving him that certain signal, the farmer looks back down on the ground and while walking at a slower pace, stares lifelessly beyond the black of his own thin shadow.

BANG

The mooing begins.

BANG

The mooing gets worse.

BANG

The mooing doesn't sound like mooing anymore.

BANG

And so, the sound of pure fear reverberates, sending a shiver down the farmer's spine.

BANG

The farmer runs as fast as he can into the big digger, slamming the door, turning on the radio and then turning it up to its loudest.

Song on the radio is some kind of classical music, quite fitting to the trauma the farmer feels.

In the distance, sick cows, one by one, are shot dead. The farmer has seen enough — he clenches his eyes shut tight — gritting his teeth and covering his ears.

The song reaches its epic part, before eventually dying down to a softer sound and in doing so somewhat lulls the farmer into a false sense of calm.

The only sound now loud and clear is the heavy breathing of the farmer trying to gather his breath back to a steadier rate.

The wrinkles beside his eyes disappear, releasing his clenched disposition and so slowly letting himself feel at least some ease, he stops clenching his teeth then opens his eyes.

Suddenly he sees one of his sick cows make a mad dash down the field.

The frantic cow runs past the digger. There is nowhere for the diseased creature to go, only into the big pit at the bottom of the field.

The cow falls head first into the big pit. The young man, gun down at his side, slowly limps past the digger and down to the end of the field.

The farmer turns his head to watch the young man in the digger mirror, turning the radio off.

The young man lifts his arm in order to point the gun at the cow, which is now struggling to its feet.

But then, he lowers his aim and does nothing.

MATTHEW BROOKES

The farmer, surprised by the young man's actions exits the digger.

The young man watches on in guilty pleasure as the cow slowly moves itself to one side of the pit, then tries climbing out but to no avail, falling down.

The farmer, from behind, grabs the gun and then kicks the young man into the pit.

The young man stands and attempts to get out of the pit, but he himself falls back down.

The farmer jumps into the pit, standing over the young man flat on his back.

He points the gun at the young man and then gets distracted by the dying cow.

The farmer steps onto, then over, the young man who squeals like a pig in the process of being stamped on.

Quickly he raises his arm, aims and fires direct at the cow.

BANG

Silence

The farmer turns around and it is Shep sitting in the young man's place, *as if by magic*.

He forces a smile, under the circumstances, ruffles the dog's hair on its head and then gets out of the pit.

Shep follows his owner, who heads over to the digger and gets in. Before he can slam the door the dog jumps up; joining him for the finishing of the job.

Dead, diseased cows are mechanically moved into the big pit. Once every single cow has been put into the pit, the farmer pours petrol all over the carcasses.

Using a flame thrower, the farmer burns the carcasses, setting them on fire.

Smoke intensifies, as does the smell of burnt carcass, so the farmer and Shep jump into the digger.

He drives up the field and back to the farm.

FADE OUT

FADE IN

SCENE 2: CAUGHT UP IN THE CHRISTIANS CROSSFIRE

INT. THE LOCH INN, LOCHEND, SCOTLAND, NIGHT

A busy pub is being addressed by a lively local speaker via microphone. It's a dimly lit atmosphere, being brought to life by flashing lights of the multi-coloured kind, like a disco only without the glitter ball. The man stands tall, on a stage that is on the same level with its drinkers. Beside the host is an aging guitarist; sat behind him remains a slightly dishevelled drummer sipping on a pint of something strong.

                    PATRICK
        And so without further ado
        all the way from. . .

The larger than life fat man adorns such a stage with a strong Scottish accent, a brightly coloured Hawaiian shirt and not to mention an unsightly kilt, tightfitting at the peril of all else present.

Forgetting an important piece of information regarding the band, he looks across at the guitarist as a cue to tell everyone where they come from.

                    GUITARIST
     Outer space

The speaker forces a smile before carrying on.

                    PATRICK
     Outer space! Lads and
     lasses, let's hope they
     have come in peace as I
     give you an up and coming
     Christian rock band by the
     name of. . .

Patrick looks embarrassingly over towards the guitarist to once more enlighten him.

The guitarist shakes his head and says nothing.

The speaker looks slightly puzzled and then the guitarist moves up to the mic, taking the speaker's place.

                    GUITARIST
     Jessie? Where's a singer
     when you need one?

Silence ensues for a few seconds, seemingly lasting a lifetime. The guitarist looks sheepishly behind him at the drummer, who openly shrugs his shoulders.

Amongst members of the crowd, drinking and waiting in anticipation of the band's performance, is standing a proud priest watching on. And so sensing the guitarist's discomfort, the priest heads straight for the toilets.

          INT. THE LOCH INN, TOILETS, NIGHT

The priest approaches a locked cubicle, tilts his head to the side of it and then hesitates slightly. He hears a forced sound of sniffing before feeling the need to knock on the door.

Knock, knock

                    PRIEST
    Jessie?

Then the toilet flushes followed by the door being unlocked. A man exits the toilet looking a little flustered and extremely sheepish. He goes straight to the sink in front of him and washes his hands. The man in question stands at just over six foot tall, wearing dark clothing that matches his mascara. The priest watches his movements from behind and looks in the mirror as the man checks himself out.

                    PRIEST
    The stage awaits you. . .
    in more ways than one.
    Wash your face, son

The man — JESSIE — shakes his hands at the sink, looks into the mirror making eye contact with the priest at a distance, does not wash his face, does not dry his hands properly, yet, leaving the tap running, walks straight past the priest and back into the plain sight of everyone waiting on the band's performance. The priest turns the tap off before leaving the toilets to watch the band perform.

INT. THE LOCH INN, NIGHT

Jessie makes his way to the stage, accompanied by a few sarcastic claps and cheers from the crowd.

                    JESSIE
    When nature calls!
    This song is called
    My Last Serenade

MATTHEW BROOKES

He runs his fingers through his mid-to-long
blond hair before addressing the drinkers —
some are sat down while others stand in wait.
As the band perform their opening song, the
priest makes his way through the crowd of
drinkers and to the bar, where he then
proceeds to tell the owner what he believes
singer 'Jessie' was doing in the toilet.

Oblivious, lost in the moment, the frontman
continues to perform 'My Last Serenade'.

The bartender/owner goes out back to
presumably call the police, as the priest
turns his attention to the song.

The song is fast-paced and very heavy for the
likes of the Lochend people who are feeling a
bit put out by it all.

Slowly but surely the pub empties as the
drinkers take themselves outside, not at all
impressed by the band's sound of an acquired
kind.

The band close out their first song to an
almost empty pub but for the barman, an old
man sat in the corner on his own and the
speaker standing next to the priest.

The song goes into a soft interlude lasting
forty five seconds, enough time for fat
Patrick the speaker and the proud priest to
hear themselves think.

> PATRICK
> Whose 'splendid' idea was
> it to put on an 'open mic night'
> in the first place?

> PRIEST
> Mine and Frank's as a matter of
> fact

> PATRICK
> Oh, and yet they say two heads are

212

better than one, well I beg to
differ, for obvious reasons

           PRIEST
Speak for yourself. Have you even
listened to the lyrics?

          PATRICK
All I can hear are the angry
remnants of what's still to
come when I get home!

           PRIEST
I'm sure your wife feels the
same way when you snore

          PATRICK
Touché

A police officer enters the pub and approaches
the landlord behind the bar.

Patrick notices this as the priest watches on,
sensing such a thing.

          PATRICK
Hey, what's he doing here?

The priest doesn't answer Patrick, but walks
over to the bar.

As the band's soothing interlude continues to
sound, so does the singer, introducing his
next song.

           JESSIE
For the few who have survived
and not to mention mister
officer of the law, who I
welcome with this next song,
it's called 'turning point'

And so the song explodes into action.

And yet, just as the song springs into life, the lights go on, not only that but the music is suddenly cut off.

Out comes the owner from behind the bar to voice his strong opinion.

> FRANK
> Show's over. Officer, arrest
> that man now

He points at Jessie.
Jessie points at himself.

> JESSIE
> Who, me?

> FRANK
> Yes, you! We here are a lawful
> People. We don't tolerate crazies —
> either you change your ways or
> we'll change them for you

Frank has short brown hair; his defining feature appears to be his big, brown and at this present moment in time, bulging eyes. His dress sense is nice and normal, along with the rest of him on the whole — he seems straightedge.

> JESSIE
> I've done nothing wrong!

> FRANK
> Don't play dumb, son, and for
> the love of God it goes without
> saying you disgrace us in your
> repulsive presence as a jumped
> up poof. Look at you — you come
> here in all your drug-giddy
> glory wearing mascara for
> Christ's sake! Who the hell
> do you think you are?

214

                    PRIEST
    That's enough, Frank

The police officer struts up to the stage.

                    POLICE OFFICER
    I am arresting you on suspicion
    of possessing and using an illegal
    substance. You do not have to say
    anything but it may harm your
    defence if you do not mention
    when questioned something which
    you later rely on in court.
    Anything you do say may be given
    in evidence

                    JESSIE
    This is horse shit!

Jessie eyeballs the priest as he is first
handcuffed and then forced outside by the
police officer.

The rest of the band pack up and leave the
pub, putting their equipment into a van and
driving off.

EXT. OUTSIDE THE LOCH INN, NIGHT

The police officer puts Jessie in the back of
the police car.

All of the drinkers are gossiping amongst
themselves as they watch on.

The priest strolls up to the police car as the
officer straps (handcuffed) Jessie in.

                    PRIEST
    For what it's worth I was
    impressed by your performance
    Jessie, you put on a good show

                    JESSIE
    Go fuck yourself

The policeman slams the backdoor shut, then enters his drivers seat, starts the car and drives off.

The fat-ass speaker appears from inside the pub, holding a pint of strong ale.

>   PATRICK
>   Well it was John Lennon
>   who once said something
>   along the lines of. . . 'life
>   is what happens when one and
>   all are busy listening to
>   a live band!'. . . Karaoke anyone?

And so most of the drinkers respond kindly by going back inside the pub.

The Carpenters — Top of the World or Harry Belafonte — Man Piaba plays as the speaker kicks off the karaoke.

SCENE 3: EMPTY DREAMS

EXT. MALTESE SEA, MALTA, DAY

THE PAST

The farmer and his wife are on a boat together. They are kitted out to go deep-sea diving.

>   WENDY
>   Let's sell up

The farmer gives his wife a mischievous smile while looking deep into her hazel eyes.

>   WENDY
>   Pretty please. . .

She even flutters her very long eyelashes as well!

>   JIM

We'll see

She looks disappointed, but beautiful nonetheless.

                    JIM
    What's wrong?

                    WENDY
    Nothing

Between them, there is something of an uncomfortable silence as they prepare themselves for a deep-sea dive.

                    WENDY
    Darling, let's go our separate
    ways

                    JIM
    What?

                    WENDY
    It's just you're always so
    slow when we explore
    whereas I want to go at
    my own pace

                    JIM
    OH!

The farmer looks relieved.

                    WENDY
    What did you think I meant?

                    JIM
    Nothing

He forces a smile, leans over and kisses her on the cheek.

                    WENDY
    And darling, let's meet back at
    the boat by 5. . .

                    JIM
     5, why 5?

                    WENDY
     Our dinner reservation. . .
     I told you to book it last
     night! Tell me you didn't
     forget

                    JIM
     I didn't forget

                    WENDY
     Good

                    JIM
     But we reserved for 8:30,
     that gives us until 7
     surely

                    WENDY
     Don't you ever listen, Jim?
     This boat has to be back
     at the shore for 7 sharp

                    JIM
     You do know you're not
     allowed to dive alone,
     don't you

                    WENDY
     We both know not to abide
     by the rules is sometimes
     as it should be

                    JIM
     You and your rebel heart,
     huh, how have I not lost
     you yet?

                    WENDY
     Because I keep coming back
     for more

Jim smiles.

She blows her husband a kiss and then puts on the remaining bits of scuba gear. Wendy gives Jim a sign of 5 fingers so to indicate the time being 5pm, then purposely falls backwards into the sea.

He watches her slender shape disappear from his sight.

INT. FARMHOUSE, TEXAS, NIGHT

The farmer is sat on the edge of his armchair, staring at a photo of his wife he holds in one hand and a bottle of whisky in the other.

The dog barks from afar, forcing the farmer up to his feet. He puts both the photo and the bottle onto the table before proceeding to let Shep in from being outside.

Then he turns off the light to the living room. Jim makes his way upstairs to bed, followed by Shep.

INT. POLICE STATION, SCOTLAND, LOCHEND, DAY

SCENE 4: A Very Rude Awakening

It's the morning after and Jessie is fast asleep. He remains the only one behind bars. A police officer enters the cell and walks up to the sleeping Jessie, who's in for a very rude awakening!

The officer throws water into the sleeping peacefully face of Jessie.

                    POLICE OFFICER
    Rise and shine

Jessie jumps up in shock, knocking his head hard on the top bunk bed.

                    JESSIE
    OHW! What the fuck?

                    POLICE OFFICER
        Wakey wakey, you have a visitor

Jessie jumps up and out of the bottom bunk
quickly. He puts on his shoes and jacket then
waits for what he believes is about to happen
next — the arrival of his bandmates.

The priest enters the cell, so the officer
steps outside of it.

                    JESSIE
        What do you want?

                    PRIEST
        To wish you a good morning,
        amongst other things

                    JESSIE
        Why don't you just wish me
        back where I belong like a
        good little priest, to keep
        the peace of course, 'cos I
        am a bad man after all

                    PRIEST
        And a bad man belongs behind
        bars, does he not?

                    JESSIE
        Touché

                    PRIEST
        I know a bad man when I see
        one. And I also know what
        a lost soul looks like

                    JESSIE
        Don't let the mascara fool
        you. I'm fine, 'Father'
        thank you very much!

                    PRIEST

    'In these days that pass
    before me there was an anxious
    feeling that would hold me down,
    tearing me inside, bleeding my
    spirit'

The priest quotes Jessie's very own song lyric
back at him.

                        JESSIE
    That's just a song

                        PRIEST
    Not a cry for help then. . .

                        JESSIE
    I appreciate your concern
    but I do not need saving
    anytime soon

                        PRIEST
    I beg to differ — you're
    the one behind bars, Jessie

                        JESSIE
    What do you want from me?

                        PRIEST
    What do you want from yourself?

There is a pause for thought. The conversation
takes a turn for the serious, as silence
brings them closer together.

                        PRIEST
    What are ya — thirty?

                        JESSIE
    Twenty nine

Jessie says defiantly, like he is not yet
ready to consider turning 30.

                        PRIEST
    And what do you do when you're
    not 'rocking out'?

                         JESSIE
          'Rocking out.' That's a good one

                         PRIEST
          Well?

                         JESSIE
          Why should I tell you anything
          about me?

                         PRIEST
          Because, Jessie, we can help you

                         JESSIE
          Who's we?

                         PRIEST
          The Father, the Son and the
          Holy Ghost

                         JESSIE
          Oh, I shoulda known. Thanks, but
          no thanks. Officer. Officer?

Jessie calls out for the officer.

                         PRIEST
          You're barking up the wrong
          tree, Jessie. He can't help
          you — not like I can

The officer responds, standing outside and
looking in.

                         JESSIE
          I want my phone call

                         OFFICER
          All in good time

                         JESSIE
          And I want him gone - now

                         OFFICER
          Father, are you finished?

                    PRIEST
    No — not yet

                    OFFICER
    Didn't think so

The officer walks away.

                    JESSIE
    What is this?

                    PRIEST
    You tell me

                    JESSIE
    This is the curse of coke

                    PRIEST
    Could it be a blessing in
    disguise?

                    JESSIE
    Don't flatter yourself, Father

                    PRIEST
    Touché

                    JESSIE
    Anyway, where did my band end up?

                    PRIEST
    Your band, I believe, have
    gone back to where they came
    from

Jessie shakes his head.

                    PRIEST
    Why are you here?

                    JESSIE
    You ratted me out!

                    PRIEST
    I meant, what brought you and

your band out here in the first
place?

                    JESSIE
Nessie!

The priest smiles showing no teeth.

                    JESSIE CONT'D
We are all young at heart,
right?

                    PRIEST
Right you are, a child of God

                    JESSIE
I don't know about that, but
to each his own way of life

                    PRIEST
Indeed, and yet your way of
life fails you

                    JESSIE
You don't know me or my way of
life for that matter, but just
'cos you 'feel the love' of God,
you think it gives you the right
to stand tall and talk down on
others less inclined by a
belief in the stuff of fantasy -
fuck you . . .

                    PRIEST
But you believe in 'Nessie' so
why not God?

                    JESSIE
Did you not detect a certain
'nuance' as of when 'Nessie'
sprang 'merrily' out of my
mouth. . . hah, I have my reasons
for feeling the need to make
fun of. . . of all things so very
ridiculous

                    PRIEST
Such as. . .

                    JESSIE
It's personal

                    PRIEST
I wasn't always a priest, believe
it or not

                    JESSIE
Oh, spare me your 'journey of
finding God' garbage

                    PRIEST
I know what it's like. I've
been there, your age, and
the search for something that
you can't quite put your finger
on, only you know it's something
more than any old words of wisdom,
maybe even more than the music in
                    PRIEST CONT'D
you. I'm talking about truth

                    JESSIE
What truth?

                    PRIEST
Your pursuit of happiness, Jessie

                    JESSIE
I have to go home

                    PRIEST
Where's home?

                    JESSIE
Good question

                    PRIEST
When was the last time you
went to church?

                    JESSIE

225

What's the 'house of God' got
to do with me?

                    PRIEST
I can get you out of here right
now

                    JESSIE
I'm waiting for the great big
'but' to breathe down my neck

                    PRIEST
Hah, there is no such thing.
This is not a negotiation

                    JESSIE
So I'm free to go

                    PRIEST
Yes, you're free to go

                    JESSIE
That's alright then

                    PRIEST
'Go with the flow' like
you always have, and then
when you end up in another
uncompromising position,
then what?

                    JESSIE
Where there's a will, there's
a way out of hell!

                    PRIEST
Very well. When you get to my
age . . . Jessie, just take a moment
next time there's something in
the air. Or for want of a better
way to give you the heads up, go
with your gut not the flow. Let
me tell ya a little something about
being true to who you really are
and not what you think feels 'good

and right' just cos everyone else
is doing the same damn thing they
always do - doesn't make them better
for it. 'The flow' is for those who
haven't got what it takes to stop
time in its tracks — cos only then,
when you're wondering what to do
or where to go - hopefully you'll have
the heart but more important than
that, the need to know what it is
you're really looking for. From
within. Without that capacity to
'call the shots,' what — are - you?

Jessie does not know how to answer such a question.

                    PRIEST
    You're a sheep. Please, listen
    to the one thing that matters most
    of all and that's instinct

                    JESSIE
    Thanks for that, I think

The priest nods and then departs.

                    PRIEST
    Wayne, we're done in here

The officer lets the priest out.

                    JESSIE
    Wait

The priest, about to leave, turns and faces Jessie.

                    JESSIE
    Take me to church

                    PRIEST
    Music to my ears

                    JESSIE

                    I'm not clapping my hands

                              PRIEST
                    No one will make you clap
                    your hands

                              JESSIE
                    And I'm not jumping for
                    the joy of Jesus either!

                              PRIEST
                    Freedom of expression is
                    a beautiful thing

                              JESSIE
                    And no way will I be
                    speaking in tongues of
                    a spasticated nature!

                              PRIEST
                    Freedom of speech is also
                    a beautiful thing

Jessie looks scared.

                              OFFICER
                    Come on now, out you get

He sheepishly leaves the cell.
The priest leads the way.

                         POLICE OFFICER
                    Seize the day!

Jessie doesn't know whether that was a
sarcastic comment or something else entirely.
Either way, they leave the police station.

                EXT. FARM, TEXAS, DAY

The farmer walks up the lane with Shep.

Smoke can be seen to come from the field,
albeit not as thick as it was yesterday.

They get to the gate, but the farmer doesn't open it because of the gross smell of dead carcass causing him to cough, covering his mouth and nose.

                    JIM
     It can wait 'til tomorrow

He tells Shep.

They walk back down the lane.

The farmer heads straight for his workshop/shed, gets hold of an axe and chops up wood.

EXT. URQUHART CASTLE, LOCH NESS, SCOTLAND, DAY

SCENE 5: FORCES ARE ALWAYS AT WORK FOR A REASON

Urquhart Castle is a well-known ruin in the foreground of Loch Ness. It's such a sunny Sunday morning and picture perfect weather for a church service. The priest has since been granted the right to take his service outside, in and around the castle.

Jessie sits at the back of the service, straight-faced and pensive.

The priest stands on a pulpit, about to deliver the word of God. He has shiny, medium in length hair, greying yet groomed. And a world-worn fire in his baby blue eyes as he stands tall at 6'2".

The village of Lochend has a small population of fifty. Each have been encouraged to become Christians. Indeed, well over half the village are in attendance this morning.

                    PRIEST
     'This revelation is the death
     of ignorance, tangled in a state
     of suffocation, slave to self-

righteousness, damnation is on
your lips'

The priest reads off a piece of paper resting
against the pulpit. His accent is not a
typical Scottish twang and yet there is some
of it in his voice. Mostly he speaks his own
way, which comes across as confident, not to
mention strong of mind and of will.

His appearance, while altogether godly, looks
as it should and good for his age of fifty —
he is certainly not fat.

> PRIEST
'From sorrow to serenity,
the truth is absolution,
from sorrow to serenity,
it's on your head
> PRIEST CONT'D
This is my last serenade,
I feel you as you fall away,
This is my last serenade,
from yourself you can't run away'

He continues to read it, without pausing so
not to make eye-contact with the churchgoers
just yet.

> PRIEST
'It's your choice, point the
finger but it's on your head,
your destination is a choice
within yourself, will you rise. . . '

The priest is abrupt to stop such a reading
and all of a sudden screws the piece of paper
up, chucking it over his head.

> PRIEST
If, and it's a bloody big if
at that! But if one of you were
to write, let's say, something
from your heart whether it be
a pretty little poem or a
short story maybe, about your

transformation, from non-believer
to believer and beyond! And you
wanted it to come from me. And
then when I read it out loud,
I'd suddenly see something in
it that struck a nerve with what
I believe. . . if that happened, do
you think I would stop? Do you
think, in my right mind I would
go so far as screw your work up
and throw your work away? Do you?
Or would I finish what I started
and in doing so show my respect
to the writer, the writer who
pours his or her heart onto the
page and for what? For you to
listen! Last night at the Loch Inn,
it was his word and the band's song
               PRIEST CONT'D
against your ignorance!

The priest appears passionate and determined
in order to make his feelings known, while
Jessie watches on from the back.

                   PRIEST
Jessie is his name — maybe if
his appearance was a spitting
image of — oh I don't know,
Jesus Christ? Maybe then would
you have stayed put? I bet the
vast majority of you took one
look at the band and made up
your mind there and then!

The priest makes the sign of the cross with
his fingers as if to say 'stay away from me,'
making a point.

                   PRIEST
Before the lyrics were sung,
before the music was played,
and before the message could
even be received! Sacrilege
springs to mind

MATTHEW BROOKES

The priest takes a sip of water from a glass
positioned beneath the pulpit.

                    PRIEST
    'Do not judge, or you too will
    be judged. For in the same way
    you judge others, you will be
    judged, and with the measure you
    use, it will be measured on you.'
    Last night, after all was said
    and done, and I lay in bed and
    my thoughts raced, yes I was
    restless! Restless as to what
    I could do today to have an
    effect on you all at once? Well
    here we are: Urquhart Castle
    certainly is a setting to be
                    PRIEST CONT'D
    reckoned with; without the remnants
    of history we are but what exactly?
    These remains represent time
    marching on and can you really
    live with yourself for being
    left behind? I'm talking about
    the outdated mind-set, such a
    subtle little thing as sense!
    Yes, of course the common kind!
    And yet to be blinded by, I
    don't know what it was, so
    compelling' bringing you to
    a 'better judgement' that would
    otherwise suit a stupid deadbeat.
    But you, Lewis, yes you, and you
    Ruby, even you too Lexi! Please, I'd
    rather not name and shame the roomful
    of wrongdoers last night that I saw
    before me. Leave, because
    ignorance is bliss. Jessie is not
    here to make peace, he's here
    for a reason beyond wrongdoing

The priest puts both hands onto the pulpit,
briefly leaning and looking down in order for
the gathering of his thoughts, then springs
himself back up straight.

He stands down from the pulpit.

> PRIEST
> Take a walk with me

The priest starts to walk through the middle of Lochend's seated Christians, stops, turns around and faces Jessie.

> PRIEST
> Come. Let us stroll
> along the loch

Jessie watches as everyone returns to their feet, following the priest.

EXT. THE LOCH NESS, SCOTLAND, DAY

The sun has gone in and clouds have gathered. The day is changing into a grey and gloomy morning, making the loch look dark and evermore mysterious. It's still, peaceful almost, but for the gathering together of Lochend and Jessie as well.

The priest stops at the shallow surface of the Loch Ness. Suddenly he bends down and undoes his shoelaces, taking his shoes and socks off before unceremoniously rolling his trousers up to his knees.

He walks into the lake. The people of Lochend stand in wait, with Jessie just displaying a look of complete and utter bewilderment.

The priest turns to face them all.

> PRIEST
> Jessie, join me. . . these waters
> are your way out. Out of the
> depths of despair, spring to
> eternal life!

Jessie steps past the people of Lochend and into the plain sight of the priest.

                    JESSIE
What is the meaning of all this?

                    PRIEST
'I am the way, the truth and
the life!'

Jessie looks around him. All watch and wait
with baited breath.

                    PRIEST CONT'D
Tell me Jessie,
are you happy??

Jessie's actions speak louder than his words
ever will. He bends down, unties his shoes,
takes them off and rolls his trousers up to
his knees. He enters the loch, walking up to
the priest as it begins to rain.

                    JESSIE
No

                    PRIEST
Deep down, how do you feel?

                    JESSIE
 Lost. . .

The priest nods knowingly.

                    JESSIE CONT'D
Otherwise, I just flap my
wings as you do — but try as
I might to fly like the chosen
few, well, you know the rest

                    PRIEST
Tell me

                    JESSIE
It's not fun anymore feeling
this way. My days as a, hah,
headless chicken, need to end

                    JESSIE CONT'D

and I mean now

The priest can't help but break into a subtle
smile before regaining his serious approach.

> PRIEST
> Keep flapping those wings
> cos it's those who stop
> flapping that freefall all the
> way down into the dark confines,
> finding themselves lost — so
> loathing themselves sick! It is
> they that have given up hope,
>> PRIEST CONT'D
> perish first in mind and then
> of their shattered dream remains
> a meaningless shell - lusting
> after the life of others, as a
> soulless little leech!

> JESSIE
> Father, I feel dead inside

> PRIEST
> 'I am the resurrection and the
> life. He who believes in me will
> live, even though he dies'

Jessie is showing his emotions as he stands
face to face with the priest.

The rain falls heavily onto them; therefore
some of Lochend retreat to a position of
shelter and warmth, while others seem
mesmerized by it all.

> PRIEST
> Do you want to change your
> life — for the better, for
> the greater good . . . of God?

Jessie glances into the eyes of the priest,
then down at the rain hitting the lake's
surface. His mascara from the night before
runs down his face. He nods slowly but surely.

MATTHEW BROOKES

                    PRIEST
        Look into my eyes, Jessie

He looks back into the priest's eyes as the
rain pours down his face.

                    PRIEST
        'Bow down, not to me,
        you know who I mean. Now
        bow down in the name of
        feeling the need'

The priest puts his hand on Jessie's shoulder
and lowers him to his knees.

Thunder sounds loud and clear, piercing the
bleak sky.

                    PRIEST
        Now repeat after me:
        'Don't ask why, I'm dying
        to live the truth is inside'

                    JESSIE
        Don't ask why, I'm dying to
        live the truth is inside

                    PRIEST
        'Day by nightfall, light my
        way with your soul'

                    JESSIE
        Day by nightfall, light my
        way with your soul

All of a sudden, the priest dunks Jessie under
the Loch Ness surface.

Lightning in the distance strikes once, fast
and furious.

The priest brings Jessie back up from under
the water.

The rain stops pouring.

He's struggling to catch his breath back.

> PRIEST
> Amen

Jessie continues to breathe heavily; he has dilated pupils as well as a white face.

> PRIEST
> Jessie. . .

His lips are turning blue. He has lost all colour in his cheeks.

Suddenly Jessie stops breathing, collapsing onto the priest who catches his fall.

> PRIEST
> CALL AN AMBULANCE!

The priest lifts Jessie over his shoulder and stumbles out of the lake, laying him onto the grass.

> PRIEST
> He's ice cold for Christ's sake

Taking off his holy attire he covers Jessie, as most of Lochend stand in shock.

Coincidently, an ambulance siren rings out in the distance.

Shockingly, the speeding ambulance drives right past them on the nearest stretch of road.

The priest picks Jessie up and struggles over to his car, where one of the Lochend residents helps out as Jessie is put in the passenger seat.

He speeds off after the ambulance.

EXT. CAR CHASE, LOCHEND, SCOTLAND, DAY

The ambulance slows up upon entering a farm. The priest is right behind, beeping and shouting out in desperation.

The ambulance stops at the front of the farmhouse as a hysterical lady runs up to it in a flood of tears, screaming.

EXT. FARMHOUSE, LOCHEND, SCOTLAND, DAY

The priest slams on his brakes, stopping the car right behind the ambulance.

Two paramedics calm her, or at least try to.

The priest jumps out of his car, hurries round to the passenger side and opens the door. He lifts Jessie out and walks towards the ambulance carrying him.

                    PRIEST
    HELP! HELP! PLEASE!

The paramedics are following the hysterical lady, yet stop in the wake of the priest's desperate outcry.

The priest falls to his knees, resting Jessie down on the ground.

One paramedic rushes over to him, while the other is taken around to the back of the farmhouse by the hysterical lady.

Jessie's eyes are closed, his face a worse shade of white, with his lips still blue.

                    PARAMEDIC
Where the hell's he been?
He's ice cold

The priest watches on in shock and horror, realising his surrounds suddenly.

                    PRIEST
    We were in shallow waters,

238

not at all deep

PARAMEDIC
We need to get him in the
ambulance

They gently lift him into the back of the
ambulance.

The other paramedic dashes into the back of
the ambulance, grabs a defibrillator then runs
towards where the hysterical lady stands in
shock.

PARAMEDIC
You need to wait outside

The paramedic slams the back of the ambulance
doors shut.

The priest takes a moment to register just
what the hell is happening here.

He hears the hysterical lady produce an awful
loud yelp in the distance, so goes around the
back of the farmhouse.

The other paramedic can be seen to give
everything he's got trying to send a
lifesaving shock to the system of a motionless
man.

Nothing doing, only the rain and that which
has been done in vain - the man is showing no
sign of life.

The hysterical lady has her hands on her head,
desperately looking down at the paramedic
crouching over her husband, doing his best to
save a life.

The priest slowly walks up to the sorry scene
and as he does so, the paramedic looks up at
the saddened lady.

PARAMEDIC

MATTHEW BROOKES

I'm sorry, he's gone

The priest shakes his head. The lady bends down and begins shaking her husband in a furious fashion.

                          ANGELA
        PETER?! PETER PLEASE!!
        WAKE UP. WAKE UP! PETER?
        PETER!

                          PRIEST
        Angela. . . Angela

The priest knows her.

The lady named ANGELA, holds onto her husband for dear life.

The paramedic gets up.

                          PARAMEDIC
        He was struck by lightning,
        God willing it to be,
        a bolt out of the blue — but
        why?

                          PRIEST
        You're asking me why accidents
        just so happen to happen?

                          PARAMEDIC
        'Accidents?' Sorry, I don't
        mean to undermine your words
        or anything but aren't you
        contradicting the duty you
        do by calling this
        accidental?

                          PRIEST
        God works in mysterious ways.
        That's all I know

                          PARAMEDIC

240

Well, Father, your boss sure is

                    PARAMEDIC
     sick

The priest doesn't know what to say, so says absolutely nothing.

A deathly silence ensues.

Suddenly, a roar of outrage from inside the ambulance, so the paramedic quickly makes his way back, closely followed by the priest, leaving Angela to cry her heart out over her dead husband.

The paramedic opens the back of the ambulance.

Jessie is being violently held down by the other paramedic, who struggles to strap him into the bed. It takes two of them to do it after an almighty scream and struggle from an unrecognisable-looking Jessie, all pale and wild-eyed.

He is sedated until his struggle subsides and the screaming stops.

The paramedics deal with the dead man now, much to the dismay of Angela. They lift him onto a stretcher and then place him into the ambulance alongside the sedated Jessie.

                    ANGELA
     DON'T LEAVE ME PETER!
     I'M COMING WITH YOU!

Angela forces her way into the back of the ambulance, but the paramedics carefully force the issue — she is not allowed in.

The priest watches on and then approaches her; she is a mess.

                    PRIEST
     I will follow the ambulance.

Let's go

Angela looks at the priest with evil eyes, as resentment towards religion reigns supreme. And not to mention anguish as she says nothing, getting in the passenger seat.

The ambulance speeds away with its siren ringing, followed closely behind by the priest and Angela.

SCENE 6: WELCOME TO LIMBO

The farmer parks his pickup truck in a space. His dog Shep jumps out the back of it.

INT. (JOB CENTRE) TEXAS WORKFORCE COMMISSION, TOWN, TEXAS, DAY

The farmer and Shep enter the job centre, greeted by a weedy-looking security guard.

SECURITY GUARD
I'm sorry, you can't bring your dog into this building

JIM
I'm not leaving him out in the cold

SECURITY GUARD
Haven't you got a car you can leave it in?

JIM
I'm not walking all the way back to my pickup truck cos I will miss my appointment

SECURITY GUARD
What time is your appointment?

JIM
At 12 noon

SECURITY GUARD

>   The only thing I can do is
>   inform my superior

A smartly dressed, somewhat attractive woman
in her forties approaches the dispute.

>   CINDY
>   Excuse me gentlemen, but what
>   seems to be the problem?

>   SECURITY GUARD
>   Can't you see? He's got a dog

Cindy bends down in front of the security
guard and pets Shep.

>   CINDY
>   I got a dog too, not as cute as
>   you though, that's for sure.
>   There's a good boy . . . you don't
>   want a 'big bad' security guard
>   to throw you out into the cold
>   do you? Oh no you don't!

The woman descends into cringeworthy baby
talk while she rubs Shep's belly. The dog
lies on his back and all four paws are bent
into the air.

>   CINDY
>   What's his name?

>   JIM
>   Shep

>   CINDY
>   And yours?

>   JIM
>   Jim, miss

>   CINDY
>   It's Cindy Sedgeway,
>   we spoke on the phone.
>   You're my 12 o'clock -
>   come to my office. As for

your friend, he can tag
along too

                    JIM
Thanks Miss Sedgeway

                    CINDY
Call me Cindy

               SECURITY GUARD
Cindy. . .

                    CINDY
Don't you Cindy me!

               SECURITY GUARD
Don't you dare undermine
my authority!

                    CINDY
Marty, I rejected you a month ago
 . . . get over it. Jim, if you'd like
to follow me please

The security guard shrinks with embarrassment.

Cindy leads Jim and Shep into her office.

INT, OFFICE, JOB CENTRE, TEXAS, DAY

                    CINDY
Have a seat. Not you Shep

                    JIM
Shep, lay down

Shep lays down near the corner of her office,
next to a big green plant.

                    CINDY
So, how long have you been
unemployed?

                    JIM
A day

> CINDY
> Ok, and what did you used to
> do?

> JIM
> I am a. . . err . . . I was a farmer

> CINDY
> For how long?

> JIM
> All my life

> CINDY
> So what happened?

Jim hesitates slightly.

> JIM
> I guess I just got bored of
> doing the same thing day in
> day out

> CINDY
> Well, welcome to the world
> of work!

> JIM
> You have no idea lady!
> I mean Cindy

> CINDY
> Anyway what do you want to
> do for a living, Jim?

Jim's face is expressionless as his mind goes
blank.

> JIM
> I don't know

                    CINDY
Was there anything in
particular, before farming . . .
something that interested you?

                    JIM
No not really

                    CINDY
And how old are you?

                    JIM
60

Cindy smiles, albeit politely.

                    CINDY
Jim, you should already
be aware, we meet today for
an initial liaison only

                    JIM
What about my benefit
entitlement?

                    CINDY
Next time, Jim, next time
that will all be dealt
with

                    JIM
I think it would be better
to sort that out now

                    CINDY
No. We operate within a very
strict system, Jim — I'm sure
you can understand that

                    JIM
So when do I see you again?

                    CINDY
Well, it won't be me you see

                    JIM

Why not?

                    CINDY
I only deal with the first
timers

                    JIM

Oh

Cindy smiles as she then begins to type away
on her computer.

                    CINDY
So I can book you in to see
Katrina Atkinson on Tuesday
at 10am

                    JIM

Ok

                    CINDY

Great!

She then types away on her computer to print
out an appointment sheet.

                    CINDY
Do you have any questions?

Jim seems depleted.

                    JIM

No

                    CINDY
Then that will be all for
today. Sorry about Marty

                    JIM

Marty?

                         CINDY
     Marty, the sorry excuse for
     a security guard. Poor guy
     spilt his guts to me and
     then expected the world!
     Well, let's just say he was
     left feeling disappointed
     and dissatisfied by my reaction
     or rejection in other words!

                          JIM
     So. . .

Cindy jumps in and interrupts.

                         CINDY
     I mean, come on! 'Cindy Sedgeway'
     ain't touching no man in pity!
     Let alone a nobody by the name of
     'who-cares-cos-I-don't!' Stupid
     pig-dog! No offence, Shep

Jim is disinterested and just wants to get the
hell out of there.

He stands up.
                          JIM
     Well thanks for that.
     Tuesday at 10 then

                         CINDY
     Don't be late!

                          JIM
     Good day

                         CINDY
     You too

Jim and Shep leave the building.

                    EXT. TOWN, TEXAS, DAY

A woman around Jim's age approaches him from
behind.

                    NANCY
     Well hello stranger

She has straightened blonde hair and big blue
eyes, she is just about average in height. Her
figure — hourglass - is so very easy on the
eye for the majority at least to behold her
attractive   appearance.   She   looks   smartly
dressed and yet not at all in a conservative
respect, but for the red dress with white
polka dots she wears it well, albeit a bit
naughtily. She must be wearing a push-up bra
and her bursting at the seams chest presents
itself as such an epic cleavage! Her white and
gold cowboy boots go without saying!

                    JIM
     Afternoon, Nancy

He tries not to look down at her 'proud body'.

                    NANCY
     What brings you out into town
     on a Sunday? Certainly not
     church, or were you hiding
     from me? I didn't see you
     there

                    JIM
     Food shopping. Nothing
     special. Shep was there,
     he's gonna fill me in with
     all the gory details on our
     way home

                    NANCY
     Huh?

                    JIM
     'Godly details'

Nancy still looks confused.

                    JIM
     Never mind

                    NANCY
     I know what you're thinking,
     Jim

                         JIM
     Do you?

                    NANCY
     Yes — 'she shouldn't be revealing
     all like that! And revelling in
     her glory, surely not at church!'

                         JIM
     You're a big girl Nancy, you . . .

                    NANCY
     Excuse me?

                         JIM
     Um I mean, um . . .

Nancy cheekily grins.

                    NANCY
     I'm screwing with you!

                         JIM
     Well, you can wear whatever
     the hell you want, that's
     what I meant

                    NANCY
     Oh I will! And for good reason!
     It's a test. I stand slap bang
     at the front for the priest
     to take a peek if he should so
     see fit!

                         JIM
     Tempting him? Hmm . . .   why?

                    NANCY
     I'm spending my spare time on
     his honest word and I want to

know just how honest it is
with the love of God in mind,
and not my 'glorified funbags'
as it were

Jim is amused and ever so slightly shocked
into a subtle bit of embarrassment at Nancy's
shameless expense. He's speechless.

                    JIM
    And does he ever, err. . .
    you know

                    NANCY
    No, he doesn't, not once has
    his eyes wandered. And yet,
    your eager eyes. . . I'm up
    here sweetie, not down there

Nancy winks. Jim blushes.

                    NANCY CONT'D
    Anyway, where are your
    groceries?

                    JIM
    My groceries?

                    NANCY
    Yes, Jim, you just said
    you'd been food shopping

                    JIM
    Oh my groceries! Yes.
    I left it all in the
    pickup truck

                    NANCY
    Right you are. Where are
    you headed?

                    JIM
    Home

                    NANCY

Where have you been?

                    JIM
Food shopping!

                    NANCY
I meant after that. Since
your shopping is in your
truck and you're right here -
where did you go, sugar?

She asks as he stands right behind the job
centre.

                    JIM

    Nowhere

Nancy glances at the job centre, bringing
about a concerned wince on her face.

                    NANCY
What's wrong?

                    JIM

Nothing

                    NANCY
Something's wrong

                    JIM
No, it's not!

Nancy bends down to pet Shep, playfully asking
the dog to kindly tell her what's wrong with
Jim.

                    NANCY
Well, Shep seems to think
your sad and all alone

                    JIM
Really? He told you that
did he?

                    NANCY

He didn't have to. I can
see it in your eyes

                    JIM

What?

                    NANCY

Sorrow

Jim's smile is a false one underneath his
spick and span vintage cowboy hat. He ever so
slightly lowers his head.

                    NANCY
I know you, Jim. Come
for a coffee

                    JIM

I can't

                    NANCY

Why not?

                    JIM

I got work to do

                    NANCY
On a Sunday, day of rest?

                    JIM
Not all of us rest today
y'know

                    NANCY
Well, you know what they say
about all work and no play

                    JIM

Nancy, I'm fine

                    NANCY
You don't look it

The farmer rests his hands onto his knees,
slouching so to humour his dog.

                    JIM
   Shep, how do I look?

Shep licks his stubbly face.
Nancy smiles.

                    NANCY
   What are you doing tonight?

Jim stands up straight, takes his cowboy hat
off and runs his fingers through his scruffy
receding hairline.

                    JIM
   I'm washing what's left of
   my hair

                    NANCY
   Good. You'll need to be
   at your best

                    JIM
   Oh, and why's that?

                    NANCY
   Pick me up at 8

                    JIM
   But…

                    NANCY
   No buts! It's a date

                    JIM
   Nancy. . . I…

                    NANCY
   Jim, I'd love to stop and
   chat but I got shops to
   drop, dresses to kill. . .

Nancy walks away with a cheeky look on her
beautiful face.

                    NANCY
    Make sure you shave for
    Me, boy!

Jim looks at Shep then shakes his head.

                    JIM
    Women!

Shep barks.

They walk back to his pickup truck.

INT. FREEDOM FIELDS HOSPITAL, WAITING ROOM, SCOTLAND, DAY

The waiting room is empty but for Angela and the priest.

He's reading the Bible, but Angela has other ideas — she suddenly grabs it out of his hand and throws it across the room.

Silence (as opposed to golden) is otherwise so very awkward.

                    PRIEST
    You're looking quite tanned
    and dare I say it - radiant

The priest tries as he might to break the silence with an untimely compliment.

                    ANGELA
    Well, that's Cor-fucking-fu
    for ya! I TOLD HIM TO
    LEAVE THE LUGGAGE ALONE!
    MEN NEVER LISTEN!

                    PRIEST
    Pardon?

The priest makes Angela laugh.

A member of staff from the hospital opens the door.

                    HOSPITAL STAFF
     Is everything ok in here?

                    PRIEST
     Yes

                    ANGELA
     NO! MY HUSBAND WAS STRUCK
     DEAD BY LIGHTNING! EVERYTHING
     IS NOT OK — FUCK YOU VERY MUCH!

The member of staff, from peeking her head in has now well and truly left them to it.

Another awkward silence prevails.

The priest feels the need to break it.

                    PRIEST
     I think it's time to call
     your son

The member of staff returns with a box of tissues.

She approaches Angela — bad idea! Handing her the box, she backhand slaps the tissues across the room and then bursts into tears. The priest gets up, retrieves the tissues and does the rest.

                    HOSPITAL STAFF
     If there's anything I can do

                    ANGELA
     You can leave me the hell alone -
     NOW!

The priest acknowledges the member of staff - she leaves.

                    PRIEST
        Your son needs to know,
        and you need your son, so
        give him a call

                    ANGELA
        I left my phone at home

The priest pulls out his mobile phone and
hands it to her.

He leaves the waiting room to give her
privacy.

INT. FREEDOM FIELDS HOSPITAL, CORRIDOR, DAY

A doctor approaches the priest.

                    DOCTOR
        Excuse me, are you associated
        with a Jessie Smith?

                    PRIEST
        Yes. How's he doing?

                    DOCTOR
        He's stable but before we
        can carry out further tests
        his mobile phone needs
        safe hands, so here

The doctor gives the priest Jessie's phone.

                    DOCTOR
        We think that was the reason
        as to why when we were carrying
        out our first set of tests. . .
        well, let's just say the results
        were far out of this world

                    PRIEST
        What makes you say that?

                           DOCTOR
        I've already said enough, Father

                           PRIEST
        So your reason being, as far as
        I can tell from your words, is an
        electrical interference caused
        something of an insufficient test
        result, right?

                           DOCTOR
        That's right, I think. Excuse me

The   doctor   rushes   down   the   corridor   and
disappears from the priest's sight.

He holds Jessie's mobile phone in one hand and
rubs the back of his neck with the other.

The priest goes outside the hospital entrance
so as to get some fresh air, followed by a
cigarette.

EXT. FREEDOM FIELDS HOSPITAL ENTRANCE, SCOTLAND, DAY

He's deep in thought, cigarette in one hand
and the mobile phone in the other.

The   priest   takes   a   lasting   drag   of   his
cigarette then stubs it out.

He looks at the phone screen, scrolls down
Jessie's list of contacts, getting to 'Dad'
and presses the green button.

INT. FARMHOUSE, TEXAS, DAY

Jim is listening to the radio in his kitchen.

Johnny Cash — Ring of Fire

He's lost in the song, upon preparing himself
something strong to drink.

Ring, ring,

Ring, ring

The telephone begins ringing. It snaps Jim out of the music, just as he cuts a lime in half. He loses concentration and slices his finger.

Ring, ring

Ring, ring

Jim runs cold water over his bleeding finger and grabs a kitchen towel on the way to answering the phone in a huff and a puff.

                    JIM
     Hello

                    PRIEST
     Hello, who am I speaking to?

                    JIM
     Who are you speaking to?
     You called me!

                    PRIEST
     Yes

                    JIM
     So who the hell am I speaking
     to?

                    PRIEST
     I am Father Clyde McCreed,
     priest at the church in
     Lochend, Scotland

                    JIM
     Scotland? This is Texas

                    PRIEST
     Is it?

                    JIM

How did you get my number?

> PRIEST
> Sir, your son. . . he's had an
> attack

Jim listens in disbelief, while watching blood
run down his finger.

> PRIEST
> Sir, are you still there?
> Jessie is stable but doctors
> are doing tests as we speak

> JIM
> Jessie has been attacked?
> By who?

> PRIEST
> No sir, no one has hurt your son

> JIM
> So why is he being seen to by
> Doctors, for Christ sake?

> PRIEST
> Calm down

> JIM
> Where is he?

> PRIEST
> We're at the hospital

> JIM
> What hospital? Where?

> PRIEST
> Freedom Fields, Scotland

The phone goes dead on the priest's side - Jim
hung up on him.

EXT. FREEDOM FIELDS HOSPITAL ENTRANCE, DAY

Angela walks out of the hospital entrance towards the priest.

                    PRIEST
    Did you get hold of him?

The priest is referring to her son.

                    ANGELA
    He's on his way. Here,
    these are yours. . .

She opens her arms as she holds his mobile phone and Bible.

The priest takes his phone from her hand, but doesn't take his bible from her other hand.

                    PRIEST
    You need it now more than
    ever

Angela lets out a big gulp.

                    ANGELA
    Take me home

The priest puts his arm around Angela as they walk back to his car.

EXT. NANCY'S HOUSE, TEXAS, NIGHT

SCENE 7: INTO THE UNKNOWN

Jim skids to a stop outside of Nancy's house. He jumps out of his pickup truck. Shep jumps out from the back.

He presses Nancy's button on her door.

Ding dong

The door soon opens.

                    NANCY
    Jim?! You're early

                    JIM
     Am I?

                    NANCY
     Very! Three's a crowd and
     you didn't even shave!
     Naughty boy

                    JIM
     Nancy. . .

                    NANCY
     For God's sake, come in!
     It's cold outside

                    JIM
     Shep, in - now

Shep runs inside Nancy's house — she raises
her immaculately trimmed eyebrows as she
smiles at Jim giving him a mischievous look of
love.

Jim remains rooted.

                    NANCY
     Seriously, it's freezing
     Jim!

                    JIM
     I have to go away for a while

Nancy's shock soon turns into bitter
disappointment.

                    NANCY
     What are you talking about?

                    JIM
     I gotta go, sorry

Her heart sinks.

                    NANCY
     Oh, so your gonna leave your

        dog with me while you go
        gallivanting at the drop of
        a hat

She is confused and upset. So she grabs his
cowboy hat, throws it on the floor and then
stamps on it.

                    JIM
        It's not for you to know

                    NANCY
        No, it's not! It's for me to
        find out but by then it
        will be too late, you'll be
        dead in a ditch and I'll be
        left to pick up the pieces. . .
        cos I care!

                    JIM
        Nancy, please

                    NANCY
        Shit, Jim! She's gone man!
        Gone!

                    JIM
        Who?

                    NANCY
        Who? WHO?! Your wife!

                    JIM
        This has absolutely nothing
        to do with her — nothing

Nancy shakes her head.

Jim picks his cowboy hat up and dusts it off
before putting it back on his head.

                    NANCY
        I knew there was something
        wrong. Why can't you just

be honest with me?

Jim rubs his forehead; he feels aggrieved and distraught.

                    NANCY
     Jim? Jim, I'm sorry for
     jumping to the wrong
     conclusion. . . it's just . . .

                    JIM
     Just what?

                    NANCY
     Well, Wendy, she. . .

                    JIM
     Don't even say her name!

Nancy has forgotten all about the cold and feels worried for Jim.

She breathes a huge sigh of saddened discontent.

                    NANCY
     What's going on, Jim?

                    JIM
     I'm going to see my son

                    NANCY
     Oh, why now?

                    JIM
     Well, why not now?

                    NANCY
     We had plans and now this?
     There's something that you're
     not telling me

                    JIM
     Because you don't need to know

                    NANCY

I wanna know! Jesus Christ,
Jim. We've been friends for
nearly twenty years!

                    JIM
And that's all we'll ever be

                    NANCY
Why can't you just let her go?
Goddamn it, Jim - move on!

Jim closes his eyes as he takes a deep breath.

                    JIM
Will you look after Shep?

                    NANCY

Why should I?

                    JIM
We're friends, Nancy

                    NANCY

Are we?

                    JIM

Yes!

                    NANCY
So where is he? Your son

                    JIM

 Scotland

                    NANCY

Scotland?

                    JIM
Look, if I don't leave now
I will miss my flight

                    NANCY
When do you get back?

                    JIM

I don't know

                    NANCY
What's going on, Jim?

                         JIM
I DON'T KNOW!
I gotta go

He gives her a hug she can hardly feel.

Jim jumps back into his pickup truck and speeds off.

                    NANCY
BE CAREFUL!

He's gone.

ACT 2: THE TRUTH WILL SET YOU FREE

INT. AIRPLANE, NIGHT

Jim is sat at a window seat on an airplane taking him to Scotland. Looking out the window, he stares at the dark orange sky while all around are different cloud arrangements sending him to sleep.

EXT. MALTESE SEA, MALTA, DAY

THE PAST

Jim is underwater. The sea is turquoise clear. He brushes past the last of the coral reef before feeling the need to rise up to the surface, passing fish of all shapes, sizes and of course, colours.

He hits the surface.

The boat is in his sights so he repositions himself and then dives underneath the surface once more.

The fish are an endless vision of wonder for his widened eyes as he swims mid-depth towards the boat.

Then, sensing his position near the boat, he swims towards the surface, soon seeing the bottom of the boat that is underwater.

Jim comes up from under the surface as he swims back to the boat.

No sign of his wife. The boat is not the biggest, so it doesn't take long for him to realise she's still out at sea.

He looks at his watch. It's ten past five. Jim begins to worry because he knows too well what his wife is like, especially where keeping time is concerned.

Jim sits on the edge of his seat at the back of the boat, anticipating the imminent return of his wife. He watches the sea's surface, sensing every single bit of movement from all around the boat.

It gets to 5:45pm and still his wife is yet to return. Jim does not know what to do. He waits with baited breath. The sun is beginning to set in the distance. It's beautiful. But Jim feels nothing without his wife to share such a wondrous sight with.

At 6:15pm, Jim has his head in his hands as the sea darkens from turquoise to a deeper shade of blue. There is a sudden chill in the air.

Jim jumps up. Pacing up and down the boat, getting more desperate by the millisecond, he feels the need to shout at the top of his voice.

                    JIM
     WENDY! WENDY!

INT. AIRPLANE, NIGHT

                    JIM
       WENDY!

Jim comes out of his dream and back to reality screaming 'WENDY' to the other passengers' dismay and confusion.

He's realised his surrounds and feels the need to have privacy so rushes to the toilet.

INT. AIRPLANE TOILET, NIGHT

Jim turns on the tap, puts his hat down, wets his hands and splashes his face. He looks at himself in the mirror, staring at the ring on his finger. He goes to take it off then hesitates. His expression says it all — blank - frankly he looks like a ghost, empty of life's fullness. He keeps the ring on his finger, grabs his hat and exits the toilet.

INT. AIRPLANE, NIGHT

Jim returns to his seat. The captain announces that the airplane will land at Scotland/Inverness airport in an hour.

INT. FARMHOUSE, LOCHEND, SCOTLAND, NIGHT

Angela and the priest are sat at her kitchen table eating dinner.

ANGELA

Thank you

PRIEST

What for?

ANGELA

Being there

PRIEST
That's what friends are for

ANGELA
Peter's funeral; will you
help me make arrangements?

PRIEST
Yes of course, so will your
son

ANGELA
So who was that man you were
trying to help? Is he ok?

PRIEST

His name is Jessie. He… err…

Ding dong

Angela leaps up and answers the door to Daniel, her son. She bursts into tears as he embraces her.

She leads him through to the kitchen and the priest stands up.

>   PRIEST
> Daniel! Look at you

>   DANIEL
> Hello, Father McCreed

>   PRIEST
> Call me Clyde, for Christ's
> sake!

Daniel politely breaks into a forced smile while looking gently into his mother's eyes.

>   DANIEL
> You have a healthy glow

She smiles lovingly at her son and wipes her tears away with her sleeve.

>   ANGELA
> A holiday in the sun, Daniel,
> will do wonders for your
> complexion! Anyway, your
> journey here — how was it?

>   DANIEL
> Ok, considering

>   ANGELA
> Are you hungry?

>   DANIEL
> No, not at all

>   PRIEST

Well, I'll leave you two to it

                    ANGELA
Don't be silly - stay

                    PRIEST
No, really, I have to go

                    ANGELA
Daniel, please! Stop standing
like a lemon and go make
yourself at home. Come on

                ANGELA CONT'D
Clyde, let me show you out

The priest shakes Daniel's hand.

                    PRIEST
You heard the lady. Good
to see ya again Daniel

Daniel nods as he smiles, showing no teeth.

                    PRIEST
You'll be ok

                    DANIEL
Thanks

Angela leads the priest to the front door.
She opens it for him. He steps out and turns
around.

                    PRIEST
I am always available.
Let me know when you're ready

                    ANGELA
I will

                    PRIEST
From my experience it's for
the best that this takes care

of itself sooner rather than
later

                    ANGELA
I understand

                    PRIEST
I am so sorry for your loss

                    ANGELA
All's fair in love and war,
right?

                    PRIEST
That's the spirit

                    ANGELA
Night, Clyde

                    PRIEST
Goodnight

EXT. PRIEST'S CAR, LOCHEND, SCOTLAND, NIGHT

The priest gets into his car, starts the
engine and drives off.

INT. THE LOCH INN, LOCHEND, SCOTLAND, NIGHT

The priest enters the pub. It's almost empty,
apart from an old man sat at the bar.

                    FRANK
Evening, Father

                    PRIEST
Frank, can I get a
glass of something
strong

                    FRANK
Coming right up

The priest leans on the bar, far from the old
man.

                    OLD MAN
    Trouble in paradise?

The old man opens his mouth while it's still
half wrapped around his pint of ale.

                    PRIEST
    It's none of your business

                    OLD MAN
    Just making conversation

Frank hands the priest a glass of 'something
strong'.

                    FRANK
    Everything ok, Clyde?

                    PRIEST
    I'm not one to pass gossip,
    but I appreciate your concern
    nonetheless

The old man downs the last of his drink and
belches loud and clear before leaving without
saying goodbye.

                    FRANK
    Can't you go easy on the old
    man . . . he's slowing down and I
    think he could be on his
    last legs

The priest stares down the glass of his drink
and doesn't say a word for a while.

                    PRIEST
    It's cold out there

                    FRANK
    Is it?

                    PRIEST
    Sure is

                    FRANK

Smoke in here then

                    PRIEST
That's not why I said it

                    FRANK
Well, regardless, it's all good

The priest starts to smoke a cigarette. Frank
puts down an ash tray at the bar.

                    PRIEST
Busy day?

                    FRANK
No, slow-going

                    PRIEST
What did you think of the
band? Drugs aside

                    FRANK
Drugs aside, I think they knew
what they were doing

                    PRIEST
Yep

The priest downs his drink, smokes the last of
his cigarette then lets out a lasting sigh.

                    FRANK
I know how you feel

                    PRIEST
Well, I'm glad somebody does!
Thanks, Frank

The priest walks out of the pub.

                    FRANK
Take care, Clyde

          INT. AIRPORT, SCOTLAND, NIGHT

SCENE 8: AN ARRIVAL TO ANSWER FOR

Jim walks through the airport, without having with him any luggage or belongings. He's in a hurry. But it's a busy place to be; people everywhere.

EXT. AIRPORT, SCOTLAND, NIGHT

He approaches a parked taxi. The taxi driver winds down his window.

TAXI DRIVER
What can I do you for cowboy?

The taxi driver appears chubby in the face, accentuated by his great big bald and very round head. He speaks somewhat with a Scottish twang and yet there is such an endearingly lovely 'like no other' aura about the way in which his words are spoken.

JIM
Freedom Fields Hospital, Lochend

TAXI DRIVER
Get in

Jim gets in the taxi. It speeds away.

INT. TAXI, SCOTLAND, NIGHT

Radio playing 'I'll stand by you — The Pretenders'

TAXI DRIVER
So where have you come from?

Jim is distant, staring out the passenger side window into darkness.

JIM

Texas

TAXI DRIVER
Texas! What's a Texan doing

in Scotland?

The bald driver keeps his beady eyes on the
road.

                    JIM
It's personal

                 TAXI DRIVER
Sure it is — so who's the lucky
lady?

He makes a basic, ignorant assumption.

                    JIM
Lucky lady?

                 TAXI DRIVER
Oh, come on man! I may drive
a taxi for a living but I'm
not stupid so don't treat me
like I'm some kind of fool

Jim doesn't respond and instead stares out of
his side window.

                 TAXI DRIVER
Oh. OH! It's like that is
it?

                    JIM
Like what?

Jim doesn't know what the taxi driver is
talking about, brandishing a look of confusion
under his cowboy hat.

                 TAXI DRIVER
I've seen it all before,
nothing surprises me anymore
— you're gay - big deal. Don't
hide under a hat. You should
be proud of who you are,
you're not the only one

The driver's hand moves swiftly from being on the gearstick to softly clenching Jim's knee.

Jim looks down at his knee being held and then eyeballs the driver.

                    JIM
    Who are you calling queer?

The taxi driver removes his hand from the customer's knee while looking at him. Jim is seething, though his eyes are darkened underneath his hat.

                    TAXI DRIVER
    I was just trying to. . .

                    JIM
    Cop a feel? Faggot. Don't
    you touch me again —
    understood?

                    TAXI DRIVER
    Yeah, sure - sorry

A very awkward silence as the song on the radio ends, so the taxi drivers first instinct is to turn the radio up a bit. Big mistake!

'Village People — YMCA' plays on the radio.

The silence between them both continues as a camp song kills them softly.

                    TAXI DRIVER
    Ahem. Do you want me to change
    Stations, sir?

                    JIM
    What I want is for you to do
    your damn job, just drive

                    TAXI DRIVER
    Fine

Another silence, as the YMCA song still plays loud and clear.

Jim turns the radio off.

There is such an uncomfortable silence lasting for what feels like a lifetime.

Jim then takes his hat off and puts it on his lap.

                    JIM
    I'm not a homophobe

                         TAXI DRIVER
    Ok

                         JIM
    Sorry for calling you
    a. . . ahem . . .

                         TAXI DRIVER
    'Faggot'. I get it all the time!

The taxi driver feels the need to make light of it all.

                         JIM
    I'm just not used to being
    'manhandled' like that,
    that's all

                         TAXI DRIVER
    It was just a 'knee-jerk'
    reaction, no big deal

A bearable silence is restored between them both.

                         TAXI DRIVER
    But you are a homophobe by
    the way

                         JIM
    Hah. And what makes you say
    that?

                         TAXI DRIVER

You don't say you're not a
homophobe because you're not
a homophobe. You say you're
not a homophobe because you
are a homophobe but because
I'm not your friend and we're
not talking like a couple of
guys do down the local. Look,
listen, in my taxi we tell the
truth — there is no time for
'polite white lies' just so
you can save face

                    JIM
Hey, you said it was no big deal

                    TAXI DRIVER
I did and it's not. Honesty
is the best policy

                    JIM
I agree

                    TAXI DRIVER
Good

Another bearable silence has been restored.

                    JIM
It's not that I. . . I don't
have a 'fear' of your kind

                    TAXI DRIVER
'My kind?'

                    JIM
Ok, queers, is that better?

                    TAXI DRIVER
Not really. You have a very
clear aversion in any case
towards what you think
'queers' stand for

                    JIM
You're right, I do dislike it.

279

Let's say you had it your way
and the whole world turned
'gay', or in other words against
'God' . . . depending on one's state
of mind. Then we can forget about
the future, that's for sure. And
depending this time on your sense
of humour, maybe you could quite
easily see yourself speaking like
the camp kind does; as for me I
wouldn't be able to stomach my own
words without throwing up

          TAXI DRIVER
It's just love man, and love,
love doesn't die a horrible death
if two men wanna 'do the dirty'.
You can't choose who you are

          JIM
But you can change

The taxi driver laughs as a way of coming to
terms with what Jim just said and it was not a
natural laugh at that.

          TAXI DRIVER
Change? I wouldn't have it
any other way

          JIM
Man and woman. Woman and
man. That's the way it is

          TAXI DRIVER
Says who? You? God? Don't
tell me, you're religious,
right

          JIM
Wrong

          TAXI DRIVER
Any unresolved 'incident' that I
sure as hell should not know about
but because I can do a pretty damn

280

convincing shrink impression, perhaps
you feel compelled to reveal all?

                    JIM
Hah, I have no history of being
abused by my late father thank
you very much!

                  TAXI DRIVER
Just checking

                    JIM
It was one of the few things
he said that stuck, and he
was a man of few words was my
father. Think it was when, well,
all I remember being, amongst
other things, was young and
reckless — those were the days.
Anyway, you come of age so fast,
as soon as he said it in fact,
I felt something strange take
place. Maybe you know what I mean
when you gain insight but at the
peril of a pearl of wisdom came
an end to the good thing innocence
was, lost and then found, by my
father

                  TAXI DRIVER
Well, what did he say?

                    JIM
'Be who you are and say
what you feel always, because
those who DO mind don't matter,
but those who matter most don't
mind at all'

                  TAXI DRIVER
My father was a no good
drunk coward and a colossal
loser who took his hate out
on anyone and I mean anyone;
nothing mattered to him,

nothing but beer or more beer. Not one word of wisdom, many a broken promise. Goes without saying; my mother, Lord have mercy, she did what she had to do and I don't blame her for, what became of my father, after all was said and done

> JIM
> Don't worry, I won't ask

> TAXI DRIVER
> Thanks. Sorry

Silence is not golden. In this case, it's something else entirely.

> TAXI DRIVER
> 'Merrily, merrily, merrily, merrily life is but a dream'

> JIM
> A bad dream

> TAXI DRIVER
> And then, when your dream becomes so unbearably bad do you know what happens?

> JIM
> Yes. You wake up

> TAXI DRIVER
> But do you? Do you really? Because snapping out of the 'same shit different day' takes breaking a great big bad habit. Such a sick creature comfort to feel 'hard done by' but by who do you feel aggrieved? God? Government? Get to know what 'your beef' means — that's

the difference between letting
yourself have a bad dream become
you, as a person of pain and
suffering from the pas

                    JIM
It was a long flight. The last
thing I need now is a long
drive if you know what I mean -
no offence

                TAXI DRIVER
Pop open the glove compartment

Jim opens up the glove compartment.

                TAXI DRIVER
There should be a CD in
there somewhere

He finds the cd and gets it out of the glove
compartment.

                TAXI DRIVER
    Put it on

Jim inserts the music CD into the cars cd
player.

Johnny Cash — A Boy Named Sue

                TAXI DRIVER
I love songs that tell a
Story, y'know

                    JIM
Yep. My boy's in a band

                TAXI DRIVER
Oh yeah? What does he play?

                    JIM
He's the singer

                TAXI DRIVER

Interesting, what do they
sound like?

                    JIM
I don't know — never heard
them play

                    TAXI DRIVER
Oh, ok - shame

The taxi driver pulls into Freedom Fields
Hospital.

                    TAXI DRIVER
Well here we are — Freedom
Fields Hospital — that'll
be thirty pounds please

                    JIM
Do you take dollars?

                    TAXI DRIVER
Is that all you got?

                    JIM
Yep

                    TAXI DRIVER
Fine. Fifty dollars will do it

Jim fingers through his wallet, gets out fifty
dollars and gives it to the taxi driver.

                    TAXI DRIVER
Have a good night

                    JIM
Thanks

The taxi driver drives off into the dark
distance.

INT. FREEDOM FIELDS HOSPITAL, LOCHEND, SCOTLAND, NIGHT

Jim walks straight up to reception.

                    JIM
     Excuse me, my name is Jim
     Smith. My son, Jessie, he's here

                    RECEPTIONIST
     I'm sorry, Mr Smith, your son
     is no longer with us

His shock can be seen on his horrified face.

                    RECEPTIONIST CONT'D
     He's been transferred to
     Fly In The Sky psychiatric
     hospital

                    JIM
     Well, how do I get there?

                    RECEPTIONIST
     A 'Father Clyde McCreed'
     said he would drive you
     to see your son. In fact,
     Clyde is sat in the waiting
     Room, just over there

The pretty receptionist points towards where
the waiting room is.

INT. WAITING ROOM, FREEDOM FIELDS HOSPITAL, NIGHT

Jim opens the door and enters the empty
waiting room.

The priest is fast asleep.

He walks up to him. The Bible rests open on
his knees. Jim gently shakes the priest but to
no avail.

Still he sleeps as his head droops.

So Jim lifts the priest's head up with a fistful of his hair, and with the other hand wraps it around his neck, cutting off his circulation.

The priest lets out a frantic cough for breath.

Jim goes over to the water dispenser, pouring him a plastic cup of cold water. He hands it to him.

The priest accepts, necking it down in one big gulp.

                    JIM
     Can you take me to my son?

                    PRIEST
     Mr Smith. . . first impressions
     sure do vary! Visiting hours
     for Fly In The Sky start at
     12noon and finish at 8pm.
     I'm sorry, you'll just have
     to wait 'til then

Jim's anguish is clear to see, but he's also very tired and the priest picks up on this.

                PRIEST CONT'D
     Where are you staying?

                    JIM
     I don't know

                    PRIEST
     Come with me. I know a
     place, it's a pub

                    JIM
     What about my son?

                    PRIEST
     Tomorrow I will take you
     to see your son. Tonight,
     get some rest. Let's go

The priest and Jim exit the hospital entrance.

INT. PRIEST'S CAR, LOCHEND, SCOTLAND, NIGHT

They get into the priest's modest car.

                    PRIEST
     So how was your flight?

                    JIM

     Long

The priest starts his car and drives out of
the hospital car park.

                    JIM
     Do I look queer to you?

He asks somewhat way out of the blue, to a
priest of all people!

The priest raises his eyebrows as he turns to
face Jim, and then casually places his point
of view back onto the dark road ahead.

                    PRIEST
     You look like a cowboy

                    JIM
     But not a queer cowboy

                    PRIEST
     I. . . my 'gaydar' doesn't
     work

                    JIM
     So you think it's possible
     then that I could quite
     easily be queer?

                    PRIEST
     Anything is possible but that's
     not my point

                        JIM
        Well, what is your point?

                        PRIEST
        I don't know! Why are we even
        having this conversation?

                        JIM
        Sorry, some chat-happy piece
        of shit taxi driver gave me
        more than his fair share of
        it to deal with! Without doubt
        the damn man misjudged me from
        my appearance alone

The priest nods as he pulls into The Loch Inn.

                        PRIEST
        Appearances deceive even the
        most perceptive of us — it's
        human nature to get it all
        horribly wrong once in a while

                        JIM
        Yeah, well, some people need to
        rein it the hell in, don't they?

                        PRIEST
        They do indeed

                        JIM
        Is this it?

                        PRIEST
        It is sure enough, not
        paradise. . .

                        JIM
        Apparently paradise is a state
        of mind

                        PRIEST
        I think therefore I am and all
        that jazz

The priest turns off the ignition.

                    JIM
Well, I'll be damned on the day
I find myself swimming in an
endless bliss of 'self-satisfied
mindfulness'

                    PRIEST
Mindfulness?

                    JIM
It's just junk mail they keep
on sending me; 'guaranteed
peace of mind in one week or
your money back'

They get out of the car, entering The Loch
Inn.

INT. THE LOCH INN, SCOTLAND, NIGHT

The pub is empty apart from Frank, the
landlord.

                    PRIEST
I've brought you some much
needed business! This
is Jim Smith — he needs a
place to stay

                    FRANK
Ok

                    JIM
Do you take dollars?

                    FRANK
Dollars? This is Scotland
man!

                    PRIEST
Leave it to me. I got

this, Mr Smith

                    JIM
Are you sure?

                    PRIEST
Yes. So what do you drink?

                    JIM
Scotch on the rocks

                    PRIEST
You heard the man and
I'll have my usual please

Frank quickly gets to it, excited to be
serving for once.

                    PRIEST CONT'D
Let's sit

The priest leads Jim to a seating area, away
from the bar.

They sit down opposite each other.

Jim takes his cowboy hat off.

                    JIM
I want to know what happened
to my son now

Frank comes over with a couple of drinks, as
well as an ash tray for the priest.

                    PRIEST
Thanks, Frank

                    FRANK
Always a pleasure

He goes back behind the bar.

The priest takes a pronounced sip of his
drink.

Jim leaves his whiskey as he waits for an answer.

The priest takes a cigarette out of his pack and lights up.

                    PRIEST
     The truth is, Mr Smith

                    JIM
     It's Jim

                    PRIEST
     Jim, in all my years as a
     Man of God, what happened
     to your son was strange
     to say the least

                    JIM
     So what happened?

Jim sips his whiskey for comfort's sake.

                    PRIEST
     Well, Jessie is something of
     a lost soul. While he was
     scheduled to perform in his band,
     and this was last night, I caught
     him using an illegal substance

                    JIM
     What was it?

                    PRIEST
     Cocaine

                    JIM
     Ok, continue

                    PRIEST
     He spent the night at the
     police station and come
     the morning after, your

son went to church with me

                    JIM
You took my son to church?

                    PRIEST
Like I said, Jessie seemed
to be displaying all the
obvious signs of a lost
soul, searching for something

                    JIM
Searching for what?

The priest takes a last drag of his cigarette
then puts it out in the ash tray.

                    PRIEST
Do you believe in God?

Jim sips his whiskey.

                    JIM
I believed in love once

The priest notices the ring on Jim's finger.

                    PRIEST
What happened?

Jim, from being tense, opens up. But of course
downs his drink first.

                    JIM
Wendy, my wife from
childhood sweethearts
who had it all and now,
well, we are not
together anymore

                    PRIEST
Divorce?

                    JIM
She got lost at sea, a
long time ago

                    PRIEST
Oh

                        JIM
And yet it still feels like
yesterday my wife was waking
up on her side of the bed and
giving me a great big kiss good
morning

                    PRIEST
Jim, I'm sorry for your loss

                    PRIEST CONT'D
I, huh, how can I possibly
react to that other than
respond by giving you my
sincerest condolences. 'Sorry'
seems to be the only way we
can say what we can't at all
feel

                        JIM
Oh, woe is me and my hard
done, deadbeat by the wayside,
sorry excuse for a life. I
'exist' not even having a
reason to go on anymore

                    PRIEST
You have your son, and your
soul

                        JIM
I dug a hole in the ground
and laid my life as I know
it not to rest; it died
of disease

                    PRIEST
Disease?

                        JIM
My farm. My home, my life!

Of Godforsaken carcass

                    PRIEST
Jim, I'm not sure you're making
sense

Jim laughs as a matter of fact. To make his
feelings known instead of finding the right
words, his expression says it all.

                    JIM
Disease. Does that 'make sense'
to you?

The priest falls silent.

                    JIM
And now this! As if things weren't
bad enough, fucking shit happens
just for the hell of it!

                    PRIEST
There may be a bit more to
it than that which we realise
is just so very beyond us all.
We don't know what will come
after the calm, but before
the storm

                    JIM
What are you talking about?

                    PRIEST
I'm talking about now! No, it's
not enough for every heart to
beat because of God's greatest
gift

                    JIM
What's God got to do with it?

                    PRIEST
Everything! And that's regardless
of belief because it's all

happening, according to the one
and only plan that made us possible

                    JIM
Well, with or without God, I got
nothing to show for sixty years
hard graft

                    PRIEST
Yet you're here, from whence
Jessie was baptized and then. . .

                    JIM
You baptized my son?

                    PRIEST
Indeed I did

                    JIM
I need another drink

                    PRIEST
FRANK — same again

                    FRANK
Coming right up

Jim looks lost for words.

                    JIM
So you baptized my son.
Fine . . . then what happened?

                    PRIEST
My sentiments exactly!
Your son went white like
limbo. Lips as blue as can
be, he lost all life, fell
unconscious and I caught
him. From the cold light
of day your son went stone
cold and I don't know why

The priest shakes his head in disbelief of his
strange retelling.

Frank brings them both another drink and then leaves them to it.

>   PRIEST CONT'D
>   It was as if his soul left
>   him

Jim downs his drink in one.

>   JIM
>   I thought that once your soul
>   leaves your body, you're nothing
>   but dead meat

>   PRIEST
>   His spirit, Jim. . . it kept
>   him here. I got him to an
>   ambulance — suddenly he woke up,
>   but he woke up screaming

>   JIM
>   In pain?

>   PRIEST
>   No

>   JIM
>   Well, why was he screaming?

>   PRIEST
>   I don't know. I was made to
>   wait outside while the
>   paramedics restrained him.
>   It's difficult to know
>   what brought about your sons
>   screaming, amongst all else.
>   So staying in a psychiatric
>   hospital will do him no harm

>   JIM
>   My son is not mentally ill

Ring, ring, ring

Ring, ring, ring

It's Jessie's mobile phone going off inside
the priest's pocket. He takes it out and looks
at the screen, reading 'Home calling'.

The priest offers it to Jim who initially
looks confused.

                    PRIEST
     It's Jessie's phone

Jim takes the phone from him.

                     JIM
     Hello?

                    CALLER
     Hello, who's this?

The voice is young, troubled and womanly.

                     JIM
     Jim Smith

                    CALLER
     Oh, are you related to Jessie?
     He's my boyfriend — do you know
     where he is? It's just I was
     expecting him home ages ago

                     JIM
     Jessie is my son. He's
     staying in a psychiatric
     hospital tonight

                    CALLER
     A what?

Jim looks stumped at what to say.

The priest senses this and offers his hand in
order to carry on the conversation — so he
gives him the phone.

                    PRIEST
     Hello

                         CALLER
        Who's this?

                         PRIEST
        I was watching Jessie's
        band play last night. I
        am a priest here — he's
        ok

                         CALLER
        So why is he in a loony
        bin then?

                         PRIEST
        Jessie is in safe hands

                         CALLER
        Give me the address

She sounds concerned.

                         PRIEST
        Certainly; Fly In The Sky
        Psychiatric Hospital, Lochend,
        Scotland

                         CALLER
        I will be there first thing in
        the morning

                         PRIEST
        Visiting hours start at 12noon

                         CALLER
        I'm his girlfriend, for God's sake

                         PRIEST
        Come to The Loch Inn,
        it's in Lochend, and then
        you can go with his father

                         CALLER
        Fine. I want to know what
        happened

                    PRIEST
    I will tell you tomorrow
    when you get here

                    CALLER
    Is it serious?

                    PRIEST
    He's stable

                    CALLER
    That could mean anything!

                    PRIEST
    I'm not a doctor

                    CALLER
    But you're sure he's 'stable'

                    PRIEST
    Positive. Try not to worry

                    CALLER
    Well, until tomorrow

                    PRIEST
    Pray for him

                    CALLER
    Bye

The priest terminates the call and then gives
Jim his son's phone.

                    PRIEST
    Jim, things don't just happen
    for no apparent reason. Destiny
    doesn't dance all over the place
    like a godforsaken drunk, does it?

                    JIM
    What do you mean?

                    PRIEST
    I mean we are already predetermined

bodies of flesh and bone born in order
to do well for ourselves, so why not go
one step further? Here we are, struggling
until it gets better or stays the same.
I'm talking about the one thing that we
need for our future to even exist. . .
with 'hope' there is vision and we breed
dreams from it. But without hope all hell
would break loose, so what's the use of
life from having hope, if for fear we
choose only to acknowledge the idea of
a future, therefore never really achieve
the true reality of it! That will require
our wholehearted hopefulness, so much so
that that hope you or me felt hellbent to
have evolved and became something else
entirely. . . eternity, to the extent of

                    PRIEST CONT'D
exceeding even our own wildest dreams.
I'm talking about transcendence,
'somewhere over the rainbow,'
beyond body, mind and above all else,
soul

                    JIM
Well, when I lost Wendy, I lost
Heart. Hell, I lost it all

                    PRIEST
It's better to have loved and
lost than not to have loved
at all

Jim lifts his eyebrows as he lets out a forced
laugh of nothing but bitterness.

                    PRIEST CONT'D
It's built into us — somehow we
are hardwired survivalists!
Man's most basic instinct is
an animal's whole life! We share
our woe, which is this struggle
for survival, with love as an
answer to the one and only question
in the world worth knowing —
WHY — ARE — WE - HERE?

RAGE AGAINST THE GAME

                    FRANK
    Because of Eve

The priest bursts into laughter from across
the table, banging his hands on the table
because of his fit of kneejerk ecstasy.

                    PRIEST
    Oh, despair for a woman and
    her wrongdoing

                    JIM
    We can't live with them and
    we can't live without them

                    PRIEST
    But it begs such a question
    then, why did she do it?

                    FRANK
    The serpent played a devilish
    trick on poor old Eve

                    PRIEST
    'Poor old Eve' gave the serpent
    her every fibre of being
    because she got bored of Adam

                    FRANK
    Maybe Adam didn't have a very big
    thingumajig!

The priest and Jim make eye contact while
laughing in light of Frank's spoken
contemplation.

                    PRIEST
    Imagine that! The fall from grace
    thanks to an 'underwhelming willy'

                    JIM
    And because of Eve's lust
    after everything and more. . .
    are all women hungry for their
    next fix of fruitfulness?

                    301

                         PRIEST
Maybe Eve felt threatened, being
in the perfection of paradise.
She saw Adam as a force to be
reckoned with, the first of her
perfect kind — competition?
One-upmanship?

                         FRANK
Well, that's women for ya - always
making things worse! Surely God
had a good idea of what he was
getting himself into

                         PRIEST
Trouble in paradise!

                         JIM
Well on the contrary, Wendy used
to love her garden down to the
ground and root of all plants,
flowers, the grass — these things
just grow out of nowhere!

                         PRIEST
Woman came from man and man's need to
have his wicked way with himself!
From woman comes the means to a
man's end!

                         FRANK
HELL YEAH! YOU'RE ON FIRE!

                         PRIEST
Frank, thanks for that but you
haven't even begun to be made fully
aware of my fire from within, even
after all these years

                         FRANK
Is that a threat?

                         PRIEST
It's fighting talk!

                    FRANK
    And for all these years here's
    me thinking that you were a lover
    of life

                    PRIEST
    I fight for the love of life with
    every breath I take; the same goes
    without saying, in every move I make.
    I make sure there is reason in my right
    mind and a fire from my heart's restless
    longing, burning until all has been put
    out of its misery — set free - made good

                    JIM
    But we are only human and like you
    Said, it's in our nature to get things
    wrong — right?

                    PRIEST
    We could go on for forever and
    a day, yet to what end does our
    curious questioning get us . . .
    closer or further from the truth?
    The redeeming feature of our
    fair lady, Eve, from being led
    astray to the make-believe of a
    brave new world where women give
    birth to a brighter tomorrow

                    JIM
    I'd drink to that, but I don't
    have a drink to drink to it!

Frank, with enthusiasm, rings the pub bell
loud and clear for 'last orders'.

                    PRIEST
    I'm tired

                    JIM
    One more for the road

                    PRIEST
    Why not!

They both stand and go to the bar.

                    FRANK
     Same again?

                    PRIEST
     Same again!

Frank gets the pair a drink each and then
makes himself one as well.

The priest raises his glass.

                    PRIEST
     To Jessie, may he make a
     full recovery

                    JIM
     Cheers

                    FRANK
     And to women — may they make
     us sweat with the magic, keep
     us guessing with the games they
     play, yet at the end of the day
     do us no harm but good old fashioned
     fun-loving

Jim downs his drink in one and the priest does
the same, so too the bartender/owner.

                    PRIEST
     Until tomorrow — I will be
     here at half past 11

                    JIM
     Ok

The priest outstretches his arm for Jim to
shake his hand and he does.

The priest leaves The Loch Inn and goes home.

Jim makes sure Frank knows he wants to go
upstairs to his room. Frank shows Jim to his
room.

SCENE 9: THE PAST CATCHES UP WITH US ALL

EXT. CHURCH GROUNDS, LOCHEND, DAY

The priest puts a bouquet of flowers down on his parents' grave; they are buried right next to one another. He looks down at them, resting in peace, showing his respect.

Leaving the church grounds, he sees Angela and Daniel walking the dog up the lane. His walking is brisk as he catches up to them.

EXT. A NARROW LANE, LOCHEND, DAY

PRIEST

Good morning

ANGELA

Morning

PRIEST

Hello, Willow! Who's a
good girl?

The priest bends down and pets the sheepdog.

ANGELA

To be carefree . . . she doesn't even
know how good she's got it

PRIEST

It is instinctual, albeit a
total lack of self-awareness,
which of course separates us
from them, yet it is also
so very ironic, don't you
think?

DANIEL

Why ironic?

PRIEST

'To be or not to be. . . that
is the question'

Daniel looks confused.

> ANGELA
> Remember the blue goose. . .

Daniel smiles by both his mouth but more so with his eyes as he thinks back to a forgotten time — childhood.

> DANIEL
> Yes

> PRIEST
> Blue goose?

> ANGELA
> Go on, Daniel

> DANIEL
> 'The blue goose has not got
> any need whatsoever, for even
> no good would a bathe do but
> waste time trying to make
> itself white. Therefore, neither
> need you do anything at all,
> only be yourself'

> PRIEST
> Well said, Daniel

Angela smiles at her son and then brings herself back to the here and now.

> ANGELA
> We were up late last night
> talking about what we want
> for Peter's funeral

The three of them (and Willow) continue to walk down the lane.

> ANGELA CONT'D
> Daniel will say a few words
> first and foremost, won't
> you, Daniel?

306

                    DANIEL
      Yes, mum

                    PRIEST
      And so you should

He glances at Daniel, who is holding Willow on
her lead.

                    ANGELA
      After the service, everyone
      will be welcome back to mine
      for food and drinks
      and reminiscing

                    PRIEST
      Yes. So have you thought about
      a day for the funeral?

                    ANGELA
      No time like the present,
      so how about tomorrow?

                    PRIEST
      Ok. Yes, sure. Tomorrow
      it is

                    ANGELA
      I've taken the week off
      work. School will just
      have to survive with a
      supply teacher

                    PRIEST
      It goes without saying your
      work commitment comes second
      to your private life

                    ANGELA
      Of course

                    PRIEST
      Daniel, will you be prepared
      for tomorrow?

                    DANIEL
I don't think anything will
prepare me for the passing
of my father, not even heaven,
and yet, that being said
I do know what I want to
          DANIEL CONT'D
say so, yeah — you know
how it is

Daniel looks like a lovely lad. He's dressed
well for his age (mid-twenties) and speaks
clearly from within — somewhere which is a
passionate, thoughtful place of wisdom beyond
his years.

                    PRIEST
That's grand. And you're
sure tomorrow won't be too
soon

                    ANGELA
No, not at all. Like you
said, the sooner the better

                    PRIEST
Well, that's alright then.
Now if you'll excuse me,
I have everything to do!

                    DANIEL
Bye, Clyde

                    PRIEST
Good day, Daniel

                    ANGELA
Take care, Clyde

                    PRIEST
See you soon

So the priest strolls further on down the
lane, leaving them to walk Willow in peace. He
sees the old man (a regular in The Loch Inn)
leaving his home.

The old man is struggling to lock his front door. The priest walks past, seeing him struggle. He thinks back to what Frank had said to him about the old man being on his 'last legs' so the priest turns around and approaches him.

PRIEST
Here, allow me

The old man has one last try before finally giving up. He steps aside and so the priest takes the initiative to lock his door for him.

The priest politely smiles, showing no teeth, then goes to walk away.

OLD MAN
When are you going to
practise what you preach?

He stops, turns his head to the side and considers the old man's words while he gets his pack of smokes out. Taking one and then lighting it with a match, he drops the match and then proceeds to answer back as he walks slowly but surely towards him again.

PRIEST
You think you're the thorn
in my side, don't you,
through the tired eyes of
an old man and his bitter
heart. Hah, has age given you
any idea yet to what it takes
for the righteous task of
fellowship, between man and his
sinful force of habit

The priest lets something strong off his chest, such words sound like they have come from way down deep.

                    PRIEST CONT'D
Because such a piercing stare
taken the wrong way will kill a
better man than me — I'm not
blind to your belligerence, Stuart,
I just tolerate it out of the purist
pity. My God old man, when are you
going to get a life?

                    OLD MAN
I've had my fun and now when
nearly all has been done,
only by words does an old man
like me see the light. I can't
journey where the rest of the
world goes, searching for truth!
The answer is always, always
within one's sorry shell, so
maybe you're right; either I find
myself some peace of mind and
in doing so stop the rot
towards darkness, suffering
for what? Other people's lot?
What of money and possessions
anyway! We all go without it
in the end, don't we, Father!

                    PRIEST
That we do, Stuart, that we
do indeed

                    OLD MAN
Pride before the fall,
for love, after all.
Clyde, I beg of you: do
the right thing

The priest squints into the old man's eyes,
seeing the unseen silence inside the windows
of his soul, leaving him feeling like a child
torn between right and wrong for the first
time in his life.

He goes to take another drag from his
cigarette but it's since gone out.

The old man searches his pocket, pulls out a
lighter and lights the priest's cigarette,
shielding the flame from an oncoming wind.

He inhales long and hard, before blowing smoke
into the old man's face.

> OLD MAN
> The years just fly by, Clyde,
> and that used to only happen
> when life was good. But now,
> it doesn't matter whether
> you're having a bad day or
> simply the best. . . time goes
> so fast! Talk about being
> out of touch. I might as well
> be out of this world, let alone
> gone from Lochend's land

The old man makes sure he has the priest's
undivided attention, speaking in an honest
respect.

> OLD MAN CONT'D
> And I don't want to die a sad,
> haggard, angry, repulsive,
> soulless son of a bitch!

The priest drops his cigarette onto the old
man's path and then stamps it out.

> PRIEST
> Blood will always be thicker
> than the dirtied water your
> words are running from; much
> ado about your dry river of
> bitter disappointment, Stuart.
> What are you trying to say anyway?

> OLD MAN
> Your brother's last act in this
> so-called life I was there when
> he. . .

MATTHEW BROOKES

The old man can't continue his sentence so
instead just shakes his head in cold
disrepute.

                    PRIEST
    Leave my brother where he
    belongs, resting in peace
    beyond the lies, deception
    and wrong of the world

                    OLD MAN
    You saw what you wanted to
    see in him

                    PRIEST
    I saw a shit-scared old man
    on his stupid little boat,
    letting life just pass by
    because of nothing better
    to do

                    OLD MAN
    You thought you could change
    him from being a bad man into
    a do-gooder, didn't you?

                    PRIEST
    I always knew there was
    something wrong with you.
    You're not right, Stuart

                    OLD MAN
    Not right about what?

                    PRIEST
    The way you choose to live
    your life — we feel for you

                    OLD MAN
    Who's 'we'?

                    PRIEST
    Who do you think? Lochend
    collectively weep tears of
    all things sad and unjust
                    PRIEST

312

Stuart, we feel let down by
your lack of life. We all feel
like your just waiting to die

The old man takes a moment to swallow what the
priest said and it chokes him up.

                    PRIEST CONT'D
The drink. The drugs.
It's a recipe for the
wrath of wrongdoing and at
your age, hey! You don't need
me to talk you up the road
of self-righteousness, as
opposed to the path that
you're rolling down

                    OLD MAN
Well, I'll admit to abusing
these surrounds so I could
quite easily score cocaine
when I wanted it but that was
a long time ago

                    PRIEST
Ok, you listen to me. We fell
from grace because of our
rebellious, disobedient,
torn and oh-so-curious is
such a thing as this. . .
self-aggrandising, sick
and tired, restless streak we
leave in the wake of our
spirited disposition!
And now, we all live in the
aftermath of fucking sin and
for what?

                    OLD MAN
Surely you haven't lost sight
of what it's all about

                    PRIEST
What's it all about old man?

313

Enlighten me

                OLD MAN
Come on, Clyde! Get with it!
Children are the only future
we will ever have to look back
on. When they are old and we
are dead and then the magic
happens for them instead of
us — that's the circle of life!

                PRIEST
I know too well what it is,
so don't go make-believing
birth into being a revelation
of life. It's life. It's not
rocket science, Stuart

                OLD MAN
It's too early for all this -
excuse me

The old man wants to walk away, yet the priest
puts his arm out, stopping him.

                PRIEST
Let me finish. Because of
'freewill' we have to put
up with the great big shit
leftover from man's basic
instinct: to procreate time
and time again and then . . .

                OLD MAN
I think you should leave me
out of your religious rants

The old man stops to do up his coat. It's cold
outside.

                OLD MAN CONT'D
Save these speeches for
your churchgoers, those who

are reborn in order to give a
damn about these certain
concepts

                    PRIEST
Concepts?

                    OLD MAN
Yes — society, community,
'togetherness' is a good one!
In our 'brave new world'
of money and meaningless sex!
There's something that we reap,
from being red-blooded and it's
the right to die

                    PRIEST
To die trying. Trying to
make the world a better place,
Stuart

                    OLD MAN
Trying to redeem being born
in the first place. Just because
of sin — it's a sick joke.
But I thank God my darling
is somewhere else — she's
so much better for it, at
least that's what I hope,
a place of peace, paradise.
Yes, please let it be there.
Oh, while here we are! 'The
land of the living' and yet,
 with every breath we take, we
give that little extra back,
laughing at life for want of
a better way to get through the
day. Crazy as a sane man in a
mad world!

                    PRIEST
So you do still think of her. . .
well, why not wonder what the
hell her eyes see when she

looks down on you now!

The old man shakes his head disgusted, looking
down to the ground.

                    PRIEST CONT'D
How much longer are you
willing to waste? When
you begrudge God, you're holding
him accountable because of
your ignorance, Stuart!

                    OLD MAN
My ignorance?

                    PRIEST
Ignorance because of the
unknown. We all feel the same,
man! Me, you and everyone
on Earth — this is not the
new world we would love it
to be, of brave heart and
of beautiful mind . . . why else
is my soul so restless?
Stuart, what will become
of one won't be merely luck!
Love or fear, or you can carry
on killing them both, but all
the booze and drugs really do,
you know as well as my word.
As a much better man than
me once said: 'In the end, it's
not the years in your life that
count. It's the life in your
years'

                    OLD MAN
I sure as hell have my hate.
You got God on your side and
yet still, look at us -
sniping opinions, sinking our

teeth into what exactly? Because
deep down we are all alone and
without the love of a good
woman. Well, what's the point?

                    PRIEST
You'd be surprised by my
creature comfort for Christ.
Because before I felt comfortable
being in the body of discipline,
lusting after the same old damsels
distressing in spite of feeling
'lost and all alone.' Oh sure, Stuart,
it seemed good enough for me.
'Desire' reigns supreme, we
are all aware of why we
act like monkeys sometimes,
pigs the next, then suddenly
we proclaim a life-affirming
moment of magic just by the
way her words spoke of love
but at the same time moved
you to tears! It is indeed
contradictory, it is certainly
crazy, and yes, I do read an
awful lot of romance! Amongst
other things

                    OLD MAN
We are, at best, our own worst
enemy - meticulous creatures
with a tragic, condemned
need to be better than everyone
else

                    PRIEST
'Survival of the fittest' is
ingrained and yet not set in
stone. When nature reigned over
me, it flooded desire — I found
                PRIEST CONT'D
myself well and truly 'reborn'
in the right light of life

                    OLD MAN
Clyde, do you have a vision

317

of Lochend? Down the line I
mean, when things change

                    PRIEST
Our future is certain to
change, just let death have
its say yet always, always
make sure you're the one who
has the last laugh

                    OLD MAN
You're not standing on your
pulpit today, Clyde. Give
me a real answer or get off
of my property

                    PRIEST
The future of Lochend depends
on one thing and one thing only
. . . the people. It is the people
we have here who want what I want -
to live in a place lest we forget God!

                    OLD MAN
If Jesus was the truth, the whole
truth and nothing but the truth -
then your word of God, of our
Saviour's Father, from the highest
horse's mouth there is, so to speak
like you do despite the deepest
secret kept dead in the water;
that truth you talk the talk of
feels fishy. Yet it's still almost
at ease because of a power your
position is possessing. So cool,
calm and calculated, Clyde. And
then I take a closer look into
those screwed up eyes of yours

The old man shakes his head and stares so very
deep into the priest's eyes as he continues.

                    OLD MAN
This is not truth, this is
not the way to go — no! Not
until Lochend is made aware

of what lies beneath!

                    PRIEST
We will sow our seeds and we
will reap plentifully from it!

                    OLD MAN
You're not listening to me!

                    PRIEST
Why should I listen? When you're
drunk, you don't wanna know.
When you're sober, there's such a
great big chip on your shoulder
Stuart, it takes the edge off of
your otherwise 'wise words'

                    OLD MAN
Lochend deserves the truth -
if all else fails, let them
have that at least to fall
back on when the end comes

                    PRIEST
The end?

                    OLD MAN
The end of your priesthood

The priest grins menacingly, looking through
Stuart.

                    PRIEST
My people of our church are
'temperamental' to strong
Words, Stuart

                    OLD MAN
And what makes you think I
can handle all of this,
this misplaced passion?

                    PRIEST
Simply because you are far
from being a 'happy clappy'

319

person in your ways of
'finding God'

                    OLD MAN
You haven't let me 'find
God' in fifteen years, yet you
preach the fine art of
forgiveness as if by black
magic!

                    PRIEST
It was because of you, Stuart,
that my brother is dead

                    OLD MAN
I don't have to stand for
this. This is my private
property — it's time you
went on your way

The priest nods accepting of the old man's
wishes.

                    PRIEST
You never even confessed,
you just let the past
stagnate. Rot. Not to mention
when you're drunk, coked up,
prevailing sin in your
very own wicked company you
keep behind closed doors.
You're ashamed of yourself,
Stuart, and so you should be!

                    OLD MAN
If you don't get the hell
out of here right now, I
will call the police

                    PRIEST
I have said all I have to
say, Stuart. Tomorrow will
be Peter's funeral. If you

know what's good for you,
you'll stay away

                    OLD MAN
Hah, I heard how he died.
God had it in for him, huh?
Hmm, I wonder why

The old man's words stink of sarcasm from
somewhere within that is crying out to be
heard. And where the truth hides, passion
remains . . . remains to be seen . . .
remains to be freed.

The priest says nothing in response.

                    OLD MAN
Give Angela my condolences

The priest turns around and walks back down
the lane. The old man stands rooted to the
spot, watching him disappear into the
distance.

INT. THE LOCH INN, DAY

SCENE 10: THE POWER OF FORLORN LOVE

MARY-JANE enters The Loch Inn with a bag on
her back and a baby bump on her belly. She has
short dark hair, bright eyes and a petite
frame. Her clothes are plain and she has not
made an effort to dress up for an occasion
such as this.

                    FRANK
Can I help you?

He cleans a glass with a dirty cloth.

                    MARY-JANE
Yes, I was speaking to a
priest last night. I am
meant to be meeting him
here

                              FRANK
      He'll be here very soon.
      Can I get you something
      to drink?

                    MARY-JANE
      No, thanks

                              FRANK
      It's on the house.

                    MARY-JANE
      No really, I'm fine

Jim walks into the bar from being upstairs.

                              FRANK
      Morning, Jim

                        JIM
      Morning

Jim makes eye contact with Mary-Jane. He knows
who she is instantly, yet the baby bump comes
as a nice surprise.

                    MARY-JANE
      I'm here for Jessie

                        JIM
      So am I. I'm Jim Smith,
      his father

                    MARY-JANE
      I'm Mary-Jane, his girlfriend

They shake hands.

                              FRANK
      Do you two, or three should I say. . .
      you're welcome to have breakfast?
      It's good food and it'll
      keep your spirits high for the
      road ahead

He glances in the direction of Mary-Jane's certain condition.

                    JIM
    Yeah, why not, thanks

                 MARY-JANE
    Ok, then

                   FRANK
    Sit, sit!

So Mary-Jane and Jim sit together. Frank rushes out back to prepare their breakfast.

The pair of them seem more or less just about content to politely smile at each other for the time being.

                 MARY-JANE
    I like your hat

                    JIM
    Thanks. Isn't it rude to
    wear one at the dinner
    table? Maybe I should
    take it off?

                 MARY-JANE
    I think you can get away with
    it. This isn't a dinner table.
    Leave it on, Jim — it suits you

Jim grins.
                    JIM
    So how was your journey here?

                 MARY-JANE
    Fine. I got the train to
    Inverness then a taxi here

                    JIM
    And what was the taxi ride
    like?

                    MARY-JANE
        Um, normal

                        JIM
        Lucky you! When I got one
        here from the airport it
        was, well, less said about
        it the better!

Mary-Jane smiles.

                    MARY-JANE
        I know you haven't seen
        him in a long time

                        JIM
        Me and Jessie just grew
        apart, that's all

                    MARY-JANE
        He misses his mum

                        JIM
        Course he does, she was
        the best

Frank brings the both of them their breakfast.
Just as he does this, in comes the priest.

                    PRIEST
        And where's mine?

The   priest   seems   overly   jovial   for
circumstances such as these.

                    FRANK
        Hey! Your cup is constantly
        flowing over, whereas some
        of us. . . let's just say our
        struggle goes on

                    PRIEST
        Not unnoticed!

                    FRANK
        God is the people-watching king!

RAGE AGAINST THE GAME

                    PRIEST
    Amongst other things, yes he
    is! Jim, morning. Did you sleep
    well?

                     JIM
    Like a baby

                    PRIEST
    Speaking of which, it's such
    a pleasure. . . you're Mary-Jane,
    aren't you?

                  MARY-JANE
    Yes, I am

                    PRIEST
    I'm Clyde McCreed

The priest stands over her, offers his hand
and they shake on it, but upon shaking hands
he leans in and pecks her on the cheek.

                    PRIEST
    Frank can I have a glass of
    grapefruit juice please

                    FRANK
    Yes — ice?

                    PRIEST
    No

                    FRANK
    Ok, grapefruit juice no ice.
    Sit down and I will bring
    it to you

The priest sits next to Mary-Jane.

Polite smiles all round.

Frank brings the priest his juice.

                    PRIEST

325

Thanks, Frank

                    FRANK
Did you want a bite to eat
with that?

                    PRIEST
I'm not hungry

                    FRANK
Ok

Frank goes back behind the bar where he
belongs.

                    PRIEST
I made a call to Fly In
The Sky psychiatric
hospital. Just so they
know we are coming

                    MARY-JANE
Can you tell me what
happened please?

                    PRIEST
As far as I am aware,
after baptising Jessie
he experienced some kind
of shock to his system

                    MARY-JANE
You baptised my boyfriend?

                    PRIEST
Yes. When he wakes up, he will
tell you how he's been feeling

                    MARY-JANE
'How he's been feeling' . . .
like I don't know how
my own boyfriend feels

                    PRIEST
That's not what I meant

326

                    MARY-JANE
    How the hell did my boyfriend
    go from playing a gig to getting
    baptised?

                        JIM
    The priest here — he caught my
    boy doing drugs

                    MARY-JANE
    What was it?

                      PRIEST
    Cocaine

                    MARY-JANE
    Goddamn it! That little liar,
    I'm gonna kill him!

Mary-Jane, not one to hide her feelings, is
upset.

                      PRIEST
    Calm down. A woman in your
    current condition should
    stay stable at all times

                    MARY-JANE
    I'm mighty fine, thank you
    very much!

                        JIM
    Isn't it time we got going?

                      PRIEST
    Yes it is — let's go

The priest downs his glass of grapefruit juice
as he gets to his feet.

Jim and Mary-Jane stand to let the priest
escort them out of The Loch Inn.

    EXT. THE LOCH NESS LAKE, SCOTLAND, DAY

SCENE 11: OLD HABITS DIE HARD

THE PAST

Stuart, the old man, has stopped his reasonably sized boat by turning the engine off, far out in the middle of the Loch Ness.

He heads to the front of the boat, centres himself, checks the time on his watch and then looks through his binoculars, skyward.

The old man has his sights set on a seaplane lowering itself from the bleak and drizzly sky.

Soon enough, the seaplane makes a good landing on the lake's surface as it skims towards the old man in his boat.

Upon stopping near the boat, out steps a shady on the eye kind of guy in his mid-to-late forties. White, shaved head, average in height and weight, he has in his hands a big bagged block of cocaine.

                    OLD MAN
          Getting good at landing
          that thing, Gabriel

                    GABRIEL
          Flattery will get you
          nowhere with me

                    OLD MAN
          Still don't know how to
          take a compliment then

                    GABRIEL
          Not from an old man - no
          offence

                    OLD MAN
          None taken!

                    GABRIEL
      Now, as much as I'd love to
      stand around and chat. . .
      have you got the money?

The old man shows him a big wad of cash.

                    OLD MAN
      Let's sample the stuff first

                    GABRIEL
      Knock yourself out

Gabriel throws the bagged block of coke at
Stuart.

It's stopped drizzling and the sky is clear. A
rainbow begins to appear — otherwise such a
thing goes unnoticed as a drug deal steals
nature's thunder.

The old man samples the cocaine and in doing
so, throws Gabriel the money.

He counts the money then and there.

                    GABRIEL
      Where's the rest of it,
      Stuart?

                    OLD MAN
      That's all I got, Gabriel

                    GABRIEL
      Well then, now we have a
      problem

Gabriel pulls out a handgun and points it at
Stuart.

                    OLD MAN
      Woah, hey, Gabriel!
      Killing me will only
      complicate matters so
      think carefully before

you make the biggest mistake
of your life

While holding the gun, pointed at Stuart's
peril, Gabriel feels distracted and glances to
the side of him. He sees a boy in a boat not
far from them both.

Gabriel lowers his weapon.

The boy slowly but surely approaches the scene
and stops between them both. He appears
fascinated by the seaplane.

                    OLD MAN
        Daniel? What the hell are
        you doing out here on your
        own?

Daniel is not yet a teenager, just a kid.

                    DANIEL
        Dad bought me a new boat
        so I'm trying it out.
        Hey mister, that's such a
        cool plane — can I get in
                    DANIEL CONT'D
        and take a closer look?

                    GABRIEL
        Course ya can Daniel, feel
        free!

The boy makes his way onto the seaplane and
gets inside, while Gabriel stands on one of
the landing pads.

                    OLD MAN
        Gabriel, I will pay you the
        rest, just give me more time

                    GABRIEL
        Forget about the rest of the
        money you owe me. I keep the
        kid and you don't die today

                    OLD MAN
   Wait!

The old man throws Gabriel back the big bagged
block of cocaine.

                    OLD MAN
   And you can keep the money.
   Please, leave Daniel alone

                    GABRIEL
   DANIEL. . .

The boy opens the door to the driver's side of
the seaplane.

                    DANIEL
   Yeah?

                    GABRIEL
   Do you wanna go for a ride?

                    DANIEL
   In this?

                    GABRIEL
   Yes!

                    DANIEL
   You bet I do!

                    GABRIEL
   Don't deny Daniel a daydream
    . . . he'll hate ya for it!

                    OLD MAN
   It's a daydream from hell!

Gabriel smiles menacingly.

                    GABRIEL
   You take it easy, Stuart

He goes to get in the seaplane.

                    OLD MAN

DON'T DO THIS!

Gabriel gets in the seaplane and Daniel straps himself in the passenger seat.

OLD MAN
FOR YOUR BROTHER,
GODDAMN IT!

He starts the engine and then winds down the window.

GABRIEL
CLYDE'S GOOD AND RIGHT,
AND BETTER OFF WITHOUT
ME

Gabriel pulls away as the seaplane gains some momentum.

Stuart watches on with a sinking feeling, and then suddenly he feels something else, something from underneath the boat take his breath away.

All he can see is a silhouette of something else entirely, lurking on the surface of the loch. He can't believe his eyes as a great big shadow swims towards the seaplane.

From beneath the surface of the loch emerges its great head of just what on Earth this breath-taking creature is with the long and prehistoric-like neck, its staggering grey body remaining just below the water's surface.

The magnificent sea creature moves its head to the side and so its neck extends fully from left to right. Then, in a moment of awe-inspiring power, it thrusts its head and uses its own neck as a catapult to fire itself straight through the seaplane.

The monster rips apart the plane and in doing so snatches Gabriel by its animalistic mouth. He didn't even have time to scream. Blood gushes from Gabriel's mouth — there is no struggle, he has been killed by a monster of myth in the most terrifying fashion.

Nessie nosedives deep into the depths of the loch, carrying Gabriel like a ragdoll down with it.

Daniel, alive, latches onto the remains of the seaplane in shock. Stuart snaps out of it, starts his boat and picks him up.

The old man in his boat takes the boy back home.

INT. FLY IN THE SKY PSYCHIATRIC HOSPITAL, SCOTLAND, DAY

SCENE 12: THE CONSTANT BATTLE BETWEEN COMMON SENSE AND PURE INSTINCT

Jim, Mary-Jane and the priest follow in the footsteps of a psychiatric doctor taking them to see Jessie. The doctor is tall, thin, Indian and compelling in the way he walks.

They walk through an airy recreational room where scattered around remain remnants of the psychotic kind. 'Ladies and gentlemen' in the bewildered wake of breakdowns, suicidal tendencies, racing thoughts etc; sedated, medicated, numbed.

It's such a godawful place made up of life's fragile few; crazy people living, or more to the raw meat of it existing, separate yet together in a world of their own insane undoing.

Some are sat down in one another's confused company, playing card games as others sit watching television, brainwashed by re-repeat after re-repeat of the same old quiz show.

A tall and skinny scruff of a man makes his presence felt to Mary-Jane in particular. He looks fascinated by her. She is intimidated to the extent of feeling discomfort.

                    INPATIENT - TRAVIS
    Hi. I see things others
    miss out on cos of my height.
    I have been burdened by much
    more than meets the beady eye.
    And when I saw the screamer come in,
    I knew he was special, extra-special.
    You love him, don't you. . . I know
    you do

He has a very deep voice. She is scared of him.

                    DOCTOR
    Travis, that's enough

                    INPATIENT - TRAVIS
    He doesn't belong in here.
    We are all the same — me,
    even you, Muhammad!

                    DOCTOR
    That's Doctor to you and believe
    Me, Travis, there's absolutely
    nothing 'the same' between the both
    of us, just so you know not to get
    any more of your funny ideas

                    INPATIENT - TRAVIS
    Ok, maybe not you but the rest
    of us, we are all too far gone
    in the you-know-what, but him,
    his suffering, it's special

Travis is speaking of Jessie as the doctor shields Mary-Jane from him and signals for a member of staff to intervene.

He takes them through the recreational room and down a long corridor.

                    DOCTOR
     You have to understand that
     what you are about to see of
     Jessie is without sedation and
     so the straightjacket, the
     padded cell. . . it's necessary
     for now

The doctor stops at a locked door, opens the sliding slot, and then steps aside. As soon as he does this the sound of Jessie screaming is piercing and raw.

Mary-Jane takes a look inside the cell.

He's wrestling with himself from underneath the straightjacket. Jessie is seen to throw himself against the four walls of the padded cell.

                    MARY-JANE
     JESSIE! JESSIE? STOP!
     STOP IT, YOU'RE FRIGHTENING
     ME

She has seen enough and withdraws her concern in shock, horror. Her hand goes over her mouth as she appears deeply affected and distraught at the disturbing sight of her troubled boyfriend.

Jim takes a look inside the cell, seeing the same sorry Jessie as she saw. He pulls away with the look of deep concern sunk into his face.

The priest feels the need not to take a look for himself, so just gathers his thoughts.

                    DOCTOR
     Before we treat him, it's
     necessary we here are aware
     of what went on. And, of course,

```
            his history proves a vital step
            in the right direction towards
            wellness

                         MARY-JANE
            He's been normal. I mean, he
            has his moments. . . this just
            doesn't make any sense

                          DOCTOR
            When you say 'he has his moments',
            what is it that you mean exactly?

                         MARY-JANE
            Well he works shifts of twelve
            hours one after the other, for
            three days straight. Sometimes
            it's nights — basically he loses
            his temper from time to time

                          DOCTOR
            To what end? Does he become
                         DOCTOR CONT'D
            aggressive? Violent?

                         MARY-JANE
            Jessie storms out of the house,
            slams the door behind him I'm
            not sure where he goes or what
            he does but I guess he's just
            letting off steam somewhere

                          DOCTOR
            Does Jessie drink? Take drugs?

                         MARY-JANE
            He drinks, not in excess. As for
            drugs . . . when I first found out that
            he took cocaine, well, I wanted him
            to stop doing it straight away

                          DOCTOR
            And did he stop taking cocaine?

        Mary-Jane looks to the priest for an answer.
```

                    PRIEST
On Saturday night I caught him
in the act of snorting cocaine

                    DOCTOR
Ok. Cocaine can cause quite a lot
of side effects: loss of appetite,
dilated pupils, nausea, psychosis,
convulsions, hallucinations, anxiety,
depression, delirium. . . I'm curious

The doctor takes his glasses off with one hand
and with the other, after fingering through
his trouser pocket, gets a handkerchief out to
clean them.

                    DOCTOR
Jessie hasn't said a word, not one,
and his screaming is constant.
'Confused exhaustion'. cocaine
interferes with the way our brain
                    DOCTOR CONT'D
processes chemicals. Jessie, as
he has a history OF taking cocaine,
needs more and more of the drug
just to feel 'normal'. Now, whether
or not this screaming of his is a
result of withdrawal, well, it's still
too early for that to happen. That he
has such a thing in his system so to
be crying out at this stage is —
strange

                    PRIEST
So are you saying then, in other words
this is not the cocaine making him
 . . . um

                    DOCTOR
I'm saying we need to be very sure
where we are coming from before we
begin considering a certain treatment.
What matters most is his safety,
to be safe from himself, because
clearly he is not in his right mind

                    MARY-JANE
Why? There has to be a reason he's
screaming. No one screams unless
something is seriously wrong

                     DOCTOR
From Freedom Fields Hospital, tests
taken there were conclusively clear
yet his screaming continued throughout.
The compulsory brain scan came back
clear. Therefore, physically, he
appears to be fine, normal, healthy

                      JIM
There is no such thing as madness
running wild, definitely not in my
nor any of my family's veins, so as
Mary-Jane just said — this makes no
sense!

                     DOCTOR
There is no easy way to know why
or what he's feeling inside; I am
not a mind reader. But of course,
I can work from my experience as
a psychiatric doctor to the best
of my knowledge. Jessie soon
will be worn down — when constant
stress exerts itself, the one and
only outcome is to each their own
undoing - it's just a matter of
time

                   MARY-JANE
So you are more than willing to do
nothing but wait, while my man has
to go through all the suffering in
the world — what sort of a sick and
twisted doctor are you?

                     PRIEST
Mary-Jane, don't get the doctor
wrong. What choice do we have?

                   MARY-JANE
The choice is certainly not yours

to 'have'. Everything was just fine
until you and your crazy idea of God
got involved, meddling with my man's
life!

                    DOCTOR
Please, let's just take a moment
to consider our options. It's in
Jessie's best interest that we
keep calm and make the right
decision, one which is based
on my diagnosis as well as your
careful consideration

                    JIM
And what is your diagnosis?

                    DOCTOR
So far, from what I have seen
of Jessie he needs restraint,
not sedation — not yet, not until
I know. . .

                    JIM
What's wrong with my son,
goddamn it?

                    DOCTOR
I don't know

                    JIM
So what are our options?

                    DOCTOR
Time being the greatest healer
of them all

                    JIM
Oh cut the crap! Come on man!
Give it to us straight

                    DOCTOR
We wait

Mary-Jane, while caressing her pregnant stomach, shakes her head and then walks away down the long corridor from whence she came.

Jim feels the need to follow her and does just that.

The priest is left to share a concerned stare with the doctor.

> DOCTOR
> I've never seen anything like
> it

> PRIEST
> Like what?

> DOCTOR
> Well, one's eyes display many
> emotions, sometimes all at once
> without having to say or do a damn
> thing. Through these windows is
> where we show our true colours -
> is it not?

> PRIEST
> It is, a soulful looking-glass

> DOCTOR
> So why is it then that when I look
> into Jessie's eyes I see a gaping,
> colourless absence so absolute that
> it brings about a basic shiver of fear
> — from me! Beneath this shallow veneer
> there are miracles taking place, just
> so I can speak my mind, and yet try as
> I might to make sense of Jessie's
> struggle

The doctor shakes his head before feeling the need to continue.

> DOCTOR CONT'D
> All I can see is suffering of
> a nature not quite right

> PRIEST
> What do you mean, 'not quite right'?

> DOCTOR
> I mean, when I take a good look
> at him I'm sure he's somewhere
> else, cos he's certainly not here

> PRIEST
> The only thing I can think of is
> post-traumatic stress disorder or
> something along those lines I will
> ask Mary-Jane if Jessie served in
> the armed forces

The doctor nods, accepting the priest's suggestion and so he walks back down the long corridor.

EXT. ENTRANCE OF FLY IN THE SKY PSYCHIATRIC HOSPITAL, SCOTLAND, DAY

Jim is comforting a crying Mary-Jane just outside of Fly In The Sky psychiatric hospital. The priest approaches with care.

> MARY-JANE
> Why now? Look at me! I'm
> the one who needs support,
> not him! I'm the one
> carrying his child and he
> should be here for me!

Mary-Jane, in a flood of tears, shakes her head dismayingly, looking at Jim for some sort of comfort.

> PRIEST
> Mary-Jane

She wipes away her tears as she faces up to the priest.

> MARY-JANE
> What do you want?

                         PRIEST
        Has Jessie ever fought in
        the armed forces?

                       MARY-JANE
        No

She answers his question and then looks to Jim
for further input.

                          JIM
        My son had no intention of
        following in my footsteps as
        a farmer — for him to even
        consider the armed forces is
        absurd

                         PRIEST
        I had to ask. I was just trying
        to make sense of it all

                       MARY-JANE
        Well, why don't you go pray to God?
        Doesn't he have all the answers?

Mary-Jane makes a sarcastic swipe directed
towards the priest.

                         PRIEST
        The doctor requires both of
        your signatures so he can
        carry on doing what he's doing

                       MARY-JANE
        Basically, he needs our blessing
        so he can carry on doing nothing
        and not feel fully responsible if
        he's the one wrong in waiting for
        something to happen instead of
        figuring it out now! Well, I
        won't do it!

                          342

                    PRIEST
I know you're upset, but this is the
only logical-looking course we have
to go on here

                  MARY-JANE
Where's the logic in any of this?

                     JIM
All I know is that's not my son
in there. Mary-Jane, I think we
have to put our trust in anything

                  JIM CONT'D
and everything that the doctors say
or do; we don't know any better
than to believe the way they work
is for the best

                  MARY-JANE
But what if it's not for the best?
What if every second we wait it gets
worse. . . Jessie is my life!

                     JIM
Jessie is my son! And I have to
believe in something that I know
nothing about. What choice do we
have, than have hope that they
know what they are doing in
there?

                    PRIEST
Mary-Jane, Jim's right. I have to
believe in something that I don't
know, not for certain anyway. We
keep the faith; if we don't do that
then it's hopeless

                  MARY-JANE
This is not about believing in
God. Jim, I'm with you, you decide
what's best and I will support it

                     JIM

Let's see the doctor, get it signed
and sorted. That's all we can do

                    MARY-JANE
Ok

Jim and Mary-Jane go back into the psychiatric
hospital while the priest watches on.

EXT. FARMHOUSE, LOCHEND, DAY

THE PAST

The old man carries Daniel in his arms as they
approach his parents' farmhouse.

Peter catches sight of them from afar and
proceeds speedily, looking concerned.

                    PETER
    Daniel! Daniel?

The old man hands Daniel over to his father.
Peter holds his son out in front of him. He
looks scared stiff.

Angela comes outside and rushes up to them,
taking Daniel from her husband's arms.

                    ANGELA
    What's wrong?

Daniel doesn't say a word.

                    PETER
    Take him inside

Angela carries her son inside.

                    PETER
    Stuart. . .

The old man looks lost for words.

                    OLD MAN
    It's real

344

                         PETER
          What's real?

                              OLD MAN
          The Loch Ness monster,
          that's what!

Peter raises his eyebrows.

                         PETER
          Are you sure?

The old man laughs as he shakes his head;
stupefied.

                         PETER CONT'D
          But the BBC recently carried
          out an extensive search and
          found nothing — they did it
          all with the use of sonar

                         OLD MAN
          Peter, take my word for it.
          There is something in the water,
          something else entirely

Peter still cannot quite register just what
the old man has seen.

                         OLD MAN
          Clyde's brother, Gabriel,
          he's gone

                         PETER
          What do you mean, gone?

                         OLD MAN
          I mean he's dead

Peter puts his hand over his mouth then lets
it slide down his chin and back down to his
side.

                         PETER
          You mean. . .

He pieces such a thing together. His face says
it all.

                    OLD MAN
    We have ourselves a
    monster here

Peter rushes inside and then quickly reappears
as he heads towards his car.

                    OLD MAN
    Where are you going?

                    PETER
    We are going to tell Clyde.
    Come on!

The old man gets inside the passenger seat of
Peter's car.
Off they go.

EXT. CHURCH, LOCHEND, SCOTLAND, DAY

Peter and Stuart approach the church. There is
a handwritten notice on its front door: *Gone
Golfing.*

They get back in the car and drive to the golf
course.

The old man turns on the radio and it's the
local news report.

                    RADIO NEWS BROADCASTER
    There has been a substantial
    spillage of toxic waste at
    Moray Firth this morning
    according to the local fishermen
    near Inverness. Details of
    how the spillage happened are
    otherwise still unknown

EXT. GOLF CLUB, JUST OUTSIDE LOCHEND, DAY

They make their way to reception.

> RECEPTIONIST
> Hello. How can I help you?

> PETER
> Yes, I believe Father Clyde
> McCreed is playing golf today

> RECEPTIONIST
> That's right. He's been here
> for over an hour or so. Should
> you wish to see him, I'm guessing
> he's teeing off on hole. . . hmm
> . . . try nine and please be well
> aware of all players as you pass
> between the holes

> OLD MAN
> Can we borrow a buggy?

Peter gives Stuart a funny look in front of
the fat receptionist.

> OLD MAN
> What? It's tipping it down!

> RECEPTIONIST
> Err, certainly. Follow
> the signposts once you've
> made your way out onto the
> course itself

Peter and Stuart go through to the golf course
itself, follow the signpost to where the
buggies are parked, pick one and then drive
off in search of Clyde.

Regardless of the rain, many games of golf are
in action.

> PETER
> I have no clue who would want
> to do this sort of thing in
> the pouring rain

347

                              OLD MAN
          Enthusiasts

                              PETER
          Otherwise known as madmen

                              OLD MAN
          Clyde is kind of funny
          in his ways, isn't he?

                              PETER
          Funny? He's hilarious! He's,
          he's. . .

They drive on in the buggy, getting to hole
nine with still no sign of Clyde.

Stuart sees a struggling golfer from afar,
trying to play his way out of trouble, deep in
the heart of a bunker.

                              OLD MAN
          He's over there! I think
          Clyde's losing his spirited
          battle against a godforsaken
          bunker

He points Peter in the direction of a golfer
frustratingly playing the same shot but once
again getting to grips with the bunker's
overhanging lip, kicking up sand and a fuss
for that matter.

Upon closer inspection of the 'golfing
incident', it is in fact Clyde.

They get out of the buggy and approach him.

Clyde composes himself before trying to hit
the ball out of the bunker. But upon doing so,
he notices the two men coming towards him and
then recognises them both.

                    PRIEST
Ah, the reinforcements have arrived,
splendid!

                    PETER
Clyde, I think you had best get
out of the bunker

                    PRIEST
That's what I'm trying to do,
damn it!

                    PETER
Not as a golfer. As a friend,
there's something you should
know

                    PRIEST
Oh. Sounds serious, just give me
one more shot at this blessed ball

                    PETER
Clyde. . .

                    PRIEST
Peter, please. . . it's important that
I take responsibility for my actions
as a golfer. Forgive me, my passion
knows no reason as to why I should
stop

                    PETER
Ok, Clyde

Clyde readies himself, swings and connects
with the ball, but the ball flies far and away
from the hole, landing in the big pond
opposite.

PLOP

The ball sinks to the bottom of the pond.

                    OLD MAN
I've seen worse shots

Clyde gets out of the bunker.

> PRIEST
> So, what brings you both here?
> Surely not the art of golf!

> PETER
> Stuart, I think it should come
> from you

The old man gathers his thoughts.

> OLD MAN
> There's no easy way to say
> such a thing, that's simply
> beyond the pale. Clyde, I can't
> quite believe this myself, but
> it's true — the truth is stranger
> than fiction

> PRIEST
> Spit it out, Stuart! What truth?

> OLD MAN
> Your brother, Gabriel, is dead

From fiddling with his golf clubs, Clyde
suddenly stops, to the undivided attention of
Stuart's sentence as it hits him hard.

> PETER
> Stuart, tell him how it happened

> OLD MAN
> Well, we all know your brother is,
> was. . . look, I can't come out of
> this as innocent so I might as well
> spill my guts. It's because of
> me, your brother. . . for the love
> of God! Gabriel was killed by the
> Loch Ness monster!

> PRIEST
> What was he doing out on the
> loch? What was he doing with

you of all people?

                    OLD MAN
He was. . . well, I was. . .
purchasing an illegal substance

                    OLD MAN CONT'D
that I was to receive from Gabriel
for an undisclosed sum of money

                    PRIEST
Why do you make it sound so proper,
huh? When all you were doing was
feeding a bad habit. But how can
'a drug deal' end this way?

                    OLD MAN
I came up short. It was not what
we agreed on, money I mean. Fine,
I was desperate for a fix. So
your brother threatened me

                    PRIEST
How did he threaten you?

                    OLD MAN
With a gun, and then Peter's
son appeared from out of the
blue. But your brother must
have been in deep trouble,
because his actions sure were
desperate

                    PRIEST
'Desperate' . . . what do you mean?

                    OLD MAN
Gabriel let Daniel look inside
his seaplane. Only he was gonna
kidnap Daniel and that was
when, well, that was when
'Nessie' showed up

Clyde looks amazed.

                    PRIEST

Are you on drugs as we speak
Stuart?

                    OLD MAN
No I am not

                    PRIEST
Peter — talk. Cos I cannot
possibly believe a word of
this unless it's . . . please
reason with what the old man's
saying!

                    PETER
Daniel looked scared stiff from
something, that's all I know

                    PRIEST
Who else knows? Who else saw all
this?

                    OLD MAN
It's between me and Daniel. Now
Peter knows, so only us three are
aware

                    PRIEST
Well, this is not fit for gossip.
It's by far the biggest thing in
Scotland today

                    OLD MAN
And I guess it's just a matter of
time before a fisherman or a
tourist. . . someone will see for
themselves. . . this is a monster,
make no mistake about that

                    PETER
What happens now?

                    OLD MAN
Well, think about what one
sighting of 'Nessie' means -
it's laughed off - common
sense dismisses such a thing.

And then another sighting, and
then another, and before you
know it we have everyone from
all over here for miraculous
                    OLD MAN CONT'D
reason. Hysteria and debate,
what to do with it? People
laying claim, making plans,
causing chaos in the face of
Lochend and our surrounds -
Scotland will be made to look
and feel like a fucking circus
-   that's what happens now!

                    PRIEST
Not if we act fast

                    OLD MAN
Act fast? What do you suppose
we are actually capable of? I've
seen it with my own eyes! This is
something slap bang out of a
blockbuster!

                    PRIEST
How big?

                    OLD MAN
You'd need to see it to believe it

                    PRIEST
As crazy as this is, I believe you
Stuart, but to give me an idea of
just what we're dealing with here -
how big?

                    OLD MAN
You don't just 'deal' with the
Loch Ness monster! Myth is myth
for good reason — it's unbelievable!
But to answer your question
in terms of size: gigantic.
Bigger than anything inhabiting
the sea

                    PRIEST

Noah had to do what God told
Him; he built the ark for
all creatures great and small!
                    PRIEST CONT'D
This is just one great creature

                    OLD MAN
One great big creature for that
matter!

                    PRIEST
This thing killed my brother.
This thing will not kill again.
'Nessie' needs stopping

                    OLD MAN
Clyde, don't you understand? It's
history being made here. How in
the world would we even come close
to justifying a revengeful killing
of a creature that could have been
around hundreds of years before us!

                    PRIEST
Stuart don't get me wrong. I was
not at all suggesting such a thing

                    OLD MAN
You just said it yourself! How else
is a monster 'stopped'?

                    PRIEST
If Noah can singlehandedly build a
big ark I think it's within us as
a people of first and foremost
peace — so by my powers that be because
of God's goodwill we do not kill this
sea creature. We contain it until the
Lord of all things gives us good reason
in order to do otherwise

                    PETER
Clyde, you're having a kneejerk
reaction to the death of your
brother, that's all

354

                    PRIEST
That's not all! Imagine Daniel
was the one on the receiving end
of this and it was his death that
we had to do something about. Don't
tell me how I'm feeling. Now we
react according to our survival
instinct and accept responsibility!

                   OLD MAN
Clyde, I think that Peter's right,
this is just a kneejerk reaction

                    PRIEST
Says the haggard drug addict!
It's simple: tranquilize,
capture and contain

                   OLD MAN
Simple, you say. Sure is
easier said than done!

                    PRIEST
And actions speak louder
than words, so come on men!
Let's get to it!

Clyde picks up his golf bag and walks over to
his buggy. Peter and Stuart walk back to their
buggy and follow closely behind the priest.

ACT 3: NEW BEGINNINGS

SCENE 13: FATE MAKES FOR A CHANGE OF HEART

EXT. LOCH NESS LAKE, DAY

Mary-Jane and Jim have taken time out from
being at the psychiatric hospital. They walk
along the loch; the day is not at all
beautiful, it's bleak.

> MARY-JANE
> I know the priest means well,
> yet I can't help but feel like
> he's hiding something

> JIM
> Mary-Jane, just remember being
> a priest must take its toll from
> time to time; I don't doubt the
> dedication in doing not just
> any old job, but a duty. Because I
> was just the same, except I wasn't
> at loggerheads with God day in, day
> out

> MARY-JANE
> And how are things - on the farm
> I mean?

> JIM
> Funny you should ask — actually,
> it's not at all a laughing matter,
> the less said about it the better.
> But what is it they say about death?

> MARY-JANE
> They say many things about death
> Though when the end is near for
> them, those so content to make
> quips up about how we can but let
> it be. . . Believe me, I was a nurse
> once upon a time and from what
> I remember of witnessing the sick
> take a truly long lasting turn for
> > MARY-JANE CONT'D

the worse, well, not one went 'gentle
into that good night', no. They
'raged and they raged against the
dying of the light!'

                    JIM
That was it; 'After your death,
you will be what you were before
your birth'

                    MARY-JANE
What does that even mean?

                    JIM
I don't know

                    MARY-JANE
Sounds profound

                    JIM
I think it came from a fortune
cookie

Mary-Jane laughs as a somewhat comfortable
silence continues to bring them closer
together.

                    MARY-JANE
Jessie is sorry for the way
he, well. . .

                    JIM
Really you don't have to say
anything on his behalf. If it
was me, and at that age. . . he
was young but still, old
enough. Now he has you and
a baby on the way

                    MARY-JANE
When I first met him, huh,
getting to know your son
was a struggle. Right from
the beginning I sensed something
                    MARY-JANE CONT'D
was missing in his life. I mean,

then as things got more serious,
I kept asking the same questions
and soon enough he told me
everything. Then we talked about
Texas. It's just I guess some
things are easier said than done

> JIM

Wendy was his rock, mine too, but
I spent most of my time on the farm
and so Jessie became more a mummy's
boy. I don't blame him for trying
to find his own way in life. . . after
all, he found you

> MARY-JANE

Jim, I'm not being facetious,
I just want to understand. Because
all of this feels beyond me —
our suffering brings us closer
together. But why? I wanna know why!
Has it always been this way? Pain,
I mean, instead of something else,
something within us. There must be
more to life than a futile feeling
of love for fuck's sake?!

Mary-Jane sounds so very emotional now.

> JIM

'I hurt myself today,
To see if I still feel,
I focus on the pain. . .'

Jim sings some of a song made famous by Johnny
Cash, 'Hurt' to answer her question and in
doing so chokes up before being able to finish
the first verse.

> MARY-JANE

'The only thing that's real'

Mary-Jane finishes it off for him. She
suddenly stops, holding her pregnant stomach,
writhing in pain.

> JIM

What's wrong?

> MARY-JANE

I think my waters just broke

Jim is lost at what to do.

Mary-Jane then begins to groan in pain and breathe heavily.

> JIM

Ok, come on - we have to
go, now

He hurries her back along the loch. The pub is certainly not a million miles away, yet it's a struggle to get there.

INT. THE LOCH INN, DAY

Jim and Mary-Jane enter the pub.

> JIM

Can you take us to the
hospital please, she's. . .
it's happening now!

Frank rushes out from behind the bar. The old man watches on.

The landlord leaves his pub. They rush to his car. Mary-Jane and Jim jump into the back. Frank skids out of the carpark.

EXT. FRANK'S CAR, DRIVING TO HOSPITAL, DAY

Mary-Jane continues to vent her pain. Jim holds her hand and she squeezes it tight.

> JIM

Just breathe

> MARY-JANE

Thanks for that! Ah!

                         FRANK
         We'll be there real soon

                          JIM
         It's gonna be ok

                       MARY-JANE
         Jessie should be here!

Mary-Jane pants.

                          JIM
         I'm sure he is in spirit

                         FRANK
         Almost there

EXT. FREEDOM FIELDS HOSPITAL, SCOTLAND, DAY

Frank skids to a stop at the entrance of
Freedom Fields hospital.

Jim jumps out and then opens the door for
Mary-Jane.

Frank runs inside so to get the attention of
hospital staff.

Mary-Jane struggles alongside some much needed
help from Jim.

A member of hospital staff appears at her aid
and brings out a wheelchair for Mary-Jane.

The pregnant woman is wheeled inside the
hospital, followed by Frank and Jim.

INT. THE LOCH INN, DAY

The priest enters the pub but can only see the
old man in his sights, sitting at the front of
the bar.

                         PRIEST
         Where's Frank?

                    OLD MAN
    Doing his good deed for the
    day

                    PRIEST
    Oh, and what's that then?

                    OLD MAN
    I believe he has taken a
    pregnant woman who I've
    never seen before to the
    hospital

Clyde turns around and heads outside.

                    OLD MAN
    Friends of yours, are they?

                    PRIEST
    Is that genuine concern or
    are you just giving out
    your daily slice of small
    talk?

                    OLD MAN
    I'm just curious as to why certain
    strangers here have compelled
    you to care a great deal about
    the goings-on in their life -
    haven't you got enough 'heavenly
    worry' to contend with?

                    PRIEST
    Take a look around you. Hazard
    your grasp at the world we
    live in — it's small, simple and
    seldom does anything go on, or
    indeed even happen here apart from
                    PRIEST CONT'D
    the obvious insignificances
    such as passing the day in a pub

                    OLD MAN
    Don't you dare resent the choice
    you made and then blame my boring

lifestyle on your wrongdoing!

>   PRIEST
> What wrongdoing?

The old man shakes his head and stands to his feet.

>   OLD MAN
> It's taken only a decade, Clyde,
> and yet your conscience sure has
> been busy. Somehow, you have found
> a way to forget what was the potential,
> let's not underestimate this, because
> this was to be Scotland's defining
> moment in history. We did not think
> up that plan of action, indeed we — me
> and Peter - were right!

>   PRIEST
> Right about what?

>   OLD MAN
> Clyde! Do you not remember? While
> you were giving golf a bad name,
> we came to offer our support at the
> loss of your late brother, Gabriel

>   PRIEST
> Of course I sure as hell remember!
> But it was you who gave me no choice!
> You were the one who said in no
> uncertain terms 'Scotland will be
> made to look and feel like a fucking
> circus'

>   OLD MAN
> I never thought I'd see the day,
> a man of God go so far gone against
> the grain, and disregard good will.
> Well, Clyde, common sense fails you!

>   PRIEST
> We are all accountable! But you

put the seeds of doubt into
place, Stuart. What has Scotland
done in a decade? Come on man,
you spend enough of your time at
home watching television

                    OLD MAN
You are asking me to tell you
what Scotland did in the last
ten years. . . this is not the
question that begs to be answered,
Clyde! Goddamn it! 'Actions
speak louder than words', that's
what you said before we went to
work on 'containing' an animal!
And not just any old animal, well,
I believe we have failed. We have
failed Lochend and we have failed
Scotland

Clyde desperately places his hands over his
face, distraught.

                    OLD MAN
And what I will say about Scotland
is this — it's confused. Our crazy
idea almost came true! To be
independent, separate from the
'United Kingdom', would have been
the beginning of the end, and indeed
it was nothing but a cry for help.
Let me admit though, it is not
enough that we speak Scottish.
It is not enough that we hold
William Wallace as high as
heaven above! Because these
things just amount to the means
                OLD MAN CONT'D
of being patriotic at all of
our peril! Hell, in hindsight
just look at what we have here!
Nessie is a national treasure
whether we believe in it or not!

                    PRIEST
ENOUGH! I know now what must be

done and I intend to do it with
or without you

> OLD MAN
>
> We set it free

> PRIEST
>
> Yes!

> OLD MAN
>
> Well, I will drink to that!

> PRIEST
>
> Stuart, you were Peter's friend.
> The funeral will be held at
> church tomorrow morning at 11am

The old man downs his drink.

The priest leaves the pub in a hurry.

INT. DELIVERY ROOM, FREEDOM FIELDS HOSPITAL, SCOTLAND, DAY

Mary-Jane is screaming and sweating. Jim is shrieking in psychosomatic pain. The doctors and nurses are at hand doing their job.

INT. RECEPTION, FREEDOM FIELDS HOSPITAL, SCOTLAND, DAY

The priest approaches reception in a rush.

> RECEPTIONIST
>
> Yes sir, how can I help you?

> PRIEST
>
> Um. . . Mary-Jane, a pregnant
> woman in the process of giving
> birth

> RECEPTIONIST
>
> Are you a relation?

> PRIEST

Yes

                    RECEPTIONIST
Can I see some identification?

                         PRIEST
Look lady, she. . .

                         FRANK
Clyde

Clyde stops addressing the receptionist, turns
to his side and acknowledges Frank calling his
name.

                         FRANK
    She's being seen to by the
    doctors. It's all good

                         PRIEST
    It's Jim I need to see

                         FRANK
    He's busy. She needs him
    to be there for her

                         PRIEST
    You're right. Thanks Frank

                         FRANK
    You look tired, Clyde

                         PRIEST
    I'm fine

                         FRANK
    Stuart told me — Peter
    . . . lightening! How's Angela?

                         PRIEST
    She's struggling. Daniel will
    do his best to be there for her

                         FRANK
    It's tragic

                              PRIEST
          The funeral will be held at
          11am tomorrow morning in
          the church

                              FRANK
          Ok

Jim walks past them both, goes outside and
gets some air.

Clyde and Frank follow him outside.

          **EXT. FREEDOM FIELDS HOSPITAL ENTRANCE,
                      SCOTLAND, DAY**

Jim has his hands on his head.

                              PRIEST
          Jim? Jim? Everything ok?

                              JIM
          Fine, I'm fine

                              FRANK
          You look really pale,
          are you sure you're alright?

                              JIM
          It's just not every day you
          bear witness to. . .

                              PRIEST
          Birth

                              JIM
          Bingo

                              PRIEST
          Jim, I need to ask you something
          personal

                              JIM
          Anything that can clear my head

PRIEST
You and your. . . well, Wendy. . .
you told me she was lost at sea.
Can I ask what you were doing?

JIM
We were having a holiday in Malta
at the time. Those were the days,
deep-sea diving...

The priest's face lights up.

PRIEST
Jim, I think you are here for
a reason

FRANK
Clyde, leave the man be!
Birth is a great big thing in
itself, obviously, let alone
hearing from your word of God

PRIEST
This is more than that, Frank.
Forgive me, I know now's not
the time to unload on you
but it's important

JIM
I am here purely for my son,
and Mary-Jane is a big part
of his life

PRIEST
I know. But at the end of the
day your life has been turned
upside down, not just cos that's
the way it is. . . something else
has been going on behind the
scenes. Forces are at work,
whether you believe in this sort
of thing, that there exists so
much more than meets the naked eye,
or rather have a mind made up
for you. Your thoughts - shut

down by society to keep us sheep
'in check', cos when we stray
you know too well what happens;
it's the 'getting lost' part, it's
into the unknown where we find
out what we are really made of

                    FRANK
Society? Getting lost? Into the
unknown? What the heck are you
talking about?

The priest ignores Frank and continues to make
some sort of point.

                    PRIEST
If we seek beyond being told
time and time again a convenient
type of truth that is lost on
political correctness, thanks
to the media and media alone.
Killer instinct sets in,
until all of a sudden, freed
from fearful living under the
manipulative influence of a
media doing its best to befriend
every fibre of your being! Making
money and then a mockery of your
better judgement! Just so you know
Jim, from my years as a servant of
God: Our Lord demands simply your

                    PRIEST CONT'D
life - if you live the truth, then
it will set you free, otherwise
'shalom aleichem'

A bouncy nurse appears at the entrance to the
hospital.

                    NURSE
Mr Smith

Jim gives his attention to the nurse instead
of the priest.

                    NURSE
        I think you should come inside

She smiles from ear to ear.

He rushes inside.

                    FRANK
        Saved by the blessing of birth!
        Thank God for that!

The priest looks at Frank, giving him evil
eyes.

                    PRIEST
        It would do you no harm but
        good, to listen at least some
        of the time

                    FRANK
        I always listen!

                    PRIEST
        Yes you do, and yet you do
        not hear!

Frank raises his eyebrows as a response to
Clyde's comeback.

                    FRANK
        Right, I'd better get back to
        work, before Stuart drinks The
        Loch Inn dry!

                    PRIEST
        I'm going to see Jessie, it's
        the least I can do

                    FRANK
        Don't you think you're. . .

                    PRIEST
        What?

                              FRANK
Well, meddling

                              PRIEST
Frank, the exact moment that
I performed my duty, to baptise
such a lost soul - all hell broke
loose!

                              FRANK
So now, out of guilt, you're
going to check on the condition
of a stranger

                              PRIEST
He was a stranger before being
baptised, and now he's my brother

                              FRANK
Your brother is dead. Don't go
making this into something it's
not

                              PRIEST
There is no harm in showing my
concern, so if you'll excuse me

The priest walks towards his parked car.

                              FRANK
Why not visit Angela and Daniel
to see if they are all set for
tomorrow?

                              PRIEST
All in good time. I've made up
my mind. Good day

He gets into his car and drives off.

         SCENE 14: GOING THROUGH THE MOTIONS

            EXT. CHURCH, LOCHEND, DAY

RAGE AGAINST THE GAME

THE PAST

The priest is seeing people out of the church, while being commended on another worthwhile service.

                    ANGELA
     Father, have you got a moment?

Angela is purposely the last person to leave.

                    PRIEST
     Certainly, everything ok?

                    ANGELA
     No, not really. I am worried
     about Daniel

                    PRIEST
     Why?

                    ANGELA
     Peter won't tell me what happened

                    PRIEST
     What you and your husband tell
     each other - that is none of my
     business

Angela gets a piece of folded up paper from her back pocket.

She unfolds it — it is a picture drawn by her son Daniel of what looks like the Loch Ness monster, with a man in its mouth and blood everywhere.

                    ANGELA
     Since when was something like
     this just a family matter?

                    PRIEST
     It's being taken care of

                    ANGELA
     When?

                              PRIEST
          Soon

                              ANGELA
          Good

Angela walks out the church.

INT. FLY IN THE SKY PSYCHIATRIC HOSPITAL, DAY

The priest is on a mission. He doesn't stop at
reception and carries on in search of a
doctor.

He walks through the recreational room and
down the long corridor, looking into each
office for the doctor treating Jessie.

Finally reaching an occupied office, he enters
unannounced.

                              PRIEST
          How's he doing, Doc?

                              DOCTOR
          Um, how's who doing?

                              PRIEST
          Jessie

The doctor it would seem is busy speaking to a
colleague.

                              DOCTOR
          Please excuse me

He gets up from his seat, stepping outside
with the priest.

                              DOCTOR
          Sorry, you can't just storm
          in out of the blue like this

                              PRIEST
          Has there been any change in

his condition?

                    DOCTOR
I can quite imagine, 'anything goes'
as a priest, but being a doctor
differs from your approach, putting
faith before fact? But of course,
 such faith in 'God', one man
sat on a throne amongst angels
and fluffy clouds speaks for itself,
so strike me down!

                    PRIEST
Excuse me! I am not about to argue
God's powers that be beyond each
and every single diagnosis you come
up with. This is not why I am here

                    DOCTOR
And I am not here for your every
whim of wonder and worry. You need
to see me? Make an appointment at
reception

                    PRIEST
It can't wait. This is serious

                    DOCTOR
If it's not a matter of life and
death then please leave me to my
mountain of paperwork, thank you
very much

The doctor tries to enter his office, but the
priest stands in his way.

The priest stands up close and personal to the
doctor for a moment of heated distain.

                    PRIEST
Please. . .

                    DOCTOR
Your passion is misplaced, and
it's wasted on me. I can't
conjure up a miracle cos your

feeling, from my perspective
at least, just a rush of blood
to the head

                    PRIEST
How old are you? Forty?

                    DOCTOR
I'd rather that we remain in
a professional frame of mind.
Do not distort your own sense
of futile righteousness. Inside
these walls all we need be are
doctors, prescribing between the
lines of objective opinion and
renowned reasoning. I think you
forget that when you depart from
your church, you have to leave
the love of God behind. Here, we
deal with a different animal
altogether - this is not the time
or place for personal indulgences

                    PRIEST
No, it's not. It's time for the truth!
I have been a priest here for over
thirty years. Jessie is the first,
and hopefully the last, person on
Earth that I have to run around for
like a headless chicken cos of a
blessed baptism gone wrong. I hold
myself fully responsible, until you
find out what the fucking hell's
happening here! You're a doctor,
for Christ's sake! Can't you use
'the science of your well-informed
mind' and make a decision NOW. . .
not later, not tomorrow, not when
desperate times force the issue.
You need to act with the strength
of your convictions as the 'superior
professional', not a floundering
doctor!

Suddenly the piercing sound of a fire alarm rings out loud and clear.

                    DOCTOR
    Get out of my way!

The doctor pushes the priest out of his way.

                    PRIEST
    Where are you going?

                    DOCTOR
    To secure the area; in case you
    have extra-special selective hearing
    on top of your extra-special selective
    beliefs, I strongly suggest getting
    the hell out of this building

The doctor rushes down the corridor.

The priest exits the building.

Doctors, nurses, cooks, cleaners and overexcited inpatients soon emerge from the building. The inpatients are forcefully shepherded to the designated 'fire zone'.

The priest waits to see where Jessie is. Soon he can hear him screaming, being wheeled out of the entrance strapped down.

Then, out runs a frantic chef, wearing a tall hat of fire. He races down the entrance steps, jumping head first into the long pond of a picturesque nature.

SPLASH

Concerned doctors watch on in shock, as do the entertained inpatients, some of whom are laughing at the chef for being on fire!

One doctor rushes over to the chef who is still in the pond and helps him out.

Now the sound of a fire engine rings out around the area as it enters the scene.

Firemen enter the building and do their thing.

The priest, not wanting to get in anyone's way, walks back to his car and drives off.

EXT. LOCH NESS LAKE, NIGHT

THE PAST

The old man has stopped his boat in the same place where the Loch Ness monster surfaced.

It is a clear evening, with about an hour and a half of light left before darkness falls.

> OLD MAN
> This is it. This is where
> I was

Peter and the priest stand together at the front of the boat.

> PETER
> So who's shooting it?

The silence answers his question — none of them know how to prepare for what they have in mind.

> OLD MAN
> Clyde, it killed your brother.
> This is your idea, remember

The priest looks at Peter, then the old man, and yet doesn't say anything.

Peter gets the tranquiliser gun and gives it to Clyde.

The old man is looking out through his binoculars.

Suddenly, Nessie's head emerges just a few feet from the front of the boat.

Its head rises up from the monster's impressively long neck, looking down on the three stunned men.

                    PETER
     CLYDE. . . CLYDE!

Clyde aims straight at the monster; it's so close he can't miss.

His hand and arm begin to shake.

                    PETER
     WHAT ARE YOU WAITING FOR?

Clyde lowers the tranquiliser; his face is a skewed depiction in the wake of awe.

Peter snatches the gun.

He takes aim and fires.

BANG

The dart penetrates Nessie's neck, causing it to make a monstrous sound of pain.

The Loch Ness monster's neck flops, causing its head to drop down onto the surface.

SPLASH

Nessie sinks.

                    PETER
     How long have we got to tie
     this thing down?

Clyde has been stunned into silence.

                    PETER
     HOW LONG?

                         OLD MAN
        Two hours

                          PETER
        Well, then

Peter forces himself into action.

The old man walks up to Clyde and offers him a
swig on something strong from his flask.

SCENE 15: SEIZE THE DAY

Hymn: 'All things bright and beautiful'

Montage: with the hymn in question carried
over for dramatic effect.

INT. FREEDOM FIELDS HOSPITAL, SCOTLAND, DAY

Mary-Jane has a hold of her new born baby,
beside an emotional-looking Jim. Him and Mary-
Jane are both being slowly seen out by the
nurses responsible for the successful
delivery.

INT. PADDED CELL, FLY IN THE SKY PSYCHIATRIC HOSPITAL, SCOTLAND, DAY

Jessie, still in a straightjacket, stops
screaming and then stops struggling from side
to side. He falls to his knees first, then
face down.

A doctor rushes in and turns Jessie over; he's
unconscious.

The doctor struggles to take off his
straightjacket.

A nurse comes in and the doctor tells her to
call an ambulance as he tries resuscitating
him.

Jessie remains motionless.

Soon enough, the paramedics arrive with a trolley. They carefully lift him onto it then quickly wheel him out of the psychiatric hospital into an ambulance.

EXT. FREEDOM FIELDS HOSPITAL, SCOTLAND, DAY

The ambulance stops at the entrance. The driver rushes around to the back of the ambulance and opens up the doors. Jessie is wheeled out.

Mary-Jane is holding her baby, about to exit the hospital alongside Jim, when they have to make way for the paramedics.

Jim immediately notices it's Jessie they are now wheeling down the corridor and follows, while Mary-Jane tends to her baby.

A doctor informs Jim of the fact that he cannot follow them into the A&E department.

Jim is forced to wait in the waiting room, along with Mary-Jane and her baby.

EXT. CHURCH GROUNDS, LOCHEND, DAY

It is Peter's funeral ceremony. Friends and family stand together in song, singing out the hymn of 'all things bright and beautiful', led by the priest.

The coffin is placed into the ground.

                   PRIEST
   Earth to earth, ashes to ashes,
   dust to dust

Slowly, the family and friends of Peter form a line. Each person bends down in order to pick up a fistful of soil, and then throws it onto the coffin in the ground.

That act of respect concludes the funeral; friends and family slowly and sadly disperse as they make their way out of the church grounds.

Jim storms past the people leaving Peter's funeral. He approaches the priest and throws a wild punch, catching him square in the nose and knocking him to the ground.

> JIM
> WHAT HAVE YOU DONE TO MY
> SON?

The priest gets up, pats his nose — its bleeding.

> OLD MAN
> I think you need to calm down

He speaks at a distance.

> PRIEST
> Stay out of this, Stuart

> OLD MAN
> What's he talking about?

> JIM
> MY SON IS DYING!

> PRIEST
> Jim, listen to me

> JIM
> NO, I WON'T LISTEN TO ANY
> MORE OF YOUR GODFORSAKEN CRAP!
> The doctors here do nothing,
> but you — YOU have done nothing
> but cause suffering

> PRIEST
> I know. . . I KNOW!

> OLD MAN

Clyde. . . I

                    PRIEST
STUART! I strongly suggest
shutting the hell up! Now is
not the time to talk

                    JIM
You damn right it's not the
time to talk

Daniel walks up to the three men.

                    DANIEL
Clyde, my mum's waiting for you
. . . your nose is bleeding

                    PRIEST
I know, I know. Tell her I'll
be there a bit later

                    DANIEL
Why? What are you doing?

The priest can't think of an answer to
Daniel's question, so instead he just smiles
somewhat uncomfortably, bleeding in the
process.

                DANIEL CONT'D
This is about the monster,
isn't it?

                    OLD MAN
Daniel, your mother needs you

The old man tries shepherding Daniel down to
the car where his mother is waiting, but he
shrugs Stuart off of him.

                    JIM
Monster? What monster?

                    DANIEL

381

The Loch Ness monster that saved
my life!

Stunned silence.

                    PRIEST
Stuart, get your boat ready
and Daniel, be a good boy -
your mother needs you

The old man nods and tries to guide Daniel
down the church grounds once more. He yet
again shrugs Stuart off.

                    DANIEL
I'm not a boy anymore! I am a
Man, damn it! And I want in on
whatever the hell is happening
                    DANIEL CONT'D
here

                    ANGELA
And what is happening here?

Angela appears as Stuart departs.

                    DANIEL
Mum...

                    PRIEST
Angela. . .

                    ANGELA
Who are you?

She looks at Jim.

                    JIM
I'm Jim Smith

                    PRIEST
He's a friend

                    ANGELA
Clyde, your nose!

Angela approaches the priest. Getting out a
tissue, she dabs his bloody nose for him.

Jim looks sheepish.

                    ANGELA
     Who did this?

                    PRIEST
     It's just a nosebleed

                    ANGELA
     But you've never had a nosebleed
     before

                    PRIEST
     First time for everything!

Angela looks confused as she stops tending to
the priest.

                    JIM
     You baptised my boy and now
     he's as good as gone, Goddamn
     it! What the hell have you done
     to my son?

                    PRIEST
     Jim, I'm sorry!

                    ANGELA
     Clyde told me about your
     son. I'm sorry he's somewhat
     out of sorts

                    JIM
     'Somewhat out of sorts'?
     Jessie is in a coma and no
     one knows why or what to do
     about it

                    PRIEST
     There is something,
     something you can do about
     it

                    JIM
What are you talking about?

                    PRIEST
I'm talking about the truth

                    ANGELA
Clyde, are you coming?
Everyone's waiting

                    PRIEST
I can't. Sorry

                    ANGELA
Oh, why not?

                    PRIEST
You know why. I was wrong
all along. Lord have mercy

Angela looks deep into the priest's eyes.

                    ANGELA
Very well. Daniel, let's go

                    DANIEL
No

                    ANGELA
What do you mean, no?

                    PRIEST
Daniel. . .

                    DANIEL
After all these years, it's time
for me to face my fear

                    ANGELA
We've just buried your father,
my husband. Daniel, please

                    DANIEL
I was chasing a rainbow when it
happened. Dad bought me a boat
because he liked to think of me

as a fisherman in the making, and
I played along with his fantasy
so I could carry on being myself.
After the monster, the rainbow
became a million miles away. And I
haven't been the same since, scared
stiff of following my heart - what
kinda life have I got to live if I
can't even be myself? Sorry, Mum,
I'm not in the mood to mourn anymore.
I'm sure you'll find a shoulder
to cry on

Angela slaps her son around the face. She walks back down the church grounds and gets into a car.

All the cars drive off together.

                    PRIEST
    Go catch up with Stuart

The priest tells Daniel what to do. Daniel does just that.

Jim gets out a mobile phone. He dials a number and then puts it to his ear.

                    JIM
    Can I have a taxi please. . .
    Lochend Church to Freedom
    Fields Hospital. That's
    fine. Bye

                    PRIEST
    You didn't just come from the
    hospital to hit me! You came
    here for a reason beyond your
    reckoning. Jim, there is
    something in the water. . .
    not only will it blow your
    mind, but what will be, will
    be — because destiny dances
    to the tic-toc of time and
    yours has come!

> JIM
> You're full of shit

> PRIEST
> These sweet nothings that I
> speak of - if you feel all
> else has failed don't you
> think it's time to tempt fate

> JIM
> Tempt fate? What do you mean?

> PRIEST
> I mean, seize the Goddamn
> day!

> JIM
> You're still full of shit

> PRIEST
> Desperate times, Jim. I'm
> talking about right here,
> right now. What will you
> do to save your son?

> JIM
> I will do whatever it takes

> PRIEST
> I know. Which is why you
> won't get into the taxi
> that's just got here

Jim turns around and sees that there is the
taxi he called for.

> PRIEST
> You will come with me, and
> I will lead the way

The priest leads him out of the church
grounds.

INT. FREEDOM FIELDS HOSPITAL, SCOTLAND, DAY

Jessie is lifelessly lying down on a hospital
bed. He's been wired up/plugged in to some
kind of monitor/machine.

Mary-Jane is sat on a bedside chair, crying
while she cradles her quiet baby to sleep.

A doctor enters the room.

                    DOCTOR
        Hi. I'm Doctor Cameron.
        Before Jessie was transferred
        to Fly In The Sky psychiatric
        hospital, tests were carried out
        to check on the condition of your
        husband's brain

                    MARY-JANE
        We're not married. He's my
        boyfriend

                    DOCTOR
        Fine. Now what's interesting,
        at least to me, is he has
        absolutely nothing wrong with
        the way his brain functions,
        so to be in a persistent
        vegetative state makes no
        sense

                    MARY-JANE
        Tell me something I don't know
        or go away and do your job
        better, because it's about time
        someone knew what the fucking
        hell is happening to him!

                    DOCTOR
        Well, where treatment is
        concerned, due to the utmost
        mystery that surrounds Jessie's
        unresponsive state, we are left
        with giving him a 'coma cocktail'

consisting of thiamin, glucose
and naloxene

Mary-Jane continues to cradle her baby in silence.

>   DOCTOR
> We are doing everything in our
> power to get Jessie better

The doctor's pager goes off.

>   DOCTOR
> Excuse me

He leaves the room. Mary-Jane remains rooted to the bedside seat with her baby.

SCENE 16: SEE THE LIGHT

EXT. LOCH NESS LAKE, DAY

The old man 'captains' his boat, controlling the boat's course as it travels along the loch.

Jim, Daniel and the priest watch on from the front of the boat.

It's clear blue skies and there is a cold wind in the air.

>   DANIEL
> I'm Daniel

The young man offers his hand to Jim.

>   JIM
> Jim

Jim shakes his hand.

The priest gives Jim the equipment fit for the purpose of diving.

                    JIM
    What's all this?

                    PRIEST
    What's it look like?

                    JIM
    I've not dived in. . .
    it's been a while

                    PRIEST
    Today's the day you get
    your life back

The old man stops the boat.

Jim takes the diving gear and goes to the back
of the boat.

                    DANIEL
    Dad never spoke a word of
    what went on, and Mum . . .
    Mum just said I'd imagined
    it all

                    PRIEST
    Your parents were just trying
    to protect you

                    DANIEL
    Protect me from what?

                    PRIEST
    The truth

The old man approaches Jim getting changed at
the back of the boat.

                    OLD MAN
    You're gonna need this

He gives Jim a knife.

Jim takes the flask from Stuart's other hand
and has a big sip.

JIM

    How big is it?

The old man laughs as he takes his flask back, has an even bigger sip than Jim did, and then wipes his mouth.

OLD MAN

    You'll see

The priest and Daniel join them both at the back of the boat.

DANIEL

    Good luck

Jim is ready.

PRIEST

    God is with you

Jim purposely falls back, into the lake.

SPLASH

The loch's surface is clear enough, but beyond that the lake looks like a black abyss.

Jim turns on his headlight to improve visibility.

He descends deeper and deeper, passing big fish in the process.

The dive so far has seen him go over halfway down, to about 120 metres deep.

Just as Jim begins to assume some kind of confidence where his surrounds are concerned, his headlight flickers off a few times and then remains off after that. He cannot see a thing.

Jim panics, first hitting the headlight with his fist, and then desperately shaking it, but to no avail as he remains amid darkness.

He repositions himself, before feeling the need to head back up.

Suddenly he notices something shining from beneath him Jim stops, mesmerized by the light that appears to be coming towards him.

The shining silhouette outstretches something that resembles an arm as an offering to Jim. He slowly lets his arm extend and makes contact with what can only be described as supernatural.

He feels a force from the bright light take him down. Jim does not struggle, letting it happen.

Jim is being guided downward.

The supernatural pull all of a sudden ceases; as if by magic the bright light illuminates Nessie.

Jim's headlight turns on, and lying in front of him is the Loch Ness monster, tied down.

He dives deeper and down until touching distance is assumed between him and the great big sea creature.

Jim gets out the knife with one hand, and then in a moment of disbelief reaches down to touch Nessie's head.

Its eyes stay shut. He snaps out of his own wonder and dives above the big body of Nessie.

Jim carefully cuts through the tight netting, starting from the sea creature's tail end and working his way towards its head.

The netting holding Nessie down has now been cut away, and just as Jim finishes, Nessie lifts its head up.

He is taken aback by surprise, accidentally dropping the knife.

Jim quickly swims upwards as fast as he can.

He soon surfaces, swimming back to the boat.

The priest and Daniel help him up. The old man takes a swig on his flask.

Jim takes his headlight off, followed by the breathing equipment etc.

                    OLD MAN
     Is it still alive?

All of a sudden, Nessie emerges, surging in an enigmatic, quite epic display, launching itself straight out of the water, roaring its release as it sounds like a dinosaur.

The magnificent sea creature catches air, capturing imagination on its way up and over the boat, before crashing back down into the Loch Ness.

SPLASH

INT. FREEDOM FIELDS HOSPITAL, SCOTLAND, DAY

Suddenly, Jessie lifts his head up off the pillow, opening his eyes as he catches his breath back, panting in a fast and furious fashion.

                    MARY-JANE
     JESSIE? JESSIE?

Mary-Jane, baby in her arms, rushes to the door screaming for help.

A nurse comes in, quickly followed by a doctor.

The doctor holds an oxygen mask over Jessie as he slowly yet surely regains his normal breathing pattern and in doing so, comes to his senses.

Then, Jessie puts his hand on the doctor's hand and takes it off of his mouth. With the other hand he takes off the oxygen mask.

He looks over at Mary-Jane, tending to her crying baby and gives her a warm smile.

Mary-Jane smiles back as a tear of relief runs down her cheek.

EXT. LOCH NESS LAKE, SCOTLAND, DAY

The old man is back behind the wheel of his boat, taking them back to Lochend/land.

Jim is reliving recent events as Daniel and the priest listen intently.

> JIM
> And then there was this
> bright light beneath me,
> so I looked down and it
> was coming straight at me!

> PRIEST
> A bright light?

> JIM
> I cannot for the life of me
> even explain it, but I knew
> then, like I know now, that
> there is nothing to fear. For
> some strange reason, this -
> thing . . . it reached out to
> me

Jim outstretches his own arm in order to best describe his experience. As he does this, he notices the wedding ring on his finger has gone. Jim suddenly stops what he is saying, stunned into silence.

                         PRIEST
     Jim?

                         JIM
     My ring. . . it's gone

The priest appears so very much touched and
indeed he is moved to a moment of profound
realisation.

                         PRIEST
     This supernatural light . . .
     it reached out to you...
     you must have made contact

                         JIM
     It took me down. It showed me
     the way

                         PRIEST
     And how did it feel?

                         JIM
     Warm, familiar, like a
     loving feeling

The priest nods as he smiles, showing no
teeth.

                         PRIEST
     She wants you to move on

                         JIM
     Wendy. . .

Jim gulps, almost choked up by this
supernatural realisation.

                         PRIEST
     Do you believe in God?

                         JIM
     I believe in love

The priest smiles at Jim.

> PRIEST
> Same thing

Jim grins at the priest.

> JIM
> Can you take me back to the
> hospital?

> PRIEST
> Certainly

CENE 17: FREE AT LAST

INT. FREEDOM FIELDS HOSPITAL, DAY

The priest pulls up to the hospital entrance.
Jim gets out, but before closing the door
turns to face the priest.

> JIM
> Can you come with me?

> PRIEST
> Yes, of course

Jim waits at the entrance while Clyde parks
his car.

They go straight to reception.

> RECEPTIONIST
> How can I help you?

> JIM
> I'm Jessie Smith's father

> RECEPTIONIST
> Just take a seat in the
> waiting room and you'll
> soon be seen to

> JIM
> Ok, thank you

Jim and Clyde take a seat in the waiting room.

There is a brief silence between them both.

                    JIM
    Sorry

                 PRIEST
    What for?

                    JIM
    For punching you in the face

                 PRIEST
    Freedom of your expression,
    Jim. I'm talking about a
    bloody good old fashioned
    'howdy partner knockdown'
    and indeed it did do wonders
    for me, so thank you very
    much!

Jim grins as he shakes his head in a bit of
bemusement to what the priest just said.

A doctor approaches them.

                 DOCTOR
    Mr Smith?

                    JIM
    Yes

                 DOCTOR
    This way

Jim gets up to follow the doctor's orders.

The priest grabs hold of Jim's arm for a
moment.

                 PRIEST
    God is still with you

The priest stays sat down in the waiting room.

They walk down a corridor in an agonising silence, until getting to a room.

The doctor stops at the closed door.

>   DOCTOR
>   After you

Jim opens the door.

Jessie is sat up, laughing, smiling and holding his baby. Mary-Jane is sat at the bedside table, glowing with love.

>   JIM
>   Jessie!

Jessie looks at his father and then hands his baby back to Mary-Jane.

Father and son share a warm embrace as tears run down Jessie's cheek.

>   JESSIE
>   I love you, Dad

>   JIM
>   I love you too, son

The doctor doesn't want to break up such a sentimental moment, but he is here for professional reasons first and foremost.

>   DOCTOR
>   Quite frankly, we don't know
>   what caused Jessie's sudden
>   reawakening. Unless of
>   course, the coma cocktail
>   took effect

>   JIM
>   'Coma cocktail'?!

>   DOCTOR
>   It's not as exotic as it

sounds. Glucose, naloxene
and thiamine. Anyway, we'll
never know so if you'll
                    DOCTOR CONT'D
excuse me

The doctor leaves the room.

                    MARY-JANE
Where did you go?

                         JIM
I had some unfinished
business

                    MARY-JANE
 Is it finished now?

                         JIM
 No, it's only just begun!

                         JESSIE
What has?

                         JIM
The rest of our lives. It's time
to make a fresh start

                         JESSIE
Speaking of which . . . there's
something that I have to ask
you, Mary-Jane, in private

                    MARY-JANE
Um . . . ok. Can you take her?

She looks up at Jim.

                         JIM

    Sure

Mary-Jane hands him her baby. Jim takes her
out the room.

                         JESSIE

Close your eyes

                    MARY-JANE
     Why?

                    JESSIE
     Mary-Jane, just close
     them

She closes her eyes.

                    JESSIE
     Where would you like to be?

                    MARY-JANE
     What do you mean?

                    JESSIE
     You can be anywhere in the
     world. Where are you?

                    MARY-JANE
     I'm right here, with you

                    JESSIE
     Ok, take reality out of the
     question cos no one wants
     to spend their days stuck at
     a hospital, let alone in
     Scotland!

                    MARY-JANE
     Can I open my eyes yet?

                    JESSIE
     Not yet. If you could be
     anywhere in the world,
     where would you be?

                    MARY-JANE
     Our own private island
     drinking a pina colada and
     watching the sun set

                    JESSIE
     Perfect. Hold that thought.

Are you there yet?

                    MARY-JANE
Yes

                    JESSIE
Now imagine me, knelt down
on one knee and then I
take your hand and place a
great big diamond ring on
your finger. Mary-Jane. . .
will you marry me?

She opens her eyes as a tear runs down her
cheek.

                    MARY-JANE
    Yes!

She embraces Jessie joyfully.

Jim watches on through the window with a
smile, sensing such a thing. Holding his baby
granddaughter, they go down to the waiting
room.

The priest stands as he sees Jim come towards
him.

                    PRIEST
    How is he?

                    JIM
    Right as rain

                    PRIEST
That's alright then

A man approaches them. He walks tall, although
the wrong side of 6". His manner appears
serious; his looks are clearly world worn or
in other words he's experienced and it shows.
There is something about him, not only by the
way he walks, but the air of importance oozing
from every fibre of his being.

                    SHERIFF
    Jim Smith

Jim turns around, responding to the Texan
twang in the man's mature tone of voice.

                     JIM
    Yes

                    SHERIFF
    Mitch Morris: Sheriff
    for the Dallas Police
    Department

Mitch is of medium build but confidently
carries himself as if slimmer than his love
handles suggest. He's shorter than Jim and a
little less handsome. There are no discernible
features that redeem the sheriff from
appearing 'average' where first impression is
concerned.

                    PRIEST
    Jim, I'm gonna go see your
    son. Shall I. . .

The priest opens his arms so as to take the
baby from him. Jim hands her over.

                     JIM
    Down the corridor, second
    door on your right

Clyde nods at Jim and then walks away with the
baby in his arms.

                    SHERIFF
    Let's step outside, shall we

Jim follows the sheriff outside the hospital.

EXT. FREEDOM FIELDS HOSPITAL, SCOTLAND, DAY

The sheriff and Jim sit opposite each other on
a bench.

                    SHERIFF
So what brought you all the
way to Scotland?

                    JIM
Personal reasons

                    SHERIFF
Care to elaborate?

                    JIM
Not really

                    SHERIFF
In that case let's cut to the
chase. 'Lester Tyler-Moore'.
Are you familiar with this
person?

                    JIM
Never heard of him in my life

                    SHERIFF
So you don't follow professional
bull riding in your spare time I
take it

                    JIM
No

                    SHERIFF
Well, Jim, in certain circles he
was known as 'Fearless Lester',
for good reason as a matter of
fact

                    JIM
What's this got to do with me?

The sheriff gets out a pack of smokes, lights
his cigarette, and then continues.

                    SHERIFF
So, no matter how good you are
at staying on a bull, sooner or

402

later you're gonna get bucked off.
For Lester it would be, on average,
after about eight seconds —
impressive, huh?

Jim doesn't look impressed as the sheriff, for
the life of him, inhales his cigarette with a
certain degree of focus.

                    SHERIFF
        Now you can be the toughest
        S.O.B there is but when you've
        just been bucked off of a great
        big bull, I don't care who you
        are, or who you think you are,
        every time you hit the ground,
        you hit the ground running and
        I mean running scared. And that's
        pure fear for ya, or survival
        instinct, call it what you will.
        Well, Lester, after being bucked off
        of course, gets up, brushes himself
        down and then slowly but surely
        strolls towards the nearest gate
        without a care in the world. All
        the while a raging bull runs rings
        around him! I mean, come on!

                    JIM
        That doesn't surprise me, you
        have to be a bit simple and
        then some. To wanna get on the
        back of a raging bull in the
        first place is just plain
        unwise

                    SHERIFF
        Suffice to say, there was
        something amiss which was
        part of Fearless Lester's
        charm. I mean, you couldn't
        help but love the guy. Every
                    SHERIFF CONT'D
        rodeo turned into a sort of
        circus, cos Lester just stole
        the show. Though, soon enough,

403

dumb luck can run out on ya
and for Fearless Lester it did
just that. He got trampled on
and ended up with a limp. No
more rodeo. And at twenty five,
for that to happen, well, what
can you do?

                    JIM
Get a real job

                    SHERIFF
Bingo. So from professional bull
rider, Lester limped along in his
father's footsteps and became a
slaughterman, until of course he
could afford to get his leg fixed,
since he spent the majority of the
money he made riding bulls on buying
his first house

The sheriff puts out his cigarette.

                    SHERIFF
But, this is where Lester
Tyler-Moore's story ends,
cos there ain't no need in
fixing a limp leg when you've
been burnt to death

Jim remains silent.

                    SHERIFF
That being said let me ask
you again. 'Lester Tyler-
Moore'. Are you familiar
with this person?

Jim takes off his cowboy hat and puts it on
the bench.

                    JIM
You know what's so special
about that hat

The sheriff squints into his eyes yet does not
have the heart to humour him on this occasion.

>   JIM
>   Nothing. Nothing but the
>   fact that it hides my hair
>   or lack thereof. Funnily
>   enough, Northern Mexico
>   was where our so-called
>   cowboy hat first came to be

>   SHERIFF
>   That hat and many more of
>   a very similar nature first
>   'came to be' by a John B.
>   Stetson in 1865, born in
>   Orange New Jersey. He worked
>   alongside his father; they were
>   both mad hatters!

>   JIM
>   Huh

>   SHERIFF
>   Why'd you do it, Jim?

>   JIM
>   I did what I had to do.
>   To begin with, there was
>   No, no nothing, nothing
>   in the air albeit for the
>   black-like eyes of a
>   godforsaken kid. I walked
>   down the field and I gave
>   him much less than a look,
>   cos I couldn't do anything
>   else, so I just . . . it
>   was a signal given against
>   my own will: to get it over
>   and done with! Then I carried
>   on walking. The
>   JIM CONT'D
>   shooting started and all
>   I can remember hearing
>   after that was the piercing
>   sound of pure fear

The sheriff gets out another cigarette, lights
up, but continues to listen intently.

> JIM
> I ran as fast as I could
> down to the digger, got in,
> and I tried to block it all
> out

> SHERIFF
> Block it all out?

> JIM
> I turned the radio up full
> blast, closed my eyes, covered
> my ears but I could still feel
> the terror, I could still sense
> the desperation

> SHERIFF
> Then what happened?

> JIM
> I opened my eyes

Jim shakes his head and draws his hand down
his face, suffering, reliving his traumatic
event in front of the sheriff.

> JIM
> One of my cows was running
> scared down the field. It
> ended up falling head first
> into the pit. 'Lester' limped
> down and he, he was just
> standing there, staring at my
> cow. He made aim. . . and then . . .

*There is a visual flashback of Jim reliving
this certain moment in time, from the recent
past.*

> SHERIFF
> And then what?

                    JIM
     I got out of the digger. I
     didn't know what I was gonna
     do. I was just too far gone,
     I guess

There is another visual flashback of Jim
reliving this certain moment in time from the
recent past.

                  SHERIFF
     Too far gone?

                    JIM
     The guy was just stood there
     for God's sake! Staring in
     some sort of twisted trance
     state at my cow while it
     tried to get the hell outta
     there, struggling, suffering,
     falling down

The sheriff stamps out his cigarette.

                  SHERIFF
     So he didn't shoot it.
     That's what you couldn't
     understand and that's what
     ultimately made you snap

                    JIM
     You cannot comprehend a man's
     actions as of when, well, what
     the hell compelled Lester to
     stand small like a lemon and
     not do a damn thing! It made
     no sense! So I grabbed the gun
     and kicked him into the pit.
                  JIM CONT'D
     Then I put my cow out of its
     misery. By the time I turned
     around all I can remember
     seeing is Shep sat there

                  SHERIFF

I take it Shep is your dog.
Did he follow you into the field?

>   JIM
> I forced Shep back down the lane
> long before my cows were
> killed

>   SHERIFF
> And yet you say you saw Shep

>   JIM
> Yes

>   SHERIFF
> Was he sat next to Lester. . .

>   JIM
> There was, sure enough, no sign
> of Lester

>   SHERIFF
> 'Sure enough'? He was either there
> or not there

>   JIM
> Like I said, Shep was just sat
> There, looking all serene and
> different. Not different
> physically, yet something wasn't
> the same, something had changed.
> Do you know what I mean?

The sheriff fingers inside his pack of smokes
for another cigarette, but there are none
left. He crushes the packet, putting it onto
the bench.

>   SHERIFF
> I don't suppose this here
> hospital sells cigarettes, does
> it?

>   JIM
> I don't think so no

The sheriff clears his throat.

                    SHERIFF
    Now, I'm no expert on matters
    concerning the mind and why it
    does certain things at certain
    times. Shep 'appeared' and
    became some kind of coping
    mechanism. Jim, you saw what ya
    had to see. Shep provided a kind
    of comfort for you to carry on

Jim's face is solemn, upon coming to terms
with what he has done.

*There is a visual flashback of Jim kicking the
shit out of Lester.*

                    JIM
     I killed him, didn't I.

                    SHERIFF
    In a moment of madness,
    Yes, yes you did

There is silence as Jim gathers his thoughts.

                    SHERIFF
    I was the one who had to
    inform Mr and Mrs Moore of
    Lester's death. The strange
    thing about it was, well, it
    wasn't the fact that there were
    no tears, cos shock comes first,
    that can last as long as a piece
    of string if you know what I mean.
    Even after that though, when the
                    SHERIFF CONT'D
    time came to cry, or release
    some sort of outburst at least,
    'mum and dad' did not display
    any sign of sadness - it was
    something else I sensed. So as
    soon as I told them the bad news,
    she sighed a sigh of relief! He
    held her hand and said to her

'it's over, darlin', no more
heartache'

Jim can only look at the sheriff with a blank
expression as he continues to listen.

> SHERIFF
> They say the truth is stranger
> than fiction. And now I know
> why they say such a thing

> JIM
> I can second that statement.
> Man, the kinda day I've had,
> hah

> SHERIFF
> She told me, Mrs Moore, her
> son never said 'I love you',
> not once. She went on to
> say many things about Lester,
> from never having a girlfriend
> to how he neglected the needs
> of their pet dog 'Pugly'. Funny
> little thing with a screwed up
> face, its tongue was always
> stuck out the side of its mouth
> — hah, yep, you're not quite right
> in the head if you don't know how
> to feel the bond between man
> and his best friend

> JIM
> I don't know how or why I
> would see Shep when in reality
> he was not there before me

> SHERIFF
> Your eyes did not deceive you -
> I have very good reason to believe
> forces were at work. Cos what I am
> about to tell you, well, let me
> begin by saying this — that the
> closest thing I think Lester came
> to being fulfilled, as a person who
> has not got what it takes socially,

410

he had to get his sense of self-
something or other from somewhere,
somewhere else; basically bull riding
made up for his failings as a kid and
beyond. From the tender age of twelve,
over half his life after that; to live
and breathe bull riding for so long.
Lester, like every other young gun,
when a precious certain something gets
taken away from you, you will do all
you can in your power for a chance at
getting that thing back before it's too
late

                    JIM
Didn't his parents recognise
something was wrong with him?
I mean, from a much earlier age

                    SHERIFF
I was sure from everything that
she had to say Mrs Moore, from
her heart; did all she could to
do good and right by her boy,
but maybe she coulda done more
as a mother. Haven't we all
entertained the bittersweet
benefit of hindsight? I am
more or less certain, Jim, from
having your recent past flashing
in front of you now — wouldn't
you like to go back in time
and make changes?

                    JIM
Yes

                    SHERIFF
Here's where I will soon enough
forgive you, if you begin to
think of me as being a bit too
'cuckoo gaga' and by that I mean
in other words so much for my
right mind kinda thing. 'Hippy
hippy shake' bonkers basically!

                    JIM
Come again, Sheriff?

                    SHERIFF
Don't get me wrong. From here on
in, Jim, the things I speak of,
strange they may be but believe
it or not — this is the truth

                    JIM
Then let me say this so you know
where I'm coming from, or more to
the meat of the matter, where
I've been - not to hell and back
but past the point of no return.
When I was 'shown the way' by a
force so far beyond any nature I
knew even existed! And now, well,
let's just say you wouldn't believe
what I've been through these past
few days

                    SHERIFF
Try me

                    JIM
It's a long story, Sheriff

                    SHERIFF
I'm sure you can make it
short, sweet, snappy maybe
. . . but for the love of God,
give it a happy ending!

                    JIM
How can it have a happy ending
when here I am on the brink of
being charged for murder and
then sent to prison

                    SHERIFF
Well, Jim, since you put it like
that. Allow me to go first.
It's time I made you fully aware
of what consequence came

over all America, after your
actions caused quite a twist
of fate! It would have been
a good two to three years before
'Fearless Lester's' time
spent slaughtering brought
in enough for the helping
hands of a surgeon or a
specialist to fix his leg.
But there are many ways we
can mend our broken dreams.
Lester Tyler-Moore was sent
an invite to the White House;
'Mr President' had followed his
progress as a fan and then felt
bitter disappointment at the
sudden demise of Fearless Lester.
Yet what he had already achieved
as a bull rider - our president felt
compelled to celebrate that in itself,
so surely Lester had it in him
some presence of mind, you'd think,
to foresee such a, well, once in a
lifetime opportunity!

The priest steps outside the hospital entrance
so to smoke a cigarette.

                    SHERIFF
     Sorry Jim, will you excuse me?

The sheriff gets up off the bench and
approaches the priest.

Jim is left alone on the bench but he too soon
enough feels the need to stretch his legs,
going over to them.

The priest gives the sheriff a cigarette.

                    JIM
     Forgive me father, for I have
     sinned. It has been a long
     time coming since my last
     confession

The priest stamps out his cigarette.

                    JIM
I killed a man

                   PRIEST
In sin, we will always strive
for the good and right, to
overpower wrongdoing

                 SHERIFF
Ahem. In keeping with the quite
unconventional manner or urge
Jim just had to confess his sin
somewhat out of place — this is
not at all ill-advised; so without
further ado and on a need-to-know
basis, before you are absolved,
believe me, I am more your
messenger than just a sheriff

                    JIM
Messenger

                 SHERIFF
Jim Smith, the world over have
you to thank. That's right.
Your 'wrongdoing' in light of
the law was a blessing in
disguise for mankind! And so
I guess it's true what they say:
'God works in mysterious ways'

                  PRIEST
Sheriff, if you will, let me
finish

                 SHERIFF
No, I won't. With all due
respect to your religious
sentiment, not everything
sinful falls foul of our
strive towards what is now
near enough; a 'kingdom come'
unto itself. If Jim did not
do as he did and don't mind

me recalling, Lester Tyler-
Moore: murdered by you, Jim,
in a moment of madness. This
is the biggest son of a bitch
'if' I've had to deliver from
evil! Lester, for the money he
needed, desperate to once again
get back on a bull, well, selling
his White House pass was what he
had in mind and we found out to
who — which led us down a
terrorist rabbit hole. When we
got to the bottom of it — let's
just say you saved the day.
Ok, cowboy, you did a bit more
than that; the President of the
United States of America can sleep
peacefully for the first time in his
terrorist-ridden reign, thanks to you!

Jessie and Mary-Jane are hand-in-hand as she
holds her baby, leaving the hospital together
as a family for the first time.

The priest feels the need to meet them at the
entrance just so Jim and the sheriff have a
moment more, for the sake of sorting this
twist of fate out.

                    JIM
    Am I under arrest?

                        SHERIFF
    Not at all. Like hell
    you are 'under arrest' !

                    JIM
    So you came all this way,
    just to tell me I. . . I

                        SHERIFF
    You're a hero!

                        JESSIE
    Dad. . . everything OK?

                    415

Jessie approaches as Mary-Jane and the priest watch on.

                    JIM
    I think so, son, I think
    so

                    JESSIE
    Well, Clyde said he'd give us
    a lift to the airport

                    JIM
    Us?

                    JESSIE
    Yes. We wanna come to Texas.
    Is that alright with you?

                    JIM
    Course it's alright! In fact,
    It's mighty fine by me!

                    JESSIE
    Ok, great! Hey, Mary-Jane, guess
    what? We're going to Texas!

Mary-Jane joins Jessie as the priest gathers his thoughts. Slowly but surely he follows her.

                    JIM
    So what happens now?

Jim asks the sheriff if he could be so kind as to shed light on the situation.

                    SHERIFF
    Why did you give Nancy your
    dog?

                    JIM
    How do you know Nancy?

                    SHERIFF
    Jim, I'm a sheriff for God's
    sake! Question is, why didn't

you just drop Shep off at the
kennels instead?

                    JIM
I didn't know where my dog goes
was such a big deal

                    SHERIFF
She told me to tell you -
you owe her a date!

Jim smiles, as do Jessie, Mary-Jane and the
priest.

                    JIM
I do indeed, indeed I do

The sheriff nods.

                    SHERIFF
Well, here's to history being
Made, and to a very bright and
forever beautiful future

                    MARY-JANE
Amen to that! Right, Clyde?

Mary-Jane makes fun of the priest but in a
nice way, while she holds her baby.

                    PRIEST
'Jesus Christ is the same
yesterday and today and
forever and ever, amen'

                    SHERIFF
And on that note, time for
me to make a move. I have
fishing and drinking, and
then some more of the same
after that, to do next on
my agenda — good day, cowboy

He goes to walk away.

                    PRIEST

Hey, Sheriff

The sheriff turns around.

                        PRIEST
Be careful what you fish for

                        SHERIFF
Not on my watch!

                        PRIEST
Well, don't say I didn't warn
ya

                        SHERIFF
Warn me? Of what? The Loch Ness
monster?! After all, with a name
like 'Nessie' should I really
be afraid?

                        PRIEST
Very afraid, if I may say so
myself — from experience of course!
Cos seeing is believing!

                        SHERIFF
Are you kidding me? Hey,
Jim, my fellow Texan, is
he for real?

                        JIM
Well, there's only one way to
find out. After all, 'the truth
is stranger than fiction'

The sheriff shakes his head and with a wry
smile leaves them to it. In other words, he
walks away.

                        JESSIE
Dad, what was that all about?

                        JIM

Buy me a drink at the airport,
. . . or two . . . yeah, make it
two. . . and then another for the
'sky above' if you know what I mean.
Only then will I tell you all about
it

                    JESSIE
And who's Nancy anyway?

                    MARY-JANE
Jessie!

                    JESSIE
What? I was only. . .

                    MARY-JANE
You were being a. . . I
don't know what the word
is, but sometimes some things
are better left unsaid

                    JIM
It's ok, Mary-Jane. Nancy is
a certain someone who wants to
be there for me

                    MARY-JANE
But what do you want?

                    JIM
I want what she wants and she
wants what's best for me

                    MARY-JANE
Good for you, Jim

Jessie cannot contain himself for much longer.

                    JESSIE
Me and Mary-Jane. . . we're
getting married!

Jim smiles lovingly.

                              PRIEST
   Congratulations!

Jessie puts his arm around Mary-Jane and gives
her a great big kiss on the cheek.

                              MARY-JANE
   Tell them about the other
   thing

                              JESSIE
   What other thing?

                              MARY-JANE
   Um, I'm holding onto her right
   now!

                              JESSIE
   Oh! We have a name

                              MARY-JANE
   Jim. . . Jessie and now 'Nessie'
   here are the only family I have
   and I was wondering — will you
   give me away?

                              JIM
   It will be the best pleasure,
   Mary-Jane

Mary-Jane hands Nessie to Jessie and she
becomes emotional, giving Jim a great big hug.

Their warm embrace is suddenly bombarded by an
overexcited dog, jumping up at Jim with its
tail wagging, and barking in a jubilant
display.

                              JIM
   Shep!

Mary-Jane ends the embrace as Jim lets Shep
jump up at him, licking his face.

                              NANCY

Shep! Don't you dare wear him
out!

Nancy walks towards Jim.

                    JIM
    Nancy. How did you get here?

                    NANCY
    Nice to see you too!

She stops in her tracks.

                    JIM
    You know what I mean

                    NANCY
    No, not this time Jim. Maybe
    you should spell it out to me
    because I can't keep on chasing
    you forever

Jim remains rooted and almost stunned stiff.

Mary-Jane distracts Shep from being in Jim's
way.

                    PRIEST
    What are you waiting for?

                    JIM
    Clyde, do you do weddings?

                    PRIEST
    Yes!

                    JIM
    Do you do double weddings as well?

                    PRIEST
    With a cherry on top!

                    JIM
    That's alright then. Nancy,
    will you?

                    NANCY
     Jim, just shut up and . . .

Jim makes his move, giving Nancy a passionate
kiss on the lips.

     FADE OUT

     THE END

CHAPTER 12: ODE TO A DREAM MOST RIGHTEOUS

29th of December, 2018

The flight from Exeter airport to Sao Paulo, long though it was, all of fifteen hours and then some, afforded Belle a lot of reflection. Because being closed in on an aeroplane made her go inward and evaluate her broken-beyond-repair relationship with Max. She realised, finally, he wasn't the man she so wanted him to be. In all the years apart, her heart yearned for what she created of him and it was just an illusion. Then, to reunite with Max was in her time of need, because she needed his support through her father's disintegration and eventual death.

Not once did she hear the words her heart waited on, 'I'm here for you'. Max was not and never here for her, Max was there for Max. She sees so clearly, her memories are not fond ones, only neutral – thoughts misspent on Max, and now, strange as it does seem to her, Belle feels free. But of course, recent past also springs to mind and her encounter with the homeless stranger – her true saviour – Francis Smith. She has at least something to look back on with a smile. And ok, yes, Isabella and Francis are responsible for the death of the Prime Minister, but to Belle, she had it coming to her. Politics is an acquired taste; if you can stomach the sheer ridiculous lingo along with the oh so grotesque posturing fit for amateur dramatics, then fine, spend your days dancing in the wake of a sanitised and deceitful profession. Because yes, Pricilla Fay, for her crimes against nature, payed the ultimate price – regardless of her immense status - she had to go.

Although Belle feels satisfied by being a conductor and accepts the great responsibility to receive her composer's symphony, she has always felt the burning ambition inside drive her towards one day making a symphony up of her own manifest. Upon receiving details from her agent Lucy, she knows it's not beyond the realms of possibility to include her very own symphony, should she be able to create it on time. Her orchestra are to play festive renditions of popular and classic Christmas songs, since it's the most wonderful time of the year after all. But Belle feels inspired by her recent set of circumstances, and knows only too well that when inspiration comes on, you must seize the moment.

Music conveys emotion; indeed Isabella learnt her craft from many a book, but it is in books you receive someone else's vision and their version of events as opposed to your own. Thus there are some things that cannot possibly be learned from reading a book; by having emotion one can harness such a thing and therefore feel compelled to create within it a masterpiece. This is dependent upon how aligned you are with the universal flow of life itself. Something, that at once comes as if by magic, takes all that you are to the place where imagination happens. Isabella always remembered the simple but profound statement made by the nineteenth century romantic composer Gustav Mahler, and so it was he who once said 'Only when I experience something do I compose, and only when composing do I experience anything.' Belle now knew not just those words of Gustav, but she resonates with them, for her feelings at this time are on fire, from whence experience has touched on that which is soulful. She is literally and emotionally high on life, looking out the plane's window to an endless lush blue view – one which further heightens her already elevated state of being. Because this was not a dream, but her reality right now, and her reality right now is of the time to go with the flow. Belle gets her notepad out, opens it to a blank page and assumes a conscious position of comfort from fidgeting on her seat, she feels such restless intensity take hold. But before putting pen to paper, she indulges in her memory of Max for one more moment.

Thinking back produces an unpleasant squirm across her otherwise flawless face. She recalls the time Max asked about his writings, to which she denied reading. The truth hurts, hence Isabella felt not the need to put a dent in this man's sure-fire pride. Indeed, she did read his writings, quite some time after that out of the blue breakup, but kept it to herself. Still unaware of her own opinion on the matter, not to mention the feelings she had harboured for such a long time, Belle only knew to keep quiet with his writing in mind. There was something that would have felt insincere about being judgemental towards his spirited outlook on life. Spirited it sure was, well-written too, but doomed to be belligerent until life let Max see why we are far from making the world a better place . . . personal gain gets in the way of everything else. She gives such thoughts a wry smile, albeit in the wake of discovering his heart was not as pure as his self-proclaimed propaganda had him and even her believe. Because his downfall lay by the beauty of one's own intimate manifest, that innocent freedom to dream up something from deep inside has become Max's life. Even though he himself had given up on breaking into the movie industry, he created that reality; it was born of selfish fantasies. Isabella understands the extent to which one will imagine and 'make-believe' in something that feels meaningful for you yourself if not anyone else.

Isabella but also recognises Max for the man he is now, and not anymore the man he wants to be. Max first and foremost is a man, made of the same human fundamentals as everyone else. His gift to write will be well-received, if only he knows and accepts his limits as a writer. But to Max, Belle believes he thinks of himself higher than that. And a dreamer's dream distorts his reality; it may even exceed or undermine a man's grasp of what is really going on in the world. We live via the story that can't help but be created by our subconscious wants and desires. As for Max's mind, it was fixed on an impossible dream. Did destiny intervene? Isabella's late father entrusted certain documents to him and his pursuit it would seem on, of course, changing the world. And yet, where was the world when presented the temptation to go your own way? The way of one's wants, as opposed to the path less travelled, and in doing so shows his true colours are tainted by burning ambition.

Belle almost feels sorry for her first true love. In his writings she can gather the frustration and fathom the battle between 'out there' where the world at once looks cold and yet feels even colder, but also she can sense such heartbreak coming from that of his old soul – the watcher within him is crying out to be heard. However, there remains more to Max than his brash raw writings, something that was crafted out of a love for film. Indeed, he does have the capacity to love, even if it's not of a beautiful woman like Belle; then only love, the one thing that truly moves Max into honest action and creative endeavour.

In truth, Belle is simply consoling herself of the man that got away. Yes, she knew him more than Max cared to question, but she did not know everything. And sad but true is how her heart must go on without him now – now she does not intend to find out who the real Max exists as. It's history, yet still Belle remembers and wonders, without the knowledge of what is certain but subtle, that a lost soul like Max must love; he has to care about something. She stops thinking, picks up her pen and titles this impending symphony: *Ode to a dream most righteous.*

Her memories of Max slowly leave the forefront from that which was on her mind and a sense of wonderment reigns supreme – she lets such a vivid imagination run wild.

What she hasn't perceived of him is for Max to only hope one day Belle will find out about. It's why he chose his movie industry dream over everything else. Story becomes us all. Our story matters because it's all we are and everything in life happens to us as individuals first, before we can share such sentiment with anyone else. A story is for the sharing. It wasn't enough for Max to share his life with just one person – Isabella. At twenty nine he had finished his film script but failed to make an impression, and that was because of inexperience. Alas, being rejected hurt his pride and crushed his spirit. At the time of trying, his hopes were sky high; he knows only how to write from his heart and soul. So the feeling was strong. To the story he gave everything, and everything in the story felt real for him.

Maybe it won't change Belle's view of him when the movie is made, but at least his innermost thoughts are to have a voice and a vision. No one but the few who are rejected at birth know how it feels to be unwanted. But Max embraced his fragility, took control of feeling vulnerable, believed in the beauty that is imagination and followed his heart. To critique the quality of his script would be to wonder how deep is his soul . . . so yes, of course there will always be a format. A set way of doing things, despite knowing too well there is limitless possibility, and despite knowing too well there can be no true vehicle for the soul. Computers are like the bicycle for the mind. Movie scripts are like an empty stage for the imagination.

Is it any wonder when aware of the life Max has that he chose to write a story like 'Nessie' . . . Jessie the young and reckless lost soul, chasing a dream of his own, only to come up against a spirited priest. That's the one thing bigger than a boy's childhood dream but chances are he has been too ignorant to truly consider where the kingdom of God is – within. Is the priest a characterisation of how Max sees Joseph Symonds?

Isabella's late father, a man of God, well-respected and wise beyond earthly years; he could have been so much more to Max but for the latter man's stubborn resilience in the face of changing one's ways when he had his heart set on something. Something that perhaps both the fictional character Jessie, and Max himself, have no idea of what it is exactly . . . they only know how to run away from the cards dealt.

It is entirely feasible to draw real-life comparisons when a work of fiction is based in reality. That's what will usually be created if the creator is not at all happy with life; he or she feels compelled to question the nature of truth. The happy writers accept the surface limits of reality, but bask in the vast, mysterious, spellbinding dreamscape potential that an imagination is for those who see such a thing as vivid and alive. Most writers write to escape life; by playing God one can create different worlds and different creatures . . . causing chaos of course is in the heart of our natural state – to play. But for Max it's much more interesting to explore reality, not escape it, and thus become the highest version of what is real. To do that, it's not all about simply 'playing' with one's imagination - a man or woman must question the reason behind being creative in the first place.

Max was probably not conscious of the decision he made to take Jessie out of the story, but instead felt inspired by an idea alone. That idea was cinematic and compelling, but it was also necessary. Because if Max does see himself as Jessie, then Jessie soon becomes a victim; a victim of the priest's deceit. Indeed, innocent Jessie, except guilty of neglecting his pregnant girlfriend, finds himself the subject of the priest's battle with his own demons. In simple terms Max is a lost soul, so by process of personal experience as an influence so is Jessie. Nessie is not a story about the origin and life of the Loch Ness monster; it's a story about a broken family - family being the central theme. Max has never felt part of a normal family; he was brought up and cared for by an aging couple who were incapable of having children. He's been alone all his life.

To set Nessie free from the hidden depths of a dark and gloomy Loch Ness was to wake Jessie up to the bright and beautiful world around him, but for being blinded by his sense of suffering from not belonging, from not feeling like he had a family anymore. And to reunite with his father Jim was to reconcile the resentment Jim's son felt towards his father for the death of his mother, Wendy. Whereas Max's soul takes shape as Nessie, the Loch Ness monster tied down and unable to be free, throughout the story. Yet in truth, Max is each and every character, trying to overcome conflict, find peace of mind amid human apprehension. After all, his writings were meant for Belle, so she could come to terms with his decision to leave the country. He wrote out of frustration and a longing for more than the simple life; a life offered to him by Belle's love but a love Max disregarded as menial. His film script came to be because love conquers all and out of love he searched his soul for something that was sincere.

Maybe Belle's not meant to know the real Max just yet. For right now she must utilize the fire in her heart, a burning blaze made out of restless passion and raw heartbreak. But both Belle and Max seek meaning – not from an outside world of feeling-less narcissistic tendency, where we people are outrageously westernized by a media that rams fame down our throat until we regurgitate the same old deadbeat dreams from film stars, popstars, or worst of all, reality TV vermin. This is not true to people like Belle and Max. What's true is what's right and what's right at once stems from within – that's where both their journeys began. Not for the love of fame; fame for the most part acts as a candy that the braindead eat with their eyes, binging on celeb-obsessed gossip and worshipping the media-driven version of perfection from the comfort of one's own home. No, at least they acted out of love first and foremost, but it is love that has torn them apart.

"Nation will rise against nation and kingdom against kingdom, and there will be food shortages and earthquakes in one place after another." Matthew 24:7

Man can choose to believe even though he has not seen, and that in itself is a miracle. However human nature acts simply upon a 'monkey see monkey do' notion. And influence reigns supreme, from all walks of life onto another. For nine days now, Rio de Janeiro remains in a state of wondrous disarray, Christ the Redeemer being worshipped like never before around the devastation of a broken city. People have been made homeless; despite it, they rejoice this seemingly miraculous result – that Christ can endure no matter what the world does because of course the world, according to scripture, suffers from the Devil's work.

Like a knock-on effect, but also because of the shock death of the Prime Minister, there is a storm coming. Untimely, yet to some and many now whose worst fears are realised, 'Brexit' negotiations are at a premature close, since Pricilla Fay is dead and patience has worn thinner than ever before. With no formal agreement reached during the dismal display of negotiation between the EU and Great Britain, it is now a 'no deal' scenario. In money terms, this means there is no legal obligation for the UK to make any payment as part of a financial settlement, thus leaving a huge hole in the EU budget that has antagonised and deeply affected relations between both the EU and the UK; legal action has been threatened to take place at the International Court of Justice in The Hague. For citizens, the entitlement of EU nationals to reside in the UK or of UK nationals residing elsewhere in the EU is no more – gone has the right to reside where one's heart desires. And so, with no new trade agreement put in place, the rules of the World Trade Organisation now apply. Tariffs are to be imposed upon goods that the UK sends to the EU, and vice versa.

Simply put, 'tis the season to go crazy. And crazy Great Britain is, now experiencing a systematic and social collapse. People all around the country are succumbing to fear of chaos. Also, with no Prime Minister to front the illusion of order there are riots a plenty . . . looting and tomfoolery, crime and wrongdoing. It's as if for far too long the general public have put up with this practised display of political posturing to no avail and now all hell has broken loose. What's worse is the further breaking news from Rio, for the world over to take note, that since such a severe earthquake has happened, an aftermath of air pollution threatens to wipe out the world population. Indeed, it's been reported upon and concluded that unless people all over the world are issued with a small earpiece device to fit in both ears as soon as possible, until the air is clear of contamination, then they will die from the highest outbreak of air pollution imaginable.

The device is said to intercept, but at the same time transfer 'pure air' via sound waves from the atmosphere in space; this is done using satellite, straight to the brain and thus cleansing a person's blood flow around the body.

President Ronald Flump, with the flair he has for melodrama, makes sure his voice is heard and has already appeared in an emergency press conference from the White House. Asking for calm from both Brazil and Great Britain in this a time of great need, indeed the US President delivered his speech with smug aplomb, not to mention an Oscar-winning sincerity. Because surely he practises such divisive sentiment in the mirror President Ronald Flump so dearly loves. But his words were also of fair warning to his fellow American citizens, concerning the apparent contamination making its way across the world and advised all people who value life to put on the earpiece and keep it on until further notice.

There's something strangely ironic about a billionaire businessman making it to US Presidency. This is a man who courts controversy as if it's Miss Universe, and a man that gets a kick out of playing up to the cameras. Ronald Flump, the man that fronts the land of the free, the man to tell you in no uncertain terms 'YOUR' American Dream is a distinct possibility. He is, or at the very least appears to be a strawberry blond buffoon and that's putting it politely. A president in keeping with the times, well, the times they are a changing and not for the better. Tweeting like there will be no tomorrow, from the comfort of the White House, doesn't Mr President have more important things to focus his outspoken opinion on? Or maybe, just maybe, he must keep up the appearance of being a buffoon in public, while behind closed doors something else entirely may well be going on. But apart from being speculative of his inappropriate methods and mannerisms as a president, it's true you must also be careful what you wish for.

Change? Well, the political posturing is now one of pure arrogance instead, and that cringe gesture Ronald does with his hand, making a circle with his thumb and his index finger really does come across as a remarkable act of supreme overconfidence. This is not the behaviour of a politician, it's the surface showmanship of a great pretender. To have him as the President it is so very vital to acknowledge the kind of culture America are fronting and encouraging. Our greedy undivided attention spent on bettering one's self, for the sake of seeking something that doesn't even exist – perfection. Then there's the pressure to appear superior, by using society as a stage in which we are part of a platform for our opinions and our material possessions.

The future will appear brighter than a fake tan, if the future is forever Americanized, and as for the truth . . . the truth of the truth that is . . . it's just not important anymore. After all, terrorists commit crimes using God's name to elevate their atrocious actions against civilisation. And this makes the sheep, small-minded and fearful, blame God, not just the misguided individual blowing things up. People follow each other for lack of a leader, and yet now with the President Ronald Flump fronting the show – Americans are being led astray by a man of complete and utter ignorance, as well as an astounding disregard for common sense itself.

Max has been lulled into his own unbelievable bubble, a bubble of which has inside it beautiful people playing the game made from what was first and foremost his story. He's just come back to his hotel room after a long day of filming. Filming which will recommence after the New Year's celebrations, so now Max has a few days off to contend with what's going on in the outside world, while his face is an irreplaceable smile stemming from the ever-so-subtle but predominant smug sense of self-importance consuming him. However, given this moment of quiet, away from all things thespian and overdramatic, Max lay on his bed to stare up at the ceiling, thinking it's too good to be true. He wonders about the director, 'Michael Gay', and how wrong he was to dismiss his ability based on the movies Michael has directed in the past.

Max has not and doesn't intend to tell Michael how he hates his other movies with the utmost discontent. They speak for themselves – movies of explosion and all the action that can compensate for an undeniable lack of gripping dialogue. But then he feels himself fidget to almost shake off this sense of artful pride because perhaps, he thinks, Michael is merely a victim of Hollywood and can quite easily be saved if presented with the right sort of script. Suffice to say, something is playing on Max's mind and it's this – why, when

Michael Gay can boast about blockbuster after blockbuster, to have worked with the A-list stars of his choosing, has he not cast one single star in Max's story?

Surely Michael knows it's the star that pulls in a big audience, more so than the story . . . after all, Max is fully aware of the risk Michael takes just by believing in this script, let alone directing it. Then suddenly, a severe rush of doubt floods his busy mind and Max gets out his smartphone for reassurance. Because now he wonders whether this is actually happening at all, or if it's some kind of fucked up power-play by none other than Oksana Kuznetsov. However, he cannot access IMDB.com to confirm Michael's commitment to his script as there is no internet connection.

Knock knock. "Room service" A member of staff from the hotel enters Max's room.

"But I haven't requested anything," Max says, as he jumps up out of bed spooked by her sudden entrance.

"You are required to wear this earpiece device for safety reasons." She gives him the device, one for each ear.

"I don't understand." Max looks confused.

"Just place both bits into your ear," She says simply, like it's an everyday occurrence to wear something inside your ears.

"Why? What's going on?" Max asks, with a degree of caution coming across his voice.

"Haven't you been watching the news?" Her smile looks forced and practiced; she too seems to be behaving like a robot but that's the system in itself.

"No I have not. There is no signal. Luckily I can live without the distraction of a television in my life." He watches her just stand there, waiting for him to put the device in his ears. Reluctantly, he does as she says. She then turns around and exits his room.

"Hey wait, what about an internet connection . . . does this hotel have WIFI?" Max asks quickly before she can leave. She opens his door, turns around and laughs at him.

"This is Loch Ness, sir, we're in the middle of nowhere . . . surely if you say you can live without television then you can quite easily live without the internet too . . . goodbye." The member of staff leaves Max to it. He fingers the device, pushing it into both his ears before sitting back on his bed.

Belle gets off the plane drained and yet excited. December is classed as spring in Brazil, with it being one of the wettest months of the year here, but she still feels the heat as it remains really rather warm, even on a night like tonight. Belle sees Lucy standing in wait for her at the arrivals point and is pleased to be greeted by a friendly familiar face. They meet with a warm embrace before her agent takes control, guiding Isabella out of the airport to where a taxi awaits them.

"The plan is we have two days to go before your performance, and your orchestra can't wait to have you back, Belle!" Lucy is a typical bouncy soul for her demanding and stressful profession as an agent. She has straightened blonde hair, long but at a controlled length, with narrow dark blue eyes like the deep blue sea, and bright red lips. Dressed immaculately, she conveys a picture of proving to the public with her appearance alone that she means business.

"Is that so . . . shame they had me replaced,

isn't it!" Belle says, staring out the window while the taxi exits the airport.

"Belle, don't take it personally, that decision was made because we all had your best interest in mind. I know how hard it's been but you're a strong woman with an abundance of ability to conduct," Lucy says, staring sincerely in the direction of Belle, who still doesn't shift her sight from the streets of Sao Paulo.

"And compose," she says softly, finally letting her head turn to face Lucy.

"Compose . . . " Lucy wonders what she means.

"Yes, Lucy . . . I have composed a symphony and I intend to conduct it as part of my performance." Isabella's mannerism is as matter-of-fact as it gets.

"So what's it called?" Her agent asks with interest.

"'Ode to a dream most righteous'," she says, shimmering with intense pride. A sheepish, unpractised sense of self-importance causes her to clear her throat; almost embarrassed by it.

"So how's your love life?" Lucy asks mischievously.

"Lucy!" Belle says, shocked and at the same time amused.

"Belle, you're a beautiful woman, not to mention talented and smart; surely you have a man in your life?" she says, glancing at herself from the mirror of her make-up, pressing her lips together after applying yet more bright red lipstick.

"Just because I was blessed with the right kind of face fit for a man's menacing desire doesn't mean I'm going to take advantage of that, and if in doing so surrender to the arms of another privileged pig – thank you very much! Do you have a cigarette?" Belle enjoys being back in the company Lucy keeps.

"No smoking in my taxi." The Brazilian man manages to make sense of the English language, looking in his rear view mirror, making sure he's been understood.

"I didn't know you smoked," Lucy says, surprised by Belle's question.

"There are a lot of things that you don't know about me, Lucy," she says seriously.

"Yes, well we'll soon see about that . . . the hotel is just up here on the right, let's get you checked in and then go for dinner . . . I know a place," Lucy says with a smile. Belle smiles back at her as they arrive at the 4-star hotel Novotel.

Max wakes up to another knock at the door. This time it's director Michael Gay.

"Hi Michael, everything OK?" Max asks standing at the door, to the tall, bombastic Michael.

"Everything is as it should be, but I have a question for you, Max . . . have you made plans for the New Year?" He sounds adamant, almost too sure of himself.

"Um . . . to tell you the truth I haven't even given it much thought," Max says honestly.

"Can I come in? This won't take long but it's not something that I want to ask out in the open." He seems serious so Max lets him in.

"Now as you're aware, because of who I am in the Hollywood world, let's just say I have friends in high places . . . so here it is: I just got off the phone with the US President." Michael looks straight into Max's eyes.

"Ronald Flump?" Max sounds astonished and

his eyes widen.

"Yep, that's the one. Well, he's just had an irreversibly bad fall-out with his speechwriter and needs somebody to fill in and write something inspirational like the 'hope springs eternal' bullshit to keep people on his side . . . so are you up for it?" Michael edges closer to Max, sensing his excitement.

"Are you asking me if I want to write a speech for President Ronald Flump?" Max echoes excitedly, licking his lips, slowly shaking his head. He is amazed.

"That's exactly what I'm asking. Can you do it?" Michael asks with a smile all over his self-satisfied face. Max readies himself, about to answer, not knowing what will exit his jaw-dropped mouth this instant but feeling like a kid that's feasting his eyes over a big Christmas tree surrounded by presents.

"I can do anything with the written word," Max says ecstatically.

"I'll take that as a yes then. Glad to hear it. There's a private jet waiting for us outside. Come on, let's go." Michael shakes Max's sweaty hand.

"What? Right now?" Max sounds nervous.

"Yes, Max, right now. No need to take your things, the White House has everything taken care of." Michael walks out the room. Max freezes, picks up his phone and then follows him out the door.

CHAPTER 13: HE WHO HOLDS THE CARDS

30th of December, 2018

Max slept for the most part of the seven hour private jet journey, and he slept in style. Never before had he experienced the superior pleasure of flying by the highest class possible, but upon opening his eyes a stomach-clenching, sick sinking feeling of fear overcame him. Still he lay back, consumed by an instinctual calling . . . inside a voice was warning him of something untoward. With delicate care, Max puts his hand in his pocket, takes out his smartphone and checks it for a connection to the internet. This time he's in luck. Looking around him, Michael appears asleep, as does the big black bodyguard, and so Max sits up to access the internet, staring down at his smartphone intently.

He goes straight onto IMDB.com (Internet Movie Data Base) and searches for Michael Gay. Max clicks on his profile after finding it with ease, that's when his sick sinking feeling returned to him in an abundantly brutal breath-taking kind of way. Because looking at Michael's directorial history, he scrolls up to the present day, hoping it would state the project now known as 'Nessie', except according to IMDB 'Michael Gay' is working on another Transformers movie. Max can feel himself shake.

"This is your flight captain speaking . . . we will soon be arriving into Washington . . . with that being said, please stay seated until the plane comes to a stop. I hope you've enjoyed your flight, and thanks for listening." The chirpy captain's announcement makes Michael wake up. Max notices this, quickly placing his smartphone back in his pocket, before feeling the need to close his eyes as he pretends to still be asleep.

"Rise and shine Max, rise and shine!" Michael leans across and nudges Max. Max opens his eyes to the smiling Michael. Quite frankly he feels paralysed by the time being now, now he knows not all is as it seems.

Belle arrives at Sala Sao Paulo, Julio Prestes Cultural Centre, to begin with her orchestra the first of two practise sessions she has before the performance on New Year's Eve (tomorrow evening). It's situated in the old north central section of the city of Sao Paulo, where the building has been totally restored and renovated by the state government. The Sala has a capacity of fifteen hundred seats; its architectural style is neoclassical, principally derived from the architecture of classical antiquity and the work of the Italian architect Andrea Palladio.

Her symphony orchestra consists of sixty five musicians separated into four groups of related musical instruments known as the woodwinds, brass, percussion and strings. She least looks forward to reconvening however, with the newfound knowledge, of which was shed to light by Lucy last night, that Belle's male violinist Stefan Hansof fancies her and has done for quite some time. This explains his impeccable timing, along with an over-the-top passion when performing for Belle and Belle alone. Unfortunately for Stefan, she does not share such loving feelings, since her initial reaction when Lucy broke it to her was one of uncontrollable laughter.

She enters the concert hall. Of course there is no one here apart from her orchestra. Awaiting Isabella already onstage are all sixty five members. But they are not sat at their rightful place; instead is a buzz of mass chatter, as conversation fills the building. Belle feels goose bumps as she walks down the middle aisle, closing in on her orchestra. For the first time since the death of her father, Belle feels alive again. As she approaches the stage, they notice, quietening down and then breaking away from being in conversation.

"You all know what you're doing here . . . however there has been an addition to the playlist. It's a symphony of my making, called 'Ode to a dream most righteous', so without further ado . . . " Belle assumes her position as conductor, and hands her composition to one of the musicians in order to be passed around the orchestra.

Max exits the private jet at Washington airport, albeit with legs like jelly; he has been stunned. But still, he follows so-called 'Michael' along with the big black bodyguard and they pass through the airport. Awaiting them remains a limousine and as the three walk toward it, the limo driver opens the side door for them to get in.

Michael sits next to the bodyguard and faces Max, who nervously looks downward while the limo driver starts the engine and exits the airport.

There is tension in the air, a tension sensed and yet endured for the forty minute trip of overriding silence. The usually free-spirited and enthusiastic Michael cuts a figure more along the lines of something else; he's serious right now, not talkative but with a strange glint in his eyes like a focus on the change of mood. Michael looks different to Max. And Max can't bear to be breathing in this sense of the unknown anymore.

"Who are you?" Max asks, still finding it difficult to look at Michael, like the truth will hurt him if he faces up to such a thing.

"Max, are you OK? You look really pale. Bill, give him something to settle his nerves . . . he's obviously overcome by the big occasion in waiting. Don't worry, you're in safe hands." Michael tells Bill to proceed and the bodyguard does as he's told albeit against Max's will. Bill shifts from his seat. Max flinches; his attempt to defend himself fails as Bill injects something into his neck, sending him straight to sleep.

Upon performing her very own symphony for the first time, Belle feels like her movements with the baton happen in slow motion. Caught up in her creation, which indeed it is as she indicates each and every instrument to sound how her heart felt when her mind did a divine dance, Belle realises this special moment must at once be seized. Almost ghostly, here the atmosphere feels electric yet empty. Not that her attention wavers because she is in the zone. Her bluey green eyes seek out the sound from her orchestra and her orchestra deliver every part without fail.

Poetry in her smooth motion and poetry by the way they play a piece of Belle's soul, so she should and does feel that same sense of self-importance but this time it's stronger, purer; her mind, body and soul are at one with what's going on. And she is so open, enough to embrace such senses as they come over her. Flashing before Belle's eyes are childhood memories, moving images of those small moments in time – time spent preciously being herself and growing into the woman she has become. It's all been leading up to this and the gratitude gathers as Belle begins feeling teary where thoughts of her late father arise. Still, she's going strong, gaining in momentum from the path of her symphony . . . until the last note takes Belle's breath away.

And then silence, a silence made golden by Belle's heavenly endeavour. Her orchestra remain motionless, still sat at their positions as such a symphony sinks into them all. It's as if Isabella and her orchestra entered a new world which was of course her secret garden consisting of emphatic emotion and burning beauty. Each and every player rises spontaneously, simultaneously.

Suddenly a round of applause fills the concert hall. Belle holds back her tears as she too applauds, directing it at all of her orchestra.

Max wakes up.

"Welcome to the White House." President Ronald Flump welcomes Max, as the former remains sat comfortably at his big office desk.

Max adjusts his position in order to assume some kind of comfort but it's useless, as he still feels uneasy. Such an adjustment then provoked a reaction from the big black bodyguard but the US President gesticulates at Bill before he can intervene.

"Max is just trying to make himself at home! I'm sorry for your discomfort, but the President's needs must come first." Ronald Flump appears smug but perhaps that's the way his face looks all the time.

"Why am I here?" Max asks confusingly.

"I thought Michael already filled you in on that," the President responds innocently.

"I feel sorry for America . . . your deceit is a disgrace." Max sits back in his chair before crossing his arms. His seat has been positioned at a distance from the President's desk.

Ronald Flump leans forward to place his elbows on his desk, looks straight through Max's disapproving glance, and suddenly laughs his head off.

"I feel sorry for 'Great Britain'! At this present moment in time and despite the futile festive cheer, you guys are pretty much fucked." The President breaks eye contact with Max and adjusts his bright red tie, before feeling compelled to continue.

"Except it's Christmas, Max and Christmas is a time for giving. And do you know what Great Britain needs this Christmas?" Ronald Flump pauses for dramatic effect.

"No I don't, but sure as hell you'll humour me," Max responds distastefully.

"Great Britain needs saving from itself. Strength in numbers. And a brand new superpower will elevate each and every citizen to the highest of heights – it's just a matter of time." The President lets himself fall back into his great big swirly office chair before spinning from side to side.

"And on whose authority may you take over my country 'Mr President?'" Max asks with a stupefied smile, shaking his head in the process of being unpleasantly surprised by the US President's audacious claim.

"Bill leave us please." The President tells his bodyguard to go away.

"This is beginning to feel like I'm in one of those old Bond films." Ronald Flump pats the top of his hair to make sure everything is in its rightful place.

"Who will authorise such a ridiculous claim?" Max asks again, and in doing so disregards Ronald Flump's lack of imagination.

"God," the President says sharply.

"God gave you his blessing, did he?" Max sounds astounded as he places his hand over his eyes and rubs his dark eyebrows furiously.

"Hah, not exactly. But if you can't be God, play God." Ronald Flump looks conniving and sounds mischievous, as Max just shakes his head despairingly.

"You see, technology these days is racing ahead

of itself. If you could change the minds of the masses, make them believe that the bright future is finally here . . . hah, Max, you poor thing. It's about to be a brave new world but a world without your careless meddling. Let me show you something." The President opens one of the drawers to his desk and gets out the classified documents concerning Nikola Tesla's pursuit of free energy. But before he can reveal them and then revel in his position of supreme power, Max has more questions.

"So, what do you know about the device that's in my ears?" Max asks with interest.

"It's like I just said; technology creates change. All I had to do was give people a reason. 'Reason' is a weak word considering." Ronald Flump, for the moment, puts the documents down in order to continue with this discourse.

"Considering what exactly?" Max is feeling restless because the President isn't being clear, he's being vague and smug about it.

"Consider your worst fear realised – death. If your life is on the line, let's say by the most toxic contamination known to man and it's in the air everywhere, well, what you gonna do? You don't know what you are going to do, you just hope someone else does, and these days it's science saving us. So people all over for fear of losing life will stick something in their ears, something that they know nothing about, something that the television tells them is lifesaving. It's basic; it's survival instinct, but truth be told it's my greatest deception." The President emphatically slaps down the classified documents onto his desk and watches on for Max's reaction. It's one of stunned silence.

"And meanwhile, we have here a small-time

'freedom fighter' or are you a wannabe writer? Wait! You're a mere dreamer, Max. I mean, come on man! What is it you actually do? You don't work. You've travelled. Drifting around the world while your farfetched dreams misguide your every move. You've become something of a self-perpetuating nightmare, your worldview looks like a la-la land and yet your destination now will bring you back down to reality my friend. Whether you wake up to that fact or not simply remains to be seen." Ronald Flump sips on his cup of coffee, feeling pleased with himself of course.

"I can just about handle being played for a fool by a fool much bigger than me, because what's a dream like mine in comparison to something far greater than that? That which is still a selfish fantasy 'to be somebody' inside a society so severely westernized it's a society fronted by liars, and of course celebrated by those who hold the cards. They are the powerful few like you, abusing such a stance to obtain yet more power over everyone else. Yes, you tricked me. Yes, you made me believe I was living the dream. I'm nothing but a man who has in him heart and soul, despite the tragedy these times are for the ones with vision exceeding greed, and belief from wanting truth before your false hope prevails. Please Mr President, don't let the illusion of power colour the world in pitch black chaos." Max pleads with the President, while still sat afar from him. He eyeballs Max and simply claps sarcastically.

"I'm glad you got to say your piece, Max, and so you should, but it is with regret to inform you of your ill-fated future for breaking the law. Your quest has come to an end. On my command, you will be arrested with immediate effect for possessing US classified documents such as these 'sweet nothings'. Is there anything further that you would like to say before I bring in the FBI?" The President is deadly serious, staring at Max, sinking his authority into him.

"I need to make a call," Max says straightforwardly.

"Fine." Ronald Flump sips on his coffee.

Max gets out his smartphone and calls Isabella but it rings and rings until eventually proceeding to the answerphone message. Belle has her phone on silent while she is practising with her orchestra. Max shakes his head but waits for the beep before leaving her a message.

"We're the same, you and me . . . you conduct your orchestra whereas I conduct my orchestra, the English language. You care about every single sound's place in a symphony, just like I care about every word that makes its way onto the page. Passion can travel via all walks of life; we are the ones with a choice as to how that passion finds its place of perfection. After all, we have already reached our destination and yet we search for it in a feeling, the feeling of coming home. Go to your place called home, Belle, because it's where you belong. Goodbye, my love." Max cancels the call.

"Touching. Truly touching. Without the distraction of the outside world, well, you'll be able to give your undivided attention to writing silly little stories for a very long time, albeit behind bars. Max, it's been a real pleasure, forgive me, but I won't shake your hand. Thanks for your cooperation . . . you played my game perfectly." The President presses his phone on the desk, picks up the handset and then tells his secretary to get the FBI in here right away.

"You walked away from one of life's greatest gifts. Max, you could have had it all, 'love', 'happiness', hell, even her father gave you a way out. You had his blessing to be with her but you chose otherwise. You chose those 'precious documents' instead and for what? Wait, what was it? 'To illuminate the world with the colour of truth'. News flash, Max: This is a world where truth has been blackened and now we need a new ruler for all the blinded minds descending into the darkest depths of despair. After all, 'hope springs eternal'." The President finishes his cup of coffee before crossing his arms contentedly.

"False hope springs eternal torture of the mind, body and soul, you sick son of a bitch." Max stands up from his seat; he walks towards the President's desk and places his hands on it to lean in close.

"Remove your filthy hands from my desk." Ronald Flump appears angered by Max's movements.

"The earthquake – was it you?" Max asks aggressively.

"All I did was give the world good reason . . . reason to believe in a miracle, the most beautiful miracle the world will ever witness," the President answers, as if innocent of causing such severe destruction and chaos.

"The second coming of Christ," Max says slowly, removing his hands from the desk to stand up straight. President Ronald Flump simply smiles menacingly, and then gives Max a wink. In storm the FBI. Max is handcuffed and then taken away.

Belle is back at the hotel having a drink with
Stefan Hansof in the bar area. She has decided to
humour his feelings for her; more importantly she
will refrain from letting him down gently until
after the performance tomorrow night. Stefan has
a good head of blond hair and he's in great shape
but remains short at only 5' 7". His eyes are dark
and yet not mysterious and his conversation tends
to centre around flattery towards Isabella, but she
enjoys being told how wonderful she is so there are
no awkward silences stemming from boredom or
disinterest.

"I raise my glass to you, Isabella, because your
symphony is a masterpiece – it's breathtaking!
Could it be but anything other than that? I think
not. Cheers." Stefan has a strong Austrian accent.
His eyes are fixed on Belle who is sat opposite,
lapping up such sweet talk.

"Thanks Stefan, for playing your part. I know I
can always count on you to be at the top of your
game. Much appreciated and cheers." She touches
his glass of champagne and they share a smile
before Belle takes quite the pronounced sip from
her glass, as she knows too well that Stefan can't
take his eyes off her.

She checks her phone and notices a new
voicemail message.

"Excuse me," Belle says to Stefan, before
putting the phone to her ear.

Politely she keeps her eyes on Stefan while
listening and then when she realises it's Max, she
breaks away from his loving gaze, looking down at
the ground.

"Stefan, forgive me, but I must go now," she
says seriously.

"Go where?" he wonders.

"Up to my room, I'm really tired. I'll see you tomorrow, ok." Belle goes to get up.

"But you haven't even finished drinking your champagne." Stefan sounds desperate.

Belle gulps down her champagne in one and then walks away, while Stefan remains sat at the peril of his sinking feeling. Isabella rushes past reception.

"Excuse me, 'Miss Antoinette'." The hotel receptionist calls out to her before she can enter the lift.

"Yes, that's me," Belle says in a spot of bother.

"Here, you have a message." The receptionist passes her an envelope.

"Thanks, is that it?" she asks, albeit breathlessly.

"Yes." The receptionist gives her a warm and yet practised smile.

Belle rushes up to her room, closes the door and calls Max. There's no answer. Disappointed and frustrated, she falls onto her bed and then opens the envelope.

'Max is in trouble. I'll tell you all about it tomorrow morning. Meet me in the hotel restaurant at breakfast: 9am. Oksana Kuznetsov.'

The name rings a bell. She remembers Max saying her name with regard to the classified documents. Isabella fidgets to find some comfort amongst feeling restless.

She thinks back to a time when Max was last in trouble, big trouble. While fronting the foxhunt saboteur team of 'The Hunt-Trap Rat Pack', Max put his life in great danger for a fox's survival. It was a significant moment for Belle, because she realised by first witness of what Max is all about. His saboteur team remained hidden in the woods, watching on as a fox was being chased down by a pack of hound dogs, followed closely behind by the huntsmen and huntswomen on horseback. Max ran like the wind towards the chase; he distracted the dogs away from the fox and then . . . then he was taken out, floored by a furious huntsman on his horse. Max was trampled on more than once as Isabella's instinct kicked in and she sprinted to him. He was in a bad way. She called an ambulance, before supporting his head held in her arms. Max did not fear for his life, he feared for the fox's life. Belle remembers being there for him, while waiting for the ambulance to arrive. He whispered in pain *'Did it get away?'*

Belle spent that endlessly limbo-like night at the hospital, waiting, worrying, and admiring Max for the bravest act she had ever seen. Indeed it was while she waited that the thought of losing him sent a sick shock to her system. And then that was when she knew, with every fibre of her being, Belle loved Max. She turns onto her side and cries into her hotel pillow, longing for the love of Max.

This time tomorrow the world will be in celebration for the new year ahead. Here and now is the calm before the storm. Except there's no such calm, for the storm of circumstance and agonising anticipation continues to spread around the world from whence recent events have caused chaos. Sao Paulo's people are truly moved by the one and only remnant of Rio - Christ the Redeemer. Much has been said regarding it as a miraculous sign of this, the time to come now soon enough, when Judgement Day breaks the world down and only the chosen few who believe will rise high while all the disbelievers shall fall.

And all is far from well where Great Britain

remains in its crazy state of disarray. The uncertainty surrounding the Prime Minister's shock death that happened when a fire broke out on Boxing Day night under 'mysterious circumstances' has since captured the frightened minds of the masses. Those whom do believe in the power of God are forming a link between the earthquake and the fire, foreseeing such a thing as 'the end'. Indeed, it is wild in the streets, yet set to get even wilder when tomorrow comes.

31st of December, 2018

NEW YEARS EVE

Belle wakes up. Her first thoughts should be filled with excitement; later she will showcase a symphony born of her heart's desire. However, now she endures her longing in a waking state, whereas last night her heart had been spared pain by that of falling asleep. She showers, allowing herself to feel all that is playing on her heartfelt senses. Isabella lets her natural waves reign free, for she has not got the time to straighten her long, dark brown hair. She applies a subtle shade of lipstick, followed by black eyeliner and then gets dressed before exiting her hotel room.

Upon entering the hotel restaurant, Isabella recognises Oksana as the same woman who was with her father the night he collapsed. Oksana is striking even from afar. Her hair remains immaculately black, shiny yet fitting to her face of flawless splendour. Dark green eyes intensified by her natural look of beautiful allure. Pale skin that stands out as Oksana adorns an attractive black business-esque skirt and suit-style shirt. She rises as Isabella approaches her from whence she sat in wait.

Oksana outstretches her arm as a gesture for Belle, but she snubs such a thing and simply sits opposite. Oksana brushes herself down in reaction to being insulted and then takes a seat.

"My name is Oksana and . . . " Oksana begins.

"I know who you are. You were with my father the night he . . . anyway, suffice to say you weren't with him out of love. You were there for something else entirely, the classified documents, so that makes you what exactly?" Belle aggressively interrupts her. She folds her arms with intent to wait for Oksana's response.

"I was working for an intelligence agency. I was a secret agent sent by the powers that be, beyond me, to protect them from losing control. All I did was my job and I did exactly as I was told to do," Oksana says directly, keeping eye contact with Belle.

"Fine. Where's Max? Because I was led to believe, by Max himself, that he had made his dream come true. Do you know where he is?" Belle uncrosses her arms and begins to rub her legs from under the table. She feels restless.

"I misled Max. He was deceived. I offered him a deal that didn't even exist . . . the documents in exchange for a dream, his dream, and it was nothing but a power play. And now, for possessing such documents in the first place, Max is . . . he's behind bars." Oksana is straight-faced and her Russian accent sounds so very robotic, inhuman almost.

"Behind bars? Max is in prison?" Isabella can't believe this; she raises her eyebrows while fidgeting on her seat. She runs her hands over her forehead and then through her hair, distraught.

"Yes, and I've been relieved of my services, so now I'm out for revenge." Oksana opens up in an aggressive fashion and betrays her robotic tone for feeling aggrieved. Isabella has been silenced as she remains in shock.

"You can remove the ridiculous earpiece, Isabella, because quite frankly your life does not depend on it. There is no toxic contamination in the air." Oksana sounds definite. Belle believes her and removes the device from both her ears. Yet still, she keeps quiet, not knowing what to say or how she should react.

"I'm here because you deserve to know. This involves the love of your life after all. And I'm here to tell you who I was, ambitious, ruthless, cold. I could do what I did because it became me. But now, now I'm no longer required . . . I was promised so much, and assured of more power than ever before because that's what it's all about. Betrayed. And of course it's karma, I'm well aware of what I've done in my many years of being this way. Yet it is 'this way' which has passed me beyond the point of no return. There is no going back. Not for me. Not now I'm nothing but a body of worthless lies. Isabella, listen to me; there is a storm coming, something that is set to change everything. If this is allowed to happen . . . " Belle breaks free from her suffocating kind of silence so to interrupt the ongoing Oksana.

"If what is allowed to happen?" Belle asks furiously.

"At midnight tonight, the sky everywhere will whiten, it will be a bright white light shining down on us all like never before. But this shall be no miracle, but a projection instead, indeed a projection of the second coming of Christ." Oksana answers her, staring into Belle's bewilderment.

"Are you serious?" Belle has gone white like a ghost.

"Deadly serious." Oksana continues to keep her eyes fixed on Belle.

"What are you going to do?" Belle asks coldly.

"I have to stop it from happening," she says desperately.

"How?" Belle wants to know; her eyes light up.

"By destroying NASA space station. I'm going to blow it up, Belle, blow it to hell and back." Oksana says calmly, like it will be a walk in the park. Belle scans Oksana's eyes, once again silenced by shock.

"But there's more than one NASA space station isn't there?" Belle still wonders how Oksana can do such a thing.

"There are eleven in all. Not including its headquarters – that's in Washington DC." Oksana says informatively.

"This is an act of terrorism we're talking about," Belle says from her head.

"This will be an act of revenge and yet a blessing in disguise - 'righteousness', Isabella. Max knows all about that, and this will set him free." Oksana defends such severe intentions, by bringing Max into the equation.

"I still don't understand just how you are going to do all this," Belle says breathlessly.

"You don't have to understand how. I have assembled a special team of freedom fighters to do what is necessary. Isabella, all you have to do is your job, but once Max is free he will come for you. You deserve each other, both of you deserve a life of happiness. I must go now. I have a plane to catch. Happy New Year." Oksana gets up and walks away. Belle watches her casually leave the hotel, before checking the time on her smartphone. It's time she went to rehearse her performance this evening.

Oksana Kuznetsov arrived at Washington airport, only to be detained and then arrested by the FBI. One of her team of 'freedom fighters' was handsomely paid off in order to reveal these 'plans' she had put in place. So now she, along with the remaining team of freedom fighters, are facing a prison sentence for planning to carry out an act of terrorism.

CHAPTER 14: ENDGAME

Belle is backstage in her dressing room. She's been joined by her agent Lucy.

"You look flawless, Isabella but what's wrong?" Lucy watches on as Isabella looks blankly at her reflection in the mirror before applying bright red lipstick.

"I'm fine," Belle says sharply.

"I know how it feels to lose someone you love, I've been there," Lucy says sympathetically.

"Who are you referring to . . . my father or my first love . . . both are gone and now I have nothing but for the times I wave a silly little baton in the air." Belle shakes her head. She takes her attention away from her reflection and looks to Lucy for comfort.

"Stop feeling sorry for yourself. Get out there and show the world why you're here." Lucy sounds direct. Belle shifts her focus back on the mirror as she powders her face.

"Everything is going to be ok." Lucy puts her hand on Belle's shoulder, before turning to leave the room.

"How can you say that when you don't even know what's going on in the world?" She snaps at

Lucy for saying such a thing.

"Belle, I don't know what's going on with you right now but you need to focus. You've got five minutes. I'll see you after the show." Lucy leaves the room.

Belle stares lifelessly at the table by the mirror, which has on it a bottle of champagne and a bouquet of flowers from Stefan Hansof. She shakes her head, picking up the flowers only to put them in the bin.

She regained her focus, so to deliver an impeccable performance while a sold out audience spirited itself away with wonder and awe. Now came the time for Belle's symphony, 'Ode to a dream most righteous.' Isabella keeps her eyes on her orchestra and begins. With hearing it right now, while behind her remains a full house, such magic comes out to play. Belle gets lost again in the moment, her moment. To the last second of sound, she did all in her heart's desire for her symphony and for her orchestra. There were even gasps happening, gasps of appreciation and amazement, until the end was met with rapturous applause.

Isabella turns around to a standing ovation and red roses thrown in adulation of her perfect performance. She motions praise at her orchestra, but it is they whom are also on their feet for Belle, clapping and cheering. And then the curtain closes. Three hours of heart-stopping passion has come to an end. She feels emotionally drained and yet at the same time she is buzzing as if by cocaine coursing through her body.

Backstage, Belle re-enters her dressing room, soon enough followed by Lucy, who opens the bottle of champagne, popping its cork into the air as bubbly goes everywhere. Which compels Isabella to take the bottle from Lucy before she could pour any into a glass, and drink it straight from the bottle. There's a knock at the door.

"Come in!" Belle says excitedly, only to be faced with her admirer, Stefan Hansof.

He greets Isabella by giving her a long one-sided cuddle and a big kiss on the cheek. Lucy smiles before raising her eyebrows sarcastically.

"You were marvelous, Isabella," Stefan says enthusiastically.

"Thanks Stefan, can I help you with something?" Belle asks cautiously.

"Um . . . no . . . I was just wanting to congratulate you." Stefan answers her question but still feels taken aback by it.

"Well, now you have, if you don't mind I was having a moment with my agent, Lucy." She sounds defensive, not to mention in no mood to have him around.

"I see you've already opened the champagne I bought for us." He sounds sad.

"Stefan, you seem sweet but I'm not interested to have anything other than a professional relationship with you." Belle tells Stefan the truth. He grins forcefully before turning around and walking out the door.

"That was a bit harsh," Lucy says, swigging on the bottle of bubbly.

"No, Lucy, telling him he's too short for me, that would be a bit harsh. How long until it's midnight?" Belle grabs the bottle back from Lucy and proceeds to get tipsy.

"It's almost 11pm. Let's finish this then get going," she says, with something in mind.

"Where are we going?" Belle wonders.

"To the best cocktail bar around." Lucy sheds light on the situation.

And so, such a night like tonight, New Year's Eve is here and Belle's work has been done. But no amount of bubbly will make her forget about the meeting she had with Oksana earlier on. Can she not confide in her agent at all? Well, what on earth could Lucy do to make everything ok except say everything is ok and yet say it with little to no conviction, let alone any belief. Belle will soon get over her buzz from being onstage, and that's when wonder and worry will kick in. Indeed there is nothing that anyone can do now but celebrate the time being nearly New Year.

Belle and Lucy arrive at Peppino Bar at 11:30pm. This gives them just enough time to get a drink at the bar before finding some space on the terrace to watch the fireworks display happening on the stroke of midnight. It's busy. Very busy. But eventually, they are being seen to by a beautiful Brazilian bartender and their drinks are soon served. Lucy leads the way while she sips on her Cosmopolitan, and they make their way outside onto the spacious terrace. It's jam-packed, but with Lucy leading the way they manage to find room to lean up against the balcony, and there is a good view of the sky above.

"Now all we need are a couple of Brazilian dreamboats to take our breath away at midnight." Lucy says hungrily, lusting after a midnight snog.

"Speak for yourself," Belle says, as she curbs Lucy's enthusiasm with her troubled disposition.

"What's wrong with you? It's New Year's Eve, Belle! Lighten up please," Lucy says, glancing around the terrace for some action.

"Well, isn't it a pity you can't speak the lingo."

she says, sipping on her champagne cocktail.

"For a kiss all you need to know is the language of love and passion," Lucy answers her back defiantly. Belle checks her smartphone. It's 11:57pm.

"You have three minutes to find yourself a feller," Belle says finally.

"I'll be right back." Lucy disappears into the crowd.

"And a Happy New Year to you too, Lucy!" She downs her cocktail before focusing her attention on the night sky. Sure enough, within a minute and a half of 'exploration', Lucy reappears with two young-looking guys.

"Belle, meet Marcelo and Fabio" Lucy introduces her to them. Belle politely offers her hand and both greet it with a kiss.

The countdown begins.

10

9

8

7

6

5

4

3

2

1 . . .

HAPPY NEW YEAR!!!

"Oh, what the hell! Happy New Year!" Belle grabs one of the guys and sticks her tongue down his throat.

Fireworks go off and fly high into the sky, but before they can climax, suddenly the sky whitens; it's a fluorescent brightness. Gasps of shock sound out around the terrace as confusion and surprise is met with disbelief. Belle breaks free from her embrace, as does Lucy from hers.

"What's going on?" Lucy says, amazed by the bright white sky.

"I don't believe it, it's happening." Belle lets slip from under her breath.

"What's happening?" Lucy asks anxiously.

And then, from nowhere, a figure appears amongst whiteness – something is in the air. Revellers are pointing at it; it is coming closer into view. Cries of 'Christ' break out amongst the crowd and chaos breaks free. Jesus Christ appears to all, and all are mesmerized. Christ outstretches his arms. Screams mix with cheers, ecstatic clapping coincides with hysteria.

Jesus speaks . . .

I am the way, the truth and the life. No one comes to the Father except through me.

All of a sudden darkness descends upon the light; Christ disappears as the fluorescent whiteness has been blackened. And there is screaming in pain, people all rid themselves of the device in their ears as it rings with a piercing sound of feedback. Black has been born of the world betrayed and chaos as the consequence is in a mad dance with itself, for the dying of the light lets us down, down until all fall from the disfigured face of the Earth, this place upon unholy ground now known to our worst fears realised. Lest we forget death, if only yet to perish then spare the people here of that thing called hell.

Oh, the irony! In no light at all but by divine intervention, now a power outage tests the patience of the people. A patience failing to take control of the rage they feel, for now enough is enough and there can only be one outcome; chaos. Those who are less inclined to fit the pieces together, they will believe because of what they saw happen in the sky. Whereas others, after experiencing such feedback happening in their ears, shall surely realise 'Christ' spoke via this device, a device that is not a lifesaver against the fake contamination, but a device that made it possible for the projection of Christ to speak to each and every one of us in the world regardless of our different languages.

Yes, this special occasion of a night, not celebrated but violated, and raped of all the revellers venturing out there for a good time. Tonight is marked by the saddest sign of the times, it's been forsaken, instead for the powerful few to try and tell us a historic story . . . yet a story nevertheless existing as nothing but a lie. The only light to be shed on such a situation as this shall arise from fire. The fire in our hearts not knowing how to handle a sadness driven insane by brute rage. The fire to burn down our surrounds out of fear, out of anger and out of hatred. Tomorrow will come undone but the natural, albeit bitterly cold, light of day, a day of days, so to bring the power back and have 'order' restored or renewed . . . no.

Tomorrow the world will react to its own devastating identity. Tomorrow the world won't be told the truth, that is in spite of a 'selected truth' that the media creates out of pure fear of being found out. Tomorrow Brazil's president will hang, while his suicide note details the true extent of this betrayal, along with his involvement where the US President is concerned and to blame for Rio's destruction amongst other things. Such a suicide note won't be revealed. President Ronald

Flump has failed. In a public display of affection and defiance no less, President Ronald Flump will be assassinated not by a crazy stranger, but by a professional called upon in order to do what is necessary now. Now the world knows not all is as it seems to be, because the pursuit of power will wrong the ones who won't stop until all hell breaks loose.

Isabella will continue to tour with her orchestra and set the world alight with the right kind of fire, a fire from within that burns because of love, true love. Max is to be set free, but the classified documents will remain that way. However, after everything that has happened, he feels a stinging sense of loss not from the documents that are out of his reach, but for the love he left behind. Belle lives on in his heart but it's bittersweet; he knows he can be nothing without the love of a good woman and she exceeds such a thing. They will meet again, when Max follows his heart to find just what he was searching for all along and that is a love done by the divine . . . indeed it is a love to conquer everything else in the world.

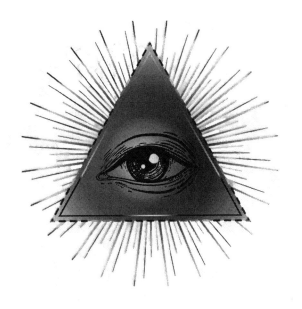

15146506R00275

Printed in Great Britain
by Amazon